The Pain We Nurture

Sarah Presley

Contents

Dedication

To My Beautiful Readers
SKP

Mental Health Matters

Mental Health issues depicting depression, anxiety, suicide ideation,
and PTSD
BDSM—Sadism/Masochism relationship
Depiction of child drowning
Intense sex scenes
Scenes in which the MMC purposefully and consensually hurts the
FMC to include: Taking advantage of injury to hurt FMC in order to
evoke a pavlovian response, choking, spanking, restraining.
National Suicide Prevention Hotline
1-800-273-talk(8255)
National Depression Hotline
1-866-629-4564

Epigraph

Sometimes life takes you in directions you least expect it to. You can be young, happy, carefree and trying to experiment and enjoy life. Thinking you're living.

The next moment the rug can be jerked out from underneath you and everything you once knew can be upended in a millisecond. One minute you're you, and the next, you're fighting for everything you want in life.

Your next breath, your next opportunity, a chance at peace maybe?

Your next love.

Do you want to miss your chance?

Fuck that. I don't think you do.

So, my advice to you?

Take *all* that shit and make it yours. Because all you've got is yourself.

Make life your bitch.

At any cost.

Let Olivia's and I's story be an example to you.

Prologue

COLIN SAT SILENTLY IN a windowless room in the two-bedroom house on his property. The sounds of the news reporter hushed in the background, and the soft pitter patter of rain beat against the roof, the only noise to break his silence.

Arms folded, Colin leaned his back heavily against the wooden chair, facing the wall that only held a handful of colorful, blown-up canvases. His chest ached as his eyes slowly roved each one, landing briefly on the black and white dog he'd loved so dearly. He had never let himself enjoy another companion since becoming an adult. His hand rubbed his chest hard, wishing he could pull his heart out and live without it.

He thought it'd feel better than walking around with the mind-numbing guilt he carried with him daily.

Seeing the picture of him and his childhood dog Marley, he gritted his teeth, feeling like a coward. As he'd never been strong enough to let himself own another dog in his adulthood. All the years of opportunities for companionship that he'd wasted. His eyes continued its familiar route along the wall, going over the other photos. Reluctantly, he looked at the picture of his father. Wondering what he looked like now, twenty-three years since he saw him last. Did he have gray hair? Wrinkles?

Was his voice still elegant, or had it grown gritty and weak with age? Did he ever find love again? Have more children? His father would be mid in his mid seventies now.

Colin wondered for the if millionth time if his father ever thought about him. His eyes flickered away from the image. He bowed his head when he stopped at the one in the middle. The picture he could never let himself focus on for too long. A tortured sob escaped his throat as he leaned forward, putting his head in his hands.

Colin groaned, the pain washing over him in waves. He disbursed an enormous amount of effort trying to calm himself from his panic attack, but it tonight his usual methods weren't working. Hands trembling, he raised his head to take a last look at the photographs before he got up and turned, hearing his phone vibrate on the lone wooden desk against the opposite wall.

Brother, I need you to answer me. I'm on my way, I'm coming as fast as I can. Please stay there. -J.

Mary knows where my documents are. Take care of her, please. You've been such a great friend to me, brother. I love you. -C

Colin felt the tears fall down his face, and he swiped them off. His chocolate colored eyes fell on his computer monitor, showing the local news.

"—thunderstorm coming in the next twenty minutes. The state of Connecticut warns all residents to take shelter immediately and do not attempt to travel. Visibility will be at a dangerous low and we are expecting high levels of-"

Colin shut off the computer with a hard stab at the monitor and sniffed. He cleared his throat of overwhelming emotions rolling through him before snatching his phone up, his eyes falling on the wall behind the desk before freezing at the contents there. Distraught at the images, his heart began racing out of control as he fought the rising bile threatening to choke him.

His eyes closed briefly, trying to fight against the gut-wrenching wave of nausea.

Resigning himself to his fate, Colin calmly picked up his keys and wallet. He bent down, retrieving his motorcycle helmet off the desk as well, before turning and exiting the room, not sparing the wall of pictures with a second glance. Looking into his wallet briefly, and hearing the comforting sound of his boots tap against the hardwood floor of the hallway, he made sure he had identifying information before exiting the small home.

Taking a quick second, he put in his ear pods and shoved his helmet on, closing the door with a click, figuring tonight was a good night as any to take a ride and join his mother.

What he should have done twenty-three years ago.

ONE
Ad Quod Damnum

THWAP! THWAP!

Olivia dug her high heels into the soft white carpet of the lush bedroom she and her client were currently occupying inside of his guest house. Raising her arm swiftly, she viciously slapped the leather barbed wire flogger against the older man's back. Her green eyes narrowed in displeasure at the weak sound that escaped her lips at the movement.

Her right arm twinged painfully. Lowering it to her side, she briefly gave herself a reprieve to rest.

I'm so tired, she thought wearily.

Closing her eyes in irritation, she mentally chastised herself for accidentally having shown any vulnerability around this particular client. She stiffly rolled her shoulder, waiting for the tingles in her arm and fingertips to cease before reaching up to push a thick lock of silky, dark-red hair behind her ear.

Breathing hard, Olivia took a second to concentrate on the fiery burn of the air going in and out of her lungs. She relished her client's pathetic yells before raising the flogger one more time. Wincing on a grimace, she barely managed to stifle a moan as her right arm spasmed in earnest this time, thankful that the older judge couldn't see her.

She blew out a slow, calming breath, wishing she had some strong pain medicine to help her tonight.

"NO, please, Mistress Kat. *I'll be a good boy!*" The man's sniveling caused her stomach to flip a nauseating somersault in her belly.

Annoying, intrusive thoughts took over, interrupting her focus on delivering for her client. Her fury at having to do this for money drove her motivation to finish this session on a high note. She was compensated for this service wonderfully, and always delivered.

No matter the intense pain, her annoyance, her hunger, or the lack of sleep.

She *delivered*.

Olivia waited another heartbeat, drawing out her client's tension before landing the flogger in a final crushing blow against his reddened back, right on the rawest part of the expansive strip of skin. He let out a pathetic howl as he strained hard against the cuffs that she'd tied him to the bedpost with.

Though his white wrists were turning raw, red, and angry looking, Olivia didn't care. Having warned him at the beginning of their session that if he pulled against the restraints, then that was the consequence. And now he was paying for it and she wanted to charge him more for his disobedience.

Olivia again considered becoming a FinDom, wondering if she'd be as successful at swindling men out of their money as she was beating them for it. With the way her arm stung, she knew she'd have to figure out a secondary plan before she caused the injury to be permanent. Stepping back, she readjusted her leather bustier before pressing her fingers into her soft flesh, biting her lip. It was sore tonight, the pain sharp. Her client said he'd pay extra for another thirty minutes of beatings, and needing the money, she accepted despite her injury.

She spent the first hour whipping him with a basic flogger, then a chain flogger that she'd cooled down in the freezer. It was perfect for dragging on the Judge's hot skin. Then she pulled out the barbed wire flogger for the last half hour, giving the man his money's worth.

She always believed in giving someone what they paid for.

But she'd worsened her injury over the last several weeks, not being used to supplying such a strenuous work over like she'd been giving the Judge. Keeping silent she bent down, vowing to go back to only spending an hour per client as she slipped her fishnet stocking feet out of her sensible black heels.

She wiggled her toes in relief, donning eight-inch, platform spiked heels before walking to the Judge and uncuffing him.

Almost done tonight.

"You've been a *naughty* boy. Haven't you, Judge Carmichael? I'm not convinced you *can* be good. Can you?" Olivia crooned, masking the pain in her voice by sheer will alone.

At his silence, she leaned down and roughly snatched his head back by his silver hair. Placing a kiss against his cheek, she left a red lipstick print on his flushed skin. She rolled her eyes at the sickening sight of the red mark on his skin, curling her lip in disdain.

Perusing his form once more, she let him see her green eyes assess him coldly, wanting him to see her displeasure.

Tilting her head, she took in the man's six-foot one frame, stocky build, and silver hair at fifty-eight years old. He was slightly hairy, and bushy eyebrows framed gray eyes that sat in a sharply defined face which boasted a square chiseled jaw, full lips, and smooth skin. He was not an unattractive man, but at thirty-three years her senior, she didn't look at him sexually at all.

That was not her understanding of this peculiar *situationship* they found themselves in.

However, that didn't stop Judge Carmichael from letting her know he wanted more than dominatrix services from her. He'd asked for more, wanting to take her out properly and offering to bring her out of the lifestyle. Professing he desired to make an 'honest' woman of her.

The first year of him commissioning Olivia's services, he'd asked constantly for sex, and she almost dropped him as a client. So, he learned to back off. Regardless, nothing had changed in the past four years. He still wanted more, and all he demanded from her was for her to give up the lifestyle, and he wanted to add something to her weekly services.

She frowned deeply, remembering the night he requested another service. His request had made her rush to the bathroom and vomit it was so disgusting, and *degrading* that she tried hard to erase the image that it brought to her mind.

Most of her clients paid her for beating, degradation, and sexual dominatrix services, however, she was one of the few females in the underground sex ring who didn't engage in sexual services. She brought pain only, and that was nonnegotiable. However, it didn't stop the Judge from asking her to do that thing he liked, and he'd recently brought it up again.

She wouldn't budge on her decision.

"Yes! *Yes, I can!* Let me prove it!" the Judge panted in his deep voice, groaning as Olivia tightened even harder against his scalp, digging her nails in and scraping gently. He moaned in pleasure as she roughly shoved his head forward.

"Lay down on your stomach, you piece of shit. You sicken me," Olivia hissed into his ear, waiting for him to comply.

As he got himself into place, she turned her eyes to the timer perched the bed, wishing the last few minutes to fly by. She was ready to go home and sleep.

Olivia gingerly placed a sharp heel into his back, and used the bedpost to steady herself as she found her balance. The Judge let out a harsh groan as both of her heels dug into his back painfully. Sniffing with disgust, she put all her weight on the delicate tips, swallowing back the revolting feeling of them sinking into the muscle beneath her.

Slowly shuffling across his back, Olivia hurtled random insults until the gentle chime of her phone alarm went off, informing them both that his time was up. Stepping off his back, she smoothed her sweating hands down her thighs.

Readjusting her lacy masquerade mask with one hand, she swiped the phone silent with the other. Untying the judge, she watched with arms crossed as he got up with effort.

Judge Carmichael rose to his feet with a grimace on his face, before turning to her with an embarrassed smile. She let him stretch in silence for a second before speaking, noting he kept himself in good shape.

"I believe the agreement was an extra one-thousand dollars for the additional thirty minutes, and another four hundred for the walking service on top of our regular hourly fee?" Olivia clipped, business-like.

She didn't want her clients to delude themselves into thinking that her services included warmth, sex, or anything mushy. She didn't do mushy; it just wasn't in the cards for her, and she'd accepted that long ago.

The Judge huffed out a breath, still trying to come down from his high, nodding before going to his closet. Olivia took off the sky-high heels, slipping on a pair of tennis shoes. She listened to the muted beeping as Judge Carmichael entered the code.

Raising her phone, Olivia beat out a quick text to her connect, Gypsy. Letting the woman know she was about to leave her client for the night. She stood impatiently listening to him rustling around for a minute before reappearing through the door with a thick wad of cash, counting out the bills.

Judge Carmichael finished and then handed the wad to her, and Olivia scrunched her nose at the sight of him eyeing her body lustily, relieved that she'd already pulled on a light jacket. Covering the bustier from his gaze, and leaving her leather pants and mask on. She didn't need him to know what she looked like, that was her business, not his.

Not that he hadn't attempted multiple times to make it his business.

Once again she'd thought about canceling him as a client, but he would not accept any other woman in the underground network that her connect Gypsy built. He iterated strongly that he only wanted 'Kat,' the name of her alter ego. And to sweeten the deal, he'd paid her more than any other woman was making at the time to keep her.

Consequently, the other clients all caught wind of the arrangement and it caused a ripple effect; the clients paid a premium to keep their services, and the women got to have steady clients.

Olivia worked hard to keep firm boundaries in place to ensure that all the men in her clientele folder knew to never expect anything more than what she was: Gypsy's top beater. The head bitch of the networking ring called Esmerelda. Which is truly the only reason she even agreed to work for Gypsy; she had a thing for fairy tales, storybooks, and escapism.

The Judge watched intently as she silently counted out the money. Three thousand, four hundred dollars, as agreed. She nodded briskly with a tiny smile before stuffing the cash, and both pairs of heels into a big tote bag. Staying silent, she followed him out of the room to the front door of the guest house on his property, briefly letting herself admire the layout of the home.

Pausing as she did every week, she stopped and stared at the imposing oil painting of him in his robes staring down at her from its place at the top of the foyer wall. The expensive crystal chandelier illuminated eyes that seemed to glint ominously down at her from his seat at the bench.

She shivered, abhorring the icy feeling of dread that suddenly enveloped her.

"See you next week, Judge?" Olivia asked quietly, allowing herself to give him a small smile as he nodded his head yes, giving her another once over.

She regarded him quizzically. His expression seemed more withdrawn tonight as he walked her out. Noting the difference in his attitude, she relented and gave him a little wave as she disappeared into the greenery of the side yard. She kept her pace brisk, letting herself through the white vinyl fence to the residential street where her car was waiting.

Olivia scanned her surroundings quickly for any intruders before getting behind the wheel, starting her old beater vehicle before driving off into the night.

***

Wearily descending the outdoor steps of her apartment complex, Olivia let herself into her plain, sparsely decorated one-bedroom unit. She lived on the basement level; it being all she could afford. She quickly latched the lock and deadbolt before leaning tiredly against the door and looking around the place with appreciation.

Nice and clean, small, *hers*. Yet, it didn't quite feel like home.

It never had.

She threw her clutch down onto the small side wooden table and kicked her shoes off one by one. Leaving them haphazardly on the rug in front of the door, she carried her tote to her bedroom, turning on lights as she made her way through the small space. Glancing at her intricately made bed enviously, she dropped her bag on it before digging out the heels and the money.

Turning, she opened her closet door and pulled out a shoebox that was hidden underneath some old scarves.

She pushed them aside and grabbed up the top, her green eyes scanning the hundreds of hundred-dollar bills nestled neatly inside.

Dumping it all out onto the bed, she counted the bands easily as she had them wrapped in thousand-dollar increments. Assuring it was all there, she placed the money she'd made tonight in with the loose bills, making another solid band. She sighed with relief, her left hand curling behind her hair, rubbing her nape.

She had just barely made the money by the deadline, same as last month.

Stuffing the bills back into the shoebox and replacing everything neatly, Olivia walked into her bathroom, eyeing the makeup brushes and makeup spread haphazardly all over the vanity. She'd worked late at her day job at a local diner and barely had time to come home, make herself up, and dress before her appointment with the Judge.

She began cleaning, quickly closing make-up compacts and putting away brushes before reaching under the sink for a Clorox wipe. She winced with pain as she gave her vanity a good scrub with her right arm.

Breathing a sigh of relief at her bathroom coming to order, she undressed and stepped into a steamy, hot shower.

"Ow!" She winced as she closed the yellow shower liner too hard, accidentally tearing it from one of its clamps on the rusty rod it was

attached to. She hummed a small tune as she relaxed, scrubbing the day away. Though at midnight it was almost a new day, and she knew she couldn't look forward to getting anywhere near a good night of sleep. Especially with her arm pulsing and burning the way it was.

Stepping out of her bathroom naked and into the comfort of her bedroom, Olivia didn't bother to put pajamas on. She crawled wearily beneath the green, silky sheets and texted her sister Vanessa that she would be at her house before the bank opened in the morning.

Yawning, she set the alarm on her phone for seven in the morning, and went straight to sleep. Forgetting the pain pill.

She was that exhausted.

TWO
Rusty Red Stress

Olivia smiled brightly as she let herself into her elder sister's small, two-bedroom house on the north side of town.

Vanessa was currently bending down into her daughter's face, pleading with her to swallow her medicine. She had tears in her eyes as the little girl stubbornly shook her head no, her cheeks puffed around the medicine she was holding in her mouth.

"*Ally*, just tilt your head back and *swallow,*" Vanessa pleaded with Allison.

At only five years old, Allison was not as vibrant as a normal girl her age, however, her spirit was just as strong and stubborn. And she had no problem demonstrating her attitude with her mother today.

Allison's green eyes flashed at Vanessa defiantly as she sputtered, trying not to choke on the medicine.

"Hey, sis. Hey, little bit!" Olivia said, closing the door behind her as she walked into the outdated kitchen.

She took a small carton of apple juice out of her bag, threading the straw through before bending down to plant a sloppy kiss on her niece's cheek. Allison quickly swallowed her medicine before squealing with happiness, and threw her arms around her aunt. She snatched the apple juice out of Olivia's hand and sucked it down. Making happy slurping noises before jumping off the chair and going the living room, launching herself on the couch to watch her favorite cartoon.

Olivia turned her attention back to Vanessa, who was pushing wispy tendrils of her strawberry-blond hair off her face, and wiping her eyes tiredly. They were red and bloodshot, with bags forming underneath, making Olivia sad. Her eyes flicked upwards, seeing Vaness'as normally bouncy hair was limp in its ponytail.

"Hard night?" Olivia asked Vanessa softly, before dropping her bag on the tiled counter and leaning forward to wrap her in a tight hug.

She rubbed her hands empathetically against her sister's cheap wool sweater, which was currently half hanging off her curvy form. Vanessa's soft body pressed into hers, so much like their late mother's, and she fought back years old grief.

"She was throwing up last night,"Vanessa said, her freckled face contorting as she leaned against Olivia's shoulder, crying silently. *"I don't know how much longer we can do this, Ollie."*

Staring up at the water-stained popcorn ceiling Olivia rubbed her back comfortingly, blinking back tears of her own. She didn't want to break down, too. Her sister and niece needed her to be strong, consistent. And as the person who had to deal with a sick child twenty-four seven, Olivia figured Vanessa deserved to cry over this situation before she did.

"Nessie, we'll get through it," she crooned, grieving that they were in this situation. Lamenting that life was so hard. Hating that little girls who had liver disease needed to suffer, and their families had to scrimp and scrounge to try to figure out how to afford the expensive drug to keep her alive until they found a liver match.

It wasn't fair.

Olivia pulled back, grasping Vanessa's shoulders firmly. Noting unhappily that her once vibrant twenty-seven-year-old sister was starting to lose her luster. She barely even sang anymore, her light beginning to dim from years of stress catching up with her. She stared in sympathy into her sisters' cat-like gray eyes, so unlike her almond-shaped emerald ones.

"*Hey*, I put an extra five hundred in there so that you can take Ally to do something fun and have a little extra grocery money this month. Spend time with your daughter. Don't pull any more doubles this month please," she said with a smile, reaching over to grab the Ziplock bag of money from her tote.

Vanessa nodded, taking the money from her with a thankful smile in return.

"Run to the bank and deposit this, and call her doctor's office. I'll finish making her breakfast, and drop her off at school. I'll lock up the house when I leave, okay? Don't sweat anything today." Olivia pressed into the sore spot on her arm, the pain stealing her breath for a moment.

"Okay, thank you for this." Vanessa's eyes searched for her's again, always more astute and observant. "Ollie," she whispered. "Please tell me you're not-*for the money*... you're not?" Vanessa's voice broke as her eyes shifted back and forth between Olivia's.

Olivia pressed her lips together nervously. She'd never shared exactly how she managed to give Vanessa twelve grand a month to help with Allison's treatments.

She smiled and squeezed Vanessa's hand back reassuringly, once again promising to take her secret to the grave.

"Never that, Nessie," Olivia whispered, leaning forward to kiss her cheek before turning to the gas four-burner stove and turning it on. "Go!" She shooed her sister towards her purse.

Vanessa mouthed an 'I love you' to her, placing her hands in a heart symbol before disappearing through the door quickly, the door banging behind her.

"Ally, do you want pancakes or French toast this morning?" she called.

"Frense oat!" Allison garbled around the straw of her juice box, which was a crumpled mess in her hands. Olivia nodded before reaching into the fridge to grab the milk and butter.

She wearily rubbed her sore arm and blinked sleep away as she looked at the oven's clock observing she had just enough time to possibly get a two-hour nap before her nine-hour shift at the diner. Sighing again tiredly, she began making her niece breakfast, trying to calm her own hunger pains.

She didn't want to eat their food and deplete their already sparse resources.

***

Thanks to a tragic accident on her way home from dropping off Allison, Olivia couldn't make it home in time for a nap.

She put a five-minute rice cup in the microwave before rushing into her bedroom, and hurriedly pulled on her diner uniform. Her arm stung anew as she yanked her dark red hair into a tight bun. Going back into the kitchen, she noticed irritably that there was no butter, no milk, no nothing except salt in her cupboards.

Groaning to herself, she dashed a couple sprinkles of salt before shoving it in her mouth while she stood at the counter, not having room in her small space for a table. She only owned a two-person used loveseat she detested sitting on.

"*Shit, that's gross,*" she complained, scrunching her nose up in disgust at the taste of the salty rice.

Vanessa offered to move her in with her and Allison, but Olivia declined, not wanting her family to see the grueling schedule that kept her coming in and out of the house all hours of the night. No, Allison deserved consistency in her already hectic world. So, Olivia worked harder. Taking on more clients than she was comfortable with to afford to stay close to them in the expensive area of Connecticut where Allison's doctors were.

However, it was getting harder to keep up. Her monthly expenses were twenty-four hundred dollars a month, and she was barely scraping up enough every month to pay for her own apartment and utility bills. Much less her car, insurance, and food. Forget luxuries and clothing. And her cabinets were bare. She'd need to go grocery shopping soon.

***

Olivia groaned as she neared the end of her shift at ten-thirty that night. For the first time, she didn't think she could make it through her shift, having to pause several times as she mopped to give her arm time to stop stinging. The pain hindered her, and she was at the diner later than she normally was during the week.

She winced with a little gasp as she hoisted the yellow mop bucket, trying to ignore the sting in her arm as she drained the water in the utility room before rinsing the bucket out, and letting it drain upside down. She locked the register for the night, pulling out her phone as she walked to the front window and turned the OPEN sign to CLOSED, before locking the door.

Putting her head into her hands for a second, she took a calming breath before she raised her head and focused on her phone again.

Anxiously flipping through her banking app, she already knew what she'd find, as she looked at her accounts multiple times a day.

Checking: -$44.02

Savings: $5.86

Emergency savings: $2.00

"Oh my God." Olivia bit her lip, unwilling to let herself feel panicked for giving the money to her sister for Allison.

Ready to go, she placed her phone down on the counter before walking back to the break room and grabbing her purse from the locker. Turning the knob on the lock she flinched in fear as a loud crack of thunder broke through the sky, sending her heartbeat sky rocketing. Unnerved, and wanting to go home, she hurriedly turned off all the lights in the back, then froze, hearing a thumping noise from the front of the diner.

Olivia stopped breathing, ears piqued for more noise. After a couple more seconds she heard a loud banging at the diner's door. Her eyes widened in surprise.

Someone was knocking on the door in this storm?

She bravely peeked her head out of the back, seeing a shadow of a man peeking in, and banging rather incessantly.

"Can someone let me in, please? *I need assistance!*" the man yelled, banging some more.

Olivia shuddered with fear as another crack of thunder lit the sky and the torrential downpour thundered against the rooftop, making it sound like the entire building would cave in under it's pressure. Though she went against her instincts, she made a split-second decision to let him in, only because she'd want someone to do the same for her.

Olivia sprinted to her phone, unlocking it and typing out a quick text to her boss and sister.

> *Still at the diner. Letting in someone who's stranded out in this storm. I should be ok. I have a taser. Can't leave him out there. Will give you an update in a bit.* -Olivia

Sharing her location with the two of them, she walked to the door and opened it. Gasping in shock as the storm blew the door further open, bringing in the man, and a ton of rainwater on the floor she'd *just* mopped.

"Oh no!" Olivia gritted her teeth, feeling annoyed as he helped her press against the door to shut it.

Raising furious eyes to him, she paled as his face came into view.

Holy fucking shit! Olivia thought, her mind glitching as she stared into a pair of the most beautiful chocolate-colored eyes she'd ever seen.

Her eyes flickered over his face unashamedly. His was brown, medium-length, floppy and wet from the rain, and his face was scruffy with a five-o'clock shadow, giving his sharp, defined features a dangerous ambiance. His skin had a beautiful olive tone, broad body type, and he was tall, almost a foot taller than her.

He looked older, well into adulthood, and confident in it.

Feeling incredibly petite next to him, she cowered slightly, biting her lip. *"Sorry,"* she murmured, backing up so she could take him in better.

He had on a felt dark green jacket, dark washed jeans, and riding boots. His broad chest and bulging biceps filled out the jacket, and his arm was wrapped around a.... *helmet*?

She frowned, her irritation growing.

"What the hell are you doing riding on a motorcycle in this weather?" Olivia blurted.

Embarrassed at her outburst, she slapped her fingers to her lips to shut herself up. Her eyes widened slightly as she remembered she was still at her place of employment, and shouldn't be talking to him like that.

Fuck, I hope I don't get fired, she thought.

The man finished running his fingers through the dark strands before glancing down at her and flashing her a devastating smile with his full lips. She balked at how *eerily* handsome he was. Her brain suddenly and inexplicably went to mush. She couldn't quite process his next words.

"Well, it wasn't supposed to rain. And I wasn't supposed to be on this side of town this late either." His accented voice was elegant, smooth as sin, with a slight growl.

Olivia felt herself go weak in the knees at his smile before determinedly slapping a frown on her face.

Nope, not going there, she thought as she fussed with the hem of her yellow diner shirt, pulling at it nervously while she took a second to gather herself. Her irritation quickly turned into something too close to desire and curiosity for her comfort.

She pointed to a chair close to the door.

"Sit there, please," Olivia ordered briskly. "I have to mop again now, because of the rainwater." She turned to walk away before stopping herself and turning back. "You're on a bike. Do you need a ride somewhere?" she asked, cursing to herself as she remembered her gas tank was almost empty. She didn't have the money to haul strangers around like an Uber.

The man dumped his helmet on the floor before lowering himself carefully into the seat, filling up the space. "No, I've already contacted someone to bring me my car, and to pick my bike up. But thank you. I appreciate the offer," he replied, flashing her another smile as he stretched out a leg and pulled out his phone from his back pocket. "They're about forty-five minutes away."

Olivia watched warily as he beat out a quick text on his phone before glancing at her once more. She again had that strange, unnerving feeling that left her rather disconcerted and unsure.

THREE

Who Are You

"I'M COLIN. AND YOU are...?" Colin waited expectantly with an arched eyebrow.

She shivered slightly at the movement, then rolled her eyes at the weakness. "Olivia."

"Nice to meet you, Olivia," Colin said smoothly, his eyes slowly purusing down her front. "I'm sorry that I'm keeping you. I hope you didn't have anything important going on later?"

Olivia stared at him and slowly shook her head, truly having been looking forward to going home and getting into her comfortable bed. She was exhausted, and had to work a double tomorrow on top of meeting another client for an hour's session later in the night. She'd needed the money badly if she wanted to eat a decent meal.

Sighing, she rubbed her eyes briefly before walking to the back of the diner, grabbing the cleaning supplies she'd just put away.

Running the mop water, she turned her head when the jukebox from the front of the diner started playing. She strained to listen, noting with pleasure at the song choice. Katy Perry *Riding Harleys in Hawaii*. Olivia was thankful that Colin put some money in the jukebox to play a song.

It'd be too cool to experience riding Harleys in Hawaii, she thought with a grin. Hoping that one day it'd be more than a pipe dream.

Rolling the mop and bucket back to the front, she mopped dark gray floor, shaking her head no when Colin offered to mop it for her in apology for getting it wet. Her normally sweet boss would skin her alive if she let a patron mop the floor.

A hilarious giggle erupted from her throat as she imagined her boss' face turning bright red as she watched Colin mop the floor through their security system feed. Envisioning the sight in her mind's eye, it took her mind off her stinging arm, and she accomplished the job without a spasm.

"Something funny?" Colin asked, glancing up at her from his phone.

She looked up from wringing the last of the water out, her eyebrow arched. "Nope," she replied, keeping it short and to the point.

"You don't talk much, do you?" Colin asked, crossing an ankle over his knee and thrumming his fingers on his thick, muscular thigh.

Olivia's eyes caught the movement, thinking he really did delicious things to a pair of pants. She wrapped her fingers hard around the handle of the mop, leaning against it momentarily.

"Would you like a piece of pie while we wait?" she asked sweetly, trying to hide her annoyance.

In other words, shut up, please.

"No, thank you. Another time," he answered, flashing her a cheeky grin as if he'd heard her thoughts.

He sank slightly deeper in the chair, really spreading his legs and getting comfortable. The sight irked her. She didn't want to find this stranger sexy and appealing. Olivia gave him another polite smile, hoping and praying he would take the hint, and stop talking to her.

She quickly rolled the bucket to the back and sorted it out before whipping her wet diner shirt off, grateful to have a white tank underneath, ignoring her tummy rumbling as she shoved her shirt in her bag.

She untied her hair from its tight bun, shaking the silky strands loose and moaning in relief as her hair fell in long waves, spilling over her breasts and down her sides before ending at her lower back.

Olivia gripped her neck hard with her hands and rolled her shoulders, wincing at the ache in her arm refusing to let up. She gathered her things again and walked back to the front of the diner, dropping tiredly in a seat, crossing her legs, and unlocking her phone, ignoring Colin rather rudely.

She twiddled with her hair absentmindedly as she scanned through the various messages from her sister and her boss. She found her foot swinging to the beat of the song, wishing she could dance to it like she wanted.

I'm alive, he's waiting for his car. They should be here in like 15 minutes. Also, not happy, I had to mop the floor again. =(. -O

I'll give you an extra $25 for staying late. You're an exemplary employee, Olivia =). Please take your time on the way home and be safe. -Boss

Olivia smiled genuinely as she sent her the thumbs up emoji. Thinking if her boss only knew about her extracurricular activities, she wouldn't be saying she was so *good*. Her chair squeaked as she startled slightly when the man's voice pierced the air. He was so quiet she almost forgot he was in the same room as her.

"You have a pretty smile. And your hair is gorgeous," Colin said, his eyes warm as they gazed at her.

Olivia shifted so she faced him head on in the seat and uncrossed her legs, planting them with a firm thump firmly in front of her. Twisting her smile into an impassive expression, she stared at him plainly, not wanting him getting the wrong idea. She lifted a haughty eyebrow, noticing his fingers twitch slightly on his right hand.

Her eyes narrowed slightly with the movement.

"If you try anything, I'll have you know that I'm *not* a screamer. I will hurt you, and won't think twice about it," she spoke confidently, her eyes dragging from his twitching hand to his. Silently conveying that he did not intimidate her, even though she knew that was a lie.

She was so used to faking it till she made it that it was not a hard, silent message to shoot across to him.

Colin mouth curled in a devilish smile as his head tilted, and his eyes flashed. A shiver shot down Olivia's spine at how dangerous he looked, and sexy.

"I believe only *one* of those statements are true," Colin said, his tongue coming out to lick his bottom lip. Olivia's gaze flicked down, observing his chest expand slightly. Putting her eyes back to his, she held his stare, uncaring that it was uncomfortably intense.

"Hey, how much longer do you think?" Olivia asked, looking away and ignoring him, preferring not to feed into his flirtation.

Turning her attention to her phone once again, she checked her credit card balance.

Maxed out.

She grimaced as she placed her chin in her hand, trying to think, absentmindedly tossing her head back and trailing her fingers through her hair repeatedly. It soothed her, hearing the thump of the heavy locks hitting the back of the chair.

She desperately wracked her brain to think of a way to get more money by the end of the weekend.

"Are you okay? You look... stressed," Colin said, placing his elbows on his knees and leaning forward, his stare slowly caressing her body from her head to her feet.

The pure, assessing way her regarded her made Olivia cease her movements, her hair falling back into place as she put her hand to her thigh.

"I'm always *stressed*." Olivia turned narrowed, green eyes on his. "You don't think I'd be working until almost midnight five nights a week at a diner in a not-so-great side of town if I were happy go lucky now, do you?"

Flashing him a sarcastic grin, she smoothly turned her attention away at the sound of her phone dinging.

> Hey, Rusty. I got a guy for you. Uber wealthy, some hotshot attorney, mid-forties. Wants one hour on Saturday night. Beating only. No need for costume, but asked if you could use a whip. Sounds like he just wants his shit rocked. He offered $2000. You down? -Gypsy

She scoffed quietly, before her eyes flickered briefly to Colin who was sitting there rubbing his thumb against his bottom lip, still watching her. He had some weird sexy thing going on that she couldn't decide if she liked or not. She promptly dismissed the thought, because what did it really matter, anyway?

Jesus, what is with this guy? She thought to herself, before flickering her eyes back down to her phone and typing out her reply.

> Did you tell him I don't do sex, or get naked? -Rusty

> Yes. He just wants to tumble. Sounded stressed. -Gypsy

> *Yeah, well, ain't we all? He can join the club. Send me his info tomorrow to my burner phone. Tell him he needs to reserve the hotel presidential suite on 3rd Avenue. I don't meet new clients in their homes. Hey, I need pain pills. My arm is fucked. -Rusty*

> *10-4 I got you. I'll drop them off tomorrow. Xoxo Gypsy.*

Feeling Colin's gaze still on her, she turned her phone over in her hands while she met his stare boldly, not offering any more conversation. She really wasn't trying to be rude, she was just too tired to talk. At this point in life, if it didn't involve money, she wasn't interested. She didn't let herself have those feelings.

It was better that way.

Her right arm spasmed just then, and her lips parted on a gasp. She moved quickly, attempting to hide the pain by pulling her hair over her arm and stroking it, pretending to play with her hair. Using that to press into the pain.

At his unwavering stare, she decided they were playing a little game of who could blink first, apparently.

Cheering silently in her head as Colin finally broke his eye contact with her, she watched quietly as he stood from his seat just as a bright pair of headlights flashed by the window, stalling outside.

"My ride's here. Thanks again, Red. I wish you well," he expressed, walking forward and offering her his hand to shake. She raised her brow at the nickname, because how coincidental after her interaction with Gypsy calling her Rusty.

Standing hastily and grabbing her things, she nonchalantly placed her hand in his. Stiffening as an electrical shock flew up her arm and exploded in her chest. She wrenched her hand away with a shocked gasp, shaking it slightly.

Her nose scrunched up. "I'm surprised you didn't get electrocuted out there," Olivia said, her brows furrowed as her already smarting arm tingled.

She pulled her lower lip between her teeth as Colin flexed his hand slowly, looking down at her with a curious expression. He smiled again, before bending to grab his helmet and opened the door to let her out first. Outside, she locked up before turning to see him greet a middle eastern man who climbed out of a big truck. Parked behind the truck was an expensive dusky blue BMW iX.

She rolled her eyes, irritated that someone who could afford such a car caused her to lose an hour of sleep tonight.

Olivia marched her way to her beater, blinking against the rain as Colin and the man heaved his sports bike into the back of the truck. She pointedly ignored him as he turned to look at her before jumping to the ground. Olivia shivered as she started her car, having no heat. She turned on her windshield wiper blades with stiff fingers and waited patiently for the truck to pull off.

"God, I'm so ready to go home," Olivia moaned to herself, tensing when she heard a tap at the passenger window. Rolling it down slowly she turned, "What can I help you with *now*?" she hissed, seriously pissed off, tired, and ready to go.

"You shouldn't be out here in the dark. Would you like me to follow you home?" Colin asked, leaning his head slightly in her window. The words took a minute to register.

"NO!" Her eyebrows slammed together as he looked at her car dash before putting his fingers to the vent.

"Why don't you have your heat on? It's cold out here!" Colin turned his chocolate eyes to her's, seemingly not caring that he was getting drenched. The rain was pounding against his back, the material visibly weighing down and plastering to his back heavily.

Olivia began rolling up the window on him, turning her face away, truly about to lose it.

"Hey hey hey," Colin rumbled in his deep voice, trying to extract himself from the window.

Olivia yelped in alarm as the passenger door opened, fumbling with her cold wet hands to open her own door to flee.

Scared, her hands slipped and grappled with the door handle. She'd just managed to push it open right as he inserted himself into her passenger seat, banging his knee on the dash on a muted curse as he kept one leg in and one leg out, not able to fit into her car. Olivia shivered as he grabbed her hand once more, pressing something into it.

Forty bucks.

She stared at him silently, breathing hard in shock. Grateful he wasn't forcing himself on her. His warm hand pressed into her skin firmly, his thumb carressing hers softly.

Vulnerable, she pressed her lips together, feeling the back of her eyes prickle.

"I'm sorry, but I don't have much cash on me at the moment. I just appreciate you waiting when you could have left me out there," Colin stated, looking at her once more before running his hand down his wet face. Her hand gripped the money and tears swelled in her eyes. With much effort she kept them from falling.

He didn't know that he had just paid for her food for the rest of the week, and she didn't want to make her misfortune obvious. But she didn't want to come across ungrateful, either.

"Thank you. I really appreciate this more than you know," she whispered, pressing her lips together even tighter, refusing to say anything else and making this already embarrassing situation even more so.

There was no way she was going to spill her life story to him over forty bucks. No chance.

Colin's fingers closed briefly on her wrist as a strange look crossed is face, and she had the reeling sensation that she'd just given him something. Something shared between the two of them that he didn't make her privy to.

"See, you *can* be nice. You're very welcome," Colin breathed, and instantaneously her nipples hardened under her wet shirt. His eyes flickered down, seeing it before rising to her's again with a slight sparkle in his irises.

"Have a safe drive home," he said, letting himself out of her car and walking to his.

They both sat there for a while before Olivia realized he was waiting for her to pull off first. She turned her signal light on and swiveled quickly into the road, watching him pull off in the opposite direction in her rearview mirror.

Olivia fell into bed in just her underwear without taking a shower.

On the way home, she'd stopped at a gas station and paid six dollars for two slices of meat lovers pizza, and a three-dollar vodka shot. Putting ten dollars in her tank before going home, she'd scarfed the food down, pocketing the rest of the money for the grocery store. Flopping to her side and placing her phone on the charger, she sent a quick text to her sister and boss letting them know she was home and okay. Her boss told her she would cover her morning shift for a couple of hours so she could sleep in tomorrow.

She reset her alarm to let herself get another hour of sleep, necking the vodka and closing her eyes. So grateful for a bed to sleep in.

***

Drenched, Colin went back into the two-story house on his property and made his way to the back room and typed the code in to let himself in. He walked in, turning the lights on against the darkness.

Facing the wall of canvases he briefly perused it, this time focusing on his mother for longer than he had earlier. He walked to her picture and put his fingers to her face, wishing he could just have twenty minutes to talk to her. Tell her about his life, let her know how much he missed her.

He stared at the image of her eyes, trying to remember her voice, the way she smelled, fighting against overwhelming grief.

"You know I'm not leaving you alone tonight."

Colin turned his head, hearing his friend Johnathan come into the room behind him, and lean against the doorway.

"I don't give a shit what you do," Colin muttered, turning away from the wall and walking to the computer behind him, seeing Johnathan staring at the wall of articles behind the desk.

"Were you trying to kill yourself?" Johnathan asked softly as Colin typed the password into the computer.

Colin stayed silent as he opened another folder, dumping the picture he snuck of Olivia into it.

"Who is she?" Johnathan pressed, not leaving him alone.

Colin took a deep breath. "I don't know yet. Will you stop fucking meddling. Jesus!" Colin squeezed the bridge of his nose and prayed for peace.

"Are you going to answer my question?" Johnathan walked further into the room. Colin!"

"I was... thinking about it. Yes," Colin admitted, unwilling to lie to his closest friend who was like a brother to him. He'd know if he was lying to him anyway, so he didn't even bother.

"What triggered it?"

"I had an anxiety attack at the office. A redheaded man came in..." He trailed off, not needing to explain himself anymore.

"*She's* a redhead." Johnathan said, leaning his hip against the desk, looking at him pointedly. "But you seem... okay. I'm still staying with you tonight, though."

"I don't know, Johnathan... I can't explain it, but she's *fascinating*. I didn't have the same reaction to her as I do other redheads," Colin mused, shutting down his computer. "Let's go to the main house. I hate it in here."

FOUR
Say Sir, I'll Pay

FRIDAY MORNING OLIVIA HAD woken up to a text from her boss asking her if she could cover a shift the next day, on Saturday morning. Groaning, she realized that wouldn't leave her much time to prepare for her new client on Saturday.

She sighed and accepted it anyway, grateful for the chance to make money. One thing to understand about her is that she wouldn't be relaxing her hustle any time soon. Her niece couldn't afford her to.

Olivia performed her morning routine before going into her living space, staring longingly at her worktable where she displayed some of the architectural work she'd managed to complete before she was forced to quit school to help take care of her grandfather. Giving up her full-ride scholarship destroyed a piece of her that she didn't even know could be damaged.

She and Vanessa had dealt with their parents dying, and having to move in with their grandpa in the last four years of school. Things seemed to be looking okay after graduation.

Vanessa had met this man, and they'd married before moving in together in the house that Vanessa lived in now. Allison was born shortly after Olivia was accepted into an architectural program, just before their Grandpa Stephen's brain tumor came to light. Vanessa's husband bailed after seeing the extent of Allison's poor health, leaving her with the expense of the house and medical bills and worry.

Due to not having support, Vanessa couldn't manage all Allison's medical appointments on her own, the house and bills, and take care of their grandpa. So, Olivia had to quit just two and a half years into her program to help.

After he died, his will bequeathed his life insurance to be split amongst them both. Olivia gave her share to Allison and Vanessa, knowing the extent of the financial strain of the monthly expense of the drug that Allison needed. But shortly after that, the money ran out. Leaving Olivia to resort to nefarious antics to help get them by.

She only worked at the diner because her rental office needed proof of employment, and unfortunately, all she could afford in Connecticut was a crappy one-bedroom basement apartment that couldn't even hold a dining room table. But she made it hold the remnants of the life she once wished for herself.

Walking slowly to her worktable, she gazed down at the blueprint of the house she'd designed as a project in the last year she attended school. It was a beautiful mansion. One that she'd hoped she'd be able to build for herself once she'd became the head of the Architectural firm she'd dreamed of opening in Connecticut.

But that dream was shot dead before it could even take root.

Her eyes stinging with tears she headed to work, and back to reality. Pushing the thoughts of mansions into the box of hurt that she kept secreted away in her brain. Only able to keep going at her back-breaking pace she'd been managing because she could compartmentalize and shut her emotions down.

Gypsy met her on her break at the diner, and they sat in her nice Range Rover.

"Here. Percocet," Gypsy said, giving her a bottle of pills.

Olivia opened it, frowning. "There's only eight pills here," she stated, looking over at her acquaintance and boss, annoyed that she didn't give her enough to at least get through two weeks.

"Hey, don't look at me like that! This is all that was available at the moment that I could trust was safe. I couldn't risk getting you something laced with fentanyl. It's killing a bunch of girls right now," Gypsy said in her smooth voice, taking a long drink of water from her tumbler.

"That's okay. I'm sorry for being snippy. Thanks for looking out, G," Olivia said, tossing the pills back and swallowing them with some water of her own.

She glanced over at Gypsy's bouncy blonde curls. She decidedly did not look like the head of the secret underground ring that Olivia circled. You would never tell by looking at her that this woman was a big boss. Gypsy only dealt with the elite of society: government dignitaries, politicians, high-powered lawyers, even a few members of royalty.

"No problem, I'll get you some more when I source them safely. How's the niece?" Gypsy asked, smiling, her icy blue eyes reflecting nothing but kindness.

Olivia eyed her regardless, not crazy about the woman, but happy that she was considerate towards her. She didn't trust many people, preferring to feed them with a long-handled spoon. The only friend she trusted inexplicably was Aliyah, and due to both their grueling schedules, she didn't get to see her as often as she liked.

"She's making it," Olivia responded quietly, not wanting to get into it.

She'd still had an entire shift left before she had to make it to her part time bartending job. She only bartended on Friday nights, as it was the only day during the week that she had free besides Sunday.

And she reserved Sunday for Allison.

"Hey, Carmichael still asking you to pi-" Gypsy paused at the alarmed look Olivia gave her. "I mean... do that thing that he'd been asking for?" Gypsy's eyes widened slightly and she blinked, waiting patiently.

"Yes. It's fucking gross. But he pays me good so I can't really drop him. I need the money."

"Well, you know we always have that back up plan for China if you need it. No one's utilizing the contingency plan, but if he becomes a problem and you need to get away for a bit to let him cool down we *can* send you away. Have a talk with him, get him set up with someone else before having you come back," Gypsy said.

Olivia nodded, amazed at Gypsy's planning. She'd told her years ago that safety was her first priority when she started this whole operation, to make sure she could always get her girls out of a sticky situation unharmed.

"I don't think that's necessary right now, but thank you for offering. Why China of all places though? Seems a bit overdramatic." She laughed, seeing her boss' wide smile as she giggled with her.

"Why NOT China?"

Olivia's eyes warmed. "Thanks Gypsy, you've been so good to me."

Gypsy nodded before hugging her goodbye, reminding her to get the lawyer's information for Saturday. Heading back into the diner, she hurried to the back to put the pills in her bag in her locker and took a second to freshen up. Coming back out to the front, she clocked back in at the register before looking up at the customer who'd just appeared in front of her. Her breath caught.

Him.

"Well, *well,* Red. Fancy meeting you here," Colin smiled down at her.

Heat blossomed in her belly as she met his eyes, her heart rate speeding up unexpectedly.

Not able to help herself, she gave him a quick once over. He was in dark gray slacks and a dark slate button up shirt that looked rather expensive. Eyes narrowing, she saw what might have been a hint of a tattoo just beneath the half of the shirt that was unbuttoned. His hair was manipulated in a tousled style, the strands untamed. His slight beard was meticulously groomed, the strands standing in deep contrast to his olive skin tone.

Fuck he's sexy, she thought. Not quite able to take his eyes off his beard, she swallowed thickly, somehow managing to smile back.

"I see you survived the storm," she winced.

"Am I ever going to get a greeting or farewell from you?" Colin asked with a chuckle, leaning a hip onto the counter as if he had all day. He crossed his arms, silently waiting for her reply.

Olivia frowned slightly. "What do you mean?" she replied, craning her neck to look behind him. There were three customers waiting to check out.

"When we met the other night, you didn't say hello or goodbye. Every interaction I've seen seem you have seems to move you on to the next thing."

"There are people behind you."

"Can you ring me up the peach pie please?" Colin replied softly, handing her his card.

Her lips pursed slightly at the shiny black Amex. A *no limit* black Amex.

Jesus, he's got money, she thought.

Careful not to touch him, Olivia grabbed his card and rang up his order before handing it back to him like it burned her. She smiled politely at him again before turning to take the other customers in line, effectively dismissing him, and ignoring him blatantly watching her interact with the other customers.

Olivia visibly seethed as he accepted his pie and opened it right at the register, eating it while she rang the other customers up. She resisted rolling her eyes, turning to him again once she had the last customer taken care of.

"Was there anything *else* you needed, *Colin*?" Her voice dripped in kindness laced with sarcasm.

Colin made her wait while he chewed another bite, his eyes downcast to his pie momentarily as if he was contemplating something important while he took his time chewing. She took the time to observe his attire better. Black belt, expensive silver watch on his wrist, however not a Rolex. She could see soft arm hair peeking out from under his shirt, and flicking her eyes back up she was struck with awe once more at how well-maintained his short beard was.

This was a man who obviously cared about his appearance.

Her mouth went dry, and her stomach fluttered as she twisted her lips in annoyance at the feelings he was unknowingly inflicting upon her. She bristled, not enjoying being made to be patient, and not appreciating these new feelings.

Colin turned, crossing the few feet to stand in front of her, and presenting her with another card. This time a business card.

C. McDermont Associates and Tech Holdings, LLC.

"*Okaayyy*...." Olivia said slowly, placing the business card on the counter in front of her.

"I'm not into tech," she said, sweeping her arm and referencing the diner.

Colin scoffed on a smile, tilting his head slightly. "No, I can see that. Give me a call, I'd like to take you to dinner." He grinned harder, crossing his arms and regarding her closely. His gaze left her eyes to slowly drag down the length of her face, down her neck to her breasts before flickering back up to her eyes.

Olivia shuttered herself closed so fast even *she* could hear the bang of the lock clicking shut.

She all but bared her teeth at him, because she knew it wasn't a smile. "No thank you," she said politely, sliding his card back to him.

Colin looked at her hand with the card before flicking his eyes to hers, grinning once more before pushing himself off the counter and leaving the diner dismissively, and without his business card.

She tore it in two and tossed it in the trash.

Olivia ran out of the diner at the end of her shift and raced to the store and then home, barely having time to put away her meager groceries, more rice and instant noodles.

She again raced to the bar she worked at and pumped out another five-hour shift. Her tips hit perfectly, and the manager of the bar gave her wages under the table. She went home beyond tired, putting the money in the shoebox before warming up the noodles in the microwave. As soon as she finished dinner, she set her alarm once again as she fell into bed, exhausted.

***

The next few weeks passed by in a blur.

Olivia beat her clients until her arm felt like it was going to fall off. She hung out with her sister and niece on Sundays, spending three days a week taking Allison to school to help Vanessa out so she could get to her nursing assistant job on time. At the end of the month, she again barely had enough money to scrape together to give to her sister, pay her rent, and afford the pain killers that Gypsy could trickle down to her.

Her reality was a distressing one.

Colin came to the diner four times a week, each time leaving his business card with her and obstinately requesting to take her to dinner. Each time her response was the same: she tore it up and put it in the garbage.

On the fourth week, she broke when she realized she had to forgo paying her electricity bill and groceries in order to not short Allison's medical bills. Bills which, for some reason, seemed to be getting more expensive.

She laid her head against the window, sobbing quietly in her car after she got off her shift at the diner. She held Colin's business card in her hand, remembering his black Amex card, now considering his offer because she was desperate for a full meal. Attempting to press the numbers into her phone through blurry eyes, she swiped at her cheeks angrily as she typed out a text.

She was hungry, irritated, needed food, and to rest her arm.

> I give, I'll go to dinner with you since you won't leave me alone-I'm free tomorrow night. -Olivia

She stared as the three dots showed up on the screen.

> Good girl. I'll text you tonight for your address. -C.

Her jaw dropped.

That's a bit...forward. she thought, frowning slightly at her phone and trying to ignore those uncomfortable butterflies fluttering around in her stomach.

> No, I don't need to be picked up. And I'm definitely NOT a good girl. -O.

> This only works one way, my way. And until you play nice, no dinner. For either of us, *bad girl.* -C

Olivia's eyes hit her hairline as she saw the text, rereading it a few times just to be sure. She bit her lip, narrowing her eyes as she contemplated her next response. Her tears were completely gone by this point, extinguished by the surprise tone of his text. Her teeth almost bit through her lip as she saw the dots again and read his next response.

> *Are you not cold in your car?* -C.

She gasped and whipped her head around, not seeing him anywhere.

> That's none of your business. -O.

> It's all going to be my business, soon. -C

> What does that mean? -O

> *Ask your boss. =). -C*

> ......excuse me? Elaborate, *please.* -O

> I'm buying the diner. I'm going to know your address, anyway. So, you might as well just give it to me, instead of playing hard to get. Isn't it tiring never being able to let go? It's written all over you plain as day. You're not doing a very good job of hiding from me,

> despite the many refusals you've made me suffer through this last month. -C

Rage unlike any kind she'd felt since the day she found out her parents died, and the day she found out the extent of Allison's medical issues filled her, seeping through her body in a white-hot inferno. She felt more so than saw her vision go red. Hands trembling, her fingers tapped out a response.

> Fuck you. You arrogant, disrespectful asshole. -Olivia.

Not waiting for a reply, Olivia threw her phone into the passenger seat and stomped on the accelerator, kicking up a dust trail behind her. Fumbling blindly for the phone once again, she quickly pulled up the google maps apps and typed in 'food pantry,' putting it as a stop in her GPS.

"*I don't need this shit,*" she mumbled to herself, her fingers digging into her steering wheel until they went numb.

Blinded by hurt and anger, she didn't notice the dusky blue BMW trailing a few cars behind her. She pulled slowly into the food pantry and glanced around nervously before getting out of her car, slinging her purse over her shoulder.

The elderly woman at the front desk gave her a list of information that she would need to submit to qualify to utilize the pantry's services, and with rising irritation, she realized she didn't have the required documentation. She thanked the lady graciously and trudged back to her car.

Stopping to throw her gaze to the sky, she once again asked God why the fuck he gave her and Vanessa this life.

In a fit of anger, she kicked her door hard, before getting in and resting her head on the steering wheel. Thinking about the money in the box at home and knowing she couldn't touch it. She was barely able to scrounge up the required money in the last couple of months before the bills went up. If she started dipping into it, then she definitely wouldn't have it next month.

"God!" Miserable, Olivia cried fresh tears at thinking about what would happen to Allison without the drug she needed for her liver.

Figuring nothing else would make her feel worse, she picked up the phone, pulled up her email and typed in 'match' in the search bar. The email she'd received from the hospital from four years ago showed up, explaining that she was not a match for Allison despite their family tie.

Letting herself have a rare emotional moment, she cried some more before putting her key into the ignition and pulling away from the food pantry. Still not seeing the BMW trailing her a few cars back.

Parking carefully in her spot, she looked at her text thread with Colin once again.

> I apologize for the last text. Though I think it's incredibly infuriating that you're buying my place of employment. I will relent to being picked up at my apartment. There better not be anything sketchy going on–I've got friends. -O

> That's nice to know. What kind of friends? -C.

> Aren't you a smart alec. You know what I meant. I'll be sending you my location tomorrow. You can pick me up at 7p. Apartment 1B. -O

5p, please. -C

7p. I spend Sundays with my niece. There was no question mark after 'please'. So bossy! -O

I am. Interesting, you don't look old enough to have a niece. -C

I'm 24. -O

Hmmm, I'll see you tomorrow. I'm really looking forward to it. Do you have a dress to wear, or would you like me to send you one? We're going to an Italian restaurant. -C

I know I don't have air in my car, but I have a dress to wear to a restaurant. I don't live in a diner uniform. -O

I was just making sure you are prepared; I never want to put you in an awkward position. At least, not THAT kind of awkward position. -C.

He sent her the demon emoji.

Olivia's eyebrow raised as she let a little giggle out at his text. The man had nerve. She briefly leaned her hips against the hood of her car, stalling walking inside of her home that wasn't a home.

Sir. Are you flirting with me? -O

Oh Olivia, the money I'd pay to hear you say 'sir' to me in person is absolutely sickening. I'd pay a lot. -C

Her eyes widened and she bit her lip, wondering if he'd be a suitable candidate for Esmerelda's ring, before quickly dismissing the thought, frowning. For some reason, she didn't like that idea at all. A tiny tinge of jealousy over this man she didn't even know surged through her and she shook her head.

Girl, get it together, she thought.

She replied to Colin's text with an angel and demon emoji as a response.

Olivia went in her apartment to see that there was no real food, so she popped a Percocet before getting ready to beat the shit out of her new client. Motivated by hunger she did so well he gave her a two-hundred-dollar bonus, which went straight into her shoe box.

***

> She said yes to dinner. She's 24 years old. -C. Kent

> Hm. You ever date anyone that young before. – J. Dawg

> No. And before you ask, no. She doesn't know I'm a sadist. Nosy as fuck. -C. Kent

> Speaking of fuck, when's the last time you got any? -J.Dawg

> John, why? Jesus. -C. Kent

Because you're about to unleash all your sadistic shit onto a 24 yr old. Maybe you should go fuck a few women first, get it out of your system before you do something to scare the poor girl. -J.Dawg.

Don't be fucking gross. I wouldn't do that. Stick my dick in some random, them stick it in her? She doesn't deserve that. She's different. — C. Kent

They're all different. That's why I'm single. Does she know you have money? -J.Dawg.

NO! God, you're annoying. -C. Kent.

FIVE

Tiganello In Mugs

SUNDAY WENT BY IN a blur: Olivia, Allison, and Vanessa binged watched movies, made cheap-fried bologna sandwiches, and played barbies until Allison conked out at four in the evening for a nap.

As she took the time to help Vanessa clean up the kitchen, she looked over at her sister, relieved to see some life come back into her eyes. She needed these Sunday family get together as much as she did.

"Hey, I'm going to head out earlier today. I have a thing. Is that okay?" Olivia said softly, crossing her arms and leaning her jean-clad hips on the counter.

She grinned as her sister's face truly lit up with happiness.

"Oh my *gosh,* is it a date?!" Vanessa half squealed, taking her arms and hopping up and down excitedly. Olivia nodded her head, smiling back at her as she saw them as they were when they were teenagers, and could afford to moon and laugh over boys.

It felt good to be able to live like that again, even if it was only for a second, and even if it wasn't true.

"Yes. And he's picking me up at my apartment, so I'm turning my location on again. Okay?" She grabbed her keys as she backed her way out the front door, leaving her sister to shimmy all over the living room in joy. She checked her phone.

> Are you absolutely sure I can't pick you up at 5? We can enjoy a glass of wine before heading out. -C

The text came through just as she pulled into her apartment at four-thirty. She hurried down the steps to her apartment, unlocking and opening the door as she contemplated thoughtfully. Not much of a drinker, she figured it couldn't hurt.

> I can be ready for company by 6pm, that's the best I can do. Also, I won't drink if the bottle has already been opened. -O

> Noted. Do you like red or white wine? -C

> I'm not really much of a drinker, honestly, so I'm not picky. I think red should be fine. -O

> I'll see you at six. Don't forget to send me your location, Olivia. -C

Olivia quickly sent him her location before looking around her apartment, self-consciously.

She shoved the two forks into the dishwasher along with the one plate, mug, and cup she allowed herself to have, turning it on quick mode. It saved on water, and dishwashing soap to only have so little. She wiped down her counter before sweeping her small kitchen and living area in a fit of OCD, even though everything was spotless because she was never home, and never had company.

Her place, though homey enough, had essentially been a crash pad for the last four years. There wasn't much to mess up, and not much to look at either. The beige painted walls were spotless still, not having any reason to be messed up either.

She threw herself in the shower, accidentally ripping through another ring of her rubber ducky shower liner. Going a little slower, she shaved quickly and washed her hair. With a frown she noticed she was out of body wash, so she finished washing up with shampoo.

Spraying her hair with volumizer, she took time to blow dry her hair and did her makeup lightly, not wanting Colin to get the wrong impression of their date tonight. She'd just wanted a nice dinner for once, and to not feel like an overworked work horse.

Cognizant of her safety, she slipped her taser in the space between her heavy breasts, snuggling it deep just in case she had to use it.

Olivia smiled with pleasure as she pulled on the only nice dress she had. An emerald-green maxi with pheasant sleeves that highlighted her eyes, cupped her breasts perfectly. It made her look taller than she really was. She moisturized the creamy swells of her breasts with a vanilla lotion, her hands gliding over her neck and shoulders gently. She finished it all off with clear lip balm and she dropped the tube, startled as a polite knock came from the front door.

Frowning, she looked at her phone, seeing that it was only five forty-nine.

Was this guy neurotic or what, she thought with irritation. No one was this polite, or on time. She wrenched the door open without looking, shivering as she felt the cool fall air brush her dewy skin.

"It's not six o'clock yet!" Olivia admonished, arching her neck and meeting his eyes before even thinking about saying hello.

The skin around his eyes crinkled as Colin hungrily assessed her face. Olivia licked her lips, suddenly feeling a hot, heavy pressure settle in between her legs, finally admitting to herself she may be more excited for this date for more than just the fact she was going to dinner. She was excited because of him.

"*See what I'm talking about?* I have yet to get a hello from you in the four weeks I've been patiently waiting to make your acquaintance," Colin teased. He flashed her a panty wetting smile and flicked his gaze to her lips. "Aren't you going to invite me in?" He held up a bottle of an expensive-looking wine she'd never seen at a grocery store.

Olivia felt herself flush in slight embarrassment at his question.

Jesus, it's like my parents didn't raise me with manners, Olivia lamented to herself as he smiled down at her. His text about her calling him 'sir' rushed through her head at that exact moment, and she blushed even harder, pulling her bottom lip in between her teeth.

She scoffed and moved to the side, gingerly pulling back so his body wouldn't brush hers as he walked in. "Watch your head, please."

He was so tall he almost had to stoop to keep from hitting his head on the short door frame, and for the very first time in years, she became properly embarrassed about her small home. So much so, her hands started sweating and she glanced around in a slight panic, suddenly wishing she'd put a few pieces of art on the wall. *Something.*

Anything to distract from how obviously boring and lifeless her home was.

Appropriate though, she supposed. Like her: lifeless and boring.

"You can come to the kitchen, I-I guess." Softly closing the door behind him, she reached over and took the wine careful not to touch his fingers. Her bare feet padded softly on the cheap gray linoleum floor as she made her way to the kitchen where she slipped behind the peninsula and stood rather awkwardly, not sure what to say as he made his way through her little living room, glancing around curiously, though there was obviously nothing to see.

"It's nice," he said simply, turning his eyes to hers and giving her a little smile.

"Thanks, it's small..."

Olivia tensed as his eyes perused her form slowly as he got comfortable leaning against her peninsula. At his compliment, she bristled with embarrassment at her lack of stools, or dining room table and chairs. She'd wanted to invite him to sit on the sofa, but wasn't sure she wanted to sit next to him that closely.

They had too much chemistry to be that close.

She could acknowledge that fact.

Placing the bottle with a soft clink on the countertop, she avoided his gaze while she desperately tried to tamp down her feelings of embarrassment. Thinking that this is why she didn't date.

"You are beautiful. *Stunning,* actually," Colin said gruffly. His eyes lingered slightly on her breasts and her collarbone. "Do you have anything for me to open this with?" he asked, reaching over to pick up the wine bottle again.

Her eyes widened in pleasure at the unexpected compliment. "Thank you. Uhm...I'm *not* sure I have a wine opener. I don't drink often enough to need one. Well... I guess I don't drink at all, really," Olivia said apologetically.

She bent, opening several drawers, and trying to ignore him curiously looking at her, and at the state of the mostly empty drawers. The few items within the drawers clanked loudly in the empty space, mentally willing a wine opener to appear out of thin air.

"Hmm," Colin rumbled again, fishing around his pocket and pulling out his key ring and unleashing an opener. "That's alright. I'm usually relatively prepared when it comes to these things," he offered, taking the wine bottle, and stabbing the opener into it.

He twisted it a few times before unexpectedly flicking his brown eyes to hers again, and she felt a heavy bang in between her legs. She sucked in a sharp breath and clenched, actually *clenched* as he raised an eyebrow at her.

She bit her lip and blinked, her eyes flickered away from his, unable to hold his stare. She swallowed thickly, feeling uncomfortable with the state of her body. She felt strung tight, almost painful so with her sudden rush of desire.

"What's wrong?" Colin asked gently.

"Oh, nothing," she said with a shy huff.

He smiled. "Are you going to get us a couple of wine glasses? Do you need me to keep telling you what to do?" he asked suggestively, tugging the cork out with a pop.

She nodded stupidly, blindly feeling for the dishwasher handle behind her. Taking out the lone glass and a mug, placing it on the counter between them. She squirmed, trying to pull the door of the dishwasher up discreetly and praying that he didn't ask questions about why there was literally nothing in her kitchen.

"No wine glasses, hm?" Colin said, with a contemplative glance at her. "Man. You really *don't* drink do you?"

Olivia let out a laugh, her eyes lighting up with amusement. "No, not usually."

His eyes roamed curiously before coming back to hers. "Do you cook at all? Your kitchen looks really... stark. No offense. Do you eat out a lot?" he asked as he poured them each a healthy amount of wine.

Goddamn it, she thought. She pressed her fingers into her arm which suddenly throbbed.

For the first time, she paid attention to what he was wearing.

He had an obviously nice watch on his left wrist, different from the one he'd worn when he was coming into the diner to ask her out. He had on slate gray slacks, and a white button-down dress shirt that he had opened a couple buttons at the top, letting his dark crinkly hair peek through. His sleeves were rolled up, revealing crisp dark hair on his thick forearms, and she saw the beginnings of a tattoo sleeve inching its way up his arm, hidden beneath his shirt sleeves.

Her head tilted as she unashamedly caressed him with her green-eyed stare.

Her mouth watered at the sight of Colin's forearms, strong and tight with roping veins and cords. His dress shoes were shiny, and he had a gold ring on his right ring finger. His dark hair was manipulated in a sexy style, and every now and then a strand would fall over his brow. Her fingers twitched to put it back in place.

Olivia swallowed a healthy drink, pausing as she looked rather bewildering in her mug. There was a pregnant pause while she thought to herself.

Maybe I'd actually drink if everything tasted like this, she thought with a small grin.

"I'm hardly ever home," she answered simply, meeting his and showing she had nothing to hide. And also that he shouldn't be looking for her here if he tried to come back. "And I can cook *some*, I guess. I just don't *much*."

Any, bitch. You don't cook at all. That voice niggled at her, taunting her.

She sucked her teeth in response. "*And*," Olivia added, her own eyes flickering over his form rather hastily again. "You don't look too bad yourself. Rather good in fact," she said with a small grin, feeling her cheeks pinken even more. The redhead's curse, always blushing. She wrapped an arm around her torso, her fingers digging into her ribs.

Colin's eyes tracked her movements, making her feel very seen.

She needed a break from the tension between them.

"Can you excuse me for a second? I still had a couple things to do before you came, *eleven* minutes early."

She edged her way around him and the counter before walking a few feet to her bedroom. She stopped abruptly, spinning around and hastily grabbing her mug of wine off the peninsula, giving him a shaky smile as she took it in the bedroom with her.

"You don't have to worry about that. I rarely come early," Colin chuckled, giving her a sexy, dangerous grin of his own as he leaned back and watched her walk into her bedroom.

How inappropriate, she thought wryly, grinning at his double entendre before closing her bedroom door and locking it.

She placed her drink down on her dresser and quickly stepped into the bathroom. She sprayed her favorite perfume onto her wrist and neck before putting her favorite necklace on that said 'Ally'. Flicking her eyes over her face in the mirror, she supposed she looked presentable before walking back into her bedroom.

Her eyes roamed to her closet, and the money hidden inside.

Eying the bedroom door, she called out, "One second, Colin," as she hurriedly took the shoebox down to removed a one-hundred-dollar bill, silently asked Allison to forgive her. She just couldn't let herself go out with a stranger with no back up-just in case, silently promising to put it back if she didn't need it.

Turning, she closed her closet door, shoving the money in her purse before walking back out into the main area with her wine, sipping it slowly as she went. She moaned a little in appreciation. Colin was still leaning against the counter, patiently watching her, arms folded as he sipped his own wine. She cursed to herself at how attractive she found him.

Colin had a dangerous aura that perplexed her, and she contemplated why it was so attractive.

Why she couldn't put him from her mind like she could everyone else.

"Thank you for waiting. This is *seriously* amazing wine. What kind is it?" she asked as she rounded the peninsula and looked at the bottle, smiling slightly, ignoring the feel of his intense stare on her face. His nostrils flared as he picked up on her scent, causing her cheeks to redden in response.

"Tignanello," he stated quickly, his voice slightly deeper than before. "An Italian wine, I'm pleased you enjoy it. It's my favorite. Gotta love a beautiful, bold red," he said to her pointedly, his eyes flickering to her hair as sipped his wine some more, groaning appreciatively.

Her eyebrow arched at the obvious parallel he made between her and the wine.

Colin ignored her surprised expression at his bold words, turning to point his glass towards the small living room.

"What's the story behind that?" Colin asked curiously. His head turned back to face her, and she could feel her face grow warm his eyes bored into hers.

Confused, Olivia scrunched her eyebrows before craning her neck to look behind him, only to see her worktable that sat across from a lamp and sofa. No furniture other than the ragged sofa and her work table.

"Oh, I don't have a dining table," she said, misunderstanding him. "The space really isn't big enough-"

"No, I'm talking about the blueprints on the worktable over there. What are they? They look important... are you building something?" His gaze met hers once more, making her freeze in place. Olivia's hand stilled on her cup as something confusing hit her, coiling hot in her belly.

She attempted to ignore it and concentrate on what he was saying, but he was just so damn handsome she couldn't manage it. She felt like she couldn't breathe around him. Like there just wasn't enough oxygen for the both of them inside her little apartment and, for some reason, it was all being allocated to him instead of her.

"Oh," Olivia paused, cradling her wine in her hand, wondering if she wanted to share this piece of herself with him.

She turned and walked to the worktable slowly, feeling him following behind her. They stood side by side, seeing the blueprints and the architectural measuring and drawing tools spread next to them. She reached forward and straightened a slightly crooked straight ruler, clearing her throat nervously.

"There's not much of a story. I used to be in architectural school at Rhode Island School of Design, and this was one of the last projects I was able to complete before being forced to drop out. I kept it because I loved it. For the memories. I always thought I'd end up building it for myself to live in, but my career didn't exactly turn out the way I wanted it to," she said, finishing the wine and turning to him.

She took a slight step back when she realized just how close he was to her, his arm almost touching hers.

Colin's eyes roamed her face with more than curiosity as her's widened, however, her momentarily shyness seemed to embolden him, and he smiled as his eyes flicked to her lips momentarily, causing her to wet them. Colin's nostrils flared again at her movement, and his eyes slid from her face as he smoothly turned his attention back to the blueprints. Olivia took another minuscule step back, desperately trying to put more space between the two of them.

The sexual attraction between them was almost too much. Forcing Olivia to question her no dating rule. Because she wasn't sure if she was up to dating, much less a charismatic man such as Colin. His energy was a lot to deal with. It saturated her from the inside out, stealing her senses.

And she needed all her senses intact.

"This is beautiful work, Olivia. You must be incredibly smart, and wonderfully talented." Colin said smoothly.

Olivia felt herself break out in goosebumps; her breath hitched slightly as he moved, feeling her clit pulsate as he leaned forward and put a hand to the paper. His fingertips spread over the drawing momentarily before he caressed it in a confidently move. The man oozed unadulterated assuredness, and she found herself inching closer instead of away.

Drawn into his aura, wanting to take some of it for herself.

"Thank you. That's a very nice compliment. Not many people have seen this..." Olivia murmured, her eyes flickering around the room as she desperately tried to pull herself together. She felt like a thread had come loose, and he was slowly starting to unravel it.

Quickly feeling overwhelmed again, she gripped her ribs tighter, needing to ground herself.

"This is my favorite spot in the home. The way you've drawn this makes an already intimate space seem more so. Almost like you designed the house around the bedroom," Colin mused thoughtfully. His eyes followed her measurements, taking in how some rooms required more and what didn't. "The spare bedrooms are so far from the main one. What made you have that idea? It's rather unusual. I wonder the reasoning as to the extreme privacy..." he enquired again, that smooth voice feeling like it was caressing straight into the center of her brain.

His head tilted as he looked down at her, expecting a reply.

She bit her lip before taking another sip. "Because it *is* intimate. And private. Where private things happen," Olivia surmised with a slight snort, wanting to say 'duh' out loud, feeling like she just told him the most juvenile thing possible.

For not the first time, she wondered how old he was.

"*Well*, I guess *all* bedrooms have private things happen in them, huh?" she tried to joke, correcting herself awkwardly, knowing she was blushing. Which was made even worse when he tilted his head to look down at her, and made a scoffing sound in the back of his throat.

"Some bedrooms need to be more private than others," he whispered, his eyes flicking down to her lips before bringing his mug up and drinking from it. "Is yours private? Is that why you locked yourself in there just now?" he dared to press, probing, trying to see an in.

Olivia pursed her lips in shock before flushing, her eyebrows furrowed. "May I have some more?" she asked dismissively, turning and walking the few feet back to the peninsula, and waving at the wine bottle.

He joined her again, and she freshened both of their cups before recorking the bottle with effort, making him chuckle. She turned to open her fridge, wincing at the eerily empty sound it made as she placed the bottle on the bare shelves before closed it quickly, hoping he didn't notice.

"So, why'd you never finish? There's got to be a story there," he pressed, wanting to know details.

"Not one I wish to discuss, and not one you need to know," Olivia snapped, trying and failing not to sound mean.

She bit her lip and closed her eyes briefly before opening them once more. His eyes were on hers intensely, and feeling too laid bare, she pressed her fingers against her hips awkwardly. Digging in. Wishing she had something to do, perhaps an amazon echo dot to put music on in the background.

The silence stretched between them.

She quickly realized this was a man who did not subject himself to coddling social cues. If a faux pass was made, he expected it to be addressed. He also didn't seem to shy down from intensity, rather seemingly inclined to relish in turning it up. She pouted her lips slightly, wishing he would say something to break the tension between them.

"I'm sorry. That was rude of me," she said, feeling her face heat up as she blushed.

Colin didn't relax out of his stance, regarding her quietly. "Apology accepted. If you don't wish to talk about it right now, I understand," he said, tipping his mug, finishing his wine before handing it to her.

He waited silently as she rinsed out the glasses and dried them before placing them into a yet again bare cabinet. Again inwardly wincing at the loud echoing bang her bare cabinet made when she closed the door.

Olivia grabbed up her purse and her phone and walked him to the door, taking a second to slide on a pair of matching green heels, using her side table to support herself as she stood on one foot and slid them on.

He watched her quietly, amused.

"Oh, *wait,*" Olivia said breathlessly.

She glanced at him before walking back to the kitchen, her heels tapping loudly. She turned on the light above her stove, then walked over to the lamp in the living area and switched that on, then hurried back to her bedroom, not caring that he'd see her purple room and the cheap frame of her bed as she walked inside.

Olivia busied herself turning on a small lamp by her bed and another nightlight in her bathroom, not wanting to come home to a dark apartment. Attention diverted; she missed the look that passed over Colin's face at her actions.

He kindly put a hand on her elbow to escort her up the stairs that led to the parking lot. Olivia pulled away once, trying to divert to her car, but he simply steered her purposefully and efficiently to his vehicle instead.

After a small tussle in the parking lot in which he told her sternly that *'under no circumstances'* would he let her drive herself, she relented, and let him place her into the passenger seat of his car.

When Colin closed the door, Olivia placed her purse on the floor and took a second to take in the soft leather seats, the muted lighting of the car, and the heavenly smell.

God, who knew a car could smell rich, her lips twitched slightly as she tried to reign in her feelings.

She was in rich people's company a couple times a week with her clients. However, she was busy focusing on inflicting pain in those scenarios, *not* worrying about her surroundings other than her safety.

"Any music preference?" Colin asked, hooking his phone up to the system and her eyebrows hit her hair line once again as 'Sex' by Sticky Fingers dominated the car, even flashing the title on his fancy computer system.

Colin didn't seem embarrassed to Olivia, and she rolled her lips as he turned the music down and stared at her intently, waiting for a response, not bothering to change the music.

"Oh, uhm.... how's Aaryan Shah?" she asked gently as he handed her his phone to put the artist in. So distracted that she couldn't tell that he pulled parking lot and into the street as the sun went down, without needing GPS to guide him.

She also missed the look he gave her at the mention of the Artist.

SIX

What Do You Want

THEY RODE IN ALMOST complete silence, apart from the music. Colin occasionally broke the silence by telling her gently which songs he liked as the phone ticked through playlist.

Putting her eyes on the clock, she'd noticed they'd been driving for almost an hour. Her eyebrows raised in shock.

"Okay sooo...are you *kidnapping* me, or what's up?" Olivia asked hesitantly, nervously checking her phone to make sure her location was still on. She sent it to her friend Aliyah as well, who she affectionately called Beau. Aliyah replied with a "?" and Olivia's brows furrowed as she sent a short text to her.

> I'm out on a date. We're out further than I expected, just pay attention to my location. If I'm not home by 1a, call the police. His name is Colin McDermont. -O

She glanced nervously at Colin, however he remained looking out the window smiled cheekily, as if he realized what she was doing.

"You're safe with me, Olivia," Colin rumbled reassuringly, placing his hand on her thigh. His accent seemed thicker, and she briefly wondered if it'd be weird to ask him to speak to her in Spanish.

The warmth of Colin's hand seeped through her dress stunned her. He gave her a slight squeeze before reaching to turn on her seat warmer and putting his hand back on the gear shift.

Her heart beat a strange tattoo, stealing her breath and making her slightly dizzy. Maybe that's why she couldn't talk, she couldn't breathe right next to him. Her stomach tangled in knots, and she briefly contemplated offering him the hundred dollars for him to turn and take her back home.

She really didn't care for these feelings she was having. They were genuinely scaring her.

"We're going to this little Italian restaurant that I know. The chef is pretty famous," Colin spoke quietly, keeping his tone neutral.

Olivia watched him steer, maneuvering them along a steep hill before turning onto a hidden asphalt road that led to a pair of gates. He grabbed his phone off the dock and quickly texted a number, and a few seconds later the gates opened before letting them into a clearing with a small parking lot.

Olivia glanced at him, observing he had a rather smug look on his face.

"*This* is the restaurant? It looks like a house!" she gaped at him, her head turning to watch the last two cars leave the parking lot, their lights fading in the background behind them. She quickly let herself out before he could open her door.

Colin rounded to her side quickly, his broad hand curling over the frame and gripping tightly before she could slam it shut.

"Olivia, when we are out together you will allow me to open doors for you. Don't do it again, please," Colin clipped, his expression turning haughty before he slid that smooth mask back in place. The transition was instant as he again became the considerate and refined gentleman she'd come to know him as.

Cocky, arrogant, ass, Olivia thought, but she stayed silent, lifting a brow in return.

She didn't argue. Admitting to herself that she wasn't used to anyone, much less a man, demanding that she let him treat her with respect.

Colin held out his hand, waiting patiently for her to step away from the car before closing the door softly. He turned to her, his eyes crinkling as if he was thinking of something amusing.

"It's a membership only private restaurant. Small and very exclusive so I had to pull some strings since you couldn't make it at five. That's why I wanted us to be here earlier. I asked the chef, staff and owners to stay later tonight," he said, opening the back door and grabbing a suit jacket.

He closed the car door and placed the small of his hand on her back, leading her to the ornate iron double doors of the restaurant. She stopped abruptly, shooting him a fierce glance as he turned and looked down at her.

"*Colin*, I would have been happy with a little bar and grill!" she said, her cheeks warming. "My *fucking* God. You didn't have to inconvenience everyone!" she whispered hotly to him.

Drawing them to a sudden stop before they reached the doors and squeezing the bridge of her nose with her fingers, trying to breathe through the irritation.

"You brought me over an *hour* for *spaghetti*?" Olivia just couldn't wrap her head around it. She glanced up at him through her lashes, knowing her green eyes were irritated, but couldn't find it within herself to care much about how he felt about her temper.

Her eyes widened as Colin stepped just slightly into her space.

It wasn't a lot, but it was enough for her to get the picture.

"You will be *happy* wherever I choose to take you, Olivia. Be it a bar and grill, or a fancy expensive restaurant... a vacation to the other side of the world perhaps. I'm not sure. But you will relax yourself and enjoy our dinner and our time together tonight," Colin all but growled down at her.

Olivia's jaw dropped, shocked at his words. Just then her arm spasmed, almost causing her to drop her purse.

She grabbed her arm in earnest, feeling the sharp burning pain there, glancing up at him again in embarrassment before placing her purse on her other arm.

Her cheeks heated. "I won't be hopping on a plane with you *anywhere,*" she whispered, attempting to get the focus off her incident.

"Are you okay?" he asked smoothly, his eyes flicked over her in concern and curiosity before he once again placed his warm hand on her lower back.

She tensed as he smoothly slid her purse off her arm and held it in his hand, guiding her through the front doors. Looking down in disbelief at him holding the feminine strap, she was happy he didn't comment on her embarrassing moment, though he looked like he wanted to.

As they walked into the foyer, she breathed a sigh of relief when she realized this was indeed a restaurant, and he didn't bring her here to kill her.

"Yes, I'm fine. It hurts, but it's nothing. I have a high pain tolerance, I'll be fine," she said before wetting her lips and stepping slightly away from him. Needing space from the magnetic pull between them.

"Hmm," his sound came across slightly judgmental, but he continued to lead them through the foyer without commenting further. He shot her another complex glance, and looked up as the host greeted them warmly before taking them through a lavishly decorated dining room. They didn't stop there, however.

He led them through the back to another lavish yet intimate deck where there were only four small tables, all decorated by glowing *real* candles, overlooking a sparkling pond that shimmered brightly in the moonlight. There were big, beautiful lights strung from beams in the air above them, lending a romantic ambiance to the serene atmosphere.

It was quiet, being enough removed from the city. The strains of beautiful classical music sounded in the peaceful air around them.

She sat down gingerly in the seat Colin held out for her, managing to say thank you to him before she realized he tipped the host two hundred dollars as he shook the man's hand. Still behind her, he reached around to hook her purse on a hidden hook under the table next to her leg.

Olivia's breath froze in her lungs as he took the opportunity to graze his nose alongside her shoulder and neck with his movement. His warm breath washed over her, and her eyes widened as she stiffened, glancing away nervously and picking up her menu. She felt her nipples become painfully hard and she bit back a soft sound trying to crawl through her throat. The words on the menu came into focus.

Fucking Italian.

Dammit.

"I'll just take a broccoli alfredo," Olivia said slowly, closing the menu abruptly and placing it carefully to the side. She winced as the menu clanked against the stemware laid neatly out for them and looked up in apology, her face grimacing slightly. "You know, this is totally *not* a first date place."

She nervously pulled the sleeves of her peasant dress up higher. Eyeing Colin warily as he smiled, picking up her menu and opening it back up, handing it to her.

"I'm glad to hear you verbally acknowledge this as a date. I'll help you order. Follow along please," Colin said quietly, his eyes meeting hers for longer than she was comfortable with. Looking down and away from her, he began to translate the menu in English so she could understand.

In the end she'd picked a salad course, a small charcuterie board, and a half plate of bolognase. Not knowing how much anything cost, as there were no prices next to the items listed, which really made her further uncomfortable.

Looking up at the silence from across the table she leaned forward, noticing displeasure in his suddenly cool expression. She leaned back in her chair and softly ran her fingers up her bare arm, feeling her flesh pebble under the stare he'd just made her endure, somehow icy and hot at the same time.

Olivia blinked slowly. "What's wrong?" she asked, meeting his gaze as he sipped on the red wine their waiter served them. His eyes were studying her fingers on her arm, watching her caress herself with interest before he turned his eyes to hers again.

"I want you to pick what you want. There's absolutely no need to spare my wallet, I have money, and I love to spend it. So, pick what you want," Colin stated simply, rubbing his forefinger holding his glass against his lips. He leaned back in his chair comfortably, placing an ankle over his knees before licking his bottom lip and giving her a sly grin.

She briefly wondered what it'd be like to kiss them, then killed the thought as quickly as she had it. "What... what I want?"

"Yes. What do you *want*?" he asked, his voice holding a seductive ring to it.

Olivia's eyes widened slightly, and she lowered them to the table in front of her, a heavy feeling suddenly coming over her and settling into her heart. She tilted her head slightly, inwardly battling emotions that she knew she could never share.

With him, or anyone else.

I want my niece to be healed. I want to be an architect. I want to stop beating rich people for money every month. I want to sleep more than five hours a night for once. I want peace. But I can't have these things. Nor wish for them, she thought, looking carefully down at the embellished menu. But she couldn't share this with this arrogant man. So, she picked something easier.

"The...the *oysters,* and.... maybe the duck with the fettuccine," she said in a sure voice, proud that she expressed it more calmly than she felt. Trying to reduce the tremors that started somewhere deep inside.

Colin appraised her over his menu, watching the candlelight flicker on her beautiful face before reaching a hand up to motion to the waiter. Never leaving her eyes, he repeated her order, and then relayed his order of lasagna.

She squirmed under his patient gaze as he just sat there with his wine glass loose in his hand watching her. His elbow relaxed gently on his knee, and his other hand stroked his fork ever so often. He seemed content to just stare at her. Memorizing her face.

"Um.... why aren't you saying anything?" Olivia said, suddenly self-conscious.

She tucked a long thick lock of hair behind her ear again before putting her gaze to the pretty pond next to them, sparkling in the moonlight. She suddenly felt unsettled, and hated that he made her feel like that. Maybe it was his age and effortless confidence making her feel out of place.

Or was it her lack of social grace? Not having hardly any opportunity in the past few years to date, or to even foster friendships that could help in this area.

"Because you're a woman of few words, I'm finding. Or, at least... words that aren't true to you. We made most of the drive in silence, did we not?" he asked in his elegantly cultured voice.

He continued to sit back confidently as the waiter placed the oysters in front of them, before placing another wine bottle in the ice holder on their table. She shivered, knowing his words hit a spot inside of her she never let herself inspect. She swallowed another small sip of wine before picking up an oyster and then looking at him rather sheepishly.

"I don't know how to eat these. I just ordered them to be difficult," she confessed. She shivered again at his sexy smile. There was a hardness to the curve of it, as if he was amused at the mouse struggling against the trap.

"I know you're difficult. I'll teach you how not to be," Colin said, continuing to hold her gaze with his.

Olivia's lips parted at his crass words, but she remained silent, feeling herself become wet in between her legs at his confident, commanding tone. She swallowed thickly, praying she didn't choke when she went to eat.

Colin smiled a wicked knowing grin at her, extending the silence out a little longer. He took a deep swallow of his wine and Olivia found herself riveted, watching his throat work around it. She bit her lip, her breathing coming slightly faster as the flesh between her thighs throbbed.

SEVEN

Oysters and 'O' Playists

"BUT FIRST, LET'S START with the oysters," Colin continued, his voice becoming gruff as his gaze slipped to her mouth. He Hummed low in his chest before ripping his eyes from hers. She clenched at the sound, feeling that hot need burn brighter in her lower belly.

Colin reached forward, snagging an oyster before she could say anything.

"Tilt your head back, chew and swallow," he instructed, demonstrating to her with his own oyster. "Make sure you get all the oyster liquor as well. Every drop," he said, sitting back and watching her place the shell to her pink lips.

"Wonderful," he congratulated lowly as she successfully ate her first ever oyster. Only dribbling just a tiny bit of the liquor on her chin which she quickly scooped up with a slender finger.

Olivia afforded him what Colin figured was a rare genuine smile before they continued to eat in silence, only once breaking it for him to offer her more wine. To which she responded no, having already had three glasses tonight.

Olivia found herself oddly comfortable with their shared silence, seeing that he wasn't uncomfortable either. He seemed to enjoy sitting back and watching her eat.

Colin tilted his head as she sat back in her seat, watching the fingers of her left arm play with the sleeve of her dress. His eyes flickered to hers as she opened her mouth to speak.

"I'm not mute, you know," she teased, referencing his comment from a bit ago as they finished their appetizer. She licked her lips and sipped on some water.

She blinked slowly as he smiled, the corner of his mouth lifting adorably.

"Could have fooled me. I was contemplating buying you a white striped t-shirt and some white face makeup and red lipstick. Maybe some white gloves to complete the outfit. I figured you could mime and maybe be more comfortable." He half laughed, running his hand down his slight beard in amusement.

She shocked both of them with bright, high laugh at his words. Throwing her head back and putting her hand on her breastbone. Tilting her head back down she wiped a tear away, cleaning her throat and grabbing her water once more. "Colin, you are so clever," she giggled.

Swallowing the water, she threw the waiter a thankful smile as he placed her entree in front of her and removed the cover keeping her food warm. Her eyes widened in appreciation at the delicious meal being unveiled between the two of them.

"And you are exquisitely beautiful, and fascinating. I don't think I've ever met anyone like you before." His confidently smooth voice floated across the table, suddenly stealing her joyful mood and replacing it with something else she couldn't name.

Olivia's breath hitched and her belly cramped slowly, heat infusing her insides as he pinned her with an innately sexual stare. Not even hiding his desire. Her eyes narrowed as she gave him a very slight shake of her head.

No.

You cannot go there, Olivia. This man will ruin you, and this is not something you can afford right now, she thought to herself, instinctively realizing this was true even without knowing him. Despite his polite demeanor, there was something dangerous.

He let it go, waving the wine away, and ordering them tea.

He ate his lasagna slowly, even offering her a bite which she surprised the both of them by accepting. He leaned back, preferring to watch her attack her duck entrée with gusto and eating his food much slower. She answered questions about the diner, though nothing inconsequential. Every now and then she gripped her right arm at her shoulder and elbow tightly when she would raise her fork for another bite with a pained look she worked very hard to hide, but she could tell he still saw.

She was too young to have such pain, and they both knew it.

He suddenly cleared his throat, and it looked to her like a pained expression crossed *his* face before he spoke. "Do you need me to feed you?" he asked, his flirtation obvious.

"No," she said, switching her fork to her left hand, slowing her movements even more. But she was determined to not appear weak in front of him. "No, I got it. Thank you."

"Do you play tennis?" Colin asked suddenly, readjusting himself in his seat and sitting back, drinking his tea leisurely.

"What?" Olivia giggled, in a rather good mood after eating, and several glasses of wine.

"Your arm. You keep holding it like it hurts. What happened?" he enquired, meeting her gaze confidently over his cup, not content to let her finagle her way out of this one. And for not the first time that night, seeing too much yet again.

Olivia's face went pale as she looked away, licking her lips before biting them gently. "It's nothing, just a minor inconvenience from working too much," she explained, not quite meeting his gaze.

He waited a beat before answering.

"At the diner? It was hurting when I met you four weeks ago?" he quipped, putting his cup on the table and placing his hand on his elevated knee. "You hid it well."

She bit her lip again, sitting back in the chair and crossing her legs. Her creamy flesh shone brightly in the moonlight against the green material of her dress. The wheels of her mind turned, and he waited patiently as she worked out what she wanted to say.

"I don't *just* work at the diner," she said, lacing her fingers together tightly to stop them from shaking.

"No?" he pressed curiously, shooting the question across the table, feeling her bristling in response.

Olivia watched rather distractedly, seeing a muscle tick in his jaw.

"*No.* I also have a couple side hustles."

"Side hustles? What's a pretty thing like you doing, working so hard?" he said lowly, almost playfully, but his face was stern, his eyes hard as he regarded her.

Her heart skipped a beat at his words, and she glanced down nervously at her almost emptied plate. "Yea... I have to work, you know." She shrugged. "I'm a part time bartender, *and* a full-time job as an aunt," she threw back, feeling his eyes settle on the necklace nestled in the hollow of her collarbone.

"Hmmm. I see." His throat worked around another deep swallow of tea. "Ally. Is that her... your niece?" he gave her a kind smile.

She nodded slowly and touched her necklace. "Allison." Olivia's voice sounded across the table sadly. Her heart began to race as that familiar, choked-up feeling slowly tightened its way around her throat regarding her niece.

"Is she what you're stressed about?" he pressed nonchalantly, carefully. Colin held her gaze over his cup as he sipped from his drink again.

Olivia stared pensively at him before her features subtly pulled into an impassive expression. She shrugged one shoulder, looking over at the pond once more. Hoping that if she took her gaze off of him, it would lessen the almost uncomfortably searing effect he was pulling over her consciousness like a cloak that's pulled so tight you had no prayer of ripping off.

"You know, I really don't care for dessert. I think I'm ready to go home. I've had a nice time," she replied, her voice sounding haunted. She turned her gaze back to him.

Colin frowned slightly, and Olivia could see something flash in his eyes again. It looked like what she felt; sad.

Olivia's shoulders relaxed and she found herself relieved when he nodded. He was seeing too much, and more to the point, she was *giving* too much.

Colin held her gaze while he finished his tea, silently signaling their waiter for the check. Throwing her off again, he handed her his phone with his apple music app open. Olivia glanced at him in surprise. He smiled a half grin at her as he took the check from the waiter.

"Set us a playlist to drive you home to," Colin ordered, reaching into his pocket for his wallet.

He fished out his card and thumbed a few hundred-dollar bills for a tip and slid them deftly into the thin black book. Her eyebrows raised as she struggled over what to concentrate on; the fact he'd just spent about a thousand dollars just in tips for dinner, or the fact she had his open phone in her hand, and he was waiting for her to start adding songs.

Olivia started a new playlist for him and titled it "O's songs."

She named it simply, making sure to add a bunch of The Weeknd songs, dotted with some other surprises like Lana Del Rey, Ed Sheeran, Jhene Aiko and Beyonce. With a smattering of Elton John, Teddy Swims, SZA and Adele. She kept the playlist purposefully young, wanting to throw him off, just like he attempted to unsettle her.

She rolled her lips when she mentally considered his age again, determining that whatever his age, she probably had no business being with him.

They stood up from the table and made their way through the restaurant to leave, and Olivia found herself oddly comforted by the feel of his warm hand pressing onto her lower back.

As Colin helped her to the already running car, she smiled in happiness as notes from her favorite song filled the night air.

She paused briefly at the door of the car and looked up at him, seeing his eyes shining in the moonlight. She pulled her lip in between her teeth and her eyes flickered between his as they stood there, close to each other next to the car.

Colin tilted his head slightly, watching her.

Olivia released her lip, feeling herself leaning into him slightly. She wondered again what it would be like to kiss him, to have intimacy with another person. Colin leaned further in and she tilted her head back, her eyes fluttering as she dropped her gaze from his eyes to his mouth. He stepped into her, putting his hand on her waist and pulling her slightly closer.

Her tongue darted out as he dipped his head and softly placed his lips over hers. Olivia moaned softly, letting herself experience being desired for the first time in years.

His hand sank into her hair, anchoring her and she giggled slightly at the feel of his beard scraping her face as his lips pressed deeper into hers. She put her hands on his chest and parted her lips, feeling his tongue stroke alongside hers. He stepped into her slightly more, pressing his body against hers and she felt her sex slicken with desire at feeling the hardness of his body against hers.

"You taste so good," he said quietly, pulling back slightly to talk to her before leaning in again. His words dropped her back to reality, and she pulled away reluctantly, her eyes falling away from his shyly before sliding into the car.

Absolutely wrecked.

Olivia shook herself out of her thoughts and shot Colin a thankful glance as he closed the door behind her, walking around and getting into the driver's side. She stiffened as his scent immediately assaulted her. He smelled like sandalwood, a fresh suit smell, and something more she couldn't put her finger on. But it was magnetic, just like him.

She glared at her purse on the floor at the side of her feet.

Staying silent while Colin snapped his seat belt and pulled them out of the spot, taking the driveway carefully. She willed herself not to lunge into it and pull out her burner phone to check for messages about the upcoming week. Which is what she'd usually be doing by this time on a Sunday night.

After a few minutes of comfortable music listening, she turned to him. Her eyes roamed over his brown hair and his side profile. She took several seconds to drink the vision of him in as she didn't plan on seeing him anymore. Planning to give him the news via text after he dropped her off.

"Thank you for taking me to dinner, the place was lovely," Olivia said softly, giving him a small smile as she clenched her hands in her seat, attempting to give him something for his troubles of showing her a nice time. She didn't want to be a complete bitch. "It was delicious, and it was my first-time trying oyster, *or duck*. And the wine really was so good. I'd drink more if I could have that quality all the time," she said with a little laugh. "Thanks for insisting on me getting what I really wanted, it was a real treat," she continued, noticing a light at her feet.

She desperately tried to ignore her purse suddenly glowing in the floor of the car, gritting her teeth.

Colin glanced at her, with a slightly amused grin on his face.

"You're incredibly welcome. A beautiful experience, for a beautiful, fiery woman." He half smiled again as if he had a secret.

She tilted her head. "So, you've really told me nothing about yourself," she continued, trying.

"I'm an open book-ask away," he stated, throwing her a grin before turning back to the road. His hand flexed on the gearshift, and she found herself once again mesmerized by his strong hands, thick wrists with crisp dark hair peeking out of his sleeves.

"Well for starters, how old are you?" she asked playfully, realizing she really wanted to know this detail about him.

"Thirty-eight," Colin answered simply, his fingers readjusting on the wheel.

He smiled wider as he felt her shock from the short distance away in the car. He didn't mind, he'd liked the fact they had an age gap, it would make things easier as he could use it to his advantage, and it was such a power exchange enhancer.

Olivia suddenly cast her eyes out the window again, her expression contemplative. Unwilling to ask any more questions.

"Are you going to answer that?" he jilted her way over the music, arching his eyebrow at her purse which hadn't stopped glowing.

She reached in quickly and grabbed the phone, seeing four missed calls from her sister.

She never calls me back to back like this, Olivia panicked, her fingers fumbling with the phone thinking something must have happened to Allison.

Her body went in overdrive; tears springing from the back of her eyes, her breathing became shallow as she shakily answered the phone, turning it on speaker as she didn't even have the strength to hold it to her ear, she was so petrified.

"Hey, what's going on?" she asked sharply, her eyes closing as she waited with her heart beating for bad news. Her hand brushed down her thigh roughly, the material of her dress scraping against her legs.

"Auntie Ollie," Allison's little voice sounded over the phone. Her breath hitched as she realized Alison was fine.

Turning her face to the window she cleared her throat gently before she attempted to speak. "Hiii, baby. What's going on, love?" Olivia gritted out in a fake cheery voice, reaching up to swipe an errant tear away.

She was conscious of Colins' movements while he was driving, he'd reached over to put the music at a very low background level.

"Auntie, I don't feel good..." the little girl whispered as she breathed heavily into the phone.

Olivia placed her hand over her mouth briefly, squeezing hard as she suppressed a sob. She quickly sucked a deep breath through her nose as she felt Colin's hand land on her leg, squeezing reassuringly, his eyes still on the road. She looked at the clock, seeing they'd been out later than she expected.

"I know you don't feel good, sweetie. What can I do to make it better?" she asked, lacing her voice with every ounce of soothing auntie cadence she could stand to muster in front of the man next to her. The heat of his palm sank into her flesh as his thumb traced back and forth across her knee.

"Can you read me a story? Talk to me a 'wittle?" Allison whispered weakly.

"Yes. Of course, I can scubert. Where's mommy?" she crooned back. Colin's hand suddenly made her feel very hot.

It laid heavily on her leg, as if he were holding her down, making her feel incredibly grounded, confusing her feelings even more.

"I'm right here. I'm really sorry to disturb your date, Ollie." Vanessa's soft voice sounded tired over the phone.

"It's okay, I don't think he's upset," Olivia peeked at Colin, seeing his slight grin., "Which story do want me to read tonight? What adventure shall we be partaking in together, little bit?" she said playfully.

"Little red riding hood," Allison said quietly.

She snuck a quick peek through her lashes at Colin who was studiously staring at the road in front of them. He shook his head yes, a brief smile gracing his lips as he squeezed her leg again encouragingly. His fingers curled around her flesh, bunching the material and cupping her inner thigh next to her knee intimately, curling around to the seat his hand was so big.

His thumb continued to sweep slow strokes over the top.

She pulled up her story book app and found the book, reading and giving her all the silly parts that she knew Allison loved. When Vanessa verified that Allison was asleep, she hung up her phone.

There was a tense silence as Olivia struggled to gain control of her emotions.

She sat back in the seat, her breathing becoming erratic as she swallowed thickly, trying desperately to get a handle over what she figured to be a panic attack. She didn't have them very often. Her grapple for control lasted briefly before she suddenly bent forward to her purse with a small noise in the back of her throat.

Fuck it, who cares? She had business to take care of.

EIGHT
Manners and Maniacs

THROWING CAUTION TO THE wind, Olivia hurriedly reached into her purse to grab her burner phone, not even pretending to not feel panicked next to this man who had just treated her to a lovely dinner. She didn't want him to know her secrets, but her desperation overtook any sense of propriety she'd attempted to have with him.

Fuck him. I'm not seeing him again anyway. Who cares what he thinks of me, she thought.

Blinking through her tears that she wouldn't let fall she unlocked her burner phone using facial recognition and called Gypsy. It rang twice before she answered, and this time she didn't turn the speakerphone on.

"What's up, love? Normally, you'll text me. You okay?" Gypsy's elegant voice sounded through the phone.

"G, I need more. Like *two* more. And I need them *this* week," she spoke into the phone urgently, leaning forward to pick Colin's hand off her knee. He put it back on the gearshift, looking at her out the side of his eye.

"But, *your arm,*" Gypsy's concern barely penetrated her consciousness.

"I don't give a *flying fuck* about my arm. Can you get me what I need? I barely had enough to make her hospital payments last month. I'm *drowning,*" she hissed into the phone.

"This week?"

"Yes, this week!"

"It may not be what you like." Gypsy said hesitantly.

"I don't care about that right now, I'll relent *a little* if it means I can get them this week. I'll text you in a minute what I can compromise on. Burners, sickers, *whatever*," she said, her voice going up an octave. "Just get me something, please! Can you take care of me? G, I *never* ask for anything! You know that! Don't make me beg, Gypsy," she all but gritted tearfully into the phone, hating to sound desperate to either of the people listening to her talk. She listened intently as Gypsy typed on her computer.

"I found two available on Tuesday night and Saturday, right after your regular with the Judge. These people are paying a premium. Thirty-eight hundred dollars an hour."

"Can you book me for a month solid?"

"Yes. Anything else?"

"Unless you can find the piece of shit who abandoned Ally so I can tear out his liver with my bare hands, then *no*. He's probably the *perfect* match." Olivia said angrily, her hand gripping the phone painfully hard.

There was a tense silence through the phone and the car, and she was acutely aware Colin was listening attentively.

"Hey, Kat... did something happen to Ally? Is everything okay?"

"No. She's *dying*, G. And if I can't get her medicine, I may be helping to plan a funeral soon," she said bitterly, bile rising up in her throat at the thought. "I'll fucking *d-die* if I have to bury her."

"Honey, I will *give* you the money. Will you please take it? You'll kill yourself if you keep up this schedule," Gypsy whispered.

Olivia felt hot tears suddenly fall down her cheeks, not expecting Gypsy's generosity. She rubbed them away harshly, turning to face the passenger side window for privacy from Colin.

Colin reached over to place his hand on her leg again to comfort her, drawing his hand away hesitantly when she snatched away at the first touch of his fingers. She pressed into the car door, the seat belt digging into her neck.

"NO. *No*, G. I will work for what I need. I don't want any handouts. But thank you for offering. It really means a lot." She said softly back, touched that she offered.

"Okay, babe. You let me know. I will help you out however I can," Gypsy said back in farewell.

"I will. Bye. Thanks again." She hung up before dialing another number.

Colin continued to listen quietly as she called her bartending job and accepted every shift for the next two weeks on their schedule. Once she methodically filled up nearly every hour of her life for the next month, she threw the phone back in her purse.

Colin looked at her out the side of his eye, seeing her chew harshly on the skin of her finger anxiously, as if she needed the pain. They rode in silence for several minutes before he spoke.

Colin cleared his throat, "When are you going to have time to sleep?" he asked softly, his deep voice carrying easily across the small space. She stiffened, not answering, still staring out the window, ignoring him.

"Do you need help, Olivia? Monetary help?" he offered, carefully peeking over and assessing her posture as she sat next to him.

She threw him a filthy look, practically vibrating in the seat next to him.

He met her stare calmly, putting on cruise control before placing his hand back on the gearshift deceptively slow. His fingers twitched.

"Not from you. I doubt you could afford it anyway," she replied in a rather haughty and nasty tone.

Colin's jaw tightened and Olivia turned to look out the window, effectively ignoring him.

Her fingers dug painfully into her shoulder as she thought about the upcoming month. She didn't know how she was going to survive it if Gypsy couldn't deliver on giving her the pills she needed, but she just knew somehow. She had to.

Allison and Vanessa needed her.

The familiar lights of her city shone through the darkness ahead, but her stomach lurched when. he suddenly pulled over onto the shoulder of the road, and put the car into park. Olivia's eyes widened, and she flinched as Colin all but slammed his hand into the overhead lighting, illuminating the space between them, and snapped his head to pin her with a level look that was equal parts frightening, and exhilirating.

She stared at him for a heartbeat. The look on his face registered in her consciousness, and fear took over. Moving fast, she tried to claw her way out of the car without undoing the seat belt.

She cried out as he leaned over easily and snatched her back to him by her jaw, his broad hand wrapping around her and hauling her to him across the console. His demeanor had quickly shifted, and she gasped as his eyes turned dark, the pupil taking over the iris. His broad body suddenly filled the space between them, one hand around her jaw, and his other arm spread outward as his fingers wrapped hard around the steering wheel.

Olivia's eyes narrowed as she felt his warm, solid fingers digging into the flesh at her jawline. His thumb pressed hard, making her clench her teeth and fight against his grip.

"I'm going to repeat myself with you *only* once. *Do. You. Need. Monetary. Help?*" he asked, his fingers digging into her jaw tighter. Olivia whimpered, her entire body flushing, she tried to unlock her jaw to reply.

"God help you if you lie to me, woman!" Colin spit out, visibly seething and miles away from the man who treated her with such consideration throughout the night.

She narrowed her eyes even further at him. "Yes. *Obviously,*" she snarled, pissed because she felt her nipples turn into stone underneath her dress. Knowing it was because he'd shown the dangerous side that he kept carefully hidden under his mask of respectability.

"*How much*?" he enunciated slowly, refusing to release his harsh grip.

"I'm going to have bruises. *Get your fucking fingers off me,*" she said, her voice hard.

"*How much*, Olivia?" he asked again.

"It's *none* of your-"

"Answer. The. Fucking. Question," Colin growled at her, lowering his brow,

She shivered against his stony stare.

"Fifteen grand a m-month," she said, her eyes lowering from his, not wanting him to see her vulnerability. Her breath came hot and fast, her breasts lowering and rising rapidly, her mouth quivering. She pulled a shaking lip between her teeth, biting down hard.

"And how do you get this money every month?" his eyes narrowed.

Olivia's eyes flew back to Colin's incredulously. She slapped a hand against her leg hard, the sound reverberating around the space between them.

"Didn't you just fucking *hear me*? I *woorrrk!*" she yelled. "I work myself to fucking death every month for that little girl you just heard me talking to on the Goddamn *phone* you arrogant, *nosy* asshole!" she jerked against him, trying to pull away.

They silently seethed at each other in the car.

She made a low growling sound in her throat as he wouldn't let her loose, his fingers tightening painfully on her chin. He answered with his own rumble, much more intimidating than hers. He leaned in closer, eyes flashing dangerously at her.

She reddened even more as she realized her panties were flooded. Not even just wet, she was soaking. His viciousness turned her on. His ability to switch from a gentleman to an interesting, hotter, more dangerous side in a heartbeat aroused her.

"There's no fucking way you make fifteen *thousand* a month working at a diner and part time bartending, so cut the omissions, *Olivia*. What was that shit with Gypsy?"

Her eyes flashed at him threateningly and she pulled hard against his hand as she shifted him her seat.

"What does it matter to you? You can't do a fucking thing about it and it's *none* of your goddamn business, you fucking bast-" she rose up on her knees, pulling against the seatbelt.

Hearing him unsnap his seatbelt, she ignored his pained grip around her jaw, and audibly growled at him before he cleared the space fast to take her mouth in a harsh bite.

Cutting off her words.

Olivia squealed and tried to pull away, her arm throbbed painfully, making her stay in place for him. She felt a vicious bang in between her legs as the pain mixed with their kiss, and she had the sudden embarrassing thought that she was so wet the material of her dress under her had to be soaked.

She whimpered as he ate her mouth in the harshest kiss she'd ever had that was nothing like the sweet kiss they'd shared before they left the restaurant. He stared back at her, both refusing to close their eyes and break contact. With an audible growl, his teeth bit into her bottom lip hard enough to bruise.

His tongue evaded her as she tried to clench her teeth down around it, and she moaned as the salty, coppery taste of her blood assaulted her tongue.

Colin finally let her go when she stopped struggling, their lips releasing with an audible smack. He pushed her rather roughly back into her seat before leaning back into his, readjusting his erection.

"Someone needs to fucking teach you some manners," Colin said, carefully schooling his face back into a picture of calm. He spent a second adjusting his erection with one firm hand, before carefully pulling back onto the road.

"Someone needs to teach *you* how to treat a woman," she bit back at him.

Colin ignoring her harsh panicked pants in the passenger seat, she didn't realize she was fueling the fire. She huddled against the car door and all but fell out of the car without another word the second he pulled into her lot, barely waiting for him to put the car in park. Stumbling from too much wine, she tried to walk faster as she heard his car door slam behind her.

He appeared on her left side and grabbed her arm harshly, pulling her against his side and ignoring her struggles.

"*Stop it, Olivia,*" Colin bit out, readjusting his grip around her arm. Olivia stilled instantly, slowing her steps, the click of her heels echoing loudly around them.

She tensed her arm against his grip. *"You're not coming in,"* Olivia retorted.

"As much as we both need it, you wouldn't enjoy it right now if I did. With that attitude of yours, I'd fuck you too hard," Colin answered back, leading them carefully down the stairs and turning her to face him.

She scoffed at him, keeping her eyes firmly in front of her.

"I'm not having sex with you-you-*you maniac!*" she whispered angrily, successfully jerking out of his grip. Her sleeves fell further down with her movements, and she hurriedly pulled them back up, trying to right herself.

"I don't know what you do extra for that kind of money, but this'll be your last month doing it," Colin said as he got into her face. He reached for his pocket and pulled out several hundred-dollar bills and tried to hand it to her.

She threw him another filthy look. "I don't want your fucking money, Colin!" she hissed angrily.

"Take it. You're going to fuck your arm up even more if you work yourself to death the way I just heard you fill up your schedule," he said, his eyes looking down coldly at hers.

At her pointed glance and refusal, he walked forward, making her press her back up against the door. Her head thumped against the wood as she craned her neck to look up at him defiantly. He folded the crisp bills before slowly inserting it blatantly into the front of her dress, nestled against the taser.

"You arrogant jerk! You just have all the audacity, don't you?" she spit out, feeling her face turn bright red. She refused to acknowledge she liked the feeling of his fingers brushing against her breastbone.

"I have all the audacity. *All of it.* And it would serve you right to remember that," he said, his eyes hard as they looked down at her.

"Motherfucker, I *said* I don't need your money," she hissed, getting in his face.

He gave her a knowing look before claiming the last foot of space between them. Olivia shivered as he stepped into her space and bent his head down to hers, keeping his mouth just a hair's breadth away from her lips. Olivia made a low, pained, whining sound. The blood rushed to her head, making her feel dizzy.

"You think you intimidate me? Hmm? *I want you. And that fucking vicious mouth of yours,*" he said quietly.

NINE
Doorway Pleasures

OLIVIA'S BREATH CAME OUT ragged, and she could feel the tips of her breasts scraping against his torso with every inhale. Not expecting his confession, she let out a whimper, slightly tilting her head back. He took the bait and closed the distance, this new kiss the exact opposite of the one in the car.

Different from their first, but burned her to her toes, no less.

She moaned low at the first brush of Colin's mouth against hers. He licked her bottom lip, swiping across the flesh there and gently stroking along the sting of the bite he gave her earlier.

"Open your mouth, Olivia," he whispered against her lips, groaning deep in his chest when she complied. His tongue dipped in, and he molded his lips to hers, exploring her mouth greedily. He placed a forearm above her head and leaned in further, tilting his head and making her tilt hers back further.

Olivia moaned as he deepened the kiss, arching her body into his.

She placed her hands against his rock-hard chest, her knees shaking as he took her mouth with so much vigor she'd briefly wondered if this is how he'd be in bed. As if he heard her, he bent down and grasped the back of her legs.

"Pull your dress up, and wrap your legs around me," Colin said, lifting her as if she weighed nothing when she complied.

She wrapped her legs high and tight, feeling her dress slip further, baring miles of shapely flesh to his gaze. His eyes roamed her greedily as he cradled her fleshy buttocks in his hands through her dress, swaying them from side to side as he took her mouth once more with a low groan.

The movement striked her as incredibly intimate and sexual; him rocking her while they were kissing. The warmth of his hands seeped through her dress, causing her to gasp in pleasure at the contact as he carefully pressed his weight into her, his muscular body molding against hers in all the right places. She whimpered again at the feel of his pants rubbing against the inside of her thighs.

His belt buckle pressed firmly against the tiny scrap of underwear she had on.

Colin experimentally pressed a little more weight against her, his hands gripped her tightly. She felt trapped with his teeth nibbling on her lip, and his fingers clutching at her ass. She briefly toyed with the idea of inviting him in, the internal struggle killing her.

What was it going to hurt if she was never going to see him again anyway?

Olivia dragged the sleeves of her dress off her shoulders, baring inches of skin to him.

Riveted by her wanton action, pulled away and stilled as he watched her movements.

His eyes met hers, his gaze burning her. "You said you didn't want to have sex with me tonight," Colin reminded her.

Her breath came short and fast and she lowered her eyes as shame started to settle in. He swooped in and took her mouth once more before it had a chance to take her over. The fierceness of his possession banged the back of her head lightly against the door, drawing a tiny moan from her.

Colin groaned deep in his chest as he felt his erection tighten to the point of pain. Her hard nipples pressing against his chest was making him crazy. He took a deep breath, smelling her unique, musky scent, his mouth watered, nostrils flaring as he breathed in her scent deeply, trying to imprint her into his memory.

Precum leaked from the tip of his dick and slicked down his length.

"You need an orgasm, baby?" he blurted.

Pulling slightly away from her lips, his head tilted, just waiting. Olivia moaned and nodded her head yes, surprising herself with her admission. It had to be the wine making her reckless.

"I can give you one without even placing myself inside you," he said against her lips roughly. His hands tightened on her ass and hauled her up the door just a hair more.

Bang! Her pussy clenched hard, shocking her, and pulling another pained whimper from her throat with its intensity.

I want something inside me, filling me up, she lamented miserably.

She hadn't felt desire like this in years.

"That's how it would feel, the first time I sink myself in deep. You'd make that same shocked noise. Like it hurt. Letting me in wouldn't be easy," he said, his lips moving to her ear. "I don't even think I could fuck you on your bed in there. It's not well built enough for us. So, I'd have to fuck you on the floor," he said, giving her earlobe a little nip.

Colin began to move her, but not straight up and down; he grasped and worked her hips, his forearms bunching as he tilted her left side up and then the right, throwing her off. The door scraped her back as he moved her, forcing her to wrap her fingers around his neck and tilt her head back slightly.

"I think our first time, I'll fuck you to this song I like. The man is so haunted by his woman that his voice sounds tortured," Colin groaned, skimming his nose along her jaw, still working her hips lewdly.

She whimpered again at the intimate act of him imitating them fucking.

"*Colin-*" she gasped, feeling the thudding urgency in her vagina, pulling her tight.

"I can hear the sound of your hips beating off the floor as I pound myself inside you over and over, *mama*," he whispered, his arousal betraying a thicker Latin accent. She tensed up, flinching as the sexy endearment caused her to become wetter. She was embarrassed as she felt her juices trickle down her buttock, right where his left hand gripped her ass cheek under her dress.

Oh my god please, I can't come on his man. I just can't, she wailed inside of her head, not even realizing that her juices had already saturated his pants, leaving a slight wet stain on the front of his dick.

Colin ground himself against her harder. His breath hitched as Olivia's fingers suddenly tightened on the back of his neck, her nails digging in.

Colin quickly closed his mouth on hers once more, stealing her breath. She moaned in his mouth, his tongue stroking alongside hers. She gasped as she felt him readjust his hands and her hips started beating softly against the door, making a muted thudding sound.

"*Yesss.* Your pussy would grip me so tightly as I stretch you out. Making those soft, erotic sucking sounds," he groaned, pulling his face back to meet her shocked expression.

He watched her for a second as he beat her hips against the door lewdly with a little smirk on his face.

"Your breasts would make a resounding slapping sound with every hard thrust," he growled.

He moved to cradle her in one arm, taking his other and suddenly whacking the outside of her hip several rhythmic times on her bare hip. Mimicking the slapping sounds.

Her face turned bright red, and her breath froze in her lungs at the sharp contact of his hand against hers.

"How do you want it, Olivia? Hard? Fast? Slow? *Soft?*" he asked, needing her to speak.

"I want it hard, slow," she said, surprising herself and turning her face slightly away trying to hide from his piercing look.

"Well, then," he said, putting his hands back under her and gripping slightly. He spread her cheeks with the movement, opening her up and stretching her sensitive flesh. She bit her lip, her eyes flickering between his. "If you want it like *that,* it would be more of a dull thudding sound now, wouldn't it, baby?" he whispered, beating her hips slower against the door, her breasts jiggling hard with every jerk of his arms.

She could feel her dress slipping down slowly with every lift and release of his arms. She made a sharp noise as she felt her nipples getting closer and closer to spilling out of her neckline.

"Tell me how you want me to fuck you." His eyes were hard on her breasts as he tirelessly moved her.

"I want you to fuck me hard and slow, Colin," she whispered.

She had no shame, leaning into this fantasy for one night that she could experience a few moments of abandon.

She tightened as he'd leaned forward and licked a trail all the way from her breastbone, up her neck and to her ear, causing her already sensitive flesh to break out in goosebumps.

Just that moment, the chilly air became even cooler with a slight breeze, sensitizing her flesh even further. She clutched at him, trying to draw him closer to her.

"Now, I want you to *beg* me, in that whimpering, soft, sexy, helpless voice," he growled into her ear, stilling his movements completely. Her heart pounded as her eyes filled with tears. She could feel the back of her dress where he gripped her was slightly wet.

"Colin, please... I'm so close," she cried out softly, trying to urge him closer to her again, but he wouldn't budge.

"*Beg me,* Olivia," he said sternly, that authoritative clip tapping what it needed to in her brain.

"*Pleaassseee* fuck me *Colin,* I want you to bruise my pussy. Fuck me hard and deep. Uhhhnnn," she whimpered, her hands came up and grasping his hair and pulled hard, almost incoherent with needing him to move.

She imagined them just like that, on the floor in her living room. Him pounding deep inside of her with his hand wrapped around her neck, and she began to sob at how strong the sudden emotion was.

Though she dug her nails harder into him, he still didn't move.

Her eyes flashed, meeting his. "I said *fuck me,* Colin," she bit out, feeling wild. She didn't even care if he pulled her panties aside and took her right against the door outside. Mentally she was gone.

"Manners. You don't get to control this. *I said beg me.* Do I need to teach you how to beg as well?" his fingers flexed hard against her as he narrowed his eyes at her, patiently.

"*Please?*" she whimpered, her eyes flickered between his as she felt her flesh burn up at the intensity of his gaze.

He gave her a slow shake of his head.

It clicked what he wanted: the text from the other day entered her head.

She licked her lips nervously. "Please fuck me, *sir,*" she said, her eyes lowering immediately in shock and embarrassment.

Oh, sweet Jesus what the fuck did I just say? she lamented, her eyes trained on his chest, not able to meet his.

Colin smiled, nice and slow. The sight made her eyes go wide, and a fission of fear and excitement slammed its way to her core, stealing her breath.

"That's a *good, gooood* girl," he said, leaning forward to reward her with a kiss, their lips smacking. Her clit twinged painfully hearing his deep groan.

He tightened his grip on her ass to the point of pain and jerked her up and down hard, pressing his weight into her lower body. Colin suddenly grabbed the ends of her hair in one of his hands at her ass and yanked. Holding her head back tight as he gave her a rough bounce, making a soft cry leave her throat.

She felt the moment her left nipple broke free of her dress and cried out once more, flinching as Colin bent down and placed his teeth around the top of her nipple and the edge of her dress where it lay. The warmth of his mouth seeped into her skin, causing her to moan long and low.

Without warning he bit down with a sharp nibble, his hot tongue lashing the tip.

She screamed in shock, cutting it off with her hand against her mouth to stifle it, orgasming so hard that she arched, sinking her fingernails into his scalp unknowingly. Her heels dug into his ass as the wet heat of his mouth seared her, and each powerful pull made the aftershocks of her orgasm longer. She hung there limply in his arms while he nibbled her at his leisure.

He raised his head back up, releasing her hair, and gave her a soft kiss.

"Fucking beautiful," he said, looking down at her, still gasping in shock.

They stared at each other while he continued to cradle her in his hands tirelessly.

Unlocking her heels, she lowered her legs as she pulled back from him reluctantly. Her breath coming in fast and shallow as her heartbeat hard against her chest, trying to wiggle out of his embrace while not meeting his eyes. She was grateful when her dress fell back into place, shyly pulling her bra and dress back over her bosom and ran a self-conscious hand down the back of her hair.

"Go inside. Tomorrow buy yourself some food, okay? I'll be in touch soon," his hand touched her cheek before he backed away.

Olivia struggled with her keys, attempting to open the door gracefully. When it unlocked, she turned in the threshold to regard him. He shook his head silently again.

And with that, he walked up the stairs slowly, hearing her slam her door behind him before multiple locks clicked in place. When he looked down, the five hundred dollars he'd given to her was torn up on the concrete floor in front of her door. He narrowed his eyes, shaking his head and heading to his car.

Olivia ran into her room, sobbing as she attempted to tear off her dress and shoes.

Gasping as she caught her hair in the zipper, she went still, willing herself to stop and go slowly. Groaning as the muscles in her arm twinged painfully.

Naked, she walked to the bathroom with a percocet. Running water into her hand, she swallowed it down before flicking her gaze to herself in the bathroom mirror seeing she looked...well.... *used*.

Her hair was mussed, and her eyes were bright, peeking through the fringe bang of her red hair. Her cheeks were rosy-red, no surprise there. But her mouth was obviously swollen. Her bottom lip slightly red and bruised looking from being bitten.

Her skin pricked. It wasn't lost on her that all he did was hold her and bit her nipple, and she had experienced the hardest orgasm she'd ever had in her life while he didn't even break a sweat. She touched her mouth gently with her fingers before her ears picked up the dinging sound from her phone.

> Meet me at my office in two weeks. The address is on the business card. I have a proposition for you. I can help-If you need it. I think we both need it. Trust me-I'll make it worth your while. -C

Olivia set her alarm and fell into bed, tired from the emotions of the night, and the wine she'd drunk. She didn't respond to him, thinking he'd get the hint and leave her alone. Colin was a complication and distraction she couldn't afford.

Still feeling empty and needy, she pulled out her vibrator that she never used and shoved it between her legs. Remembering his mouth on her, her fingers pinched and pulled the nipple that he'd bitten. Crying out, she finished what they started outside before falling deep asleep. She missed the text he'd sent.

> You did so good tonight. I'm so proud of you. Rest well. Goodnight, baby. -C

***

Colin arrived home, pulling into his garage and threw his car into park. He unbuckled his belt and undid his pants, pulling his cock out and fisting it hard. Tilting his head back he imagined himself back at Olivia's apartment, and instead of this time just holding her, he was pulling the small scrap of underwear to the side and thrusting himself into her sweet, tight body.

He spent a long time jerking off.

Every time he got close, he slowed, edging himself. His chest burned and his heart raced painfully as he mentally replayed the entire night over in his mind from the moment she opened the door, their sweet kiss in the parking lot, the harsh kiss in the car, and them almost fucking against her door.

There was a particularly sexy sound she made that he thought about and it threw him over the edge.

He ejaculated with a harsh growl, imagining pressing into that spot in her arm, hearing her shocked sound as he forced her to orgasm while experiencing pain. Grimacing, he grabbed some spare tissue from the glove compartment and cleaned himself up before checking his phone.

She hadn't replied. He prayed to God that she'd show up at his office when he asked her to. If not, he refused to think about what would happen if he couldn't have her. There had to be a way to get her to want to stay around him so he could figure out this fascination he had with her. What this feeling was.

His thoughts turned to her disturbing phone conversation.

Money. Something he had plenty of and liked to spend. His facial features tightened as he wondered what she could be getting into. His thoughts wandered to the extreme, and he found himself uncomfortable that she could be dabbling in trouble.

I'm going to follow her, see what the hell she's doing, he thought. *In the meantime, I have a contract to draw up. I'm going to do what I do best: business.*

TEN

The Meeting

Two weeks later Olivia sat in the locker room of the diner, gasping as tears fell from her eyes while she dug her fingers hard into her hurt arm. She'd just closed, but couldn't bring herself to walk to her car just yet.

Her fingers trembled as she took her last Percocet and swallowed it dry.

God if you're there, she started, then scowled and cut the prayer off as quickly as it started. *No point in praying when you're abandoned. If God can't help a little girl to live, why should he be bothered with my arm?*

Olivia hadn't heard from Colin except from him reminding her of their meeting the next morning at ten o'clock. She'd appreciated the space, still reeling from the hottest sexual encounter she'd ever had, and needed time to think.

Their night together, she'd waited until Colin left before going back outside, scooping up the money and taping it together. She'd placing four of the five hundred dollars in Allison's shoebox, and then used the other hundred to buy a few groceries.

Olivia walked wearily into her apartment the most exhausted she'd ever been. and took a few minutes to warm up some chicken noodle soup. Spacing out as she stared at the food rotating in the microwave. Her vision was blurry, and she swayed rather unsteadily on her feet.

She'd barely been sleeping. Working almost eighteen hour days for the last two weeks on top of seeing her new clients, and she knew she looked rough.

She ate and laid down, hearing her phone ping.

> See you tomorrow at 10a. -C

She tried to type out a response before her phone hit the pillow and she fell asleep, not having sent it.

***

Olivia woke up the next morning feeling slightly more refreshed, having been able to get a solid nine hours of sleep for the first time in about four years. Picking through her closet, she contemplated what to wear, deciding to the meeting with Colin to turn him down in person.

It was only the right thing to do after he treated her to such a lovely dinner and had given her money.

She'd even bought and sent him a thank-you card to his office over a week ago. To show him she had manners. The necessary manners that a person needed to have.

Asshole, she thought to herself again for the dozenth time. There was something about him she couldn't place, something dangerous simmering beneath his cloak of magnetism.

Mindful of her arm, she pulled on a cheap department store cream linen dress, accessorizing with her 'Ally' necklace, and stylish dark green ballet flats. She didn't put on any makeup aside from mascara and gloss, and brushed her hair into a shiny, flowing mass down her back. Humming gently, she got into her car and put Colin's office address into her GPS, wincing as he was forty-five minutes away.

Paranoid, she checked her gas level, relieved as it was fine for now.

She smiled the closer she got to Colin's office, imagining the look on his smug face when she turned him down. Telling him she never wanted to see him again. The truth, as she just didn't need the complication. She wasn't sure exactly what he was looking for, but she knew she wasn't it, she didn't belong in his world.

And thanks to Gypsy coming through with the extra clients, she'd almost had all the money she needed, and she was only halfway through the month. She sighed contentedly, happy that she didn't *need* what he alluded to in his text two weeks ago.

Olivia pulled next to a tall glass office building, making sure it was the right one. Seeing C. McDermont and Tech Holdings, LLC. in large, intimidating, shiny chrome letters above the glass doors, she glanced quickly around at the parking outside of the building, seeing no empty spaces.

She parked illegally, not having change to put into a street meter.

I'm only going to be in there for a few minutes, anyway, she thought to herself, smoothing her cream dress with her hands before walking confidently through the double doors.

Swanky, she thought, admiring the tastefully done architecture and interior decoration.

Spotting one of the two pristine receptionists seated at a long mahogany desk with a marble countertop, she introduced herself sweetly. The letters C. McDermont and Tech Holdings, LLC. striking an imposing presence on the wall behind them, the chrome letters backlit against white lighting.

She frowned slightly, not realizing that Colin was such a big deal.

Nibbling on her lip, she suddenly found herself shy and uncomfortable. Wondering who she really went to dinner with. Feeling inadequate, her eyes fell on the mounted letters again.

It further solidified her decision to let him down, but maybe not with glee this time.

How could she involve herself with someone so apparently well off and connected? Would he know her clients? If they became involved, she wouldn't be able to continue to work if he ran in the same circles as the people she serviced. That was too big of a risk to take.

No, it's better to just cut it off at the pass and keep it moving.

"I have a ten-o'clock with Mr. McDermont," she stated confidently, inspecting the extensive area with a keen, curious eye.

There were several banks of elevators to her left, men in suits walking around, well-dressed women with their heels clacking on the marble floor. One of the receptionists walked her to the bank of elevators, sharply turning to the right to face another lone elevator. This one was flanked by huge potted ferns.

She watched curiously as the woman entered a code into the wall before pressing her hand to her ear and spoke into it softly. "Ms. Cameron is on her way up, sir."

The receptionist nodded, and waved her into the elevator before disappearing down the hallway once more.

"Wait," Olivia called, hastily. "I don't know what floor to pick!" The elevators closed in her face, and she scowled before looking at the panel and seeing only one button. Up.

She pressed it, suddenly feeling even more unnerved. She smoothed her hair, pulling half of it to drape across her right arm and chest, wanting its protection from his gaze in case she had another embarrassing muscle spasm.

Get it together bitch, it's just a freaking elevator, she thought.

A few seconds later the elevator doors opened, gracing her with a breathtakingly beautiful view of the skyline of Connecticut just in front of her. Her lips parted as she gasped in pleasure, forgetting herself as she felt her feet take her to the wall of windows. Mesmerized, she peered in awe at the sight outside of the windows, seeing beautiful fall-colored trees amongst the downtown buildings.

"Hello, *mama*," she heard from across the room.

Turning in surprise, Olivia's hand flew to her throat, having been so immersed in the view that she'd forgotten for a second why she was even there. She flushed, remembering what happened between them after dinner. And seeing him now in all his CEO power had her second guessing all her confidence.

Her eyes met his from across the expansive and lush space of his office, backlit against the singular wall of glass that sat behind his desk.

She remained silent. For once in her life, she was not sure how to conduct herself. Colin looked cool and in control in a dark blue suit, his blue tie matching his socks. His brown hair was styled in a sexy tousled mess on top of his head, or maybe he'd spent the morning running his fingers through it.

She wondered if he was anxious to see her.

Colin arose from the seat at the head of his desk and swiftly walked around it, his gait relaxed and controlled, before bending to press his lips to her cheek. He placed a hand to her lower back, and walked her over to an intimate sitting area. It was intimate, and inviting.

Her eyes roamed, seeing the coffee table in the middle of the space held a manila folder and a small remote. Presumably to the flat screen TV above the drink cabinet in the room.

Olivia lowered gingerly to the loveseat, trying to ignore Colin lowering next to her. She curiously caught his gaze as he offered her a drink, surprising him as she said yes.

"Sure, I'll take a vodka," she smiled nervously. He stood up once more to walk to the drinks cart.

Must be nice to blatantly drink on the job with no one to reprimand you for it, she thought wryly. She felt her mouth tip up in an amused smile. Her eyes fell to his backside, and her mouth suddenly went dry, and she struggled to smile.

What does he look like when he's thrusting into-

"Ice?" Colin half turned his head at the drinks cart. He startled her out of her musing, and her lashes fluttered as she brought her gaze up to his, attempting to focus.

"Yes please." She licked her lips.

That's okay. I'll just fantasize about his tight ass when I'm home.

She smiled again. Tilting her head as her eyes lowered to the folder curiously.

"Chaser?" Ice clink into glasses as he moved, working to make their drinks.

"No." *I'm not going to drink it anyway,* Olivia thought as she smiled prettily at him. Knowing she had asked him to make her a drink so she could manipulate the meeting as she wanted a bit of control.

"Ladies have chasers, Olivia," he murmured quietly.

She snorted slightly, looking away from him and placing her gaze to the corner of the room.

Fuck you, she thought.

His eyes crinkled as he finally turned and looked at her with a brow raised, as if he heard her curse him out. She cleared her throat slightly and gave him her most polite smile.

Make him work before you turn him down, girl, the voice niggled gleefully in her head, bouncing around with joy while outwardly she stared at him silently as he made his way to back to the loveseat.

Influenced by the look of the mouthwatering drink he'd handed her, she changed her mind and decided to partake, finding herself suddenly needing the liquid courage. He just looked too delicious, and she needed to settle her nerves.

Colin sat back down next to her, handing her hers before taking a sip of his own. He licked his lips while she shot her drink back and sucked on the lime that he offered, grimacing slightly as the burn immediately hit and spread. A dull thudding hit her vagina, reminding her of why she didn't drink.

She became insanely turned on when she drank hard liquor, and she *really* didn't have time for that.

Colin's eyes flicked down, observing her legs clenched together tightly. He took his time to rake his gaze over the sight of her curvy calves and knees, exposed by the dress she was wearing. His eyes suddenly landed on her right arm, the one that he knew bothered her. Thick wavy locks of dark red hair currently covered it.

She'd accepted the glass and drank with her left hand.

"You're still keeping your right arm close to your body," he said quietly, observing her slender hand and fingers wrapping around her ribcage. "It's been two weeks, and you haven't had it looked at because I can tell that you, at the very least, need a sling."

His eyes landed back on hers as he took another deep drink of his glass, and she could tell he attempted to hide the irritation that flashed across his features. She saw his fingers twitch, and her brow raised haughtily.

"I haven't had it looked at," she said simply, not bothering to elaborate. He nodded, seeming to breathe through his irritation.

His eyes found hers before he spoke, breaking the silence between them.

"I would like to buy the rights to the blueprint renderings of the residence I saw in your home," he stated, snagging the folder off the table. He folded his ankle over his knee and leaned back, placing the folder on his elevated leg and watching her patiently.

Olivia's brow furrowed as she carefully placed the glass on the table, the heavy mass of her hair tumbled forward to spill across her front with her movements. She glanced at the table as she obsessively made sure to put the glass on a coaster.

His eyebrow twitched.

"I'm not sure what you mean," Olivia said, blinking at him as genuine confusion and shock colored her voice. She truly didn't expect this, out of all the things he could have said. She thought he was going to ask her out on another date.

Colin handed her the folder, and she took it slowly before opening it with shaking fingers. Her eyes widened seeing her drawings that were currently in her home, now in black and white on paper in front of her. Looking quite professional.

Out of her peripheral she saw as he turned the TV on with the remote.

A 3D-colored rendering of the home she'd designed a few years ago in college popped up on the screen. The images turning in slow motion to see all the angles of the exterior of the house.

The house he'd coincidentally designed the same color she wanted her herself; a tasteful blue-gray, and white in some places.

Olivia sat back against the plush back of the couch as her jaw hit the floor. The images on the television screen continued turning as the they faded and reappeared with new ones, showing multiple angles of the home, landscaping, as well as dozens of interior pictures. It was an impressive presentation, and looked even better than she'd imagined when she originally drew it up.

The color was broken up by stone pillars, and more stone fireplaces dotted all throughout the house. The presentation even showed recessed lighting in the house, and there was a rather impressive outdoor terrace off the master bedroom that hosted a private hot tub, and outdoor television area. A screened in day bed was on the other side of the terrace.

The man had been busy in the two weeks they'd last seen each other.

The slideshow finished as Olivia came back to her senses.

Closing her mouth, she realized her face was wet and raised a trembling hand to her face to touch her cheek gently in surprise as she stared at the dark television, lost in her thoughts. Not noticing his eyes turned a warm brown at her crying.

Colin waited patiently.

"Do you know what you just did... what you just gave me?" she whispered, her eyes now sliding to meet his. It didn't even bother her to cry in front of him, because he'd given her a precious gift: the ability to see her vision played out in real life. She'd only ever imagined what he'd just shown her.

Colin tilted his head at her and regarded her slowly.

"How much do you want for the drawing? What does this mean to you?" Colin asked again calmly. She met his stare silently, and he forced himself to wait patiently as he could see a dozen thoughts crossed her mind at once.

"What's the *catch*?" she asked, her eyes narrowing suddenly, her tears drying up.

He cocked an eyebrow and grinned wickedly.

His eyes flicked down with interest as he saw her breath hitch, and her nipples poke through the thin material of her dress before landing on her eyes again.

"Very smart, Olivia. I'm afraid there's three catches. When you sell this to me, you can't sell it to anyone else. You are not allowed to *build* this rendering for anyone else. This is a one and done deal. Not even for yourself," he smiled at her, not unkindly. Noticing his own breath had become strained as his body tightened with tension.

Olivia narrowed her eyes slightly at him as she blinked, attempting to process this information. She realized that in giving her one dream, he was taking away another; her dream to live in said house, or even a smaller rendering of it. And then she scoffed at her own foolish thoughts, because how was she ever even supposed to afford to build it to begin with?

It was and continued to be a pipe dream that haunted her from the corner of her living room.

Her mouth turned down in a slight frown, and her eyes slid down to the empty space between them. Colin stretched a leg out, the material of his pants pulling tight across his thick legs, momentarily distracting her. He cleared his throat, causing her eyes to lift back to his.

"So, I need you to think hard about the amount. What do you think you're worth?"

A small flashback of them at dinner when he asked her a similar question of what she wanted came to the front of her mind.

"You went through my things when I was in my bedroom?" she said in disbelief, for some reason, that being the first thing she wanted addressed.

She shot daggers at him across the seat. He nodded solemnly, unashamed, arrogantly. Though it irritated her, she dismissed it as momentarily inconsequential. The man wanted a monetary figure for her work, she didn't have to figure out how to turn down his romantic advances.

Olivia crossed her legs and turned her gaze away from him once more to rest on the drinks cabinet.

She narrowed her eyes as she picked through each drink displayed at the cart. Wondering for the millionth time which brand of liquor the drunk driver who'd killed her parents was drinking the night of their fatal accident.

Silently, Olivia focused. She considered multiple facets about her life; thinking about her student loans, finishing paying off her sister's house, and the various medical bills and quickly came to an amount she thought might be suitable. However, she didn't want to play her hand too soon.

"I guess that would depend on what can you afford?" she asked plainly, turning her eyes to his.

Colin gave her another one of his slow smiles, except this one seemed much more self-satisfactory. As if he had a precious secret she wasn't privy to yet.

"Just give me a number, Olivia," Colin said, leaning back further in his seat and taking another drink.

"Two hundred and seventy-five *thousand* dollars. All cash, and all up front. Then the blueprints will be yours," she said. "If you're serious?"

Colin arched his brow as a slightly surprised and impressed look flashed across his features. He studied her for a minute, before nodding thoughtfully. He made a low humming noise, his thumb rubbing the knuckles of his hand which was draped across the back of the loveseat.

Olivia felt herself give him a small satisfactory smile of her own, feeling like she was having an out of body experience.

See? Can't afford it. Not able to help herself, she smiled wider at him for some reason. Then her smile disappeared as soon as it came with the next words.

He exhaled heavily before speaking.

"I thought you were going to lowball yourself, so, I created a third catch. This one more, mutually beneficial. I've been working on this for two solid weeks while I waited for you," Colin said darkly, running his fingers across his slight beard.

His eyes flitted to her mouth, and she swallowed hard, noticing he was remembering the brutally intimate kiss from two weeks ago. She touched her fingers to her own lips before accepting the folder he'd presented to her, and fought desperately to ignore the butterflies tightening her stomach.

ELEVEN
Page 3

CAREFULLY OPENING THE FOLDER with her left hand, she scrunched her face up in annoyance seeing a rather official document. Multiple money figures. Bullet points. The document was a few pages long and looked incredibly complex.

She didn't have time for this.

Not bothering to flip through it, Olivia quickly checked her phone to see how long she had until her shift. "What's this?" she asked irritably, her eyes snapping to his. He stared at her as she hoisted the document slightly between them.

"Read it please," he responded, just as shortly.

"My shift at the diner starts in two hours, so I apologize, but I truly don't have time for this, Colin. I need to leave soon, or I'll be late. I can't afford the luxury of taking an extended break out of my day for random nonsense." Irritated, her voice rang out in the expanse of his office.

The damn man smiled at her before taking his phone out of his pocket and speed dialing a number. A few seconds later he spoke, his eyes tight on hers.

"Ms. Belinda, I am truly sorry to call on such short notice, but I am going to need you to close the diner down for the rest of the day, something's come up. Yes. Yes, with pay for all the employees affected today. The food will of course be reimbursed. Yes. Thank you,

Belinda." He kept Olivia's eyes with his own while he finished the call and hung up.

A minute later she was still staring stupidly at him as her phone chirped with a text from Belinda teliing her to not bother coming in for her shift, and she would still be paid regardless.

Her mouth fell open.

"Sit. *Down*," Colin ordered.

She'd started rising off the seat, slowly shaking her head as the last forty minutes of being in his office hit her all at once. She plopped back down, hearing her purse hitting the floor with a thud, ripping open the folder and tearing it slightly she was so angry.

Smiling, Colin freshened their drinks, pouring her a little more as he knew the fury was really about to come. He quietly thanked God for a private, soundproofed office. He closed his eyes and inhaled with pleasure at her indignant gasp. It didn't take long.

"You-y-you... *you...*" she whispered, her wide eyes scanning the document, stopping only to flip the page to continue reading.

Colin almost groaned with pleasure he was so happy to stand there and watch her eyes flickering back and forth as she read. Her eyebrow arched at one spot in the document, and he smiled. His eyes lowered as he let his eyes wander freely, glancing slowly down at her legs, now crossed again, swinging her food anxiously.

Colin leaned against the drink cabinet, crossing his legs too, getting comfortable watching her as she got to the delectable part of the document. Her little noises of disbelief bounced around his head, and he committed them to memory as he wanted to hear them in other scenarios.

Olivia titled her head as she stiffened, and almost damn near stopped breathing. Colin watched with amusement as her eyes went wide as saucers. His own breath hitched as his need got hotter, watching her struggle for breath.

He slowly came to stand in front of her before lowering to the table and sitting. Waiting patiently as she flipped to the last page, the signature page.

"It's going to be so good between us." He leaned forward and pushed back a lock of silky red hair behind her ear.

Tempting fate, he leaned in further and placed his lips to hers, tasting her cry of surprise and the vodka she'd just drank. He licked inside her mouth deeply, chasing more of her scent.

"*None* of it's negotiable. The contract stands as is. I want your blueprints, and I want your body, *and* your time," he said as he pulled back and looked into her eyes.

"Why me... can't you have anyone you want?" Olivia asked, her voice quivering as he fluttered his thumb across her cheek. Her brow furrowed as she stared rather seriously into his eyes.

His heart squeezed painfully.

"I'm a fucked-up person Olivia, as evidenced by the contract in your hand. That day you let me in from the rain you saved my life, and you didn't even know it. I wasn't there by chance, I was trying to wreck. Praying for someone to hit me in the darkness out in that storm." He stopped, seeing Olivia's shocked expression. "But then I saw you through the windows, and something about you called to me. I stood there watching you for a while when you were closing that night, and your determination fueled me. I want *you*, Olivia."

Her eyes bored into his, her pain recognizing his in his eyes. Knowing he was telling the truth. Trauma understood trauma.

Olivia gasped, her heart skipped a beat. "You were trying to kill yourself?" she was barely even able to make the words escape her mouth. She felt her heart breaking for him. She'd never had anyone tell her they wanted to kill themselves before, and it was *jarring*. "Why?" She felt her hand slide forward towards him, before pulling back.

She paused another second before reaching out again and touching her fingers to his, gripping his hand tightly with hers. They were both trembling.

Colin tilted his head again, a deep exhale leaving him. Olivia tensed, feeling his breath brush her hand. She flexed her fingers, waiting for a response.

"I want you to know that I am in therapy, and I see a psychiatrist as well. That was my first ever attempt in twenty-three years, but I had a horrible trigger that day, and could not pull myself out of a panic attack. I cannot talk about the why right now. Just know you won't have to worry about that."

Olivia nodded; not quite sure she believed him.

"Um...because no offense, but I don't think I could mentally handle walking in on a... on a..." her eyes met his before looking away hastily. "Just please don't, ok? Talk to me first if you're feeling...sad. Or triggered." She wet her lips, changing tactics. "It takes an awful lot to sh-shock me, Colin," she whispered, holding the contract to her chest, and meeting his gaze. "I'd have to do these th-hings, with you. To get the terms of the contract? No, this is too... *convenient* to be true."

She refrained from saying good.

Some of the stuff described in there wasn't good at all. She blinked away from him in embarrassment, flushing a deep red as she thought about the acts listed on page three of the contract and swallowed hard.

He nodded solemnly.

Swallowing the rest of his drink, he leaned forward and held her gaze once again. Something clicked in her head and her eyes narrowed as her eyes flicked to his once more, narrowing.

"Wait a fucking minute..." she said tightly, her eyes flashed dangerously at him. "Are you doing this because you think I'm a *prostitute*? Because of my *phone call* the other night?"

He shook his head no, eyes still calm and steady on hers. Her eyes narrowed him even more, her face reddening further. A low rumble started in his chest.

"Take the offer, Olivia." Colin's eyes turned hard once more, losing their softness at the threat of her refusal.

"*Why are you doing this*? This is *insane*. It's certifiable!" she said softly, turning away from the document and placing confused green eyes on his.

"Because sometimes the difference between those who are successful, and those who aren't is only opportunity. They just need someone to give them a chance," he said quietly, turning his brown eyes onto hers. "But my chances come with a hefty cost, I'm afraid."

She silently stood, watching him stoke his five o'clock shadow thoughtfully.

Please. Please say yes. I'll help you make a beautiful life, baby. Don't be stubborn, Colin thought, a small grin touching his face as he silently willed her to accept the agreement. His eyes flashed threateningly as he noted her pregnant pause, and then he tightened as Olivia bent to snatch her bag up off the floor.

"I would be interested in selling the blueprint. Not the contract. It sounds like I damn well would be a *prisoner,*" she said, folding her arm across her torso as she regarded him.

"The two offers are joined, if you do not take the contract, then I will not buy the blueprints." he said softly. He stood up and folded his arms tightly, looking down at her.

"That's nonsense, you literally offered me the-"

"I said *no.* They're offered together. And I know how much you need the money." he said seriously, tilting his head. "We both do."

She met his glare head on, her plump lips pressed tight together. He took a step forward into her space.

"You are so fucking arrogant, it's *sick,* " she whispered, goading him.

"I know. I am what I am, and I make no apologies for it whatsoever," Colin replied, seeing her gaze rake down his front rather judgmentally.

"See, proving my point. No deal. I couldn't fucking survive living with your ego for two hours, much less two years," she quipped, her voice going slightly higher as she stepped into his space. "And you'd want me to call you '*Sir,*' too? Please, get the fuck out of here. I wish I *would.*"

Colin smiled at her and bent his lips to her ear. She tensed.

"We'll be testing that theory on your back, on your knees, with you screaming and clawing beneath me on every surface in my house. You may be right, you might not survive two years, but it won't be because of my ego. It'll be because of my cock, baby. I have *very* demanding, *voracious* appetite for sex, as you read. That business against your apartment door was nothing compared to how I'm going to fuck you. I'm not just going to fuck your sweet tight body, but I'm going to fuck your mind, too. And I'm going to make sure it *hurts so that the lesson sticks.*"

He brought his hand up to her arm and pressed slightly into the spot he'd seen her clutching during their date.

Feeling her panties soaked with his words as her clit twinged painfully, Olivia hissed and cried out as his fingers pressed into her arm at the same time he grasped a straining nipple in his fingers of his other hand. She leaned her head forward to rest onto his chest, and she moaned miserably, the two sensations clasping and making her knees buckle as she felt a weak orgasm roll through her body.

Olivia shivered as she felt skin break out in goosebumps.

She raised her head after a few minutes, staring helplessly into his eyes.

What the hell was that? Olivia thought, her eyes flickering between his.

His hand moved from her nipple to the back of her neck, feeling the warm dewy flush of her skin.

"You have a little girl, who would be most appreciative of her aunt's decision." he pressed, not at all ashamed to use what little collateral he had against her. "It's only for two years."

"Yes, but you can add on time as you please, it seems like?"

"Within reason." Colin said, smiling slightly at her as she frowned at him.

"Within who's reason?"

"Mine." His chocolate-colored eyes turned darker, the irises dilating suddenly.

"*Obviously.*" She snorted. "What's to keep you from taking advantage of me?"

"The whole point *is* to take advantage of you, and in doing so you'll become a very rich woman," he said, pressing his thumb slightly deeper into her neck, watching her green eyes lower slightly.

Colin smiled wider as her lips parted slightly in surprise.

She nodded silently, her eyes going back to the blueprint of the house she desperately wanted for herself, but knowing instinctively that it was a pipe dream. It would be better to cut her losses and get the money they so desperately needed while there was a chance.

She blinked back tears, giving away her dreams for this home, to this man she barely knew.

"I don't think I like page three, though," she whispered, her eyes trained on his chest, unable to look at him. His chest expanded at her words, and she shivered, hearing a deep sound emit from him.

"Out of all the things, page three is the least negotiable one. But that particular act will take months of us building trust," Colin assured her.

"I don't even know you. How do I know you're even telling me the truth about all of this? About if you can even afford it?" she bit out, narrowing her eyes again at him.

He narrowed his back, preferring to remain calm until after she signed.

Opening his phone, he logged into his banking app before pulling up his accounts. He couldn't help the smirk that he felt on his face when she clocked how many zeros were after each account. Her face was priceless. She closed her eyes on a deep exhale, and he could see her resolve leave her in waves.

Colin turned on his heel, snatching up the document from off the couch and walking to his desk again so that he could sign the contract, before turning the packet and presenting Olivia with the signature page.

He felt his body catch on fire as she slowly signed her name on the paper in a big, beautiful scrawl.

He leaned back, regarding her intently as they both stood there in complete silence. Neither of them speaking for long minutes as the shock set in.

"I will have you know that I don't do things like this. I don't let men fuck me, and I definitely don't get ordered around by them. I'm *only* saying yes, because my niece's life is on the line," she said, her voice sounding hollow.

"Hmm-hmm," Colin hummed, his finger rubbing his lip. They both knew what the unspoken irony was between them.

If she didn't then, then she does now.

Colin made the first move.

Noticing Olivia's hands shaking, he walked her to the couch before dialing her apartment complex on his own phone, putting it on speaker. He sat back and watched with pleasure as she broke her lease, giving up her home that had been hers for the last four years.

He nodded at her as she took out her burner phone and dialed Gypsy, telling her that she needed to cancel her appointments for the rest of the month, that she would no longer be utilizing the service, and her phone would be cut off permanently. She then handed him the phone, and watched silently as he placed the burner phone in his pocket.

Olivia's next call was her boss Belinda, and tearfully told her that she'd be quitting, but she would still be seeing her as she would drop into the diner sometimes.

Colin hummed in pleasure as she then called the bar to officially quit there as well.

At his instruction, she made another call to hire a moving service to pack up her apartment, reading off Colin's Amex card information to pay for the men to pack up her things and take them to a storage unit. Which again, he arranged a two year, fully paid agreement. Her next move was to send him an encrypted email with all her banking information, as well as her credit card information.

After a tense conversation about Allison's medical expenses where Olivia was unable to tell him how much her care would be for the next two years, he had her call her sister to get her banking information as well. Promising to dump an undisclosed amount of money into her account so Vanessa would be able to pool from those funds, instead of relying on Olivia every month.

Olivia shook her head rather numbly, dreading having to deal with explaining that to her later. Her sister sent the account information, and Colin stepped aside to quietly make a phone call to his bank to expedite the process.

Olivia then signed a release of information to relinquish medical information, and an airtight NDA. She'd sent him her body measurements, her foot size, her preferred hair style, and had her college transcripts electronically sent to him.

She then waited patiently as he called some big wig dean at the Architectural school in the area and got her enrolled for the rest of the school year, starting in the fall session. And was somehow able to plan out the rest of the classes she needed to graduate. Adding an additional four months onto their contract as a few of her credits didn't transfer, and she'd need to retake them.

They had to revise and resign the contract to add the extra time.

Two and a half years almost, she was tied to him.

He then had her pull up her student loan information and pay off the entire balance, one hundred and twelve thousand dollars, erased at once. She then called her sister again, promising that she would be over later to explain.

Explain what exactly? Olivia didn't know...the temporary signing away of her life? The fact she agreed to be a move-in sexual submissive to this sadistic, powerful man who apparently was Oprah-rich.

Olivia sat on the couch, her chest heaving raggedly, tensing in distress as her heart pounded uncomfortably at the magnitude of what she'd just done, and the ramifications of her actions.

This man was going to fuck her, probably hurt her.

When, she didn't know, but it was coming at some point. Her face flushed, and her hand came up to her throat knowing that they were both thinking it. She shuddered and kept her eyes averted from his as desire and fear of the unknown filled her, making her weak.

She turned her gaze to him and blinked slowly. "I literally only asked you to make me a drink because I just wanted to have you do something for me that I would turn down. Because I wanted some semblance of control. Now I feel so stupid," she whispered, swallowing thickly.

Her eyes searched his desperately, thinking about how passionately he'd treated her when he'd had her against her apartment door, and she flushed, feeling dizzy.

"Will you be gentle with me...sometimes?" she whispered, too shocked to cry, and not knowing if crying was what she needed.

Colin furrowed his brow and tilted his head slightly, seeing her face pale slightly.

Seeing her expression, he made her lie on the couch, and got her a small bottle of water to sip on. He knelt down next to her, holding the water to her lips, and running a soothing hand down her arm and hip.

Olivia closed her eyes, overwhelmed.

"I will not mistreat you, Olivia. We will work on building our trust. That's why the contract is so long. A lot of my pleasure is going to come from taking care of you." His deep voice wrapped around her almost hypnotically.

The stroking rhythm of his caresses barely penetrated the sudden onslaught of her emotions. She lay there deathly still, in shock.

She literally signed herself away to someone else for two and a half years. *Like a sexual slave.*

Olivia made a small sound in her throat, her eyes popping open and finding him watching her carefully. They stared at each other in silence as he continued his long sweeping motions down her body.

"Think about what you're gaining. You'll get to finish your degree, I'm going to help you start your business, you don't have to cook, clean, lift a finger for anything really, other than to please me."

"But I'll have to call you 'sir', kneel, let you have access to my phone, you can do... whatever you want to me."

"Not without trust. We will build this relationship together. I'm not going to throw you off the cliff headfirst, baby. And to answer your question, *yes*. There will be times when I am gentle with you, but there will also be times I will not be gentle with you. But I *will not* be unkind to you. And I will not treat you badly. I just want to be close to you." Colin's voice became deeper and softer at the same time as his fingers stroked her cheek.

"Okay...uhm...I'm actually really tired. Like *really* tired," Olivia felt a tear escape her eye as she looked at him, her cheek resting on the couch cushion. He leaned forward and caught it with his tongue before kissing his way to her lips.

"Then I've got the last phone call."

She sighed as he made the last call on her behalf; instructing a tow truck to pick up her trusty beater off the street. He had the woman who put her in the elevator come up to grab the keys to give to the tow truck guy who was hauling it off. The white ticket flickered on her windshield gently in the breeze as it rolled away.

Then they were alone, with no more emails, phone calls, or loose ends to tie up. She'd sat back up and stared at him across the intimate expanse of the loveseat, watching him play with a long lock of her dark red hair.

"What now?" Olivia whispered, shell-shocked.

She blinked at his slow grin as he leaned forward, grabbing her and pulling her into his lap.

He leaned his head down, placing his lips on hers gently before tilting his head and licking deeper. Taking his time as he explored her mouth thoroughly. Their lips smacked together, and she blushed as he spent long minutes groaning as he made a meal of eating her mouth.

Pulling away, he whispered into her ear. "*Now*, I get to take my time discovering every inch of you. Now the *real* fun begins," he said, grasping her hand and hauling her up gently by her left arm. "Welcome to your new life, baby." He smiled, escorting her to the elevator with his lips to her hair.

Colin led her to his car, where she waited patiently for him to open the passenger door.

Sneaky bastard put that in the contract; she was no longer allowed to open her own doors.

He was a self-professed sadist, and she'd just signed her life over to him.

TWELVE
Muscle Tears and Family Ties

AFTER THEY'D STOPPED BY her apartment to grab the original blueprints and the shoebox with the money in it, he'd surprised her by taking her to the doctor. The doctor huffed as he took her through a string of exercises that left her depleted and in tears.

"The tendon's torn. You'll need a minor procedure, and physical therapy. No lifting and all that jazz. The nurses will walk you through it. Healing time won't take long. How long did you let it go like that for?"

The handsome blonde-haired doctor pushed away from her in his chair, swinging around to type into his computer.

Colin kept an impassive look on his face as she told the doctor how long she'd been suffering with the injury, but inside he was silently seething with the need to punish her for neglecting her body and her health to that extent.

"Do you play tennis? Shot put? Despite the injury, your arms are quite strong. You're well defined. Recovery shouldn't take too long," the doctor said rather absentmindedly as he typed some more.

"No...I don't play anything. I'm not very athletic," she joked with a small grin.

It was the truth. She chanced a glance at Colin before looking away quickly, seeing he looked rather irritated.

The doctor turned to give her a quick glance before arching his brow. He didn't believe her. She crossed her legs and arms, looking away from both men, her own mood souring. She knew she had secrets, but she didn't consider herself a liar. Not really.

"Okay, let's go over some basic questions. Some of these are quite personal, so it's up to you if you would like Colin to leave the room," the doctor asked, still facing the computer as he pulled up some sort of document. She peeked at Colin, who shook his head slightly. Her jaw dropped before his eyebrow raised.

"It's fine," she gritted her face heating up. She threw Colin a filthy look.

"Okay, any chance you are pregnant?"

"Nope, *I'm* not sexually active," she answered, with a big emphasis on the 'I'm,' leaving that up for the doctor's interpretation. She hoped Colin was as embarrassed as she was.

The doctor glanced briefly between the two of them before putting his eyes back on the computer. Colin's crossed his ankle over his knee and began tapping the toe of his shoe on the tiled floor, the action making her nervous.

"How many sexual partners have you had? Would you like us to do an STD test while you are here today?"

"W-what?" she sputtered. "Aren't these questions more appropriate for a gynecologist, Doctor?" she said, pissed.

The man swiveled all the way in his chair, his hands clasping between his knees. "These are all normal questions. I see that you haven't been to a regular doctor since you were seventeen years old. And if you're going to be a patient of mine, I need basic information about you for your file. If you would like, I can refer you to a female Doctor here in the office, but her next available appointment isn't for another three months. Seeing as you need your arm attended to, I am the quickest option at the moment to get you referred for surgery. You let me know what you're comfortable with, Miss Cameron," the doctor finished, rolling back and forth slightly in his chair, regarding her kindly.

Olivia calmed herself with a deep breath, not even daring to look at Colin. She felt his energy from across the room choking her. She blew out a breath and nodded.

"It's fine, sorry. I'm just a little nervous. I'm on edge because of the pain." She put a hand up to her hair and tugged, breathing a sigh of relief at the tingles breaking across her scalp.

"I can prescribe you something for that. Can we continue?" he replied, turning back to his computer when she nodded her consent. Olivia felt her face flush.

"I've only had one sexual partner six years ago. And I don't need an STD test, but he does. Can we make *him* an appointment?" she said, referencing Colin. His lips twitched in amusement.

"Yes. We can get him in right after you, actually."

Olivia looked at Colin and gave him a self-satisfied smile. Her phone dinged.

> Keep it up. I dare you.-C

She smiled brighter.

> Just giving you your money's worth. -O

"Date of your last period." The doctor's voice interrupted her glee.

"Two and a half weeks ago." She pursed her lips, turning even more red. She threw her phone back in her purse and pushed it away from her.

The doctor proceeded to ask her all kinds of questions before doing a careful exam of her body. Worried about any freckles or moles, and instructing her to keep a good eye on any changes in her freckles, as any change might be a sign of cancer. There were more and younger people dying of melanoma, unaware of the risks and what to look for.

He gave her a couple of recommendations for a dermatologist, which she shoved into her purse.

They got her surgery scheduled for a couple of weeks out, due to a patient dropping out of their surgery date. Colin put his arm around her comfortingly at her shocked look, staying quiet as they walked hand in hand to his car. He apparently didn't need any testing, already having had all of that taken care of because he was responsible. She bristled when he told her that.

Her hand felt slightly clammy in his warm palm.

Olivia bit her lip, suddenly missing her parents.

Colin started his vehicle and patiently waited as she called her sister to tell her the news, and to let her know that she was bringing dinner over, ignoring her usual 'can we afford that' statement. She looked at Colin, thinking that because of him, they could now afford just about whatever they wanted.

He called the local Chinese restaurant over the car system while they drove, putting in an obnoxiously large order. She raised her eyebrows at the price, but stayed silent.

It was more of an effort to stay silent as she watched him add his facial recognition to her phone, before making her do the same to his. As well as adding her phone to the car's bluetooth system.

While they were on the way to her sister's house, he'd called a dealership and ordered her a cherry red Porsche. Taking her hand in a vice grip as she'd snapped, trying to stab at the many prompts on the touch screen to disconnect the call before he could complete the order. His hand stayed tight on hers until his GPS pulled him up to her sister's house.

He finished up the call and got out of the car, rounding it and opening her door.

Olivia glanced at his hand as he held it out, her eyes flickering between his as she slowly met his gaze. Blowing a breath out to clear her nerves, suddenly almost terrified as she'd never brought a man to meet her sister, or her niece. She swallowed hard, imploring silently with her eyes for this to go okay. She grimaced past the pain as she extended her arm, letting Colin help her out of the car.

He grabbed the Chinese food out of the backseat, and then gestured for her to lead him.

Colin's eyes scanned the worn-down house with its downtrodden yard that was missing grass in places. He made note of the white picket fence in the back missing posts and half it's white paint. Vanessa's semi collapsed car port that just barely missed touching the top of her dark blue SUV, making him frown in displeasure.

Her house paint was faded and peeling, and the door looked scuffed from years of neglect. The grass was half swallowed with weeds as tiny dots of white flowers littered the lawn. The short driveway was a sorry mess, half missing its asphalt in some places.

Colin wryly thought if Olivia's sister had checked her bank account yet. Knowing Olivia hadn't checked hers, and he was revving himself up to deal with that when she finally got around to it when she had time.

Olivia glanced silently at him, praying and hoping that it reached where it needed to go this time. She led him through the carport, through the side door, into the kitchen and into the clusterfuck that was her and Vanessa's life.

***

"Tee-Tee Ollie!" The little ball of strawberry blonde curls hurled its mass at Olivia as she tried unsuccessfully to walk through the door. Olivia hissed around the pain, and fell back a step. Hauling the quivering mass up her body as best as she could with her left arm.

Colin reached out a hand to help pull Allison the rest of the way up, balancing the Chinese on his leg via the foot that was resting the top step. He watched as Allison squealed and planted a big slobbery kiss on Olivia, and he winced as Allison left drool on her chin.

His heart warmed as the cute little girl squirmed and threw her hands around Olivia's neck, who was still trying to walk into the house.

"Ally, calm down, calm *down,* sweetheart." Olivia laughed softly, finally able to finish getting through the door. She pulled back to look in the girls' eyes, which were the same stunning shade of green as hers. "I have someone for you to meet."

Olivia smiled at Allison as she placed her hands on either side of her face and squashed her little nose into Olivia's.

Colin chuckled at them as he carefully placed the overflowing bag of Chinese food on the table in the kitchen. Allison clocked his presence with her eyes before ducking quickly under Olivia's chin, snuggling in tight, and peeking out at him from her hiding spot.

"Who are yoouu?" she trilled the word out in her high-pitched voice.

Her shy grin revealed a missing tooth. Olivia stayed quiet as Colin assessed Allison. His eyes roamed, taking in her dark eyes and ashen skin tone. She watched a momentary flash of sadness at cross his features at seeing how frail and tiny her little body looked. Oddly, she felt better knowing he had compassion for others.

***

"My name is Colin, it's nice to meet you, Allison." he answered softly, extending a hand to take her outstretched finger in two of his and shaking it gently.

"Collie!" Allison suddenly yelped, sitting back up and looking into Olivia's eyes. *"Ollie and Collie!"* Colin chuckled as she cheered while yanking at Olivia's hair. She tsked and put Allison down gingerly, being careful of her shoulder.

"Hey sis," Vanessa called from somewhere down the hallway. "I just checked my bank account. Something's wrong, so we need to call them together tomorrow; I think the clerk must have added some extra zeroes to the amount you deposited." There was a slam before she spoke again. "Whatever happened, they *maaaajorly* screwed up. I hope they can fix it before her bill is due this month." Her voice got louder as she walked up the hallway. "And thank you for putting it in the bank for me early this month. Last month the doctors made it a big deal-" She paused as she emerged from the hallway into the kitchen, spotting Colin and breaking out into a bright smile.

"Hiii! *Oh*, you must be Ollie's date!" Vanessa said brightly, hurrying to straighten her messy bun, coming towards him with her hand outstretched.

He took it warmly, flashing her his most charming smile as he regarded her intently. The woman was gorgeous, with strawberry blonde hair rather than the dark red locks that Olivia boasted. She had a cat eye shape, but her's was a light gray instead of green. She was taller and curvier than Olivia, probably due to having a child.

Colin frowned slightly at her tired countenance, though Vanessa tried hard to hide it. He noticed she was slightly pale under her smattering of freckles, and his eyes softened slightly. He knew exhaustion when he saw it. Vanessa was young, too young to be dealing with a sick child.

"It's *Olivia, not* Ollie." Olivia hissed to Vanessa as she shook his hand. Colin smiled teasingly down at her.

"Hi Vanessa, it's so nice to meet you and Allison. I've heard great things," he responded, grasping Vanessa's hand firmly in his before leaning back again and sharing a quick glance with Olivia.

"Ooooh!" Vanessa said suggestively, wagging her eyebrows and giving Olivia a look. "He has an accent!"

Narrowing his eyes slightly, he silently encouraged her to explain the banking 'mishap'. Olivia took the hint, thankfully.

"So um... Nessie. About the banking stuff, can I talk to you really quick?" she asked, reaching forward to pull her to the back bedroom and leaving Colin alone with Allison, who was currently rifling through the Chinese food. Getting one of the cartons open, she took a piece of chicken and shoved it in her mouth with her fingers.

Colin moved quickly, gently taking her off the counter and placing her onto a counter height chair before unwrapping and pulling out a plastic fork out for her to eat with.

His ears strained to hear the girls talking, but all he could hear was furious whispering and then a "Oh *hell* no Olivia! What the FUUUCK?" Before Vanessa hurdled herself down the hallway and snatched up Allison, who was busy trying to shovel another forkful of noodles in her mouth.

Vanessa walked backwards until she bumped into the loveseat in the open concept living room. Turning, she placed Allison down before snatching up her food, placing it on the coffee table in front of the little girl, and turning on a cartoon. She turned back, seething, her arms crossed as she walked back into the kitchen. Somehow, her gray gaze was even more piercing than Olivia's.

He could tell this was the 'older sister' gaze. He raised an eyebrow, never having had one, so it didn't bother him.

Vanessa rounded the counter fast, and got in his face.

Lowering his chopsticks, he placed the carton of sweet and sour chicken down, amused by Vanessa's flash of temper. He cleared his throat and folded his arms as he leaned his hips against the sink, biting back a grin.

"Explain yourself. What the fuck is she talking about? That's way too much money. Are you *crazy*?!" Vanessa bit out, her eyes flashing dangerously at him. He saw Olivia appear in the hallway timidly, looking at her sister as if she was superwoman. She inched closer.

"I'd like to think I'm pretty sane," he said, putting his eyes back to Vanessa in amusement. They were both adorable, and no match for him.

"For what!?" Vanessa hissed, narrowing her eyes even further. "What the fuck did she promise you for that money? That's more than most people see in a lifetime!" she whispered angrily, trying to not be overheard by Allison.

Vanessa squeaked as he suddenly picked her up, placing her on a stool and shoving an unopened box of chicken kung pao in her hands firmly with some chop sticks. He threw Olivia his brightest smile in repentance for touching her sister, however innocent.

"There's not much to explain. Olivia and I came to an understanding. She agreed to give me two and a half years of her time in exchange for money for Allison's treatments, finishing architect school, and giving me a three percent profit from her future architect business. Along with some other bonuses. Simple."

He watched her face slowly turn redder with each word, and wondered how long that could go on before her head popped off.

"She couldn't give me a numerical value on Allison's treatment, and her contribution to this household. So I took it upon myself to estimate two million should suffice for a while unless something major happens. And in that event, I expect you to call me." He met Vanessa's stare just as directly as she gave it, waiting patiently.

Silently letting her know that she didn't intimidate him.

"She-she said something about a binding agreement..." Vanessa turned and threw Olivia a filthy look, getting up and pacing the small kitchen back and forth. "Well, she gets to finish architect school...Gramps would like that," she mused to herself quietly, tapping a fingernail against her tooth. "But, okay... what happens if you guys don't like each other? What if something happens, and she wants to break the agreement? *Well*?" Vanessa asked, turning on both with incredulous eyes.

Colin waited for Olivia to tell her, putting his dark chocolate eyes on her green, still shell-shocked ones. When no explanation was forthcoming, he had pity on her, answering her sister himself.

"Oh, she'll be stuck paying me back every cent every day for the rest of her life. Even if she leaves a day early." His voice came out rough, his eyes still on Olivia's. His own crinkling as he felt that illicit pull between them.

Christ, he hadn't even touched her properly yet, and he was a fucking simpering mess. He didn't know what was going to happen when he finally got inside of her. Maybe they'd burn each other up with their passion, and neither one of them would have to owe anyone anything.

Vanessa's head cranked to the side, looking at Olivia in sympathy.

"Oh, Ollie! I *knew* you were getting into something you shouldn't have." Vanessa put her head in her hands, taking a deep breath. "The way you consistently brought in all that money every month for four *years*. Damn you girl." She leaned forward, placing her forehead against Olivia's, giving her a soft kiss on her cheek.

Colin studied this interaction closely. Olivia's relationship with Allison and Vanessa would be one he would have to protect.

"I've *been* telling you! I wasn't sleeping with anyone to get that money!" Olivia flashed angry eyes at Vanessa's before pulling open her own carton of food.

Colin watched, enamored as she poured an interesting amount of sweet and sour and soy sauce on her food, before mixing it with a different beef dish. His nose crinkled in surprise, and he frowned.

Gross, he thought with some amusement.

"What else brings in that kind of money?" Vanessa shot to Olivia, and he could hear a smidgen of anger in her voice. She cocked her head at Olivia. "Drugs? You're in with the cartel?" Vanessa asked.

Olivia rolled her eyes.

"*Stealing?*" Vanessa pushed.

Olivia shook her head no, starting to dissociate and get annoyed, putting some more food in her mouth. Colin noticed she ate a lot neater than her sister, who dropped her food to her carton with a horrified expression on her face.

"Trafficking? You fell into the black market, *didn't you?*" Vanessa whispered, her face going pale instead of red.

Colin's eyes slid to Olivias, desperately wanting the answer as well.

"It's not your business. Just accept the money and *shut up*." Olivia hissed, leaning forward and pinning the two of them with angry eyes. "Stop *pushing* me. I wouldn't do anything that would potentially put you and Allison in danger."

Colin, who had been silently eating and just observing them, got an incredibly painful hard on at her sudden attitude. It was almost like she flipped a switch on for him internally. His eyes narrowed.

"Yeah, okay. Either way, I'm thankful." Vanessa tilted her head up and regarded Colin with a haughty stare. "And *you*, if this goes bad, I hope you know I'll kill you first before she spends the rest of her life doing whatever she did to fuck up her shoulder to pay you back. So, I really hope for all our sakes this works out the way it's supposed to."

Colin nodded solemnly, understanding her need to push back.

He picked up more rice, preferring to lean against the counter and watch Allison fall asleep on the couch, having barely finished her food. Olivia padded over and pulled the blanket over her before efficiently cleaning up the mess her niece made. They ate for a while, and Vanessa and Colin sized each other up, talking about each other's jobs and interests.

She was quite impressed when he told her what he did for a living. Telling her about his tech company which supplied safety features for car brands.

Colin hurriedly put the food in the fridge with Vanessa, who snatched the kitchen towel out of Olivia's hand, making her stop cleaning.

"Your arm, *Jesus* woman!" she admonished.

Colin realized his girl was just Uber independent and couldn't wait to beat that out of her, instinctively knowing her attitude was going to be a problem. He dismissed Vanessa's need to be there during the surgery, knowing she'd need to be available for her daughter.

He traded contact information with Vanessa, giving her his address and code for the house so Olivia wouldn't feel so ostracized.

Colin tensed as Vanessa caught them on the way out the door, placing her arms around him and hugging him tightly. "*Don't* hurt her, she's special," she said before whispering a tearful "thank you" in his ear.

He softened slightly, patting her back and gruffly saying goodbye and placing Olivia in his car, watching she waved goodbye to Vanessa when they finally pulled off in the late evening.

Letting his eyes roam her face and body, he noted she looked exhausted.

He knew the revelation of her surgery came as a shock, and she didn't really react much today besides annoyance at the doctor's office when he wouldn't leave. Guessing the shock of it all was dampening her usual temperament, he treaded carefully. He'd caught her checking her student loan account already, almost as if she thought the zero balance was going to magically reappear with over one hundred thousand dollars to be owed.

No, I got you, baby, Colin thought to himself, knowing she just needed time for it to sink in.

She fell asleep quickly, the Chinese food and excitement of the day finally catching up to her. Colin reached over and traced a knuckle over her exposed chest before turning the soft music slightly up, and settled into the half hour drive to his house.

It wasn't lost on him that Olivia had no clue where she was going, had no clothes or belongings with her, save her phone and her purse. For her to fall asleep without being curious as to their destination meant that she'd finally found a modicum of peace. His chest once again swelled with pride at being able to put that much money into her sister's account without having missed it.

He looked over at her beautiful face, illuminated by the setting sun, and smiled slightly.

Enjoy your rest now, he thought. *You're working off every cent whether you break the contract or not. We just need to get you healed up first.*

He turned on her seat warmer on low before placing his hand back on hers, his thumb stroking over the delicate blue veins under her skin.

THIRTEEN
Decidedly
Disrespectfully

COLIN HAD THE FORESIGHT to wake Olivia up before he pulled into his neighborhood, idling at a stop sign in the nice neighboring residential area, rubbing her thigh firmly and watching her pull herself out of slumber. Her lashes fluttered as she inhaled quickly, her eyes flying open in surprise before she looked around, disoriented. He thought she was adorable when she woke up.

"Welcome home, baby," he whispered quietly as he watched her blink drowsily.

She looked around, and he tried to make himself see what she saw. Remembering the first time he was able to afford a house of this magnitude in a prestigious area like this. He remembered it to be quite overwhelming, and exciting.

However, it had been a very long time since he let himself appreciate the grandeur and scale of it all, and he let himself go back in time just for a moment, imagining himself in her shoes.

His own gaze roamed, seeing wide streets, with no line dividers, and lots of lush, green grass. He resumed driving slowly, giving her a chance to see the enormous mansions behind the tall gates. The deeper they journeyed into the residential area, the denser the foliage became, the bigger the houses and property grew, and the less of the houses you could see behind the gates.

His neighbors' lights were on and twinkling in the yards, the homes and surrounding property lit up by outdoor lighting systems. He took two more turns before rolling up to a pad in front of a six foot tall, iron double gate. Colin lowered his visor and pressed the button hidden there, and rolled them slowly down his curved driveway onto the property.

Watching her exquisite face light up as his house came into view.

Not able to help his reaction to the awed look on her face, his dick twitched with excitement, and his breathing became slightly labored as he watched her eyes widen like saucers when she got the full magnitude of his property.

Damn, the fucker was worth every bit of twelve million for this look on her face, he thought.

Colin parked the car out front next to the fountain and hopped out fluidly, walking around to her door and opening it. He stared enraptured at her as she slowly looked from the front of the house to his hand, as if she was in a trance she couldn't shake. He could sympathize.

Olivia placed her hand softly in his, and he let out a nervous breath when she stepped gracefully out of the car without any fuss. She craned her neck back to look at the tall white home, that was trimmed with black windows, and had an enormous double door entrance of glass. Most of the home was glass as well, but tastefully so.

While she was distracted he took the opportunity to admire the curve of her neck, the light blue vein he could see just under her jaw line. His dick hardened impossibly further, wondering if she would like for him to nibble at the vulnerable flesh there.

Colin desired for her to enjoy this arrangement just as much as he planned to. And so he began to scheme, to find out what made her tick, what turned her on. Unbeknownst to her, he hadn't planned on unleashing himself on her right away. He really wasn't a monster like he suspected she might think he was, truly wanting for this to be mutually beneficial in more ways than one.

He wanted her to enjoy *every* aspect of her new life.

Even the pain he brought her sexually, he'd just have to tread with caution.

She licked her lips, regarding what was to be her home for two and a half years, according to the contract. She tried to open her mouth to speak, but nothing came from her lips. Curiously, her eyes flicked back and forth, finding something new to pause and focus on with every pass.

"Your landscaping is....is...." Olivia tried, and smiled at her struggle.

He remembered hiring the company initially, and then the absolute glee he felt putting them on payroll. He almost wished he could turn them around and start all over from the beginning so he could better appreciate the experience of her seeing it all over again. There were so many nuances to be found within her expression, within her gaze. Her wonder.

He wanted her to look at *him* like that.

To see him and have the same exact overwhelming expression on her face. He thought he'd might feel joy then, as she seemed to be the closest he'd ever felt to the emotion.

He closed the car door softly behind her, handing over her purse before taking her soft hand and leading her up the stairs. He rubbed her fingers encouragingly with his thumb, feeling her trembling and looked down in curiosity at the box within her other hand seeing she held it clutched tightly to her stomach.

Olivia paused as Colin opened the front door and she turned for a split second, looking over her shoulder at the expansive front yard, as if she was looking for something nostalgic and familiar to rest her eyes on. He knew there was nothing. Just beautiful roses boxed in with bushes, fountains, and pretty trees and other flowering bushes.

Her breath hitched as he placed his hand on her lower back again to get her attention, and she raised those startling green eyes to his again. Colin found himself losing himself in her, drawn to her like the same night he saw her through the diner.

Swallowing hard, he jerked his head towards the foyer, his eyes crinkling slightly, indicating for her to go inside before him. She took the first step into his home, and he heard her take a deep breath as the smell of lemon chicken assaulted her senses as she crossed the threshold into the foyer.

Her head tilted way back as she looked around, taking in the pretty buttery foyer, and noting the dark uniquely planked wooden floors flanked by the gorgeous double staircase leading to the upper house. In between the staircases hung an incredible crystal chandelier.

An enormous bouquet of dark pink earth angel roses graced the table in the middle.

She looked to the left, seeing a lovely library room that he remembered costing a ton of money to build, as well as a formal dining room to the right with two tastefully large sideboards on the opposite wall. The colors in the home were so rich it was homey, and not stark at all. He couldn't have lived in this house if he didn't make it warm.

He remembered the day he sat down with the first interior designer when he built the home. She didn't get a sense of what he wanted for the home, so he fired her after too many attempts at her trying to make the house modern instead of what he wanted.

He turned his head from Olivia as Mary, a brown-haired, middle-aged Spanish-American came through the foyer from the back of the home.

"Mr. McDermont, how are you? And you, miss?" She greeted them in her elegant Spanish accent. Her heels clicked rapidly as she strode through the foyer, taking off her apron and presenting a smart, polished outfit.

Colin smiled, feeling settled in her presence and greeted the house manager warmly with a chaste kiss on her light brown cheek before stepping aside to introduce Olivia. He found himself suddenly tense, worried at how Mary would like Olivia as he'd never brought another woman home before, and he felt a vicious pang in his chest, wishing he could tell his mother about her.

He supposed Mary was a more than suitable replacement, not that anyone would ever replace his ma.

He turned back to Olivia, seeing her smile broadly at Mary. His momentary sadness dissipated as her beautiful smile hit him full force.

He cleared his throat softly. "Mary, this is Olivia. She'll be staying with me for the foreseeable future. Olivia, this is Mary. She's my house manager."

"Mijo, don't forget the cook as well, huh?" Mary's eyes sparkled as she teased Colin.

The woman smiled kindly at Olivia, her eyes crinkling at the edges as she held her hand out to gently shake hers.

"It's so wonderful to meet you. You're so pretty, and your accent is *so beautiful!*" Olivia gushed, walking another step towards Mary, betraying the pain in her arm. Colin reached out and grabbed her hand softly, giving Mary an 'I'll explain later' look.

He saw Olivia's eyebrow raise as Beth, a young brunette in a professional cleaning uniform, quickly and quietly walked across the landing upstairs, she hadn't even made a sound. The only reason he noticed her was because of his past military training. Beth disappeared into the hallway like a ghost, almost as if she'd never been there to begin with.

He smiled, because that's why he loved having **Beth around**; she was smart to avoid him, they gave each other a wide berth, and she handled what needed to be done efficiently.

He took note that Olivia was a keen observer.

"Ms. Olivia, it's lovely to meet you as well. Please make yourself at home and do not worry about a thing! If this tyrant bothers you, you come see me. Okay, Amore?" Mary smiled warmly at Olivia once again before turning her attention to Colin. "I am headed out for the day, Mijo, but I've left a lemon roast chicken with vegetables in orzo rice in the oven. The wine cooler is stocked, and I put in an order of tignanello you wanted but they said a full case would be ready tomorrow, and you'd have to pick it up. Do you need anything else before I leave?"

Mary reached forward and took Olivia's purse, her eyes widening as she watched her place it in a hidden closet under the stairs.

He noted she didn't like anyone touching her things.

Oh well, he thought. *Because all of her things are going to be touched. Respectfully of course.*

Colin grinned as he realized that was a lie. He'd be touching all her things, decidedly disrespectfully.

His smile broadened as he reached into his pocket for his phone. He wondered again for the hundredth time why Mary never had music playing over the home surround. She knew he liked it.

"No thank you, Mary. I appreciate you," Colin said, turning his attention to his phone momentarily.

"Ms. Mary, it's so nice to meet you again. Thank you for dinner," Olivia said softly, and Colin kept his gaze on his phone as Olivia stood there rather awkwardly as the Mary nodded, grabbed her own purse and belongings, and let herself quietly out the door.

Colin made another mental note that Olivia hadn't disclosed to Mary that they'd already had dinner. He liked this about her, she seemed to care about others feelings, even strangers. He watched through his peripheral as she attempted to look around her surroundings without appearing obvious.

After a few taps, soft music began playing throughout the house through a customized sound system. Colin took her hand again and led her through the foyer into the back of the home, where there was a vast, homey kitchen. And across from the kitchen was an informal lounge with comfortable furniture, a fireplace, and a tastefully big flat screen television.

He was incredibly proud of every aspect of his home, and though he knew she was tired, he couldn't help but want to show it off. Just the highlights. He paused briefly at the drinks cabinet in the kitchen while she walked to the wall in the back of the home, working quickly to make them both a drink.

The back wall was nothing but sliding glass doors leading to an indoor-outdoor style dining room and outdoor kitchen with a fireplace/pizza oven. Beyond that was an immense pool with a grotto that was currently glowing purple, and spitting out water over the top. Water was splashing everywhere, and in another corner was a hot tub, also glowing.

Colin grabbed both of their drinks and walked the few feet to her, seeing Olivia staring at the grotto, smiling to herself.

"Do you like what you see?" Colin asked softly, coming up from behind her with two glasses of white wine, handing her one. She took it hesitantly, managing a cautious sip before smacking her lips in surprise. He'd purposefully picked a delicious and refreshing sweet wine.

Her eyes widened in pleasure. "Mmm...You're going to make me become a lush," she said with a small laugh, "and yes, you have a beautiful home. Though I think the grotto is very playboy mansion like." Her smile faltering as she noticed he was staring rather intensely at her, sipping from his wine.

He made a soft sound in the back of his throat, remembering a rather salacious party at the aforementioned mansion when he'd first started making serious money. That was his first and only time there, he didn't want to get caught up in the partying lifestyle.

"Nonsense, it's *nothing* like their grotto. *I've been in it.* This one is more intimate, and not made for an orgy," Colin said, smiling cheekily at her.

Olivia's piercing eyes flickered away from him and perused the kitchen slowly, taking another cautious sip. He wanted her to like to drink, however he knew given her past with her parents that he'd have to tread carefully there too. He didn't want to, but if she truly needed him to, then he'd be willing to give up alcohol for her.

That's how badly he found himself wanting her trust in him. Wanting this relationship to work out.

"May I show you some more of the house? I know you're probably tired after the day, so I'll just hit the highlights so you can at least get your bearings, and then you can get comfortable. You're more than welcome to explore all you like tomorrow if you wish," he said, mentioning for her to follow him.

She clutched her box tighter to her, the cardboard starting to bend beneath her fingers.

He placed his hand on her back again, taking her downstairs through the staircase so she would at least know where it is. After a tour of a two-lane bowling alley, a media room with leather sofas and a popcorn machine, he took her to another spot that hosted a small indoor jacuzzi.

"Impressive," Olivia admitted, her eyes widening with pleasure at seeing a jacuzzi nestled into the floor next to an indoor pool room. Which had more glass doors that opened to the grounds outdoors.

"Thanks. I had it set up like this for the wintertime, if we don't want to be outside," Colin explained.

She raised her eyebrows at his use of 'we' but didn't comment verbally.

According to the timeline, they would celebrate three sets of holidays with each other. *If* she successfully lasted that long, that is. And he found himself really hoping she could.

Colin took her to a little spot in the wall, near a door that had a set of stairs that led to the first floor, and pushed a button, showing her a hidden elevator. Her eyes lit up.

"It goes all the way to the second floor. In," he said, ushering her in and closing the door quickly. She stood next to him with her glass still in her hand, cradling it against her breastbone as she stared straight ahead, obviously trying to get her bearings.

He had another moment of appreciation of her. He knew it was one thing to design a house like this from imagination, but another thing entirely to be in one. Every inch of the home exuded wealth, and he could tell that it made her slightly uncomfortable. However, she kept her thoughts to herself.

Exiting the elevator on the top floor, she stepped out before him, looking left and right down a long, wide, and beautifully decorated hallway. He'd lined the walls with beautiful old art that cost a small fortune, with chunky elaborate frames, and thin tables laden down with small lamps and more flowers.

The cream colors up here seemed even more rich looking than downstairs, and the view through the windows was beautiful.

"Hey, where's the cleaner I saw a little bit ago? I haven't seen her since we got here," Olivia asked, suddenly realizing Beth was nowhere to be found.

"Oh, that's Beth. She comes five days a week to do laundry, clean the rooms, and dust. She also takes care of the guest house and puts together the flower arrangements that Mary orders for the house. That sort of thing. Mary manages her. She won't talk to me; I *never* see her. Mary said she's slightly terrified of me, which is fine. You'll probably never see her either," Colin said, his eyes flicking over the grounds of the property.

"You don't have any pictures of your family?" she asked suddenly, turning a curious eye on him.

She'd been looking at the walls, only seeing beautiful paintings, but no canvases of any family members, or pictures anywhere. He knew it was strange, how it must look, and how lonely it came across. He felt the familiar tightening in his chest, that cloud of anxiety looming closer.

"I have no family," Colin replied, leaving it at that. Thankful that Olivia wasn't pushing her luck by asking questions either.

She snuck a curious look at him before he placed his hand once more on her lower back, and began to show her to the right of the elevator where there was a small powder room. Past that was a small foyer entrance that hosted carved double doors set into an alcove that was lit by a stunning chandelier.

Books filled the inlay of the foyer wall flanking the door. It was spectacular, because he designed it that way.

The fight with the third interior designer was well worth making his bedroom look like a retreat. He smiled, remembering how he fired the second interior designer within the first half hour of meeting her, because she told him he was stupid for wanting a bedroom in his guest house with no windows.

"My *intimate* master bedroom," Colin explained simply.

Cautiously, Olivia peeked her head in. Her eyes flickered around the space curiously, seeing a gas fireplace and a lounge with gold fabric that offset the green of the room perfectly. A large flatscreen hung above the fireplace, and a California king sized bed was on a platform that dominated the far side of the room.

It was formidable, nothing like her flimsy bed that he saw in her bedroom. He meant what he'd said two weeks ago; he'd break the hell out of that fucker and hurt them both if he attempted to fuck her on it.

No, he needed room, and stability to work her over the way he planned.

His bed sat next to a giant wall of windows overlooking the pool. A small drinks cabinet was by the window, next to a tall and obviously expensive and intricately curved floor-to-ceiling mirror which faced the bed.

He frowned slightly, not liking she hadn't stepped into the bedroom.

"It's very nice, I like it. The paint color is pretty, and unexpected. Do you choose it yourself?" Olivia smiled at him, turning to peek at him, taking another sip of wine before she backed further into the foyer, not even having gone through the threshold.

Colin furrowed his brows at her before giving her a not so gentle nudge back deeper into the room.

FOURTEEN

I Can Show You

"Hey!" she snapped, spinning to face him, trying not to spill her wine or drop her shoe box. "I just wanted to keep going so I can see where I'm sleeping. I'd like a shower, and to figure out what I'm going to wear to bed."

Her eyes flicked over Colin slowly, lighting up in surprise. He had stretched his arms to grasp the door frame above him, giving her a delicious muscular view of his body on display. His chest swelled proudly, he knew she couldn't know how hard she was stroking his ego at this exact moment.

He kept his body in pristine shape, and he wanted her to enjoy it just like he enjoyed hers.

"This *is* where you're sleeping," Colin said, licking his lips. "Hmmm.... Did you forget that detail in our contract? Should we go back downstairs and read it again? It could be a *great* bedtime story. Maybe I could read it to you." He cocked his head again, perusing her face once more.

I could lay you out over the couch, make you read me the contract slowly. I'd spread your legs and eat you out until you can't talk anymore, then punish you for not being able to read the contract by biting and tugging your clit. I wonder how sweet you taste, or if you taste deeper, like the earth? I wonder how many of my fingers you can stand to take inside you? How do you sound when your limits are pushed. How red can

I make that body get. Would you be scared if I used a whip on your back? Does being scared turn you on? he thought.

Olivia recoiled her head as she turned away from his stare. He couldn't blame her, he probably looked like he wanted to eat her. Because he did, thoroughly. All night. And then when she couldn't take anymore he'd tied her up, strap her down, and make her take it anyway.

Olivia's eyebrows rose slightly again as she backed deeper into the room.

Colin came into the room with her and she backed up a few more feet, this time away from him. He gave her a knowing smile before heading left to the closet door, entering a code to unlock it. Opening it, he turned on the light, showing her yet another room that was three times bigger than her former apartment bedroom, and he found himself wondering how she felt about that.

He kept quiet though, not wanting to say anything to make her feel less than. He'd told her he had plenty of audacity, but he never wanted to intentionally offend her with his wealth.

She hesitated in the doorway, same as she did when she first entered the master bedroom.

He watched as she looked around the room slowly, perusing the expansive shelves backlit with warm lighting that matched the hallway lighting. There was a mechanical tie rack, an area in the back with hooks for hanging hats or purses. So many color coordinated tailored suits lined in perfect rows that it he knew, without even asking, that made her eyes cross thinking of how much money was just hanging on one rack alone.

It was a lot.

The room was very comfortable, hosting the cream color from downstairs, and had a thick carpet. He bit back a grin as she wiggled her toes in it experimentally. Then he stared riveted, not having given her feet much thought, and he felt precum dripping down his dick at the sight of her pretty toes.

Jesus Christ. I've never been a feet guy before, he thought.

The defining feature in the room was the massive marble top island stationed in the middle of the large space. It hosted cabinets all around, painted the same deep green color as the bedroom. The island was the only pop of color in the room, aside from the clothes hanging from hangers on racks against the wall. It was all cream and marble. Making the room feel even bigger than it already was.

Above the island hung another smaller, but beautiful crystal lighting feature, drawing her gaze to the decanter of whiskey gleaming in the light next to a colorful bouquet of flowers.

She wrinkled her nose, and he tightened his lips at her reaction, knowing there was liquor all over the house.

Please don't be a problem.

Olivia's eyes narrowed.

No bueno.

He'd have to give her something regarding this. To buy himself enough time to show her he was responsible. He built his entire brand on safety and responsibility, and he really didn't want her to take this away from him.

"You *suuurreee* like to drink, don't you?" She didn't bother masking the slight contempt in her voice as her eyes turned to his.

Colin nodded once, giving her a slight up and down once over. His mouth tipped up on one side.

"I enjoy it in moderation. Everything I buy is expensive top shelf liquor.... so, it doesn't take much to feel good. And I don't drive drunk. And in any event my car's software doesn't allow it. I also don't drink to get drunk. And I will make sure you won't, either, unless you just need one of those nights. And maybe on the occasional girl's night out-*if you ask for permission first,*" Colin replied rather absent-mindedly, before turning to an extremely expensive-looking cabinet.

Olivia scoffed. She wouldn't be asking permission for things like a girl's night out, but resigned herself to broaching that topic another time. Today had been stressful enough.

He turned back to face her, leaning back against the drawers and folding his arms and legs. His tattoos bunched and flexed with his muscles, and that sexual tension between the two of them tightened as he watched her eyes do another slow meander down his body. He spoke quickly, knowing if she didn't stop looking at him like that, he was going to drag her to his bed and do unspeakable things to her.

And he knew she couldn't handle it, not her first night.

"If you ever feel triggered by drinking, or *my* drinking, please let me know right away. You can safe word with sex, and drinking. Nothing else. Would you like to pick a safe word now? I left it optional in the agreement. I wanted it to be something you were comfortable with, and would be easy for you to remember." His eyes bored into hers as she cradled her glass closer and shifted from foot to foot.

"Um... it can be anything?" Olivia asked hesitantly. Her eyes flickering from his to his chest and back again. She looked unsettled, even though she knew what she had signed up for. She clutched the box even closer to her, the cheap particle board slightly crunching under her fingers.

He tilted his head, wondering if it was a sex toy.

Whatever it was, she hadn't wanted the movers to see it. It was the only thing she elected to carry out of the apartment, aside from the blue prints.

"It needs to be something easy that you can think of, in times of... sexual distress. For when you're being punished, et cetera," Colin said softly, his head tilting as he studied her reaction, biting back a sly smile.

Olivia's body looked like it had caught fire as her face, neck, and shoulders flushed a beautiful red color. His eyes wandered across her skin greedily, wondering just how much she could flush in other places. Her nipples hardened, and his eyes flickered back to her's as she took a cautious step back.

Still he waited, silently.

Olivia cleared her throat. "Bunny," she whispered, bringing her glass up to her lips and downing all the wine inside. He selfishly felt minutely relieved that she didn't seem to be demanding he stop drinking-at least tonight anyway.

"Bunny?"

"Yes."

Colin nodded, turning and began pulling out drawers, motioning silently with his hand for her to come and see. Olivia leaned against the doorway, refusing to enter the space with him just yet, however spacious. She craned her neck slightly to see.

"Bras, panties, socks, tanks, tees, sweatshirts, sweatpants, pajamas are in these drawers. Courtesy of Mary." Colin showed her one by one. She cocked her head, and he noted that Mary had picked all very feminine and skimpy undergarments.

He took pleasure in rifling through them curiously, as if he pawed through women's undergarments all the time. He didn't. The lace looked even more delicate in his powerful hands, and he let himself imagining ripping them off her body slowly. At four hundred dollars a set, it'd do much to take him over the edge sexually, buying her something expensive just to rip it off. To prove to her that he could afford it. Afford her if he so chose to.

He'd never tell her how much her things cost. She'd never let him tear it off her if she knew, it'd have to be his secret. She cautiously walked a few feet to him, and reached out and grabbed a white tank top with spaghetti straps and a matching sweatpants, gasping at the buttery feel of the material.

Olivia held the fabric to her face. Rubbing the material on her cheek, she closed her eyes and cooed at the whisper soft feeling sliding against her skin. He held his breath against the painful tightening his dick did at the sound.

Slowly, as if she was scared to move too fast around him, she re-opened the intimate drawer and saw there was no cotton *anything* inside. He grinned happily. *No cotton for you, senorita.*

"There's no... comfier... undergarments?" she asked hesitantly.

"No. I didn't instruct her to get any. For the most part, I'll want you with no panties. There might be the rare occasion where I'll like you to walk around in lace. That's what this is for," Colin rumbled in his deep voice, reaching out to brush her hair behind her shoulder. He relaxed his hand on the back of her neck.

"Oh." Olivia's cheeks went bright red, and her eyes looked down fast.

"Does this bother you? Can you not wear lace? You were wearing a lace bra the night of our date." Colin said, tilting his head and staring at her as his thumb rubbed gently on her nape. The movement served to comfort her, like they weren't discussing something he could tell she felt incredibly embarrassed about.

Though he wasn't sure why. Panties were panties.

"I-I *can*. It's just... on the days I have my period, I'll want something more comfortable, please." Olivia's eyes practically glued themselves onto the drawer in front of her.

Colin inhaled sharply, and adjusted his stance slightly, in pain.

The thought of giving her a mind-numbing orgasm while her body is its most sensitive. Oh my God. Would she cry? I need her to cry when I fuck her. I want her wrecked from the inside out, he thought.

"Of course, and about that... are you comfortable with period sex?" Colin looked at her curiously, his thumb still caressing away. As if he didn't just ask the most embarrassing thing in the world. As if it actually mattered, because he'd fuck her regardless if she was comfortable with it.

Olivia's lips quivered as she suddenly gasped. Her face turned an even brighter shade of red, her breath audibly caught in her chest. Her shoulders shrugged up hard, and added to the ever increasing mental note he'd been keeping on her that this was a serious tell of hers.

He heard the crinkling of the cardboard as she inadvertently pressed the box harder into her stomach. The stress of the day weighing on her. Her eyes closed briefly, as if that would save him from her.

Her big bad wolf.

"I-I d-don't know -look, I really need a shower, Colin. Is that okay?" Her voice sounded hoarse as it scraped through her windpipe, making his jaw tick.

I need to hear that sound as I rim her ass. Specifically. I want to hear her stutter my name just. like. that.

Colin closed the drawer quietly and turned to face her, his eyes falling to the shoe box still clutched tightly against her stomach.

His chocolate eyes met hers briefly before he turned and opened a dark green cabinet door underneath the island. Exposing another door that he pressed lightly to release a latch, and opened that as well, revealing a black safe hidden within the doors. He quickly entered a code, and the safe unlatched.

He held out his hand for the box, turning his head to look up at her.

Olivia paused for what felt like an eternity, her fingers digging into the box. Her hesitation betraying she didn't want to give it over to him. Colin waited for a few heartbeats before standing back up and closing the distance between them. Her eyes stayed trained on his chest, refusing to meet his. Colin took the wineglass out of her hand and placed it on the island countertop and Olivia took a tiny step back.

"Look at me, Olivia," he ordered softly, placing his hand against the side of her face.

She slowly looked up at him and he grinned at her wickedly, seeing a flush start in her cheeks.

"If there's a sex toy in there, maybe we should move it to the nightstand instead?" he teased. He smiled wide when she blushed even deeper as she shuffled from foot to foot.

Lowering his hand, he grabbed the shoebox and began to pull. Olivia pulled back. His eyes narrowed.

He stepped slightly to the side and then walked a step into her, trapping her against the island. She attempted to control her sudden ragged breathing, her eyes trained on his chest.

Give it to me, he thought. Yet, he forced himself to stay silent. He had to give her tonight.

Her fingers cramped as they clawed tightly around the cardboard. He stayed silent, their battle of wills playing out uncomfortably in the space of his closet. The air thickened in a tense inferno around them as she tensed further, and he knew her arm had to burn with the strain of how hard her arm was visibly locking up and the knowledge made him painfully aroused.

Eyes on hers, Colin suddenly flicked his hand and easily ripped the top off. Ignoring her little groan and her tightening her lips. Looking down, he stilled, before his body as well as his erection stiffened to its fullest extent at the sight of money, and not just any money. *Her* money.

He groaned as a muscle ticked in his jaw. He let out a long exhale, the air puffing out between them, and ruffled the red hair laying against her breast. She watched with a miserable expression on her face as one of the many hundred-dollar bills fell over onto it's face.

He went deathly still, his eyes flickered up to hers and narrowed.

"I don't want this shit in my house," he said, plainly, keeping his eyes steady on hers.

I don't know or care if you fucked for it. Killed for it. Drowned babies for it. Stole it. I didn't give it to you, so you can't have it. You're done with this. And if I could reach inside your head and rip out every memory of you fucking yourself up for it, I would. So, you can't spend it because it'll make you think of what you had to do to earn it. And you're so done with that lifestyle, baby, you may as well forget you even had a life before me. I'm your prize. Every fucking step you've taken in your life has led you to me., he thought.

Everything that he wanted to say to her, he kept to himself as he made the decision to maybe take one step back in their fledging trust in order to teach her a valuable lesson regarding his personality. He could show her better than he could ever tell her.

The first lesson in pain would be tonight, after all.

The corner of Colin's eyes crinkled as he slowly reached into the box and pulled out a hundred-dollar bill. He held in the air between them, carefully observing her watching his movements. With an audible rip, he tore it up into pieces in front of her.

Olivia gasped and placed the back of her free hand over her mouth, her eyes impossibly wide, her expression slightly horrified. She lowered her hand quickly before he could reach in and grab another one. *"No!"*

Her fingers spread wide over the money, and she bowed her body slightly over it, trying to keep him from grabbing more.

"No Colin," she gritted, her voice thick with emotion. "You don't know what I had to do for this-please stop. *Don't do this!*" she cried out, trying to back away, but she was trapped against the island.

She let out a yelp as his hand suddenly grabbed her jaw hard, and jerked her head up.

His eyes flashed dangerously at her. "Remove your hand, or you will get your first punishment tonight," Colin said, his face hard and impassive as he looked at her.

Olivia shook her head, tears welling in her eyes, but remained unmoved. Unwilling to be manipulated, no matter how fairly.

"*Colin,*" she whined, pulling her lip between her teeth as she implored to him with her eyes.

Please. she mouthed. Closing her eyes at his slight head shake no. She let out a sob, removing her hand slowly. She stared at his chest again, refusing to meet his eyes.

"I want you to think about whatever the hell you did for this money," Colin said in a hard voice. The ripped sounded out between them loudly as he tore another bill up, before grasping another.

FIFTEEN
Bathtime Talks

OBEDIENTLY, OLIVIA THOUGHT ABOUT the two weeks of torture she'd just put herself through. Her arm throbbed painfully as image after image of the sick stuff she had to do for that money flitted through her head, accompanied by a loud rip.

She was left reeling, every tearing sound she heard making her feel less tethered to the life she'd led *just* this morning. She let out another pained sob, somehow keeping the tears from falling.

Colin spent the next ten minutes grasping individual bill after bill, only stopping to roll his neck slightly and take a deep drink of his wine. He groaned contentedly, and leaned forward to place his lips on the side of her neck. Giving her a wet kiss there, followed by a lewd lick that made goosebumps break out on her body.

He proceeded to slowly rip up every bill, one by one that was in the box until they were both standing in confetti made of money. With a small, shocked and defeated sound, she let the empty box fall from her hands. They stared at each other for another, the tension almost unbearable in the room.

"Got it?" he exclaimed softly.

Olivia swallowed and nodded. She was too shocked to respond with anything else.

"Do you mind if I take a shower now?" her voice came out hollow as she half turned toward the closet door, waiting.

He looked at her, over the rim of his wineglass. "It's not time to beg yet, Olivia. You don't have to ask for those things. There would only be one reason I wouldn't want you to take a shower. Of course you can take a shower. Or a bath, even. That might be better for your shoulder," Colin said softly, observing her closely as she was unconsciously pressing into her arm.

She gave him a slightly bewildered look, ignoring his comment. Thinking of how long it'd been since she had a proper bath. He led her out of the pile of money and into the bathroom.

She frowned, reluctantly looking at him once more.

"What do you mean 'there's only one reason you wouldn't want me to take a shower'?" she asked with a slight frown on her face. She backed up a step as he came closer.

"There might be times I want to fuck you straight when we get home from a long outing. I like it hot and dirty sometimes. And I love your smell... thinking of fucking you after we've been out all day is just...*delicious*. That reminds me, we need to make an appointment with a perfume house to tailor make you some scents that go well with your body chemistry. I don't want anything masking your scent," he explained, taking another sip of his wine.

Olivia bit her lip, deciding she was through talking to him for the night. The man was a freak.

Olivia's lips parted as she watched him swallow the liquor, his throat working hard. Her sister's voice echoed in her head. *"Oh Ollie, what have you gotten yourself into?"*

She took a deep breath.

Because out of all the things she could have gotten herself into in all the years she'd been struggling, Colin was proving to be the most disconcerting decision she'd ever made. He seemed sweet... emotionally attuned. But the man just ripped up fifteen thousand dollars that he knew she worked herself to death for. Slowly, and relished it.

She blinked blankly, suddenly thinking about judge Carmichael.

Are all men with money like this? she thought pensively.

"What you *can't* do is lock the bathroom door," Colin stressed, watching her pupils dilate, and her cute gasp as her nipples hardened under her dress. "I'm going to park the car in the garage, and put the food away until tomorrow. I'll be back in a bit. Relax." He closed the bathroom door in her face and walked away confidently.

Olivia stuck her tongue out at the door, imagining the look on his face if he'd have seen it.

Taking her first true deep breath in hours, she smiled, relived to finally be alone.

Sighing, she turned to the bathroom properly and her eyebrows raised, except this time in pleasure at the sight of an enormous soaking tub with jets. She'd hurriedly started the faucet on the tub, pressing a lot of buttons on an electrical panel attached to the wall to get the thing to work. In the recessed spot in the wall were shampoo, conditioner, body wash, body cream, loofahs, towels, face masks, and bubble bath.

She poured a generous dollop of bubble bath, watching it sud a lot better than the cheap stuff she buys Allison at dollar general.

Sipping her wine again, she tried to listen for movement in the house but could hear none. The house was enormous and she was pretty sure noise didn't carry. Confident she was alone up here, she stripped and got a good look at her body in Colin's huge bathroom mirror and dimmed the lightning.

Her breasts lay heavy against her ribcage, standing proud and making her thin waist look thinner next to its mass. Pointing to the sky were dusky pink nipples, elongated against slightly wrinkled areola.

Her milky white skin looked creamy, and was thankfully blemish free. And her hair hung long around her like a flame, highlighting her freckles, and making her tired face look even more youthful.

Her plump lips glistened wetly from the wine, and she licked them lightly, liking the taste. Her hips flared out almost indecently. Nestled between them was her mound, bare and plump. She wondered if he'd like that, and then immediately chastised herself for caring.

Seeing the tub filled sufficiently, she turned the water off and plunged in, groaning as the heat and the jets soothed her arm. She'd looked out the window, seeing the sun had finally set, leaving the stars and dots of mood lighting all around the property glowing in the window.

Olivia craned her head back as the Weeknd's voice crooned inside the room suddenly. Colin must have activated the sound system in here for her. She smiled, thinking that was thoughtful, before she frowned again, thinking about some of the things she'd read in that contract earlier that day.

She shook her head, still feeling like she was in a fever dream.

Moving slow, Olivia proceeded to wash her hair, enjoying the smell of the expensive shampoo. She sputtered, cracking her eye open and tensing as she heard a noise.

The bathroom door cracked open slightly before Colin's deep smooth voice came through.

"Do you need help washing your hair?"

He thankfully stayed behind the door, giving her space.

"No, thank you!" she squeaked, pulling the bubbles to her chin just in case he decided to push through the door and invade her privacy.

Her eyebrows raised at the thought. *What privacy? She didn't technically have any anymore.*

"Okay, call for me when you're done. I'm going to help you out, so you don't accidentally slip." He cracked it wider so he could hear her when she was ready.

Her face reddened.

No man had seen her naked since she lost her virginity in high school. But then she remembered the agreement, and checked her attitude quickly, wondering if she'd fare better if she took the pleasant route this time. He'd already ripped up all her money, betraying his sadistic tendencies so, what did that make her for being turned on so violently by his actions?

"No please, that's quite alright. I can see myself out just fine. Thank you for offering, though." Olivia rinsed the soap out of her hair quickly before adding conditioner and unplugging the stopper, wanting to rinse out the conditioner and the suds off her body with the above head shower spray before exiting the tub.

She pulled her knees to her chest, and lowered her forehead to them as she waited patiently for the water to sink down low enough to justify running the above spout. Taking long minutes to settle herself.

Olivia glanced up, attempting to navigate the buttons to start the above-head waterfall spray, when she saw a dark figure in her peripheral. She froze in shock, too frightened to even scream.

Olivia slowly turned her head as the water shot from the above spout to pour down as if in slow motion. Seeing Colin's dark figure leaning against the vanity, his legs crossed, his elbows were bent, his hands propped his body up on the vanity. Watching her without saying a word.

She'd hadn't even heard him come in.

She shivered with nerves as he just stood there regarding her quietly, his gaze so penetrating. After a few tense minutes of her trying to wait him out, she turned her head, sighing. She slowly rotated herself, so her back was to him, and began to raise up. Fully aware that his eyes were on her ass.

She pulled up on her left arm until she gained her footing, and commenced to rinsing her hair and body clean of the conditioner and suds. Her thick hair brushed her ass lightly as she swished the conditioner out, stubbornly staying under the spray a lot longer than was necessary, but she didn't know how to get out of the tub without facing him.

She gasped as the water suddenly shut off, and a towel came around her from behind, cocooning her in its warmth, almost like it was straight from the dryer.

Colin's arms followed, wrapping around her and lifting her up and out the tub, protecting her modesty. He carried her with one hand banded under her knees, and another underneath her back. His body felt hard against her soft wet skin.

A hilarious giggle broke from her mouth at the thought.

Modesty?

She won't have any left once he finishes his mission to turn her completely inside out, courtesy of their contract. She looked into his dark chocolate eyes and sobered instantly, her flesh burning under his stare, desire as plain as day on his face.

His face was tight with the emotion, a vicious look in clouding his eyes.

Colin remained quiet as he placed her gently on the vanity. He leaned forward and placed his lips to the top of her head, and she could hear him inhaling, his minty breath brushing against her ear as he exhaled. After a few seconds, he gently pulled her wet hair to tumble over her left shoulder, baring the right side of her neck and arm.

The music continued to pulse around them, cocooning them in a sultry beat.

Still silent, he reached next to her to grab a small, expensive looking ointment bottle. Scooping up a generous amount, he rubbed it into his broad hands before massaging his them into her shoulder, kneading the surrounding muscles. Her brow furrowed as he gently raised her right arm to access the muscles underneath.

She closed her eyes, moaning gently as he hit sore spots in her muscle from where her body was trying to overcompensate for the injury. He suddenly hit the truly painful spot, and a whimper left her lips as she tugged her arm away. She shot him an embarrassed, pained stare. Her eyes were shining with tears.

Sultry music added to the romantic ambiance between them.

Anxious, she broke their eye contact, looking to the side, embarrassed.

To top it off, a hot throbbing settled in her sex as she remembered the orgasm he gave her as he pressed slightly into her sore spot earlier in his office.

Colin stopped her massage before turning her back to look at him with a finger under her chin. She clutched the towel tighter to her chest, her eyes lowered to his waist, not able to meet his intense gaze.

"Look at me," he said, her eyes fluttered up from his waist and onto his. Olivia quickly lost herself in the dark chocolate depths. He stared openly into her face, holding her gaze hotly. "You don't have to do that *ever* again. Do we understand each other? I didn't even want you to spend the money you earned from it. *That's* why I tore it up. Not because I don't respect, and even admire that you worked for it. But to show you that you are done with that life."

Olivia regarded him with sad eyes.

Nodding, she looked away again as he resumed massaging the ointment into her muscles until the jar was gone and she was completely relaxed, almost sagging into him once he was done. The ointment heated against her skin, deliciously tingling and making her feel oddly safe.

He blow dried her hair, sipping his drink while she pouted at him, finishing the last of her wine. When he was done, he put a finger under her chin again, tilting her head up and lowered his lips to hers, stopping just shy of grazing her mouth with his.

"Who do you belong to?" he whispered, holding her stare with his as he stood there patiently waiting for her.

Olivia's eyes widened slightly, and her breath hitched again. Sudden memories of him holding her up against her apartment door assaulted her, and she blushed deeply, her skin prickling. She wondered if he thought about the night incessantly the way she did.

"*Say it,*" he said, his fingers tightening slightly.

"*You*. Sir. I belong to you," she crooned softly.

Her tongue sneaked out to lick her bottom lip, inadvertently grazing his in the process. She briefly wondered if that was what she truly wanted as well. To belong to someone.

To belong to him?

Old desires resurfaced, stealing her breath just as much as he was.

"Good girl," Colin said lightly against her mouth, the words rolling off his tongue in a seductive purr.

He gave her that devastatingly handsome smile that made her weak, even more so than the easy endearment resonated in her brain.

Leaning down, Colin licked into her mouth. Giving her a taste of what he wanted to do between her legs. He spent a couple of leisurely minutes sucking her lips, giving her gentle bites and nips before groaning and deepening the kiss once more. He put his all into her, sweeping his tongue over hers, and sucking hers into his mouth as well, swallowing her little moans and whimpers.

He didn't let it last long, however.

Olivia's tongue tangled shyly with his, squealing quietly as he suddenly picked her up again, towel and all, and carried her into the dimly lit bedroom where he laid her on the turned-down bed, breaking their kiss. He pulled the crisp covers up over her, and pressed the remote to the television in her hand. "Watch something while I take a shower."

She nodded, her gaze falling to the foot of the bed where he'd put her sweats in case she wanted them. He disappeared into the bathroom, keeping the door open. She looked over at the bedroom door, seeing it closed and wondering if it was locked.

Olivia was much too relaxed to care to check.

Raising from the pillows, she looked around, relishing the juxtaposition of the gas fireplace going and one window slightly cracked. Her dewy skin pricked as she felt the coolness of the deliciously crisp fall breeze blow gently into the room before being warmed again. She pulled on her sweatpants and tank top before covering herself back up, and looking around for her phone to set her alarm for the morning.

Pausing, she'd realized that she didn't have to get up early in the morning for anything anymore to set an alarm for right now until school started.

Until school started, she thought again.

A fission of rare happiness ran through her.

She listened to the muted shower sounds for a second before looking at the nightstand on her side of the bed. Her phone was attached to a charger and turned it on silent. Opening it, she quickly made sure her location was turned on and sent it to her sister, before gleefully deleting every alarm she'd had pre-programmed on her phone.

She scrolled through several texts, a couple from Aliyah as well asking if they could get together, stating she was going to be in town in a couple weeks and wanted to hang out. She beat out a few "I'm okay," and, "yes, let me know when" texts and a, "kiss Allison goodnight for me."

> I can't stop looking at my bank account. Ollie you are the craziest, most beautiful person in the whole wide world. Send me a picture. Love you 4eva.-Sissy.

She'd turned and snapped a picture of her with the windows in the background, her still in the bed before sending it and typing.

> Pray I last. I think I might actually like him Nessie. And you know I don't like anyone! -Ollie

> That's a nice place, sis. And I really hope so. What's in the contract?-Sissy.

> I can't tell you-I signed an NDA. And it's not appropriate anyways. You don't want to know. I love you! Going to bed. -Ollie

> Ew, bitch. Please get on the pill ASAP. One day, we'll have to talk about your penchant for risk taking. Night! -Sissy

Olivia hit the love emoji, before sending her the picture she snapped.

Turning the TV on, she selected a streaming app and found a show about an English time traveler, excited as she'd been wanting to watch the show, and had never had time.

She settled deep into the big pillows, smiling wistfully as the theme song began to play. The fireplace flickered romantically, and she found herself mesmerized by the show and wondering when Colin was going to come to bed. She didn't get to see much of it before she drifted off, finally succumbing to the day's adventures.

***

Three quarters of an hour later, Colin turned the light off in the bathroom before padding quietly into the bedroom.

Stilling, he saw Olivia had fallen asleep half sitting up and his cock thickened at the sight of her curvy breasts rising and falling rhythmically in her sleep. Her hair cascaded around her and against the pillow, its tresses tickling her waist with its length. And her puffy areola and soft nipples were slightly noticeable through the white fabric of her tank top. The swell of her breasts gleamed in the small light of the fireplace.

He'd left it on knowing that she didn't like the dark and wanted her to feel comfortable.

Walking to her side to turn the lamp off, he noticed the TV flickering gently. He glanced at it for a moment, seeing a man and woman walking through a dilapidated old building they called "Fraser's Ridge" before getting it on in the basement. He grabbed the remote, rewinding the show a few minutes so she could start off where she finished before shutting off the TV.

Seeing it glowing faintly with a message from her sister, he unlocked it before checking to make sure Allison was okay, knowing Olivia's worry and not wanting to wake her up unnecessarily. Unable to help it, he saw their former texts where she'd discussed the NDA and explained that she couldn't share much.

Truthfully, he shared enough with Vanessa in her kitchen earlier, and that's where he wanted her knowledge to end. She didn't need to know the filthy, kinky things he'd had planned for her sister.

He then turned his eyes again to her sleeping form when he read more.

'I think I like him. And you know I don't like anybody.'

Colin put her phone face down on the nightstand and walked to the other side of the bed, grabbing the remote there and turning the fireplace on low before crawling in and laying there quietly. Trying to regulate his breathing after masturbating for well over half an hour in the bathroom.

His restraint was costing him dearly.

Just smelling her next to him made his dick hard again. He willed it down and attempted to fall asleep next to her.

First Lesson is Pain

COLIN WOKE UP EARLY the next morning, bringing his work laptop to bed, wanting to watch Olivia wake up. Finishing out an email, he sipped deeply from his coffee cup as she stirred, watching her open her eyes slowly before arching into a deep stretch, and moaning.

He felt himself flinch in sympathy at her small hiss of pain as her arm pulled with the movement, but not able to stop her body's re-flexes.

Her body slithered half down the bed with her stretch, and she took a second to roll before her eyes really focused and she looked up the big bed to see Colin sitting up next to her. Having had a early morning meeting, he was already dressed comfortably in black attire.

He smiled at her, holding the corner of reader glasses in his mouth.

"Good morning pet," he said gruffly, flicking his eyes over her mussed appearance. Her hair was wild, and her shirt had ridden up with her stretch, revealing inches of creamy skin of her torso. "Sit back on your knees, and face me," he ordered, not bothering to close his laptop.

His eyes quickly flicked to hers as her hand reached up to pull her shirt back down.

"Leave it," he said sharply.

Olivia's hand faltered as she slowly sat back on her heels.

Her shirt had ridden up indecently high, bunched against the heavy swell of her right breast, revealing several inches of under boob. Her waist dipped in indecently, and he took in the shadows of the curves of her body against her heavy breasts. He was so thankful for her flared hips, he didn't know if he could fuck her if she was petite everywhere.

He would break her.

He made an elusive humming sound of pleasure at the sight of her nipples visibly bunched with his request, pressing against the white fabric.

"Come here. Get in my lap," Colin said, closing and placing his laptop on the portable table he had next to him in the room. She paused, her eyes flickering quickly to her phone and back to his again. His eyes remained on hers while she obviously warred with her mind.

"Did you sleep well?" she asked, licking her lips, shuffling slightly on the bed.

Her sweet question warmed his heart, easing his irritation at her hesitance slightly.

"I did, eventually. Thanks for asking," Colin answered, patiently waiting. His hand flexed again, and her eyes flickered to it and back, her eyebrow arching.

"Can I-" she started, her eyes flickering to her phone again.

"*No*. They're fine. I already checked in with your sister," he said, cocking his head at her patiently.

She'd better be thanking God her arm is fucked right now, he thought to himself; fighting rising irritation, because he didn't usually exercise this amount of patience.

She shuffled to him awkwardly on her knees, wisely not to hurt her arm, before tossing her right leg over his lap.

Colin chuckled, thinking it was adorable that she'd settled almost on his knees, like that was going to save her. He flashed her another heart-stopping smile before leaning forward, and sweeping his hands over her fleshly backside, yanking her gently to him and settling her against his erection.

The action caused her pants to catch and slide down her legs slightly, revealing the very top of her bare mound. He fisted his hands in her sweats and yanked, pulling the fabric back up, pressing the seam flush against her vagina. Her heat seared him immediately, and he suppressed a low groan at her whimper.

Colin's eyes flew to her breasts as her nipples tightened even more at the rough movement.

But she looked anywhere but at him.

"So, tell me, what are we going to do today?" Colin asked conversationally.

He leaned his head against the headboard, finally capturing her eyes with his and squeezing her ass in his hands over her thin sweats. His fingers worked her flesh in a firm massage. She licked her lips before responding, and swallowed hard as his rather impressive erection jerked against her.

"You don't have to work?" Olivia asked.

She leaned slightly back in surprise when Colin suddenly dipped his head forward and took her left nipple in his teeth through the material of her thin tank top. He groaned to himself at the feel of her nipple in his mouth again.

He felt her jerk as she cried out, her left hand quickly sinking into his dark hair as the warmth of his mouth quickly sank through, wetting the material against her.

He nipped experimentally.

A rush of heat suddenly flooded the space between their legs where she was pressed against him. He pulled back slightly to look at the v of her body, seeing the material of the sweats were slightly damp.

Colin leaned back again, ignoring her mortified expression as she placed her hand there, blocking the sight from him. He let her take a brief comfort in hiding from him before he picked her hand up firmly, placing it next to her thigh in a silent warning. He flattened his hand against hers, holding her there, his warmth seeping into her skin and grounding her.

Colin watched his thumb flutter back and forth across her wet nipple, pleased with how fat it was, and how responsive *she* was. He tightened his fingers, digging his nail in slightly and hearing her breath freeze as her eyes widened.

He caught her eye again with a smile. "Not today. I took the day off work so we can get you some clothes and shoes. Mary just got you the basics yesterday." His hand stilled as he heard her teeth grind together. *"Stop that,"* Colin said sternly, reaching up to grasp her jaw rather roughly.

"I can shop for my own clothes! I have money now. Just because I'm here, *doesn't mean you do everything for me!"* Olivia said indignantly, her green eyes flashing adorably in her face.

He placed his fingers against her lips and pressed hard, relishing her shocked expression.

Good, she'd better get used to it because I have a feeling I'll be slapping that mouth often, he thought.

He took a steadying breath.

"You never answered my question about period sex?" he pressed, back to her nipple, beginning to roll it between his thumb and fore-finger. She squirmed, her body doing dangerous things to his erection. He regarded her patiently, just playing with her as he watched her green eyes go stormy.

"*Colin,* do we have to talk about this?" she whined, and he loved it.

"Yes," Colin said, pulling and tugging at his leisure, enjoying the wet spot slowly spreading in her sweatpants. He moved to push the shirt that was bunched up against her right breast the rest of the way up, baring her creamy flesh to his gaze, before baring the other one.

Her breasts bounced slightly with his movement, and his mouth watered at the sight of her heavy naked breasts and fat nipples. He suddenly made a deep growling sound in his chest, a muscle ticked hard in his jaw. "Oh, *fuuck.*"

His eyes snapped back to hers when Olivia knocked his hand away. Irritated, he moved quickly, feeling her tense as he grabbed her left wrist hard, keeping it pressed to her thigh, slapping her cheek lightly before grabbing her jaw again.

"There's that obstinate spirit," he growled.

It was coming back out having gotten over the shock of yesterday.

"You slapped me!" she bit out, her expression furious.

"Par for the course, sweetheart. You need to answer the question!" he bit out in a short tense tone.

"I'm not a fucking *idiot, I know,*" she hissed at him, struggling against his hold with eyes were so narrow they were almost slits.

Olivia cried out as he suddenly yanked down her sweatpants at her hip and gave her five hard cracks across the flesh there. The blows sounded loudly throughout the room.

Pure unadulterated joy met desire at feeling his hand slap against her.

"Who do you think you're cursing at, huh?" Colin said sharply, maintaining eye contact as she wiggled on top of him, her butt burning. She pressed her lips together in a pout, refusing to speak. "Did you speak to all of your lovers like that?"

"I haven't been with anyone since high school You heard me tell the doctor that!" she almost yelled, trying to put her hand back there to rub her tender skin.

Colin's eyes widened, and he tilted his head suddenly.

Olivia blanched as he leaned forward into her face.

"I thought you might have been lying, because you didn't want to talk about your side hustle. You actually, *knowingly* entered into a relationship with a sadist no better than a virgin?" he growled into her face.

"I *know*," she hissed back at him, struggling against his hold, groaning as her arm twinged and she gasped, curling in on herself and placing her forehead against his hard chest.

He let her go immediately and rubbed his hand down her arm gently.

"I don't like *that* kind of pain," he murmured into her ear as he cradled her close for a second until her gasping stopped. "I'm not fucking you until your arm is recovered. Don't worry about that. I won't relish you being in pain that I don't cause," he said against her hair, his warm hand stroking soothing down her back, her shudders taking a moment to subside.

Colin stilled as she nuzzled into him harder, feeling the hair at her temple brush against his beard softly.

His heart beat painfully.

How long has it been since I had true intimacy? he thought sadly.

"I'll make us breakfast, then we need to pick up your pain medicine," Colin said, reaching over when his phone lit up and answering the incoming call.

"Mr. McDermont, this is Dr. Healey's office calling. I'm sorry to disturb you, but we have another cancellation for tomorrow and wanted to know if there was any way we could expedite Ms. Cameron's procedure?"

"Sure, give me a moment, please."

Colin quickly placed the nurse on speaker before moving Olivia off his lap, putting his computer back onto his lap, opening it. Olivia watched closely as he pulled up a rather complex calendar and began clearing his schedule for the rest of the week. He tagged one of his employees with each click, moving it onto their schedule instead.

He paused at Monday, his cursor hovering intently over the day before he resumed the clicking quickly, crossing off his schedule for Tuesday as well, leaving Monday alone.

He would never not go to therapy on Mondays. Johnathan would kill him,, and he'd been skating on thin ice lately with his best friend/brother.

"What time?"

"Six in the morning, sir," the receptionist replied. They both listened to the click of her keyboard in the background.

Colin looked at Olivia, who was settling back into the pillows on her side of the bed. He put the phone on mute.

"Would you ask your sister if she could come stay with you Monday? I have an appointment that I can't move," he said gently, taking the phone off mute and turning back to his computer.

She nodded, turning to grab her own phone.

"And when should she stop eating?" Colin addressed the receptionist once more.

Olivia silently took a second to appreciate him taking control of the situation, not having had someone truly looking out for her in years. She sent him a quick text before texting her sister, he looked at it briefly before going back to his laptop screen, smiling at her display of manners.

Thank you, Colin. -O

"Twelve hours before the procedure. Only water after six tonight."

"Okay, I'm ready. Give me the information." Colin listened intently as the woman gave him instructions to the surgical center, reiterated the fasting schedule, and verified that Olivia would have a ride back home and be monitored after her surgery. He slid off of bed and disconnected the call, looking down and seeing the text she sent.

Welcome, baby.-C.

Colin's eyes crinkled again as he looked up, seeing her sitting cross legged on the bed with her back to him as she spoke on the phone. He smiled slightly, waiting patiently for Olivia to finish her conversation with her sister.

Soon, she hopped off the bed herself, turning to face him.

"She can be here Monday, but she'll need to bring Ally. Is that okay? If not, I'm sure I'll be perfectly fine without any assistance," she said dismissively, rounding the bed to head into the bathroom.

Colin didn't bother to respond to her ridiculous comment as he sat at the end of the bed and watched as Olivia brushed her teeth and hair, observing how neat she was as she washed her face gently with a dark green towel, before folding it, and placing it on a nearby towel rack.

She came out quickly, throwing him a cute glance before veering off into the closet. He heard some rustling around before she appeared again, dressed in a clean white t-shirt, and comfortable black sweats. She'd put on sleek black tennis shoes that Mary had the foresight to pick up in her shoe size.

Leading her out of the bedroom, he watched as her red hair swished.

"I'll give Mary a heads up so she can prepare a guest room for them." He took her left hand, pleased to see that she only pulled away a little, still not used to that kind of intimacy.

He guessed neither of them were, but they'd navigate it together.

Colin took her downstairs, making her the most ridiculous breakfast possible of pancakes, turkey sausage, complete with sunny side up eggs. Her favorite, and he was so happy that he'd paid attention to his mom when she'd taught him how to cook before she died.

He could barely remember what she sounded like anymore.

He listened to Olivia teasing him, giggling as she got a kick out of watching him freshly squeeze her a second glass of orange juice. She glanced at him with a brow arched, and grinned. He grinned back, arching his own in response, noting how easy they were together. He handed her a glass of juice.

"Man, what you must have thought of my place!" she said with a little giggle, leaning back to look at the long skylight above the island.

He gave a half laugh that ended with a sexy hum, watching her lick her lips at the erotic sound.

"I was highly concerned. Thought you might be a serial killer, there was no sign of life in there until I got a peek at your bedroom," he teased with a grin as he finished off a piece of sausage. She watched him chew with interest, and he decided he loved how astute she was. Wondering if it spoke to deeper issues to how carefully she paid attention to her emotions.

When Colin was sure she was full, he cleaned up efficiently, making her sit at the island and watch him, ignoring her irritated look. He led her into the garage, through the mudroom off of the kitchen. He smiled, ignoring her shocked and slightly judgmental expression at the multitude of expensive cars and multiple bikes.

Colin made a mental note to make space for her Porsche that was being delivered the next couple of days.

SEVENTEEN
The Rich Live Fine

OLIVIA WATCHED AS COLIN efficiently backed them out and revved the engine as they roared around the house and up the drive. Olivia was struck by the difference between getting out of his property and backing out of her sister's tiny driveway, not having a driveway of her own to think about.

Man, the rich live fine, Olivia thought. Then she was stuck dumb again by the realization that her sister was now a millionaire, thanks to Colin.

She chanced a small peek at him out the side of her eye. Colin was studiously driving, seemingly lost in thought, as he navigated the car confidently. He'd slipped on a pair of sunglasses that set off his skin tone handsomely. The windows were down, and the eastern breeze ruffled her hair comfortingly as she picked up her phone to shoot her sister a message, asking her if Ally was feeling better.

"Are you on the pill?" he asked suddenly,

She paused, remembering the text from her sister. "Nooo..." she stated slowly, her eyes turning to his.

Did he read my shit?

"I need you to set a doctor's appointment. Call them real quick and see if they can squeeze you in," Colin murmured, resting his elbow on the window, and checking carefully before merging onto the highway.

"Okay." She watched him for a minute, the slight dark hair and his tattoos on his arms doing something to her brain, making her blank out momentarily. Once he merged, he put his hand on her leg, curling it under, thumb stroking the top of her knee like that was their thing.

He seemed to like that spot on her body, and she realized she really enjoyed his hand there, too.

She pursed her lips and called her doctor's, asking if the nurse could see her quickly for a quick appointment for birth control. The woman said yes, but she'd have to come in within the hour. Thankfully, because she'd always stayed up to date on appointments and pap smears, she didn't have to be a new client anywhere and deal with their wait.

She set her phone navigation and listened as the car did a fancy beeping, moving the music to the background, and giving step-by-step instructions. Her phone went black, but the GPS kept playing.

She frowned, tapping the screen, giving it a little shake as if that'd help.

"It's my software," Colin explained. "When I synced your phone to the car, I installed the software that would disable your phone to keep from using it if the software notices you are texting, or using apps on the phone that would distract you. It also pings the nearest police station if your car is driving erratically. Such as if you're swerving or driving dangerously, and the software gives them your car information and location."

She gaped at him as the GPS chirped in the background, decidedly non-distractible.

"That's...helpful," she mused, thinking about her parents, wishing this technology was around back then in order to save them from the drunk driver who hit and killed them when she was in middle school.

Too little too late to save them, she thought sadly to herself as they sped off down the highway. She smiled when he reached into the console and got out a pair of her sunglasses for her.

Olivia placed her hand softly on his, entwining their fingers as he drove, and she felt her heart flutter as his thumb captured hers, pressing firmly.

***

The rest of the day went by eventfully. She got a prescription for three months of birth control, and he took her shopping at her favorite store. They only fought twice; once when she tried to buy her own clothing and realized just how much money he'd deposited in her account. And another time when he took her to some really fancy boutique to get some dresses for some upcoming charity events and galas that he wanted her to attend with him.

Olivia relinquished to not paying for her clothing. But when he pulled her into a Nordstrom rack and some sort of expensive boutique, she saw a dress he was trying to get her to try on that was worth over four grand. She dug her heels in obstinately.

"I don't need a *pretty woman* moment, Colin! *Literally*!" she muttered angrily at him, shaking a thick lock of her red hair in his face and storming off, cursing him out under her breath.

"*Fucking what am I, Julia Roberts?*" she hissed, before learning a valuable lesson that day about disrespecting him in public while she was with him. He'd grabbed her elbow and quietly walked her to the intimate dressing room with his hand at her lower back and dismissed their shopper.

"Colin," she hissed as he closed the door behind them, backing her knees into a plush seat in the middle of the room. "What are you doing? That was *rude!*" she gasped at him, feeling her face flame with embarrassment.

He walked past her to sit on the bench before reaching forward, taking her left arm and maneuvering her easily to drape over his knees.

"Wait!" Olivia squirmed against him.

"You will not storm away from me while we're out. You will listen to what I say. If I want to buy you a four-thousand-dollar dress and make you wear it once just to take it off and burn it, that's my prerogative. Understand? These are not your rules anymore, and when you signed that agreement, you relented to obeying me."

She wiggled as she felt his big hand press down on her shoulder blades, stilling her.

'Colin, not here. *Please,* not here. This is embarrassing," she whimpered, feeling her sex slicken with his words. But she was angry with him that he dismissed the shopper and embarrassed her.

"How do you think I felt when you cussed at me then stormed off in front of our shopper? I pay good money for you to enjoy, and now I'm afraid I'm going to spank you harder because you have robbed me of being able to absolutely relish spoiling you to my fullest extent today. Hold still, pretty girl. This might hurt." Colin's said sternly, and she knew better than to try to continue to fight with him over this.

Her heart pounded in her chest, her head falling as she went limp over his lap.

Colin slowly lowered her sweats over her ass and spanked her so hard he left red handprints on the tender white flesh. Surprisingly, the hard punishment made her more wet than she already was, and he wouldn't do anything about it, because he wasn't touching her like that until after her surgery.

Olivia sniffed as he helped her off his lap and leaned against the doorway, with his arms and legs crossed, quietly watching her pull herself together. She wiped a tear from her eye before they left the room and he had the shopper finish picking out dresses, more intimates, and shoes.

Olivia was fuming, not wanting to admit to herself that she was turned on from the pain.

The rest of their interactions were mutually stoic, and she accepted every dress that he and the shopper threw at her, closing herself off in an obstinantly.

She observed rather nervously that Colin hadn't lied to her when he told her that her interaction stole his joy; he was completely stone faced when the shopper presented him with the bill, a tall forty-five grand.

He paid quickly before loading up the SUV with their purchases, before opening her door again.

"Ahora," he said sharply, jerking his chin towards her seat.

Olivia slid in, keeping her eyes averted from his. Leaning in close, Colin's minty breath washed over her face, and she pouted, lowering her eyes to her lap. Her hands wrapped around her torso tightly as she blinked away tears.

"Don't look at me. I'm sorry for fucking up so soon," she thought, but couldn't bring herself to say it out loud.

She made a small sound when Colin suddenly leaned forward and took her mouth in a gentle kiss, uncaring that they were in the middle of the parking lot in view of others.

Olivia trembled as he savored her mouth slowly.

His tongue coaxed hers gently, parting her lips and slipping inside to tangle with hers. She made a hurt noise and tried to pull away, but he just pressed deeper, putting a hand to the side of her face and cupped her intimately, his warmth seeping in. She melted, nuzzling into him, starting to kiss him back.

After a minute, he pulled away and stroked his thumb across her cheek, staring into her dark green eyes.

"Thank you, sir. For the dresses," she whispered, telling him in her own way she was sorry, just as he showed her with his kiss that he was sorry.

She supposed they were going to have hiccups as they got to feel each other out, and their roles in this arrangement.

"You're welcome, baby," he said, leaning forward and pressing his lips to her forehead, leaving her stunned at the small action. She blinked in surprise as he closed her door and rounded to the driver's side and slid in smoothly.

Colin drove them home and reheated Mary's chicken and squash orzo in the oven while he made multiple trips bringing all the bags upstairs, just on time at five in the evening. Olivia mixed them a drink for dinner, having observed that he'd loved a drink in the evenings, before shouting in surprise as he poured hers out, stating that she couldn't have alcohol before the procedure, but he made it better by mixing her a delicious mocktail.

"Colin," she said softly, watching him take a couple of plates from the cabinet. He looked over at her, pausing at her expression before turning to lean a hip on the counter next to them. He gave her undivided attention and she appreciated that. "I'm nervous…. scared about tomorrow. I've never had surgery before. And I don't know how I… act."

Colin tilted his head, giving her a low slow smile. She wasn't sure if she imagined his intense stare soften slightly with understanding, but she relished it all the same. He stepped towards her, spreading his hand against the side of her face and kissed her forehead again.

Her eyes closed briefly.

He can be gentle.

"You don't have to worry about a thing. I'm here, Mary is available, and your sister and Allison is coming too when Allison gets out of school to spend the night. I thought of everything, and I believe you'll be too drowsy to have to worry about how you might act. So, stop stressing, and lets enjoy our food and the rest of the evening."

Olivia let her tension go with a sigh of relief as his effortless confidence settled and soothed something inside of her she didn't know needed tending to. She snuck him a look, wondering if all the shit he'd put in the contract was just a front. He couldn't have been serious about some of that stuff.

Then she remembered him ripping up the money, and him spanking her in the store and blinked. Not a front after all.

Just because he was a sadist, doesn't mean he can't be decent, she told herself.

Colin plated their food and took it out on the outside terrace, where they settled against the cushions of the outdoor furniture. He busied himself turning the outdoor flatscreen on to the Outlander show she'd had on the night before. She breathed deeply, she took in the unique, crisp smell of the evening fall air, and sun starting to set.

As they dug into the food.

"I've never had orzo before, it's really good?"

"Really?" he asked, swallowing his drink and chuckling when she snuck a bite off his plate. "Well, I'm glad I get to watch you enjoy it."

They finished eating, and Colin pulled her against him, careful not to jostle her shoulder too much. Though she was tense and shy watching the initial love-making scene with him, she'd got through it. She ignored him chuckling every time she blushed, and hid her face in his chest shyly. It'd been so long since she'd been able to sit through a show that wasn't a cartoon.

They finished the show right as six o'clock rolled around, and he let her know it was time to get ready for bed.

Olivia had helped him clean up after dinner as much as he'd let her, before they went upstairs together to get ready for bed ahead of her procedure.

She'd showered, and he tenderly rubbed the muscle ointment in again before placing her under the covers. He slapped a brief kiss on her plump mouth, and said he was going to work in the bedroom lounge for an hour, ordering her to relax before briefly disappearing to grab his work laptop from his study. He returned quickly, settling into the wide leather seat facing the television.

Scrolling through her phone, Olivia glanced over to the other side of the room contemplatively.

Colin had his bare feet propped up on the coffee table, listening to the news with his laptop screen, working with a glass of whiskey in his hand.

He looked delectable with nothing but some dark grey sweatpants. Olivia briefly thought how comfortable the day had been, except for the event in the dressing room today. Remembering the hot sting of his hand on her bare flesh, she blushed, betraying complex feelings.

Olivia sighed, missing the exhausted feeling of working herself to the bone like she'd been for the last four years.

She'd relished the feeling of letting go as Colin was spanking her, as well as the pain it had provided, and wrapped that feeling close to her. Frowning, she realized she felt slightly unsettled even now, propped up against the huge comfortable pillows in bed, scrolling through her phone as if she had all the free time in the world.

Which she supposed she did, technically.

She checked on her sister and Alison, and soon settling in between the covers and willing herself to sleep. Not feeling when Colin crawled into bed behind her. He nestled in and touched her hair, his eyes skimming her sleeping form before he nestled in close and curled around her, following her into sleep.

EIGHTEEN

Pink Bunny Fresh Victim

OLIVIA WAS GRUMPY WHEN Colin woke her up at three in the morning to prepare for the procedure. She grumbled moodily, not wanting to wake up. So, resigned to her early morning attitude, and lack of response, he had to pick her up and walk her into the shower, pajamas, and all. Two hours later they'd pulled up to the surgery center, and Colin sent the vehicle off with a valet and checked in with registration.

The nurse settled them in a private room, where she had to wash down with special wipes before dressing in a hospital gown and cap.

She made Colin leave for that part.

"So sexy, huh?" Olivia huffed, not appreciating looking like an invalid next to this beautiful man who'd just spent a small fortune to get her to bend to his every desire.

He responded pleasantly, and told her she should think of it as her investing in her future. And she hammered that into her head on the times she found herself lost in thought, ruminating over the various clauses in their contract.

The fact that he'd not listed much of any hard limits was a little scary. Only a safe word that was of her choosing, but implying that almost nothing was off limits, and her mind went wild with possibilities.

The anesthesiologist came in and ribbed her good-naturedly about being a redhead, explaining that he might need to up her dose depending on how she falls asleep, and the possibility of her waking up on the table during the procedure. Which almost made her call off the whole thing. It scared her so badly.

At Colin's stern look, she bravely listened to the man, and asked him a few questions to help soothe her mind. Grateful that Colin was there to hold her hand while the anesthesiologist ran her IV in order to distribute her medicine.

"You're so brave," he said, and her eyes watered as Colin softly kissed her goodbye, whispering in her ear that she was going to do so well.

Olivia indeed woke up on the table, but then was quickly put under once more.

In recovery, Colin raised his eyebrow at her when the doctor explained that she was hard to put to sleep. They explained that her injury was, in fact, a minor tear that most athletes get after years of being in their career. They went in microscopically, so the scaring should be minimal. The post-surgery grogginess helped her to keep quiet about what she did to cause the injury, simply thanking the doctor before he left her to get dressed.

At her insistence, the nurse helped her dress and then strapped her into a sling.

Ignoring her pleas to walk, they wheeled her all the way to the front entrance, and she grumbled once more when Colin had valet bring his vehicle to the front for her so he could be with her every step of the way.

Bending down, he scooped her up from the chair and deposited her carefully into the passenger seat that he already had reclined.

Olivia giggled groggily as he produced a small pillow to place under her arm to help prop it up. He flashed the nurse a megawatt smile when she praised him for taking such good care of her, before gently closing the door, getting in the drivers seat, and pulling off.

***

On the way home, Colin voice texted Vanessa to inform her they were on the way home, and sent her the address to the house again. Then he preordered take out for them all for dinner, pizza this time, something easy that he knew Allison should like.

Olivia succumbed to her medicine, and slept reclining on the way home. So, he took advantage of the opportunity to stop at the pharmacy drive through, and pick up her prescription medicine and her birth control pills. Now and then he reached over to run his hand down her bare arm affectionately, proud of how brave she'd been despite her grumpy mood.

Colin found himself trying to think of ways to reward her.

Pulling onto the property, he parked in the front drive again by the fountain, and lifted her still sleeping out of the car. He carried her into the house and placed her in the informal lounge by the kitchen, covering her gently with a blanket so he wouldn't wake her.

Fiddling with his phone, he turned the sound system to some soothing music to create some white noise so that he wouldn't disturb her while he pitter pattered around the house.

Four hours later, he was sitting on the couch across from Olivia on his computer, enjoying an expensive scotch, and watching the news when his phone pinged with a text.

> Hi! I'm off work and on my way with Allison.
> -Vanessa

Colin went upstairs to check that the guest room and the ensuite were suitable, and he opened the doors to their private terrace, letting a breeze in.

He smoothed out the cream sheets on the four-poster bed, turning on the two lamps on a low setting before fluffing the stuffed unicorn that he had Mary pick up for Allison. Then headed into the bathroom, making sure there were enough toiletries for them and towels.

After a few seconds of running around, he stopped, realizing that he was trying to impress Olivia's sister and niece, wanting them to know she was being taken care of.

The thought of caring enough to prove his intentions slightly disturbed him, so he put a lid on the whys, and went downstairs to grab the pizza and pasta delivery.

His phone rang. Vanessa.

He answered it quickly, looking over to see Olivia still deeply asleep.

"Hey, Vanessa," he turned, making his way down the hallway.

"Hey, Colin," Vanessa sounded slightly irritated. "I think we're lost."

"Did you put the right address in the GPS?" he enquired.

Stepping quickly into his downstairs study, he sat down at the mahogany desk and pulled out his personal laptop. He put her on speaker while he jiggled the screen awake. He winced as the bright light assaulted his eyes and reached for his readers to slip them on quickly. There was a light shuffle in the background.

"Yes, but I barely see any houses, and everything's gated. I pulled over just to make sure. I didn't want to bug you, but I thought it might be worse if we were truly lost." Her soft voice carried through the phone along with Alison's murmuring.

Colin typed in his password and pulled up his favorite search engine. Leaning back into the seat, he settled in comfortably, hearing the creak of the leather of his expensive office chair.

"It's no bother at all. Send me your location really quick," he said, putting her on speaker.

His phone pinged, and he checked Vanessa's location.

"You're in the right place. You have a few more minutes to drive. The code is nine-four-two-ten. By the way, I put two million dollars in your account, Vanessa. Where did you think I lived exactly?" he chucked down the phone, teasing her.

He listened to her shocked scoff and wished he could visualize her face.

"These are insane homes, not your regular mansion. I didn't know. We didn't exactly grow up around wealth to know the difference. I mean, you've seen my house, right?" she said tiredly, and he felt bad for making her feel less than. So, he pulled up a webpage and bought a ridiculous unicorn and flamingo floating device for the pool, hoping that Allison would like it.

Then immediately felt torn again for trying to impress them.

"Just for the record, neither did I. I'll see you when you get here, park by the fountain. If you still can't find your way, call me back and I'll jump on my bike and come find you." Colin disconnected the call, texted her the code as a reminder before he went back towards the lounge to check on Olivia, who was still sleeping.

But she'd moved at some point, her blanket slipping slightly. He pulled it back on her, careful not to disturb her.

He grabbed Olivia's pills and a bottle of water from the kitchen counter, quietly placing them on the table in front of her so they could be handy when she woke up.

Heading out the front, he stood on the stairs, seeing the sun setting into brilliant shades of blues, pinks, and lavenders. Throwing the property's lights on, and illuminating all the various landscaping, the fountain, and the home in the dusky atmosphere of the evening.

A minute later, he looked over at the unmistakeable sound of Vanessa's car pulling up; the engine was knocking, immediately causing his mood to turn irritated. It seemed that when Olivia wouldn't be testing his patience, her sister would be stepping in to substitute in some way, shape, or form.

God, that irks. he thought, just wanting everyone to behave, and not drive a car that sounded like it was going to blow up.

He walked down the stairs to meet her, raising his hand in hello. Stepping out, she was so busy staring at the house that she couldn't even speak at first.

"H-hey Colin. This is a nice..." she said, her head craning back to take in the architecture.

She snapped out of it and bent down, grabbing Alison from the car, and putting her briefly on the ground so she could reach back in to grab their overnight bag.

"Thank you," he chuckled, amused. His irritated mood dissipated quickly with the compliment. He didn't bother to correct the fact she didn't finish her sentence.

He smiled wider as he watched Allison's slight body toddle back a few steps, her own head craning this way and that way to look all around her. She was holding a worn, pink bunny in her hand, one of the floppy ears dragging on the ground, looking like it's seen much better days.

She'd suddenly spotted him in her perusal, and rushed towards him, saying "up, up" while making little grabby hands and grunts. He bent down and picked her up easily, placing her in one arm and reaching out to grab the bag from Vanessa.

Allison smiled. "Is this *your* castle?" she whispered excitedly, grinning at him. She placed her hands on his cheeks and stared into his eyes and his heart tugged at how dull her eyes looked.

Poor little chica shouldn't be having to go through this at all, he thought, planning to take time to say extra hail Mary's for her with his mother's rosary.

"Yes," he whispered back. "Your aunt's inside. Would you like to go see her now?" he asked, grinning.

He turned jerking his head to Vanessa, who was busy feeling the top of her hood. He rolled his eyes, not sure what she thought feeling the top of her hood was going to do.

"You have to lift up the hood and look inside of it, silly," he shook his head, already resigned to fixing it.

She glanced up and walked back over to him with a slightly embarrassed look on her face, bumping her shoulder against him lightly. He bumped her back. causing her to grin at him.

"You know I'm going to look this place up on Zillow as soon as we get settled in, right?" Vanessa teased, not even trying to hide being nosy and making Colin laugh the hardest he's laughed in weeks. "What's the taxes on this thing?"

"Vanessa, I'd think something was wrong with you if you didn't, you nosy woman." he'd ribbed back, escorting them into the home and dropping the bag on the floor.

Allison fell over her rabbit's ear, yelling, "Tee-Tee! Where are you?"

Colin winced at her high-pitched voice. "This way, chica." He ushered them around the foyer table with the roses, and into the lounge across the way from the massive kitchen. On the couch, Olivia was stirring, finally waking up.

"Ally! Hi baby! I missed you!" Olivia crooned, sounding groggy.

With his help, she gingerly pushed herself up to an incline as Allison first ran towards her, then stopped, tiptoeing as she got closer to her aunt. She finally made it to her, and her green eyes stared into Olivia's as she leaned in, careful not to touch Olivia's arm. Allison wrung her fingers in front of her small body, unsure of herself.

Vanessa settled onto the opposite couch after leaning in to give Olivia a kiss on her forehead.

Colin motioned for her to grab the matching Hermes blanket for herself as he turned the television onto the app store. The fireplace was gently roaring, and he made sure the iron gate was nice and secure. Safety was always his top priority.

"Auntie Ollie, are you okay? Does your arm hurt a lot?" Allison whispered, trying to snuggle, but careful not to touch Olivia's arm.

He paused, looking at Olivia contemplatively for a second before reaching onto the couch behind him and grabbing a thick throw pillow. He walked to her and leaned her forward slightly, placing the pillow behind her back and helping her to settle more comfortably. She smiled her thanks at him, not able to talk as Allison had one hand around her jaw, and was shoving her face into her neck.

He chuckled in amusement. "Please, help yourself to something to drink," he said to Vanessa, resuming flicking through the apps.

Olivia helped Allison settle against her in a way that was more comfortable before replying to her. "Only a little, sweet pea. It's better now though, because you're here." She smiled, leaning down to give her cheek a kiss as she giggled. Colin's heart swelled just a little watching them.

"So, how'd it go? Okay?" Vanessa asked, pulling out her phone and snapping a quick picture. Colin's phone dinged a second later, and he opened it, seeing she'd sent him the picture of Olivia and Allison.

Smiling his thanks, he quickly saved the picture to an album he mischievously titled, "Ollie."

He resumed scrolling through the apps on the television he never watched unless he had the news on. Suddenly feeling three pairs of curious eyes on him, he sat on the couch, realizing just then he was the only one standing. He wasn't used to having others in his home.

"So, what do you want to watch?" he asked, leaning back and sipping his whiskey, looking over at Allison.

Her eyes went wide as she stared hard at him, contemplating. "Do you have the Little Mermaid?" she said excitedly, clutching her bunny so hard he wondered if the thing would still have ears by the end of the night. The seams were splitting rather alarmingly.

He was happy that there was a fresh victim upstairs just waiting for her to mangle it.

"Do I? I don't know... *let's see,* "he mused out loud, working to put it on. He glanced over at Vanessa, and leaned forward. "Can you get the pizza and pasta out of the oven, and the plates and napkins while I work to get this movie on? They're in the kitchen in the warming drawer in the island, to the left."

"Sure can." She nodded and got up gracefully, padding to the kitchen.

He heard a bunch of rustling before she appeared with the two pizza boxes, thoughtfully spreading a huge kitchen towel on his wood table, before laying the pizza boxes and spaghetti down. "Thanks, Vanessa," he said nodded his thanks, locating the movie, and pushing play.

Allison got on her knees in front of the table as the opening of the movie started. He watched her reach in the box for a cheese pizza before carefully placing it on a plate with the help of her mother. She took a bite before turning and offering it to Olivia to have.

Everyone smiled. Colin chuckled, thinking kids were cute. He'd never really thought about having one of his own.

His eyes slid slowly to Olivia.

Knowing Johnathan was right to assume he was crazy, because he couldn't help imagining her pregnant. With his child. Children he'd never thought about having until he met her. This stranger who really didn't *feel* like a stranger. He felt like he'd known her his whole life.

"No, sweetie. Thank you." Olivia shook her head before leaning back once more, and sighing.

Colin contemplated her for a second before reaching forward to unscrew her medicine bottle, dumping out two pills in his hands. Handing it to her with some water.

"You need to take this before the pain starts to take over," he encouraged, placing the tablets on her tongue, and watching her sip the water carefully.

She shakily smiled her thanks before leaning back and settling deeper into the pillows.

They watched the mermaid movie and ate all of the pizza. Colin assumed his usual position, ankle over his knee, propping his head against his fist. Finding himself ironically thinking that this was the most red-head action he'd ever had in his house. He watched with interest as the purple sea witch rose out of the sea ominously. Her stolen crown separating the Princess and the Prince, forcing them to plunge into the sea separately, only to come together in the end.

He rather enjoyed it.

He'd gotten a tremendous thrill from hearing Allison yell with excitement when he took her and Vanessa up the elevator to their ensuite, showing them their bedroom, and bidding them goodnight.

He paused outside of the guest bedroom to text his good friend and business associate, Johnathan, that he needed a new car delivered tomorrow; worried about the engine knocking on Vanessa's vehicle.

Going back downstairs, he rubbed his eyes. Beginning to feel pangs of fatigue from constantly going since three in the morning.

Colin scooped up a sleeping Olivia, and took her to their bedroom, laying her in the bed and covering her up gently. He went out in the hallway checking the guest bedroom and seeing their light was turned off. Activating the house alarm on the phone, he showered and brushed his teeth before donning a pair of pajama pants and crawled into bed next to Olivia.

Making sure to place an extra pillow under her arm so she wouldn't jostle it in her sleep, he leaned in and kissed her lips goodnight, settling in close and drifting to sleep facing her, with his hand on her belly.

NINETEEN

Adequate Math

THE NEXT MORNING, OLIVIA woke up and noticed she was alone in the bedroom, the door slightly cracked. Sucking in a sharp breath, she took a moment to take stock of her body.

Her arm was sore, but this was now more of a dull burning pain than a sharp stabbing pan. Turning her head, she spotted her pain medicine and birth control already thoughtfully popped out of the package next to a glass of water on her nightstand. The glass was sitting in some sort of holder, to keep the drink cold. Her throat burned, the condensation on the glass making her parched.

Taking the medicine and checking her phone, she winced, seeing that it was almost nine thirty in the morning.

She never slept in that late.

Rubbing the sleep out of her eyes, she made her way into the bathroom to brush her teeth, wash her face, and comb her hair before stepping into the shower. Keeping her sling from the spray, she washed quickly, scrubbing herself, not liking the post-hospital feel, making an astronomical mess as she didn't have the use of her right hand.

Stepping out and drying off one handed, she assessed herself in the mirror and smiled at her reflection, observing she looked better already. The pinched, pained look lessening on her face. Leaning further into the mirror her eyes roamed; between the days of rest, her eating full meals, and now the sharp pain gone, her features were softer, fuller, more youthful.

Making a face at the sling, Olivia went into the closet and grabbed her preferred sweats and tank top, pulling them on. Wondering where Colin was, she journeyed the hallway to find the guest bedroom empty. Pivoting, she rode the elevator downstairs and stepped out to the comforting smell of biscuit and gravy.

At the sound of Allison talking, Olivia warmed at her little lisp.

Walking into the kitchen, her smile broadened seeing Colin leaning against the sink with his arms folded in his usual relaxed stance, talking quietly to Allison.

Olivia sucked in a deep breath when his eyes turned to hers, freezing her in place. She blinked, feeling the sharp sexual tension between them, and turned face away to focus on Allison in an attempt to distract herself, and calm the sudden butterflies in her tummy.

"Aunt Ollie!" Allison sat at the vast island, devouring a bowl of sausage biscuits and gravy with a side of scrambled eggs.

Olivia crossed the space to her. "Hey, lil' bit," she said, bending down, rubbing her nose on the girl's cheek before looking at Colin. She gave him a sheepish smile. Her eyes fell to the counter, seeing another barely touched bowl of food sitting there next to Allison's. But no Vanessa. Her eyes flicked back to his.

"Why aren't *you* eating?" she enquired quietly, looking around for his food, pushing some hair behind her ear anxiously. She didn't mean for him to play host while she couldn't help.

"I was waiting for you to wake up so we could eat together," he said simply, silently flicking his eyes down her front, tilting his head. She blushed, feeling very laid bare and guilty. Finally, a familiar emotion next to all these decidedly *unfamiliar* emotions he evoked.

"You didn't have to do that," Olivia said, clearing her throat and averting her gaze.

Colin caught her attention once more and silently jerked his head in a come here motion. Her core heated in response, and she peeked a glance nervously at Allison, who was now playing on her tablet and scarfing down her food, unconcerned with them. She walked around the massive island to stand next to him, feeling small against his big build.

He unfolded his arms and pulled her in to him, leaning down to take her mouth slowly and thoroughly. His thick forearm tightened around her waist when she stiffened and attempted to pull away. Her heart began to raise, and her cheeks warmed at feeling him against her.

As if he knew he was torturing her, Colin leaned in even more, deepening the kiss.

Olivia moaned low into his mouth.."Colin, this is not an appropriate kiss for the morning. *Or in front of Allison,"* she mumbled against his lips when he wouldn't let her up.

He reluctantly pulled away with a low chuckle, staring down at her with a arched brow.

"Well, that's something you're going to have to come to terms with and quick now, isn't it? And besides, she's not watching," he said, swooping down and giving her another kiss. "You smell *gooood,"* he drug the word out on a sexy growl. "Did you shower?"

"Yes." She smiled against his mouth as he pulled her closer, careful to keep her right side tilted so he wouldn't bother her arm.

"Why didn't you call for me? I would have helped you," Colin whispered, pulling her bottom lip into his mouth and tugging with his teeth, not giving her a chance to respond.

The front door closed loudly, and he groaned, reluctantly pulling back from her lips as Vanessa entered the kitchen.

"Okay, Colin. I got the car situated. Again you really didn't have to. The engine was probably a simple fix," Vanessa said breathlessly, placing a brand-new set of keys in her purse before placing it on the table in haste to get back to her breakfast.

She held her hand out to fist bump Colin while she took a big bite, causing Olivia to turn a questioning look to Colin who merely gazed down at her with a mischievous glint in his eyes. He stayed quiet, holding her eyes as he brought his coffee to his lips for another deep swallow, and Olivia felt those butterflys errupt in her stomach once more.

Vanessa's voice brought her back to reality, and she turned her head to look at her sister.

"He got me a Range Rover. It's white and *freaking beautiful!*" she mumbled around her food to Olivia, who raised her eyebrows in surprise. At both Vanessa's new car, *and* at the way she was shoveling it down like she hadn't eaten in forever.

"Vanessa, oh my *God!* Why do you have to eat like that!" she admonished, before turning to frown at Colin. "You bought her a *car?*"

"Yes." He couldn't help the wicked smile that broke free now, looking incredibly pleased with himself at utilizing the contract so soon. "Johnathan will be here any minute with the paperwork for you to sign, Vanessa."

Turning dismissively from Olivia's sudden, irate expression, he grabbed a bowl and began crumbling her biscuits in, adding a generous ladle of sausage, gravy, and eggs.

"What do you say?" he asked lowly, holding the food to her.

"*Thank you,*" Olivia gritted her teeth, clenching her left hand. "How much time did this add to our agreement?" she whispered, furiously accepting the bowl, but not being able to do much about the dilemma in front of her sister and niece. Feeling stuck, she became further irritated, her earlier good mood dissipating.

His jaw twitched as he bit back a knowing smirk. "For the car? Only three months," he said, ladeling up his own food.

Olivia's jaw dropped. *We're up to almost three years now!* she thought incredulously.

Her eyes slid back to Vanessa, who was oblivious to her dilemma.

"Oh, your Porsche is so nice, Ollie! It's so *cute,* have you seen it yet? Colin showed me pictures!" Vanessa exclaimed, licking her spoon. Allison watched her with interest, giggling.

Olivia turned narrowed eyes at Colin, who was eating his food nonchalantly.

"Take a bite, Olivia, and calm down," he chastised, his eyes flashing dangerously as he put a forkful of his own food to her lips.

Colin chest tightened with pleasure as she bit the fork hard, before jerked it out of his hand, pulling the fork out of her mouth and tossing it in the sink, then walking away from him.

She bristled as he chuckled at her back as she placed her food on the island, preferring to eat standing. He reached forward, attempting to open the utensil drawer she was blocking for another fork when an almighty crash came from the foyer.

"MY MAN, *WHERE ARE YOU?* Oh, hey, Beth. I didn't see you there. How's it going, pipsqueak?"

"Where in the kitchen, Johnathan!" Colin called out, placing a bite in his mouth and groaning contentedly.

All the girls' red heads swiveled like something out of a movie in alarm towards the foyer as his best friend's tall, broad frame entered the kitchen. He was dressed in expensive black slacks, black graysons, and a matte black shirt that probably cost as much as two months of Olivia's rent.

Johnathan walked in with all his confident swagger, his deep tan skin glowing against his dark goatee.

He smiled brightly when he saw Vanessa, and it took Colin a second to realize that he'd briefly lost his easy gait, carefully covering it up with that devilish smile of his.

"*Johnathan*," Colin's voice came out clipped. "If you break my front door, you're going to be paying for a new door *and a new face*," he said, efficiently breaking him out of his spell.

Johnathan and Vanessa had been staring each other down with slightly bewildered expressions on their face.

Curiously, Colin watched as Vanessa looked away, quickly blushing.

Johnathan turned to Colin again and flashed another bright smile as he saw Olivia standing next to him. "We'll see about that. Here's the paperwork. I just need a signature here," he said lightly, unconcerned with Colin's threat. He slid the paper over to Vanessa with a pen. "Hi cutie," he said to Allison.

She'd finally finished her food, and was holding her bunny to her chest, looking up at Johnathan in awe.

Colin grinned at the sight, seeing the girl visibly melt. Thinking if Allison cheesed any harder, she'd have hearts in her eyes.

"Hey, Johnathan. Nice to meet you, too," Olivia said with a slight laugh, flashing him a bright smile of her own.

Colin turned and narrowed his eyes down at her.

"*What*?" Olivia mumbled sheepishly. Shrugging and leaning forward, she grabbed Allison's plate, watching as Vanessa damn near drooled over Johnathan while she signed the papers without even looking at them. She'd peeked at Johnathan, who seemed to be making the same strange lovesick face.

Colin abruptly took Alison's bowl from her with a disapproving noise. He shooed her out of the way, rinsing it off quickly in the sink before loading it in the dishwasher.

"*Eat*," he said firmly, pushing her bowl closer to her and leveling her with an assessing stare that made her core tighten. "You look good, baby. Not so weary. Like you're starting to get your health back."

Colin turned to offer Johnathan some breakfast while Olivia blinked over at him, shocked at his words.

"Is it halal?" Johnathan asked, scrunching his nose up at the bowls in front of the rest of them. Vanessa frowned, looking at her bowl before glancing at Johnathan.

"Hermano, you know I've *never* fed you pork before. Jesus. I made it with turkey sausage, estupido." Colin rolled his eyes at his friend irritably.

"What do I have to do to get you to speak to me in that sexy accent?" Olivia teased, looking over at him as she chewed her food slowly.

Colin met her stare intensely, giving her a slow once over with his eyes. "Estoy seguro de que cualquier cose que hagas para provocarme bebe requerira que seas castigado. Lo cual hare con mis manos, no con mis palabras."

I'm sure whatever you do to provoke me, baby, will require you to be punished. Which I will be doing with my hands, not my words.

Having not understood a word he said, Olivia blinked. "Okay then," she said, turning back to her food with a satisfied look on her face.

They discussed their car business with the women a bit, sharing information about the software business, and how their cars were shipped all over the world.

Johnathan was the owner of a reputable, prestigious car brand. He spent a year testing out Colin's software on cars in Germany before moving on to other countries. The business move was a lucrative one, catapulting both men into billionaire status.

The women stopped chewing, slowly raising their eyebrows and glancing at the men.

"*What?*" Olivia asked, swallowing her food and glancing over at Colin with an incredulous look on her face. "Did you say 'illionaire' with a '*b*'?"

Colin bit back a smirk, willing to bet every red cent that she was thinking she should have made him pay more for the blueprints.

"That's correct. Like Oprah," he added, just to really make it fun.

"Jeff Bezos,'" Johnathan chuckled.

Colin shot over to him the name of a famous prince. This was a fond game they engaged in.

"Not yet, I asked him," Johnathan said around a bite of gravy.

Olivia's fork clattered on the countertop. "*What?*" she gasped, her face flushed a bright pink.

Johnathan nodded, eating another big bite. "He will be, though, *I think*. Just give him a few years. It's coming. They're good people."

Colin raised an eyebrow as he observed Olivia's features settle into a peculiar expression. He reminded himself to remove the picture of himself, Johnathan, and the prince that was in his study. She didn't need to know everything. And especially didn't need to know anything that caused her to look like she was intrigued by the thought of another man, royalty or not.

"Yeah, that's enough Johnathan," Colin said, slightly irritated at the way Olivia's breath hitched excitedly when his friend mentioned the prince.

Johnathan ignored him. "Why do you think y'all have *fifty bottles* of tignanello wine in the cellar? The prince's wife first gifted it to Colin, and now he's hooked."

Oliva whipped around and gaped at Colin. He just smiled at her, the corner of his eyes slightly crinkling in amusement, and his facial expression making her go a little weak in the knees.

So much for trying to hide that, he mused.

"So, what are we doing today?" Vanessa enquired, turning to check on Allison who took her tablet to the living room and plopped on the couch.

"Well," Colin said, clearing his throat. "If Olivia feels up to it, I thought we'd spend the day looking for a new house for you." Vanessa's brows raised as she flicked a look at Olivia, but stayed silent. "I found a bunch of open houses that I thought you might be interested in. Since we're off today, and together. If you're okay with it."

"Not.... *here*... in this area, right?" Olivia said slowly, flickering a glance at Vanessa, who was turning to look at Colin slowly.

I wouldn't do that to you, baby. There's no fucking way you can work the cost of a several million-dollar house off in this lifetime. Even if you worked twenty-four seven, he thought.

Colin hoped she didn't think he was that crazy. Johnathan did, and he didn't care. But he cared a lot about how she viewed him as a person. Even if he was fucked up, he wanted her to not think he was completely crazy.

"I found *reasonable* houses that I would like to help gift a down payment for," Colin said carefully, hoping to not overstep his mark so soon. Olivia narrowed her eyes, tightening her lips.

No such luck.

"Can I speak to you?" Olivia hissed, snatching him up by his hand and pulling him towards the foyer.

Colin quickly took control, pulling firmly on her hand and making her slow her gait. His grip tightened around her and he heard her sharp inhalation of breath at the action. He led her through the wide hall, bypassing the foyer and leading her to his office through a hidden door. Just the simple act of taking control of her in this way wet his appetite.

The tension between them was thick enough to cut with a knife.

Colin pivoted on his heel to look at her haughty expression. He could tell she would take a lot of humbling throughout their time together, and considering she'd just had surgery, he would be creative about it.

This morning, anyway.

"I want to stress that I *technically* don't need your permission to do this, but would it make you feel better if I can make it a tax write off?" he asked firmly. Seeing the bewildered expression on her face, he walked to his desk and leaned against it.

Olivia observed him for a minute as he crossed his arms and legs, settling himself in to get what he wanted.

When he was done, she snapped.

"You just gave her *two million* dollars! Vanessa can buuuyyy a *house!*" she yelled at him, her face blazing. She placed a hand on top of her head, and her green eyes widened, looking at him like he was insane. "You're just flinging all your fucking money around like...like...like..." she trailed off, looking to the side with a huff.

"*Like* a billionaire. Which is what I am, so you need to accept that. And while you're busy learning to accept it, you can go ahead and take it one step further and get the fuck over it," he said sternly, cocking his head at her shocked expression as he raised an arrogant eyebrow at her.

Olivia's brow's furrowed. "But...but the two million-"

"You and I *both* know that's not enough money. Not for her to live comfortably and take care of Allison without worrying about money over the years," Colin volleyed back quickly, unrelentingly. "Come on, she wouldn't even use it to get a car, and when she pulled up yesterday, her engine was knocking. She drives Allison around in that thing, so she's probably not going to prioritize the house. I don't like their neighborhood *and* they could have a place much closer to us, closer to her doctors, and in a better school district. Allison's about to start kindergarten next year. Do you really want her in the school district your sister lives in?"

Colin shot all this to her quickly, not giving her a chance to think. Olivia tapped her toe.

"God damn you, Colin. How much time is this going to cost me?" she hissed, her eyes narrowing at him in irritation. "I don't want her to feel like she owes you *anything*." Her eyebrows raised and she stepped closer, bringing herself within reaching distance. Colin smiled wickedly, his eyes crinkling at the edges.

No but you will sweetheart. You'll owe me everything by the time we're done, he thought.

"Well, if you want to play it like that, we can negotiate," Colin said, rubbing his hand on his jaw and regarding her with interest. "How much time do you think a six-hundred thousand dollar house is worth?"

He reached forward to grab her left arm and pulled her firmly to him, leaning down to kiss her. His tongue licking into her mouth erotically, his cock jerking excitedly at the sound of her hitched breath.

Colin bent, picked her up with an arm under her hips to turn and put her on his desk, uncaring of the couple of items he had on there clattering to the floor. He pulled her face back to his when she turned to look at the mess on the floor in surprise.

"Don't worry about that. Look at me," he said, needing to fuck her. Taste her.

Subdue her.

Ruin her so she wouldn't be fit for anyone else except him.

She lowered her eyes, watching him push his way between her legs. He drew a hand slowly up under her shirt to mold his hand to a breast, making a pleased sound in his throat at the feel of her nipple pressing into his palm. Fueled by lust, he slammed his mouth over her's roughly, groaning as he flexed his fingers around the round curve of her breast.

"You want extra time already, and you haven't even tried the goods yet? That's not a good business move. I hate to be the one to tell you that," Olivia whispered between kisses, moaning as his fingers pulled and twisted her sensitive nipple. Her hand settled against the back of his head and pressed him harder against her.

"Well, since you insist on schooling me, lay back. I'll sample the goods while you think, and they have time to get to know each other." Colin murmured as she gasped in shock.

He tugged on her bottom lip, his teeth worrying the plump flesh before placing a hand against her breastbone, and pressing her back to the desktop gently.

"*Colin*!" she squealed as he pulled up her shirt, baring her breasts to his gaze.

He groaned at the sight of her puffy pink nipples.

Bending down, he sucked one into his mouth, relishing her whimper. Ignoring her hand clutching at his hair, he drew on her hard as his fingers hooked the waistband of her sweatpants and panties and pulled them down.

She slammed her knees shut, preventing him from seeing her. Making a displeased sound, he bit her nipple as a slight punishment, his dick jerking at her sudden cry, and he smelled her unique scent perfume the air. He yanked her sweatpants the rest of the way off, pulling her legs apart.

She squealed as the sudden rough move excited her, and at the sound, he raised his head to meet her gaze.

"You're supposed to be thinking. I'll want an adequate answer when I'm done eating you," Colin said simply, pushing her knees up and back. His mouth suddenly went dry as he got his first look at her naked flesh, and he licked his lips as his heart beat faster, his body filling with lust.

Oh Jesus fucking Christ. Colin cursed to himself.

She was beautiful.

Her plump, creamy mound sat atop perfectly rosy red lips that hid her clitoris. Her slit was small, and he got a thrill at how smooth she was. The lips of her sex glistened with moisture, beckoning to him.

He walked around his desk, rotating her slowly on the surface as he went, hearing more items fall. She placed her left hand to hide herself from him and he hurriedly snatched it away, setting it firmly against the desktop.

"You don't get to cover yourself from me. I thought you got the hint yesterday morning," Colin warned, making a fresh wave of lust ripple through her at his words.

He lowered himself into his office chair, feeling the seat give with his weight as he got himself good and comfortable.

Olivia wet. her lips nervously. The sound of the leather and the chair's mechanisms creaking under his weight made the act they were about to partake in seem so much starker.

Colin looked down at her once more, his eyes drinking in the sight of her greedily. *Jesus, she is succulent,* he thought.

He placed a kiss on the inside of her bent knee, sneaking out his tongue to draw it between the bunched halves of her legs before slightly biting down. She leaked out, her juices dripping on the table. He noted she very much liked that.

He put a hand to the top of her mound and pulled up slightly to expose her clit to his gaze, ignoring her tensing up.

"Do you like oral, Olivia." he asked, looking up at her face flushed with embarrassment.

"Uhm...I've never had it. I don't know," she whispered, turning her face from him.

He cocked his head, rubbing both palms on the softest inner thighs he'd ever felt in his life.

"Normally I'd give you *much* more foreplay, but we have guests, and I have no clue how long I'm going to be drinking from you until you give me the right answer," he said.

He looked down at her legs again, seeing a delicate vein just there under her skin, close to the juncture of her thigh. Just like with the vein at her jaw, he wanted to bite it, but he'd vowed to be decent this morning, considering their company.

Then she had to open her fucking mouth.

"I can't think while you're doing this to me at the same time!" Olivia cried out.

Colin looked down, seeing her belly trembling with nerves. Needing the sadist cravings somewhat appeased, he removed his touch and leaned back, settling in the chair once more and watched as her nerves visibling ramped up even more. His cock tightened even more in pleasure at the sight of her discomfort.

"Raise your legs and bend your knees back. I want your feet in the air and off my desk," he waited patiently while she complied.

"Now, this is my pussy, isn't it?"

"Yes, sir," she said shakily.

"You're not in control. Are you, Olivia?"

"No, sir. I'm not."

"Good girl. That was the perfect answer. A plus. Now, I want you to pull up on my pussy for me. Expose your clit to me. I want to talk to you for a second," Colin instructed smoothly, leaning in the chair slightly to have a more direct gaze on her face.

He waited until she slid her hand down, cupping her mound in her delicate fingers before pressing and pulling up on the plump flesh there. His cock hardened painfully tight when her clit peeked out from between her middle and forefinger.

He let out a slight snarl, his chest rumbling and vibrating with the sound.

"Since we're talking mathematics, let me give you a brief lecture, *mama,*" he chastised sternly, his eyes boring into hers.

Olivia shivered under the intensity of his stare, seemingly unsure of herself. He smiled, loving the fact he could throw her off. The feeling was amazing.

"My requirements are this, and I consider them simple ones; you're going to learn to have multiple orgasms, you're going to learn to fuck for multiple hours, and you're going to learn multiple ways to please me. Or, we start subtracting pleasure, and adding more pain," Colin paused, letting the words sink in.

Olivia's eyes widened at his words.

"And if I instruct you to think of something while I'm playing with you, and for you to give me an answer when I'm done with this tight little snatch of mine, well, then that's what you will do. *Or else,* Olivia."

"Colin!" she cried out, forgetting herself. Her breasts heaved with her struggle to catch her breath.

His eyes narrowed in displeasure.

She hissed as he suddenly slapped the inside of her left thigh right over the vein he coveted; more of her juices dripped down, and he saw her pussy spasm. He tilted his head curiously.

"I will also begin to add on more time if I find myself constantly having to correct the way you address me. *Fix. It,*" he said sharply, causing her to flinch.

Colin could see she was making a puddle underneath her on the desk. He bit his cheek to keep from grinning.

"Sir," Olivia corrected herself quickly on a hitched sob.

Colin reached over and grabbed his coffee that he'd placed on a warmer by his monitor and drank deeply as he watched while she dripped onto his desk. He enjoyed that she found his words highly arousing. He groaned as the hot liquid saturated his mouth, and the smell of the roasted coffee grinds mixed with her sweet, musky scent.

He drank more, rolling the liquid around his mouth, wanting to get his tongue and lips nice and hot for her. His eyes roamed her greedily.

Olivia's clit was pulsing between her fingers, Colin's words traveling through her veins and helping to make the flesh swell with need.

He really enjoyed the fact that she'd tried to hide herself from him and he made her expose herself instead, when he knew all she wanted was to close those fingers against his gaze. Watching her hand there, powerless.

They both knew it.

Tilting his head, Colin wondered briefly if he could get her off just by talking to her long enough. He chuckled darkly, putting his coffee back down and dipped his head without warning.

Olivia tensed and cried out as Colin suddenly leaned forward and licked her from her opening, and straight up her seam. He flicked his tongue from side to side to open her lips before landing straight on her clit between her fingers.

Hmmmmm, Colin hummed inside his head, not even able to form a coherent thought.

Her taste flowed across his tongue, her flesh felt like velvet against his mouth. He groaned, suckling slightly harder before pulling away slightly.

"Your cunt tastes amazing." Colin complimented her, pulling back slightly to give her a provocative look.

Taking both his hands, he moved hers away, and spread her firmly open for him ignoring her unconsciously trying to close her legs in embarrassment. He pressed his mouth harder against her, settling his lips around her clit and sucking greedily. Stabbing at it with a medium pressure.

He ate her with his lips and tongue for long minutes, getting her nice and swollen before experimentally scraping his teeth over the tip of her clit.

Olivia made a sharp sound as her legs shook. He growled in pleasure at her attempt to pull her knees back even further with her excitement.

The smacking sounds his mouth was making as he ate at her flesh added gasoline to an already raging inferno, and she broke with a sharp cry, her legs jerking as she arched, orgasming.

Colin groaned deeper as she arched her back with the strength of her orgasm. Olivia was crying out softly, her taste flooded into his mouth making him even more aroused. He sipped it down happily. Pleased, he wiped his face on her inner thigh before getting up and leaning down to her, watching her come down from her orgasm.

She looked up at him shyly, still trying to close her legs, however, Colin pressed down firmly against her thighs.

"How much time should I add to the agreement?" he asked. "I'll have you know, being able to choose isn't a luxury you will be afforded in the future. I'd take advantage of it if I were you." He sternly looked at her, her slight panting subsiding as she gazed at him.

He leaned down to take her lips in a rough, bruising kiss, swallowing her moans.

"I'm going to keep eating you until you give me an answer that I can live with. I don't care how sensitive you are," he said against her mouth, before sitting back down and placing his mouth on her again. This time he'd added a thick finger to test her tightness, groaning as her slit clenched him greedily. A muscle ticked in his jaw at how narrow and tight she was.

"Baby, you feel so perfect."

She whimpered as he thrust his finger back and forth while he sucked harder on her clit.

Feeling her pulse around him, he added a second finger. She flinched on the desktop, trying to push away from him. He growled in irritation, taking her by the hip and roughly jerking her back into place, his middle finger now fully joining the first. The muted wet noise as her flesh parted for him caused pre-cum from the tip of his dick.

Groaning, Colin sucked harder, feeling like he was trapped in a circle of hell denying his body the pleasure of hers. He spread his two fingers hard, punishing her.

She flinched, crying out as her juices flowed over his fingers.

"Four months!" she moaned. "I'll give you an extra four months, Oh *God*," she said breathlessly, trembling with her orgasm.

Colin raised from his seat and laid his body over hers, pressing his weight on her left side, surprising her. He ran a hand down her hair, feeling the silky strands glide over his fingers. He began to thrust, beating his hand hard and slow against her, taking a second to enjoy the sound of his fingers moving in her juicy cunt.

He smiled, watching her face break out into a light sheen of sweat.

"We have a serious problem, baby. I thought you did well in school. That's not the right answer. Think over it again, carefully, because I *will* keep you in here all day," he said, licking her flavor from his lips.

"You told me I could *choose*." Olivia retorted, her eyes flashing as a pissed off expression clouded the desire on her face.

He smiled dangerously, because the fact she was pissed only made him want to make her suffer. He pressed a little more of his weight into her as he added a third finger, ignoring her squirming and ragged inhalation of air. Their gazes locked as he worked it inside of her.

"I said your answer has to be *adequate*. Four months is *not* adequate. Think back to the kitchen, baby. Did I not just buy your sister a car? How many months did you give me for that?" he said in a dark voice, leaning down and rubbing his lips along her jaw.

"Three months," Olivia whimpered, tensing as his fingers twisted inside of her and pressed upwards. She slammed her hand over her mouth, whimpering. His lips went to her ear.

"And do you know how much a range rover costs?" he whispered before pressing a kiss against the shell. He pressed harder, feeling her knees slam shut, bracketing his hips.

"Don't run, I won't let you," he smiled, finding her g-spot and agitating it mercilessly. He dipped, taking a straining nipple into his mouth and nipping hard as he sucked.

"Colin," she gasped. "Let me up, I think have to pee," she cried out, embarrassed, trying to scoot away from him. Like the devil he used his fingers to pull her back to him, sliding her easily on the polished wood top of the desk.

He pulled away from her breast.

"Oh no, baby. That's not your bladder, that's your g-spot. Relax. And answer my question. How much do you think it costs? You wanted to school me so bad just a few minutes ago, you obviously are well educated in these things." Needing something to sooth him, he gave her jaw a little bite.

She let out a pained moan as his thumb started flicking her clit.

"I think.... almost one hundred thousand d-depending on the model." She let out a strangled moan, clenching hard around his fingers.

"*Close,*" he rumbled into her ear, leaning back and sitting down once more. "So let's try again. Put two and two together and give me an adequate answer. I'm not expecting an A plus." He put his mouth on her again and she moaned, arching and sobbing as he nibbled at her clit in earnest. He groaned as her juices squirted onto his hand as she orgasmed again.

Not letting up the pressure let it drip onto the table, uncaring at the moment of his furniture.

"Col-"

"*Excuse me,*" Colin said sharply, looking up at her, offended.

"S-sir, please, *please, please,*" Olivia chanted as he continued to suck her clit, not giving her a reprieve from her orgasm. She was sensitive, and he was loving it.

"Tell me, baby. Give me an answer I can live with," he mumbled around her flesh, his fingers pressing deep as he sat back, watching her come completely undone on his desk and knowing he would never get rid of it now.

"Eighteen months. The answer is *eighteen months!*" Olivia keened, her hand reaching down to grasp his wrist, digging her nails in. Colin stilled his movement, feeling her pulsating hard around his fingers.

"And how did you figure that out?" Colin said, amused. Almost annoyed he didn't get a chance to give her another orgasm. He slid his fingers out, seeing how wet they were, and her pussy, and his desk. He put them in his mouth, sucking them clean.

"Because if I give you three months for a car slightly over one hundred grand, then mathematically it makes since that I'd give you another three months for every hundred grand from now on," she breathed, her voice sounding weak.

He stood up to lean over her again, situating himself on his forearms and bracketing her in with his body.

"Good girl. We'll get her a six hundred-thousand-dollar house, and I'll require another year and a half of your time. Pretty good deal, don't you think?" he whispered, leaning down and kissing her, letting her taste her own juices on his mouth.

All I want to do is take my cock out and shove it into your tiny slit while you lose your voice screaming for me. I want it to feel so good it hurts, I want it to see your eyes widen in disbelief that you can even fit me inside of you. I want you to scratch your nails down my back and make me bleed because you have such a mind-numbing visceral reaction it terrifies you. I want it to scare you so that from now on every time you look at me your body only recognizes what I can do to you. So there's no room for anything or anyone else. All I want is for you to see me. So I can save you, and maybe you can save me too.

Colin stayed silent, kissing her deeper. The act embarrassed Olivia, and Colin felt her tighten and hunch her shoulders.

He knew that the act of tasting one's own juices was considered a humiliating one, but that's what fed the sadist tendency in him. He basked in it, and wouldn't let up until he was sure she got every bit of the taste on her lips and tongue as well.

"Fine," she growled.

Her cheeks flushed as he rubbed his nose alongside hers. Colin helped her up and into her clothes, being careful with her arm. He ran a hand down her hair, smoothing it before letting her go in front of him.

He dipped into the powder room to wash his hands and his mouth.

As he was cleaning up his desk, he wondered if he should tell her that she'd agreed to him buying the whole house. Instead of only the down payment that he'd originally offered and decided against it. He'd won fair and square, and since she was determined to be difficult, he would take his wins where he could.

A few minutes later, he heard Olivia tell Vanessa that they would be going house hunting, watching as she excitedly hugged Olivia with a little squeal. It warmed him to see that a little life was returning to Vanessa, knowing that this would please Olivia.

He quickly realized that he'd do anything to see that look on her face. However, when she caught his eye it wasn't just the house that seemed to make her happy; she was looking a little dazed from their morning romp.

He didn't bother telling anyone that he'd already found and bought the perfect house less than twenty minutes away. Preferring to spend all day exploring and seeing what the local architecture was like. Colin considered it an emmersive field trip for Olivia to review other architectural work before she resumed school in January.

TWENTY

Kneel For Me

Olivia sighed happily as her and Colin pulled back up to the house as the sun was going down, pulling into the garage and coming through the kitchen. They'd looked at five houses extensively before Vanessa picked a beautiful one about eighteen minutes away. She tearfully hugged all of them, almost breaking down so hard she couldn't sign the papers. Vanessa and Allison went home that night, leaving them to themselves.

"Something smells gooood!" she sang appreciatively as they rounded the island and peked curiously in the warming drawer.

"Oh my gosh, Colin. What is this?" she asked.

He reached in, pulling it out and placing it on the stove.

"Mary's famous paella," Colin said, shooting her a thrilled glance. "She doesn't make it often, but when she does, she puts her *foot* in it." He leaned down and placed a firm kiss on her lips. "Hey, do you mind if we take this to the patio and watch a movie on the flatscreen? Or is it too cold for you? I can turn on the outdoor heater and grab us a blanket." he mused, his eyes flickering to her hard nipples poking through her shirt.

She blushed instantly, noticing him ogling her without a care in the world. He turned suddenly to open a cabinet and pull out a glass pyrex dish and put a couple of large scoops of paella in the dish before snapping the lid on. Colin turned to open a drawer, grabbed a sticky note and a black sharpie before writing 'Beth' on it, and placing it on the top of the dish and placing it in the refrigerator.

That's so freaking thoughtful, Olivia mused, hiding a small smile.

"Well, that depends. Will you please pick the movie, and can we eat it straight out of the pot?" she teased back, grabbing two big spoons and raising her eyebrows inquisitively.

Colin glanced at her, flashing a big smile, his eyes crinkling slightly around the edges.

"As long as you don't eat like Vanessa! My God, that woman, how does she do it?" Colin teased, grabbing the pot and jerking his head at her to follow him. He started the gas fireplace outside before turning on the tv and picking a movie.

Olivia had been too busy blowing on a spoonful of rice to see the title, and looked up as the haunting music started. "What's this?" she asked, still feeling a little shy from him putting his mouth on her earlier, and had a hard time meeting his stare now that they were alone.

The stuff he said, Olivia thought, her heart beating faster at remembering his words while he was making her orgasm over and over.

The man was a true born manipulator and smooth talker. Olivia supposed she should know all about that, the problem was, she couldn't manipulate *him* like she could with her clients. He never gave her an opportunity to vie for control.

In a way, it was a freeing to not have to play those games.

But his forward style of approaching things was rewiring her brain chemistry, changing her outlook. She'd considered what she did for work as a sickness, but Colin was showing her there was more than one way to skin a cat. She didn't feel gross like she did when she had been beating her clients.

Olivia still felt dirty, but a *good* kind of dirty. She wanted to please him, and would even go so far as to say she had this weird *need* to please him. She pursed her lips, uncomfortable with feeling as if she'd want to cater to another person, specifically another man.

She shivered.

Oh my God this is bad bad, she moaned in her head, closing her eyes briefly.

Resigning herself to focus on the movie, she opened them and saw a shadow in the window above the kitchen sink. The top of Beth's head appeared before Olivia saw her turn towards the refrigerator and grab out the paella before disappearing from her view. Olivia's eyes slid to Colin who was making his way to her where she sat.

"Braveheart," Colin answered. "You've never seen it? It's a classic!" He sat next to her and tucked into the food himself, they ate in silence for a while with nothing but the sounds of the movie and their utensils scraping the stainless-steel pot.

When the gift of a thistle scene came on, and the little girl gave William a flower, she'd surprised him by wiping a tear away.

"I'm sorry I'm crying, it's just the soundtrack is so beautiful," Olivia whispered tearfully.

He leaned forward and brushed his thumb over her cheek and hummed deep in his throat.

"You can cry, Olivia. It's a touching movie," Colin said, leaning back and putting a bite of rice into his mouth. He frowned as he suddenly found himself wishing it was Olivia's taste on his tongue instead of the paella. He didn't get enough this morning.

His eyes narrowed as they slid to the pot on the table between them before sliding to the side of Olivia's face.

She was picking a mussel out of its shell with her fork. He wanted to watch her wrap her lips around the shell and suck it clean, then he wanted to take the shell from her and scoop it up her center while he sucked it clean next. His heart banged in his chest as he watched her.

That's never happened before, he thought with interest.

Paella was his favorite meal.

Colin always told Johnathan it was better than sex and he meant that. He chewed the inside of his cheek, pushing the thought away. He grabbed his phone.

> Johnathan. I'm in so much fucking trouble. I've only known this woman for a month. She's making me lose my mind.-C. Kent.

> Shiiiiiiiiittt. You've been half crazy for a while. Let her finish you off. If she's anything like her sister, I feel sorry for you. Her sister's been on my brain since I met her this MORN- ING! I haven't felt this way since Ezra, and you know it took me a while to feel that with her. What the fuck dude, do red heads have some sort of voodoo magic? -J Dawg.

The three dots came back up, indicating that he was typing still. Colin waited.

> Do you mind if I ask Vanessa on a date? -J Dawg.

Colin frowned, raising a brow as he looked at Olivia, wondering what she would think. He moaned to himself as she began sucking the shell of the mussel clean.

> Why would I care about that? -C Kent.

> Because, if things don't go well with you and Olivia, I don't want you going off the deep end because I'm seeing her sister, ghabiun. Jesus, I swear something's wrong with you. -J Dawg

> Fuck you, Johnathan. Nothing bad is going to happen with Olivia and I. We have an air-tight contract for about four years. -C. Kent

> You're the stupid one. You could have just dated her like a normal person. What's the plan after the contract dummy? She's going to leave. -J Dawg

The hell she is. He bared his teeth, typing and sending the next text without thinking. The possessive part of him ruling out common sense.

> I'm marrying her.-C Kent.

He winced, not really meaning to send that. Surprising himself because what the fuck.

Ok, that might have been too far. He thought.

> You are not thinking straight. You just met her. You are a Latin American man and you're setting up some arranged marriage shit for yourself? In my culture, the parents handle that for us. You're crazy. Don't make me fly my mom down here to set you straight. -J Dawg.

> Listen, she turned me down four days a week for a month after I met her. She wasn't

budging. I was looking for any way in possible and I found it. Why does that make me crazy? Aren't you doing the same thing by wanting to date Vanessa who you just met mere hours ago? We didn't get where we are in life because we play the safe games, Johnathan. We have to go after what we want. And I want her more than I've ever wanted anything. Don't worry about us, and go after what you want.-C. Kent.

Colin put his phone down, not caring to read Johnathan's response.

They finished eating in silence, riveted to the movie. He leaned back sideways on the couch and pulled her back towards him in between his legs with her head on his chest so they reclined together. To say she had visceral reactions towards some of the scenes was an understatement, and he spent more time watching her than he did the movie; having seen it several times.

He rubbed the skin of her arm gently throughout the movie, fascinated with how soft her skin was.

"Your breasts are prettier," he said when the honeymoon scene came on.

Slowly dragging the material of her tank down, he bared her left breast to the open air and began to play with her nipple.

Colin teased the hard bud throughout the whole movie, only letting up when they got the intensely violent parts. He groaned to himself as he felt her squirm and realized her breasts were an immense turn on for her. He plumped the nipple between his thumb and middle finger, squeezing tightly and scraping the nail of his forefinger across the tip.

Olivia cried out and arched, moaning as she settled back down.

"They're really sensitive, huh, baby?" he teased, sucking her earlobe into his mouth.

"Colin..." she moaned, circling her hips.

"Shhh...be still and let me do my job while you do yours. I want you to cum, beautiful. I fucking love the way you sound when you orgasm." he rearranged them slightly so he could reach with his right hand, plunging it into her sweatpants and under her panties, finding her soaking wet.

She wiggled against him slightly.

Colin growled audibly as he rolled her clit in his fingers, feeling more of her juices coat them. She was gasping and whimpering, still sensitive from their earlier escapade.

He took a minute to thank God he wasn't a lesser person, because surgery or no surgery he wanted to tear her pussy up. She didn't deserve that, though, and the only thing keeping him from solidifying his place in hell was the fact that he had home training.

Taking a calming breath, he grabbed the remote with his left hand and scrolled through several apps until he found a sensual playlist. Music took the place of the movie. He ignored her small hand trying to still his movements and wrapped his body more securely around her.

"Do you know how long I've wanted to do this? I thought about touching you every day since the night I met you at the diner. The moment you erased that pretty smile from your mouth and faced me with that challenging fucking look on your face, I knew *then* you were going to haunt me. But my fantasies pale in comparison to the real thing."

She whimpered in response, unable to speak.

He clenched his jaw, placing his hand back on her breast as he pressed a finger into her, making himself follow the slow beat of the song.

She pressed her head back against his shoulder, turning her face into his neck and gently nipping at his skin. Snuggling to him.

He bent his left knee back, resting his foot against the cushion close to her hip and pulled her left leg up and to the side, hooking her leg over his and opening her wide. He pressed his wide, warm hand to her leg for several moments, settling her.

Olivia gasped at the movement, pleasure filling him at the sight of her face flushing hotly.

He lowered his head and took her mouth in his at the same time he pressed a second finger in her, the thick digits spreading her. His tongue dueled with hers wetly as he curled his fingers up inside of her, trying to find her g-spot. Her legs shook as he found it, and he worked it a little faster with the beat.

"You're so fucking beautiful shaking for me while I pleasure this pretty cunt. She's mine. Isn't she?" he growled, losing his mind.

His nostrils flared as her scent sharpened around him. He thrust his fingers hard inside her, pressing his knuckles against her and twisting.

The wet sucking sounds became louder as she became wetter, her moans against his lips turning him on and he briefly pressed his hips up into her lower back to ease the ache between his legs. He pulled away to catch her gaze as he introduced a third finger, feeling her start to slightly recoil her hips away from him.

His left hand tightened harshly on her breast, keeping her in place, his eyes hard on hers. A low mewling sound escaped her lips as he pressed harder, feeling her tight flesh give.

"Take. It," he bit out almost angrily, feeling his ring finger slide deep in next to the others. She was so warm and snug, and he prayed silently he didn't die when he slid his cock into her.

It was a sudden worrying thought.

Olivia threw her head back, her mouth opening as he curled his fingers against that delicious spot, and pressed the palm of his hand hard into her clit. His hand encompassed her small pussy easily as he worked her mercilessly, groaning himself at the feel of her narrow channel pulsing around his fingers which he suddenly spread inside of her without warning.

"Noooo-oo-oo!" she whimpered, gasping for air.

Not wanting to misunderstand her use of 'no', Colin was about to ask her if she needed to use her safe word. Just then, she let out a sexy series of broken sobs as she orgasmed again. His firmed his grip on her nipple even more as he slowly thrust in and out, lowering her from her orgasmic high gently.

He gently plucked her lips with his as he let the night air and music encompass their moment, swelling their emotions. After several minutes, he kissed her lightly again and shifted, pulling out his fingers, straightening her top, and letting her lower her leg.

Olivia panted, having just had two very strong orgasms in just half an hour. His lecture about learning how to have multiple orgasms bounced around her head. She'd never come this many times in one day in her life. Her skin sizzled as he spent time manipulating the two of them back into order.

She sat up gasping in shock as she leaned forward and felt just how wet she was. She put her left hand to her sweatpants. They were soaked. Her face reddened, and she froze, not able to move.

Colin began to sit up himself, noticing she wasn't moving, and continued to face away from him. He looked her over and saw how uncomfortable and embarrassed she was.

Her shoulders were raised, her telltale sign.

"What's wrong?" he asked softly, already knowing the answer but wanting her to begin to feel comfortable enough to discuss these things with him.

She glanced back over her shoulder with a nervous expression and spoke so softly he barely heard her. "M-my pants," she stammered, her face beet red.

He looked into her eyes before reaching down, wedging his hand between her ass and the cushions, feeling the extent of the mess they'd made together. He smiled as he gripped her firmly.

"I like it." He seductively hummed deep in his throat. "Stand up. I want to see."

"But-" she whispered, getting a horrified look on her face.

"You'll do what I ask the first time, or there'll be consequences, Olivia," he said sternly, her name rolling off his tongue like velvet.

His chocolate eyes flashed at her as he squeezed her ass sharply.

Colin swallowed hard as she stood up in such a way as to try to hide her ass from him. He smacked her hand away gently with a light scoffing sound.

His cock twitched painfully at the sight; her sweats were indeed soaked.

The wet fabric clung indecently to her plump ass, highlighting curvaceous round globes. He leaned forward and pulled them down, then helping her step out of her underwear, baring her ass to his gaze. Turning her around, he held her eyes as he pressed the lacy black scrap of material to his nose and breathed deeply.

He groaned, letting her know without words how much she pleased him.

He smiled wickedly at her as Olivia's mouth parted and her pupils dilated. She shifted nervously from foot to foot, feeling very out of sorts in her sling. Her vagina was almost mouth level with his mouth, and she whimpered as he leaned forward and furrowed his tongue into the slit between, locating her swollen clit quickly, and grasping onto it with his teeth and tongue.

She suddenly screamed as he bit down and pulled sharply with an animalistic growl, tugging the sensitive bundle of nerves away from her body before burrowing his tongue into her and lapping her up. She moaned weakly through another orgasm as she swayed gently in his arms; her left hand burrowed into his hair.

They stood there like that for a few minutes, rocking against each other.

Colin moved, and she felt a thud at her feet.

She looked down, confused, seeing the thick couch cushion at her feet in between his legs.

"Kneel down," Colin ordered, spreading his legs and leaning back slightly. Her eyes searched for his.

Conceding what she saw there, she lowered her eyes as she went to her knees, with his assistance. She sat on her heels as he helped her out of her tank top.

"Lay your head in my lap, Olivia." he said in that sure voice, digging its way into her brain like it was searching for something.

She mentally cradled her box of hurt closer to herself, hiding from him. It was too much to reveal. Her hurt, and her secret she was hiding from everyone, her old lifestyle, her wants and dreams. She stared at him for a tense minute while she worked it out, then, she slowly leaned forward and laid her head on his lap.

Olivia settled into him, leaning into the intimate feel of his body against hers, and her breasts pressing against the couch cushions between his legs.

He moved firmly and without hesitation; closing her in with his thighs and placing a heavy hand on her head, and another on her bare back. She tensed, her shoulders hunching with a ragged inhale that burned her lungs. He hummed low in his throat, his thumb at her head starting to move, stroking her temple firmly.

His hand on her back steadily seeping warmth into her, before running down her back in a wide sweeping stroke. Patiently, he repeated the movement for long minutes.

Olivia felt a tear escape her eye.

She wiped it away inconspicuously as she felt him move against her. His broad hand at her back stilled and calmed her as his other hand firmly held her head to his thigh. She had a niggling thought that this was oddly too intimate. She'd almost rather he kiss her.

A weird, warm sensation overtook over her body and she relaxed, breathing out a breath.

Colins administrations comforted her. However, she stubbornly tightened her hold on that box of hurt inside of her.

"There we go, I got you baby," Colin said after a few minutes, slowing his movements and leading her down gently but firmly.

Soon, his hands stilled completely against her, but she stayed there for a while longer with her cheek pressed to his thigh. Slowly, she raised her head up, her eyes not quite meeting his, feeling something she didn't know she wanted to examine just yet.

Colin stood up and shoved her panties in his pocket.

"I don't think you'll be getting those back," he said, bending down to grab her sweatpants and slinging them over his arm before grabbing their pot.

Jerking his head at her to follow him, he led her into the kitchen where he rinsed the dish and whistled as he loaded the dishwasher and locked up the house.

He had her shower carefully with her sling using a detachable overhead spray, and then put her in bed, this time making her stay naked. She lounged tiredly against the pillows, flickering the television and putting on some sort of comedy. She fell asleep before she even got five minutes in. The day completely exhausted her.

***

Colin went into the shower, this time roughly masturbating. He scraped his nails down his abs, imagining they were Olivia's instead, and pictured himself pounding into her helpless mouth.

Mentally replaying her cries and moans of pleasure, he growled low in his throat as he slammed his palm against the tiled wall as his seed spurted out almost painfully.

Shuddering hard and trying to catch his breath, he took his time soaping up while torturing himself dreaming up ways to take the woman in his bed. Having a carnal, vicious need to possess her. Groaning again, he placed his forehead against the shower wall, wondering how much longer he could wait until the day he could sink his cock into her sweet warmth.

Colin got into bed, this time staying close to his side, scared to smell her, knowing she wasn't ready. He fell asleep after a couple of hours, his erection preventing him from sleeping deeply.

TWENTY-ONE

Expectations vs Reality

OLIVIA SPENT THE NEXT several days beginning her day with Colin's mouth between her legs. Though it was embarrassing, she eventually got used to how many times they had to put fresh sheets on the bed. One morning, her curiosity got the better of her and she asked him if he had left the laundry for Beth to do.

She felt self-conscious of another person knowing the intimate details of their sex life when she was barely wrapping her head around it herself. Not used to having a person in the home doing basic help.

Colin's answer was a solid no.

He washed their sheets daily himself in the king-sized washer and dryer that was stowed in a hidden room off their closet. He showed her the secret door, and her eyes went wide as she saw the personal laundry set up. Happy that he had multiple spare sets of sheets and a waterproof pad to rotate.

They also made good use of their brief time off, moving Vanessa into her new house.

Olivia was a wonderful patient, healing nicely from her surgery just like the doctor promised. She only had to be reprimanded five times for doing something she wasn't supposed to.

And though it was more than he liked, Colin knew it could have been way worse, and it pleased him that she was at least trying to behave herself.

Vanessa's new home was a beautiful, contemporary, two-story house. It boasted dark gray siding, chunky trim, two glowing lanterns flanking a beautiful mahogany door. She had a three-car garage and gorgeous wrought-iron fence with a play area in the back for Allison. Johnathan was able to join them for a couple days, helping to unbox while Olivia couldn't help.

She started working her way out of her sling, feeling a slight soreness from not using her arm for so long.

Colin made her sleep in her sling, however, and that irritated her. He took the pleasant route more often than not when she was in an irritable mood., kissing her senseless instead of doling out a punishment like she thought he would.

It endeared her to him.

Olivia found herself often craving his kisses, wondering anew how she went so long without intimacy. Colin was affectionate and loved touching her.

He also surprised her by helping her do her physical therapy, making sure they got it in before he went to work in the mornings. The first few days he had to go back to the office she went with him as he didn't trust her arm to drive, and he'd wanted her close until he was confident that she was able to drive on her own.

The habit became a beneficial one and after a couple of weeks; it was comfortable.

She was making use of the sizeable space, and his staff enjoyed having her around, often inviting her out to lunch with them. Colin went along a couple times, but would stay behind at the office trying to play catch up, and was apparently working to solidify deals with other countries.

Johnathan stopped by on multiple occasions to talk business, and she found his brotherly nature with Colin sweet.

Even when they cursed each other out, it was with a tinge of fondness.

***

It was a cool Thursday afternoon when Colin took Olivia to see Johnathan's office for a business meeting. She almost peed her pants with excitement at Johnathan's compound of multiple office buildings. And her eyes widened with disbelief at the expansive glass warehouse used to store luxury cars.

Apparently Colin's best friend was a formidable force in car manufacturing, and she was kicking herself for not googling them both to do more research into their business and philanthropic interests.

They were fascinating separately, but a force to be reckoned with together.

She suddenly felt incredibly shy, feeling inadequate in their presence. Still in disbelief that she was plucked out of obscurity and dropped into this world she would never know. It all felt surreal.

Yet, it solidified her motivation to make something of herself. Even if it couldn't be at their level, she never just wanted to be regarded as that poor project that Colin found and polished up. She narrowed her eyes in concentration, watching the two men discuss a company that was based in France.

Two men who were speaking French were standing with them. They hadn't journeyed into the office yet, so she was sitting in a little seating area nearby on her phone., minding her own business and waiting for Colin to finish up.

She noticed that one man in particular kept turning his head to eye her curiously.

Olivia smiled politely, watching with interest as Colin side eyed the blonde man in front of him.

It didn't take him long to catch on, and Olivia observed him quietly. Seeing Colin's posture become more stiff with obvious irritation that the man was constantly turning his attention away from him. Colin's eyes met hers briefly before he turned back to the man with a stern look, and said something in a sharp tone in French she couldn't decipher.

Biting her lip, she grinned with a little giggle.

She twisted her lips and turned away in her seat slightly, crossing her legs and moving her head so her hair shielded her face. She concentrated on her phone, looking up current academicic books on architectural studies and sending a few of them to him with a question if she could buy them.

"Olivia!" he snapped.

She lifted her gaze off her phone his, surprised. She hadn't intended for him to interrupt his discussion, that's why she'd texted him. However, she raised a brow, choosing to stay silent as she didn't want to get involved in whatever they were talking about.

"Come here," Colin ordered with his arms folded tightly.

Her eye roamed quickly, seeing his legs were spread in a power stance.

Olive licked her lips nervously, not desiring to go over there with the group and embarrass herself. But his eyes were hard on her's as he gave her a look that let her know she'd better obey.

Sighing to herself, she uncrossed her legs and stood, leaving her bag and her purse in her seat. Her red bottomed heels clacked on the marble floor as she advanced to the men, thankful that dress she was wearing covered her from her neck to her wrists, and all the way to mid-calf. But it hugged her curves almost indecently.

Still, she felt too exposed, however Colin had insisted on this outfit. Telling her he wanted her in green today as he had a present for her.

She'd almost fainted at the sight of two big emeralds and diamond watch.

They sparkled in her ears, and the expensive watch encased her left wrist, weighing her down as she approached warily.

She tentatively held out her hand with the diamond watch, assuming they were about to do introductions but Colin's hand reached out and snatched hers up into his before the Frenchman, who had been staring at her, could even raise his own. Her mouth dropped slightly at how rude it was.

Colin's eyes sparkled at her before speaking, however she doubled down on her irritation as her face heated.

Introductions? What a stupid thought, she hissed in her head.

"Doesn't she look expensive, Francis?" Colin said, letting out a long exhale before turning cold eyes to the dark haired man who'd been eyeing her.

Not expecting that, Olivia recoiled her head and blushed at his tone. Not sure what to do and always slightly off kilter with this man.

Francis glanced at Colin before his eyes turned back to her, clocking the emeralds in her ears, and the diamond watch Colin gifted her with. Olivia bit her lip, swallowing hard.

"Oui, McDermont." The man switched respectfully to using his last name, but she knew Colin didn't care. A lesson was going to be taught today and Olivia stood there silently, not knowing if the lesson was for her, or his business associates.

Johnathan rocked back on his heels, a little sound in his throat. He clicked his tongue, but Colin ignored him.

"Too expensive to look at. Wouldn't you agree?" Colin pressed, seemingly unbothered, but his energy said otherwise; it draped over the group as if he'd flung a bucket of icy water on them all.

Slightly offended, she stiffened.

"Col- " she started before being interrupted by a deep, warning sound emitting from his chest. She froze in shock, her eyes widening as she attempted to school her features.

"Your company wants *my* reputation," his voice came out rough, and made the hair on the back of Olivia's neck stand on end. *"You* need my business. I don't need yours. You keep your fucking dick in the other associates' wives if you want to, but if I catch you even so much as *breathing* in *her* direction from here on out, I will fuck your entire world up. Don't play with me, you shitty, Toyota driving *cabrón.* "Colin's deep voice echoed threateningly around them.

Olivia's heart thudded painfully, and her fingers trembled within his strong grasp.

Johnathan covered his mouth, clearing his throat gently, looking away and rocking on his feet once more.

Olivia bit her lip and hurriedly lowered her gaze to Francis' feet, blinking, thinking about her Honda he made her get rid of.

Oh. My. God. What an awful fucking insult, she thought to herself.

Francis turned his eyes back to Colins. He looked incredibly nervous. "You're right, McDermont. Too expensive for me to afford," he said with a carefully hidden shocked look on his face.

Colin smiled a truly genuine smile before leaning to her and placing his lips against her ear.

"You buy every fucking thing you want, Princess," he breathed deeply, giving her ear a little kiss right next to the emerald before turning back to the men, wrapping his arm around her waist and keeping her close.

Olivia stood there, perplexed.

Despite her being quite literally right in front of him, standing next to Colin as they finished their conversation, Fracis did not even so much as flick his eyes in her direction. And even though he hadn't even been addressed, the other man didn't either. She didn't know whether to be embarrassed, or relieved at Colin's jealous outburst.

Not even just an outburst, but a ruthless *chastisement.* Publicly ousting Francis as a serial cheater with wives that were in the men's circle.

Olivia peeked at Colin through her lashes.

Truly appreciating for the first time that he was *powerful,* wrapped in audacity, and plated with cojones bigger than Texas. No wonder Johnathan always called him crazy. He said and did what he wanted with no fear whatsoever. It was intimidating, but admirable that he could live so eloquently in his truth.

Respect swelled inside of her for him, so strong her lips curved in a smile as she watched him continue his discussion. Colin flicked his eyes to her and ceased speaking mid-sentence. "Why are you looking like that, Amore?" he asked softly, tilting his head.

"Because I respect you so much. Your balls are absolutely enormous, Colin. It's a sight to behold," she said, holding back tears of laughter. His eyes widened before narrowing in shock.

Johnathan roared with laughter, coming over to give her a big hug. Laughing so hard he couldn't even get words out; he gestured a hand to his office and ushered the French men away. *"Serves you right, Francis,"* he said before the door clicked shut, leaving just her and Colin in the small seating area.

She let out a little giggle, wiping her eyes as Johnathan's laughter was contagious.

Colin's gaze flicked over her face before he closed the foot of distance between them.

"And what do you know about my balls, missy?" Colin breathed, wrapping his hand around her upper arm and pressing her into his torso. The action made her have to stand up on her tip-toes, and she let out a low moan as he lowered his face to hers to barely graze her lips with his.

"Nothing," she whispered. "And well, if we have to talk about them, then maybe everything's so very small down there. Surely that's why your ego is so fucking big," Olivia said with a straight face, giving him wide doe eyes.

His lips twitched with amusement as he let out a deep sexual chuckle, and that was all she needed to know that he was, in fact, not small down there.

A man would never make the noise he just did if he didn't have what it takes to back it up.

As if he heard her thoughts, his hand traveled down her arm before grabbing her fingers, making her bend down slightly. Her eyes widened as he yanked her down further, to a spot on the inside of his thigh and then pressed her hand in. She averted her eyes from his when she felt the *very* thick tip of his dick where it rested quite a way down his pants.

Her panties flooded as their eyes locked, and she whimpered, her face flushing as she realized what an incredibly inappropriate position they were in.

"You tell me, Olivia. Is this *small* enough for you?" His face was impassive.

She swallowed hard before pulling her hand back. "Well, it's a dick for sure," she said, giving him a little wink. Not betraying what was really going on in her head.

Like how she was never ever going to find herself in this position again. How the hell did she sign that agreement without asking him to show her what he was packing? She was going to void it anyway when she couldn't fit it inside of her. He wouldn't pay for what he couldn't use.

A fresh wave of insecurity and fear washed through her, and she paled.

He saw it. Of course he did.

"Ohhhh," he tsked. "Poor thing. Did I just scare you?"

It took everything in her to keep his eye contact as she trembled inside with intimidation.

"You can take it, Olivia. You're going to have to." He smiled at her, giving her cheek a little pat before he turned on his heel and disappeared through Johnathan's office door.

The pat was all it took to switch her fear to desire. Like a light switch going off, her panties flooded, and she felt a harsh throbbing between her legs.

She unclenched her legs and let out a choked noise. Turning to grab her bag and phone, she ran into a nearby executive bathroom, uncaring that the men saw her running through the glass door of the office. Closing the bathroom door and locking it, she took a second to breathe before looking over at her reflection in the mirror with her heart hammering inside of her chest.

She looked wild, her eyes tortured.

On a hitched sob, she dropped her purse and her phone to the floor and yanked her dress up.

Looking down and seeing a covered small trash bin, she placed a heel gingerly on top of it, rested her back against the wall as she bent her leg and opened herself up for her fingers.

TWENTY-TWO
Worth It

OLIVIA PLUNGED A HAND into her panties, knocking the back of her head against wall when she grasped her swollen clit. A little moan flew past her lips as she worked it furiously, thinking about the possessive man across the office. With her other hand, she squeezed an aching breast.

Seeing her nipple jut through the fabric in the reflection of the vanity mirror, she grasped it, digging her nails in and crying out at how good it felt.

The sound startled her and she stopped, covering up her mouth with her hand, breathing hard. Her fingers worked her flesh for a few more minutes, and she shuddered as she felt her orgasm looming, the wet sounds of her fingers slipping against her flesh. She was so close.

Just then a knock sounded at the door, throwing her off.

Her brows furrowed. "Just a minute," she called, her fingers still circling her clit as she desperately tried to finish.

"*Olivia*? You've been in there for a while. Are you okay?" Colin called through the door.

She tossed her head back, seething. *What the fuck. Fuck fuck fu-uuuck!* she screamed in her head.

"Yes, I'm *fine*. I'll be right out."

He was silent. Seeing he wasn't leaving, she hesitated, dragging her fingers from her panties and lowering her leg.

"Let me in," he said, his deep voice coming out stern and demanding.

"Colin! I need privacy," she gritted, now pissed because her orgasm was receding.

"It wasn't a question. *Now*," he said through the door.

Panicking, she hurriedly went to the door and unlocked it before lunging to the sink as he walked in and shut it behind him. She squealed as he grabbed her elbow and pulled her back from the sink before she had a chance to put her fingers under the water. He pressed her hard against the wall, his eyes lowering to items scattered on the floor before roaming all over her body, taking in her disheveled, panting state.

His lip curled.

"I can *smell* you," he rasped, taking a deep breath.

Olivia paled, yet her heartbeat raced again. Her sensitive body misting with a fine sheen of perspiration as desire slammed into her at his proximity. She cried out as he took her hand and held it up between them before slowly placing it to his nose, inhaling deeply.

"*Colin*," Olivia whined as he lashed his tongue out to lick her before slipping her fingers into his mouth.

He sucked her fingers, biting down harshly on the spot she normally did when she was upset. The action caused a shocked whine to escape her throat, and she gasped as he tightened even further before releasing her.

"*Finish,*" he ordered, his eyes intense on hers.

She shook her head. She'd never masturbated in front of anyone before.

"We need to have a talk about expectations, I see," he bit out, running his nose along her jaw before stopping at her ear.

He pulled her earlobe into his mouth before tugging on the emerald. Olivia's breath sawed in and out of her lungs as she felt his hard chest pressing into her breasts firmly, pushing her harder into the wall.

"I am not a man who likes to repeat himself, and you know this. *So,* when you put me in a position to repeat myself, I have to ask myself what the reason is. The only answer I can think, is that you *want* Francis to hear you screaming my name. Is that what you want, baby? Because I'm prepared to make that happen, if you don't do what I've just requested of you. I will fuck you right here in this bathroom and not stop until all of Johnathan's office knows what's going on. Just keep testing me. Your choice, baby. You've got to the count of two. *One.* T-"

At his hard tone, Olivia scrambled to pull her dress up. In her haste, she almost knocked her head into his.

Without thinking, she placed her heel on the trashcan again at the same time she plunged her fingers into her panties, rubbing furiously. However, because she didn't get her balance before she did, her foot rolled, and she toppled to the side. Colin caught her up quickly as she tilted, and righted her back, keeping his hands firmly on her waist.

Panting, she rested her head on the wall and closed her eyes, her lips pouting sexily as she fought to get her impending orgasm back.

She felt a violent tugging on her body and opened her eyes to see Colin fisting the material of her dress in his hands and yanking the tight fabric up her legs until it bunched at her waist.

He stared intently at her fingers swiping under her panties, that wet clicking sound filling the area and making her cheeks redden in shame.

"Almost there, baby," he said encouragingly.

She inhaled shock as his hand suddenly raise to pinched and rolled her right nipple through her dress, keeping his gaze nailed between her legs. She keened as a wave of pleasure broke over her, and she orgasmed with a soughing sigh, feeling her juices leaking down the inside of her leg.

She stayed there against the wall, panting quietly in the aftershocks, her leg bent outward at the knee as Colin raised his eyes to hers. They silently looked at each other for a long minute.

It was the hottest, most forbidden thing Olivia had ever done in her life. Colin smiled at her again, as if he heard her.

"Do you feel better? No, no, no. Leave your leg right there, mama. I didn't say you could move yet. I said, do you feel better?" His eyes flickered between hers, waiting for her response.

"Yes, sir," she answered.

"Do you want me to clean you up now?" he asked, cocking his head.

"*Yes, sir,*" a tear slipped from her eye and she bit her trembling lip to stem them.

Why does he have to talk to me this way, make me feel like this? she thought as she inwardly retreated, scared he was getting too close.

He brushed a tear away with a thumb. "Why are you crying, baby?" he asked.

"Because I hate the way you make me feel," she whispered, slipping her fingers out of her panties.

She didn't care if he punished her for it.

"And what way is that?" Colin asked gently, treading carefully as his eyes stared deep into hers.

"Like I'm wanted. Like you care about me." she said simply, feeling a shiver crawl down her spine. She went to move her leg, but he stilled her with a palm against her thigh.

"Yet, you *are* wanted. And I don't think I care about anything as much as I care about you. Let me take care of you, baby. *Promise* me you'll let me take care of you," he said, a sudden desperation coloring his speech.

His head tilted closer to her's, and Olivia's breath hitched. However, she remained silent as his hands tightened on her hips.

"Promise me, and then I'll get down on my knees and clean you up, sweet thing. I just need you to say it first," he said, a hair's breadth away from her lips, his eyes still hot on hers but they narrowed at her hesitation.

Olivia couldn't breathe, she was so choked with fear.

"*Say. It,*" he growled, his hands shaking her hips where his hands were fisted in the material.

Her face contorted slightly with emotion. "Yes. Yes. I promise you can take care of me sir, I'll let you. I promise," she whimpered, tears falling from her eyes.

A triumphant look passed across his face before he sank to his knees with a growl. He traced the trail of cum up her leg. Lapping it up until he reached the sensitive flesh between her thighs.

Eager for her taste, he snatched her panties aside and buried his face hard into her pussy.

Olivia threw her head back and wailed, so lost in him that she was uncaring about who might hear. His growls and sex crazed sounds filled the small bathroom, and after a few minutes of him smacking on her flesh, she broke so hard she collapsed down the wall.

Colin sank to his knees and propped her up, pressing deeper, sticking his tongue inside her. She squealed, trying to get away from the fresh sensation. She pressed a heel into his leg and pushed, crying out as he snatched her foot up and held her up with his other hand.

Her eyes rolled to the back of her head.

"*Sir, please,*" Olivia cried out, her body bowing as he unrelentingly feasted on her.

Colin's phone suddenly went off with Johnathan's ringtone, scaring her.

She tried to reach for it, but slipped. Her back slid the rest of the way down the wall, and she hit the floor on an arch, hissing as she tried to claw at Colin's hair.

A sharp snarl filled the air as he moved with her, knocking over the trashcan next to them. Colin's hand raised up and searched for the folded towels that were kept next to the vanity before his hand disappeared with a bunch between her legs.

He suddenly did something with his teeth and tongue that had her whole body seize up and she broke with an ear-shattering scream. She felt him press the towels to her as she broke, and was thankful for his foresight as she squirted hard. He caught it all with the towels and thankfully none got on her dress or on his suit.

She lay there panting in a daze, her vision hazy as he kneeled over her, wiping his mouth.

"How do you...*do* that?" she wheezed, pressing a hand to her chest, feeling like her heart was going to stop.

"It's a gift," Colin murmured, seeing his phone light up again. He answered it.

"MOTHERFUCKER, I HAD TO MOVE EVERY *FUCKING* BODY INTO MY OFFICE BECAUSE YOU CAN'T CONTROL YOURSELF YOU HORNY PIECE OF-"

Colin clicked the end button, cutting him off. Olivia covered her mouth in horror, her face beet red as he looked at her, amused.

"I'm sorry if I embarrassed you, baby. It'll be okay. You just did something to me when you promised to let me take care of you. I couldn't help myself. Is your arm, okay? I tried to not let you hit the floor too hard," Colin asked, rubbing her legs and pulling her dress down.

He righted the trashcan, disposing of the towels he used on her before helping her up gently. Olivia winced, his words reminding her of her pain.

She jostled her arm when she hit the floor, and briefly wondered if that was the reason she'd orgasmed so hard.

"A bit," Olivia admitted, wincing at the look of concern on his face as he busied himself fixing her dress and went to smooth his hand down her hair. She eased away gently and combed her fingers through the strands with a little smile. Turning to the mirror to fix herself up, she grabbed a lipstick out of her purse and smeared it on before wetting a towel and dabbing at Colin's mouth.

"Thank you," she whispered, her eyes flickering to him briefly, back to being shy.

"You're welcome. Now, I have to calm Johnathan over before he kills me. He's quite capable of dolling out extreme pain, and I don't want you to have to see that," Colin chuckled, leading her out of the restroom and into the severely deserted lobby and reception area.

They drew up short, glancing at each other.

The receptionists' phones were ringing off the hook with no one at the desk to answer them. She peeked a bit to the right and looked through the glass window of Johnathan's office and inwardly groaned. Johnathan in fact did have his staff in the office, and they were all talking around a boardroom table while passing around a couple of decanters of liquor.

Her phone beeped.

She opened her text to dozens of demon and eggplant emojis.

> *Oh, sister, sister, I heard from a little birdie that you are getting your shit absolutely ran through at Johnathan's business. *giggle* I am jealloouuussss. Btw, Johnathan's mad as shit at you two. I told him I'd say something*

to you so: Can't y'all just suck face like normal people? -Nessie.

"Oh my Goddd!" she muttered, putting her hand to her forehead and rubbing.

"Don't worry about it," Colin said, stepping forward to wrap on the office door, getting Johnathan's attention. He looked up from the table sharply, and arched a brow. Colin motioned they were leaving before grabbing her hand.

Olivia gave Johnathan a little embarrassed wave as she clicked in her heels after him.

Back at his office building, she sat in his lounge and downloaded architectural books on the kindle that he'd bought, trying to get a head start on studying before starting school in January. She then bit the bullet and bought her books for her first semester early, and pored over them. Taking time writing notes and highlighting, as well as making electronic flash cards.

At the end of the day, Johnathan sent Colin the bill for the money they all lost while he and Olivia were in the bathroom. Two million dollars, and Colin paid the invoice happily.

Olivia was more than worth it to him.

TWENTY-THREE

Evil Sister

OVER THE NEXT SEVERAL days, Olivia put herself into her own world, refusing to be an ornament in his office. Or like a third limb for him to always carry around with him. Although she appreciated the clothes, and jewelry, she didn't dream of being a trophy wife.

She wanted to hold her own next to him.

Colin would watch her during his online meetings, how studiously she worked and pushed herself. She brought up paper and tools and spread out on an obscure corner of his office floor to refresh herself on design and measurement. He would cross an ankle over his knee and observe her intently as she practiced designing various structures.

His eyes perused her designs thoughtfully, nodding at her and telling her how brilliant she was. Because he truly thought she was.

But deep down, Colin was worried. He noticed exactly how brilliant she was and saw a lucrative career in her future that he wanted desperately to help bring to fruition. Ideas of how to use his influence to network to give her the best possible start flirted with his conscious. Even though he instinctively understood when the time came, she would try to shut down any help.

He struggled anew with his irritating fresh wave of insecurity.

He massaged the back of his neck, struggling with the need to have this woman the way his body craved, yet needing to make sense of her first.

A week later on Friday evening Vanessa and Johnathan stopped by the house before they all headed out for some fun. They were going to chill out a bit before going to a karaoke bar. It was Vanessa's idea, not wanting to go dancing and have Olivia be uncomfortable. She wasn't ready for that quite yet.

Olivia rolled her shoulder, feeling less and less of the twinge the more the days went by. She stood there in the kitchen with Mary watching her cook up a lamb and rice dish. The house manager seemed to be a little short-tempered today, and Olivia was sharing a bottle of wine with her while she cooked.

She helped her by cutting up onions but that's all Mary would let her do.

Olivia was wearing another long-sleeved dress, this one cream colored with a singular aquamarine necklace. She wanted to ask Colin if it was real, but considering he took it out of the safe, she felt like she didn't really have to ask. A simple gold bracelet cuffed her right wrist, and Vanessa gasped as she saw it.

"Oh my God, that's a Tiffany cuff bracelet!" she breathed, turning it this way and that. Olivia scrunched her nose and pulled her hand away, still very uncomfortable with wearing jewelry.

Colin walked into the room with a bottle of whiskey for him and Johnathan, and she watched as they clasped each other's back in greeting. Thankful that whatever he did to smooth over the office fiasco they created last week worked, and there was no tension. Really, the big man was all softy on the inside.

She was happy for Vanessa.

She said they were dating, and things were going really well, and Allison obviously adored him.

"Mary," Olivia said, turning to the woman again. "Can I give them a little to taste? It really looks delicious," she asked.

"Sure," Mary said, scooping few pieces onto a plate.

Olivia was busy trying to grab some forks when Johnathan suddenly spoke, and then all hell seemingly broke loose.

"Hey, Mary. Is that ha-" he shot across the island to Mary's back, who suddenly stiffened and pivoted on her feet to face them.

Everyone jumped when she slapped her hand on the island. Olivia's hand flew to her breast in surprise.

"HALAL? *Is it HALAL?*" she shouted. "You dense man, I've yet to serve you anything that's not halal! Do you even bother to notice?" Mary bit out with tears in her eyes.

Johnathan's eyes rounded in shock as he sat ramrod straight in his chair, shooting a panicked look at Colin who slowly set his whiskey down on the counter.

Inhaling on a ragged breath, Mary put a hand to her forehead, shaking. Vanessa's eyes widened as she leapt off the stool she was sitting on to hurry to Mary. They both surrounded her, touching her arm as she suddenly began crying into her hands.

"Mary, oh my goodness, what's wrong?" Olivia asked softly. Vanessa took the spoon out of Mary's hand and placed it back on the stove.

Colin walked to them, gently pulling Olivia and Vanessa out of the way and wrapping Mary in his arms. "Ma, what's wrong? What can I do? Tell me please," he said, concerned.

Mary sniffed and wiped her face with a shaky hand, patting his arms and stepping back. With red eyes she turned to Johnathan, who was still sitting there looking quite disconcerted.

"Nothing. I don't feel well today. I'm sorry for taking it out on you. But it's true, we don't ever serve you anything that's not halal, so please, the next time you say halal to me, I'll halal you straight in your throat." Mary said softly, looking over at Johnathan who had winked at her and was sipping his whiskey. Colin laughed softly, running a hand through his hair.

"Oh, Mary. Say less, I like it when you talk dirty to me," Johnathan said, cracking a joke and easing everyone's tension.

Boy, he's really been getting the shit end of the stick lately, Olivia thought, wincing.

Colin stepped away cautiously. "You still didn't say what's wrong."

"It's women's problem, mijo. I apologize. I shouldn't have talked to a guest of yours like that. I'm so sorry. I can resign for being so disrespectful."

Olivia and Vanessa shared a knowing look and cooed in sympathy.

Johnathan and Colin both erupted in outrage at the same time, scaring the women who were sharing a moment.

"Take that back, Mary," Johnathan said rather loudly with an of-fended look on his face.

"Never! How dare you suggest such a thing. Mary, what is wrong with you? This sickness better be something serious for you to say what you just said. I'm with Johnathan. Take that shit back *now*, right now," he growled at the Mary with a thunderous look on his face.

Mary stared at the two men before breaking out into tears again. "I'm going through menopause and I feel so-so.." she broke off into sobs again, looking like she was about to have a complete meltdown.

Colin and Johnathan both paled, their eyes flickering everywhere, not sure what to say.

"Well, uh." Colin cleared his throat. "I mean, um...That's alright. You can't resign, though. Please, take the other guest bedroom if you need to rest, mami. Don't worry about going home tonight, unless you just need to, then we can take you. And please take a few days off. Do you need one of us to take you to the doctor? We can do all kinds of stuff now with..."

Seeing Mary becoming visibly weary the more he rambled, Olivia turned and threw him a very obvious 'shut up' look. Taking the hint he snapped his mouth shut, and looked away sharply at her expression.

"Mary, what do you need? What can we do to help?" she whispered softly, pulling her out of the kitchen and into the powder room with Vanessa following.

Mary looked at her with red eyes. "Thank you Mija, their energy can be a lot, you know?"

"Yeah, we know,'" Vanessa said sarcastically. She took a small hand towel and wet it before pressing it into Mary's hand.

She smiled her thanks and put it to her neck.

"Oh yeah," Olivia giggled. "Hey, take off a couple days next week and take a four-day weekend. Don't worry about money or *anything*. And besides, we can manage for a little while before we starve to death, I think."

Vanessa let out a hilarious giggle before looking down sharply and picking at a nail. Olivia tilted her head as she just now noticed a beautiful sapphire on her right hand.

"Vanessa! Oh my gosh, did Johnathan give you that?" Olivia whispered as a smile break out on her face.

Vanessa nodded, blushing as she showed Olivia and Mary.

"I'm so glad you two came into my boy's lives. It's about time they found some happiness. Thank you," Mary whispered, leaning over to wrap them in a hug.

They walked her to the car without letting the men interfere and waved as she drove down the driveway.

Turning to each other, they smiled.

"So. Have you and Johnathan bumped and grinded yet?" she teased her sister as they walked to the front door.

"Not yet," Vanessa laughed. "I'm holding out. I just have to live vicariously through you!"

"Vanessa, we haven't had sex yet." She giggled, bumping her shoulder with her left.

Vanessa turned a disbelieving face to her. "Now I know you're freaking *bullshitting* me, sis. I could sort of believe it before, but now? Come on, you've been here how long, and then the text I got from Johnathan at the office last week?"

Olivia giggled again, opening the door with a wink. "Nope, I guess I just got the gift of driving men crazy." She laughed again, walking straight into Colin and Johnathan, who were waiting for them.

"You got that fucking right," Colin growled, stalking forward, bending down and picking her up. She wrapped her legs around him. "You ready to go, baby? We got some terrible singing to do," he teased as he gave her a soft kiss.

Johnathan took Vanessas hand and pulled her out the front door. "Hey!" she yelped, "My purse!"

"The babysitter's got my number. Stop worrying, and let's have some fun. Trust me?" Johnathan said, looking down into Vanessa's face as they descended the steps.

Olivia saw Johnathan look at Vanessa tenderly and Olivia's eyes widened at the look on her sister's face. Her lips pursed.

No crying tonight, Olivia thought, turning back to look at Colin, who was still holding her cradled in his arms. They climbed into Johnathan's car and sped off to the karaoke bar.

***

"Okay, this is what we're going to do!"

They all leaned in intently to hear Vanessa, who was trying to yell over the noise of the bar.

"We're going to each pick three songs to sing. And make them *good,* dammit."

Vanessa slammed a shot, fanning her flushed face. Johnathan took the opportunity to run a hand down Vanessa's hair.

Olivia looked at Colin. "I don't sing, I dance. Vanessa's the singer. Like she can blow. Seriously. I sound like a strangled cat," she explained, slightly embarrassed as her cheeks flushed.

She finished her half shot of vodka, grimacing and sticking her tongue out before sucking on a lemon.

"Shit, that's *strong!*" Olivia gasped, scrunching her nose as Colin leaned back and sipped his whiskey. He'd put on a blue shirt that matched her aquamarine necklace and she warmed with pleasure that he'd worked to match her like a real couple.

"Vanessa, do you want to make our third song a duet?" Colin tossed across the table at her.

Vanessa looked at him in surprise.

"You can sing?" she asked, a look of disbelief on her face. "No offense, but I don't want to taint one of my turns if you aren't good!"

Her eye sparkled as she laughed at him, and Olivia watched her sister happily, seeing a lot of the stress from her face had dissipated, and it further solidified her choice on taking the contract with Colin..

Olivia glanced at him. *The man's just full of surprises, huh?*

"I guess I'm okay. I need to hear your first song, though, before I decide if you can share a microphone with me," he threw back, sipping his whiskey again.

His own eyes shining with happiness as they stared each other down.

"What's the song?" Vanessa asked as she accepted another drink from the waitress.

He wrote it down on a napkin and passed it to her. Watching as her eyes widened before she broke out in a smile. "Yeah.... I can do this one. But it needs to be the second song for us. I have something different in mind for my third song," she said quietly, folding the napkin and sticking it into her bra. They all raised an eyebrow, and Johnathan chuckled before taking another sip of his drink.

"So." Colin said, "What songs are we doing?"

They wrote all their songs on the cards, giving it to him and he got up to take it to the DJ with a hefty tip.

They cheered hard when a woman got up and absolutely slayed a rock cover.

Olivia whistled, jumping up and down, clapping. It was Johnathan's turn next and he sang *Leaving On a Jet Plane* by John Denver. His voice was not professional in the least, but a few women were looking at him enviously.

Olivia was next, and she sang *Yellow* Kina Grannis' cover.

She was nervous and avoided looking at anyone when she was singing, and her bravery touched him.

Colin was proud. Her voice was sweet, innocent, stroking over him like a balm. Then it was Vanessa's turn.

She took the microphone and his jaw dropped as she belted out a song that had him standing up and whistling along with everyone else in the building. Even the servers stopped serving and were staring.

He gaped at Olivia, who was staring at the stage with a proud, albeit watery, expression on her face. He leaned over to whisper in her ear.

"You *never* said your sister could sing like that," Colin accused her, taking her hand as Vanessa exited the stage. He gave her a squeeze before he went up to the stage and grabbed the microphone, adjusting the stand and signaling the DJ. The lights went down in the building, surprising everyone before a spot-light shined on him.

Olivia gasped as he began to sing a salacious song, her face heating as he watched him basically fuck the microphone, his eyes on hers as he took complete control of the stage, his voice coming out growly, strong. She shrugged her shoulders as she felt her nipples hardening, the song and his singing turning her on.

Oh yeah...this man can fuck me any day of the week. This is so hot. Olivia thought, squirming uncomfortably in her seat.

Vanessa's jaw was on the floor as she turned her head to look at her, giving her a 'What the hell?' look. She shook her head as Colin exited the stage, only to be met by four women who had come up to him, fawning over him.

Uh-uh. No. Olivia's face settled into a scowl as she got up and stomped over to where he was, taking his hand and jerking him hard behind her. He gave her a chuckle as he followed, rubbing his thumb across her fingers and not caring how pissed she was.

She practically threw him in his seat, though he went willingly, snatching up his whiskey and downing it before he picked up his fresh glass. He gave her a fiery look, making her stomach do somersaults.

"That song was for you, miss," he teased, giving Johnathan a high five.

"You can sing like that?" Vanessa half screeched at him from across the table before slamming another shot and sucking a lemon. Just when Olivia opened her mouth, about to tell her to slow down, Johnathan leaned over and placed his lips against Vanessa's suddenly, surprising them all.

Vanessa's brows scrunched together as he pulled away, blushing furiously.

"John," she said, looking away shyly.

Olivia grinned, scooting out of the booth as it was soon her turn. She horribly belted out *Harleys in Hawaii*, picking it because it was the song that Colin played at the diner when they first met. She made up for her amateur singing by moving her body in a seductive rhythm to the song, causing more men than Colin was comfortable with yelling and cheering for her.

Colin scowled as he shot back the rest of his whiskey, slightly slamming the glass on the table. He held up his hand for the server to bring him another one, along with a pitcher of water for the table.

"I think we might need to be done drinking after this round till we get back to my place," he said to Johnathan as Vanessa stood up in the booth.

Her hands were in the air as she cheered Olivia on, who was gyrating into the microphone stand too sexually for his tastes.

Over it, Colin got up, striding to the stage to reach forward to snatch her off mid song. He snagged her calf, pulling her off the front stage, uncaring of what the employees thought. The bar booed as the music came to a stop and announced Johnathan's song.

He got up and did a rock soung, making up for Olivia's dancing fiasco. The Bar cheered.

Then it was Colin's turn.

He picked a touching cover that was meant for Olivia, and several people in the audience came to the stage and began clapping along to the song. Olivia stayed in the booth with Johnathan and Vanessa. Her eyes were wide as she listened to him sing the lyrics as he faced her from the stage.

Her heart beat painfully as his eyes trained on her, only leaving hers to close briefly as he sang passionately into the microphone.

She sat there blinking back tears as Johnathan reached over to take her hand. The look he gave her made them spill out, and she wiped them away quickly, shooting him an embarrassed glance. Johnathan leaned forward as Colin continued to sing into the microphone.

"Do not ever be embarrassed for your emotion, Ollie," Johnathan said quietly, chucking her slightly under the chin.

The big man's use of her nickname made her give him a watery smile, and she nodded her understanding.

As she took his hand and gave him a slight squeeze as Colin finished his song. The karaoke bar erupted as the DJ's voice came loud over the speaker, struggling to regain control over the bar as people began cheering so hard the tables shook. Olivia placed a hand on her throat as her chest swelled with pride.

This man's mine, she thought, and her eyebrows raised, startled by the thought.

She noticed Vanessa had slinked away to join Colin on the stage. It was time for their duet.

The bar finally hushed, realizing the two best singers of the night were pairing up for a song together. Everyone's phone was out and even the kitchen cook was leaning on the wall by the kitchen door with his phone out. *Senorita* by Camilla Cabello began playing over the speakers.

Johnathan and Olivia looked at each other, smiling with excitement and sprang into action.

"Let's dance," Olivia said, grabbing Johnathan's hand and yanking him up laughing.

TWENTY-FOUR

I Said No!

"THEY SOUND AMAZING!" JOHNATHAN yelled over the noise of the bar. Since their significant others were tearing it up on the stage, they proceeded to tear it up on the dance floor. More couples came up and began dancing as well, the whole building just comfortable with the chaos that was erupting.

"I can't remember the last time I had this much fun!" she yelled as Johnathan dipped her backwards, making her hair swing wildly. She giggled as he righted her, and then they performed a complicated spin that startled her.

"*Johnathan*! You never *ever* said you could dance!" she gasped, rather accusatory.

"It never came up!" he laughed back at her. And he really could dance. The man had rhythm. She swayed in his arms as they looked up at Colin and Vanessa.

"Olivia, I really like her," Johnathan said quietly as they spun on the dance floor. He turned his dark eyes back to her, and she smiled in return.

"She really likes you too, Johnathan. Nessie's been alone since her husband walked out on her four years ago," Olivia said, a sad look coming over her eyes. "It's just been us for so long that I don't think either of us had much hope that anything was going to change. Everything just seemed so *hopeless, and* no one wanted to be with someone

with a sick kid...and a busy schedule. And chaotic sister," she dramat-
ically whispered the last part, looking away and clenching her jaw.

Johnathan looked at her sharply.

"Don't do that, Behan! It's bad for your teeth, you're going to
tear small holes in them and then Colin will never shut up about it.
He'll make you rip them all out and put veneers in. You'll look like
those freaks on Instagram," Johnathan said seriously, his dark brows
furrowing over his eyes as he attempted to lecture her.

They stared at each other before erupting in laughter as the
song ended. Tears streamed down her face as she fell apart, giggling.
Johnathan, as intimidating as he looked, was the perfect mix of humorous and dangerous.

"Johnathan, did you just curse me out? What's 'behan' mean?"
Olivia asked, giggling as she wiped a small tear out of her eye. He
turned to watch Vanessa and Colin, who were making their way to
them. Johnathan tore his eyes away from Vanessa to look back at her.

"It means sister," he replied, before turning back and meeting
Vanessa and Colin halfway, leaving her standing there, stunned. A
warm feeling rushed through her he swooped Vanessa up and turned
her a few times, causing her to yell out excitedly.

Colin finally got to her before swooping down to land a juicy kiss
on her mouth. Her hands sunk in his hair as he tilted her backwards,
deepening the kiss to lewd cat calls from nearby people.

He pulled away and assessed her hungrily. She smiled and jerked her
head at the couple next to them, talking as they began walking back to
their table.

"Ohhh they are *so* knocking boots tonight," Olivia yelled to him
over the rock music that blared over the speakers.

And then it was her turn to share in laughter with Colin, who put
his arm around her and began to lead her to their table. They slid across

from Johnathan and Vanessa, who were both tearing into the food that the server put in front of them. The bar was backed up as the employees took the time to enjoy the evening, too.

He took their plates from the server and handed Olivia's hers, who was busy staring in alarm at the couple across the table. Apparently, they both shared a love of food, a very violent love.

Jesus, he thought, his eyebrows raised as Vanessa stuffed a rather large bite into her mouth, making her cheeks stuff out.

"That's a good sign that she can do that, Johnathan." Olivia pointed at Vanessa's full mouth rather suggestively.

Colin gave Olivia a shocked look, a bark of laughter rumbling from him at what she just suggested. Olivia cut a piece of boneless chicken in half and put it in her mouth, shrugging her shoulder unashamedly.

"So damn beautiful," Johnathan complemented rather reverently as he leaned forward to Vanessa and kissed one puffed up cheek, before turning and putting another bite of his vegetarian meal in his mouth. They'd had to deal with the "halal" speech, along with a threat to sue if he got sick from any pork contamination. They'd all followed suit and ordered everything non pork.

"So, Johnathan, where are you from?" Olivia said conversationally.

They'd not had too much time to talk, and she wanted to get to know him better since he was obviously enamored with her sister. Olivia's eyes flickered between them in amusement. They were currently looking at each other like they could race down a church altar to say vows. She let out a giggle at the thought. Because they just met each other, and who would be that stupid? Not her sister.

She'd made her ex-husband wait almost three years before they married.

"It's my turn," Vanessa said, putting her phone down. Olivia glanced down as her phone lit up. She picked it up, swiping it unlocked.

> Make sure Johnathan's okay. I need to get this song out, and I don't know how he's going to handle it. -Nessie.

Olivia frowned, not knowing what she was talking about. She glanced up at Vanessa and nodded. Colin looked at her for an explanation, and she lifted her shoulder and reached for her water. She sipped slowly as Vanessa took the stage and took a seat on a stool in front of the microphone.

Olivia's breath froze in her lungs as the music started, and she stiffened as chills saturated her body. She stared at Vanessa wide eyed as she began to softly sing a song of a woman who could never love again.

Olivia trembled with nerves and emotion, suddenly understanding why her sister wanted this to be the last song. The emotion she had to expel to get this song out was probably going to ruin them all and she wasn't ready.

She didn't think any of them were.

Her watery eyes slid to Johnathan, and she realized the man looked absolutely petrified. Gutted.

Johnathan stared at the stage rather blankly, but his hand was trembling on the table.

She reached forward and softly placed her hand on his as she felt the tears slide down her cheeks, dripping onto her dress. His hand unclenched before wrapping around her tightly where they trembled there together. Colin placed his lips against her temple and leaned her against him, wanting her support too.

She let go of Johnathan's hand momentarily as she looked over at Colin and leaned forward, pressing her lips hard to his, surprising him.

She moaned as he sank his hand into her hair, holding her still so he could take control.

They pulled away as a woman loudly wailed in the back of the bar, and there was a sudden commotion as a couple of people went to assist. She had collapsed crying and was yelling, *"Oh my Goodd!"* over and over again. Yet, Vanessa still kept singing, lost in the song. Probably couldn't even tell she was making people absolutely sick in the audience.

The woman's friends escorted her to the bathroom, as she was inconsolable.

Olivia placed her hand back in Johnathan's and squeezed as Colin rubbed her shoulder, rocking her slightly, his lips still at her temple. She clung tight to Johnathan, feeling her hand go numb as he squeezed her back hard. Overwhelmed, she leaned forward and placed her head down on the table, crying quietly. Just done.

She wanted to go up to the stage and smack her sister. Colin's hand settled on the back of her neck as she felt Johnathan's hand slide from hers abruptly. Johnathan got up and walked away and she got up, crawling over Colin's lap to follow him. Johnathan disappeared in the hallway to the bathroom, and was leaning against the wall with his hands on his face.

He put them down as she approached, his face drawn tight, looking tortured, and a tear slipped down his cheek. Olivia felt her heart break for him at the misery and open grief on his face and rushed over to wrap her arms around him.

"I'm sorry," she blubbered.

They stood there, crying together, hugging as Vanessa continued to croon into the microphone. Colin walked up to them, staying silent, just watching. He put a hand to Johnathan's shoulder and squeezed.

"I'm so sorry. I think you got the evil sister, bro," she whispered, smiling as he chuckled through his tears. He pulled back, running a hand down his face, his eyes haunted as he looked at her.

"My wife died eight years ago... freak heart attack," Johnathan explained, his eyes lowering to the ground. "I've never been with anyone else since. It just hurts too bad. All those years of planning our life gone to waste."

"You don't have to talk about it. I know what it's like to not want to try. It *does* hurt, and it doesn't feel worth it. It hurts too much to let go of the pain," Olivia whispered, glancing up at him.

Not embarrassed to share this part of herself with this man who just bared himself to her, and everyone else in the bar with his emotion.

Colin made sure they were okay before he walked back into the main room, not wanting Vanessa to be completely alone with them gone.

Olivia stayed silent, rubbing his arm sympathetically as Vanessa finally finished the song. The woman who had to leave the room when the song first started walked out of the bathroom, patting her eyes with a tissue, looking slightly better. She gave her an apologetic smile as she walked past.

"Come on, let's get back," Johnathan said to her, leading the way around the corner back to the main room.

Olivia's eyes widened in surprise seeing Vanessa hugging the woman who'd broke down crying. She hung back, seeing a crowd of people were congregating around her, vying for her attention, and to congratulate her on busting out a difficult song.

Johnathan let her arm go, swiftly making his way through the throng of people, snatching Vanessa to him and kissing her as everyone pressed around them.

Olivia smiled, turning to their table to find Colin, freezing when their eyes locked.

He was watching her with a tortured expression of his own on his face.

He jerked his head at her to come to him.

Olivia approached hesitantly. That song meant something different for each one of them, and her and Colin didn't know the depth of each other's emotions. Whereas Vanessa and Johnathan were laying themselves bare to each other. She wished her and Colin could be that brave.

But she couldn't.

How could she ask for more, if she was unwilling to disclose the hell that had been her reality for the last several years?

Colin held out his hand for Olivia to take, turning in the booth to pull her in between his thighs. Looking up at her, he reached around and ran his hand up her thighs and to her back, pulling her close and resting his head on her stomach, just holding her.

Her fingers caressed his jaw as they swayed like that to the instrumental music the DJ began playing. Who'd paused karaoke performances after Vanessa's performance, stating they all needed an emotional break before disappearing himself.

Probably to cry too.

Vanessa and Johnathan made their way over, looking emotionally wrecked, however Olivia was happy to see them smiling tenderly at one another. Vanessa's song seemed to bond them, and they were holding hands and leaning into each other as they walked. Colin stood up, pressing Olivia to his side as he addressed the pair.

"I already paid, so we can get going."

"Wait! I had one more song," Olivia teased, smiling at him prettily.

Colin's eyebrows raised as he turned his eyes onto her. "And you can sing it to me later, baby. I promise." He smiled back before glancing at Johnathan.

The man nodded at Colin's unspoken question, clearing his throat.

"Excuse me Miss," a man's voice penetrated their group, and they all turned as a tall, African American man approached them, holding out his hand to Vanessa, who took it tentatively. When she pulled back, a business card was in her hand.

"You can call me Vanessa," she said softly as she squinted at the card.

Olivia bit her lip, leaning forward, and sniffed. Heart pounding, her eyes widened when she realized the man smelled familiar. She gasped as Colin suddenly yanked her back to him.

"Did you just sniff that man?" he said in her ear incredulously, a tinge of jealousy in his voice.

She struggled against his hold. *"Sir,"* she said to the man, trying to get his attention. She let out a pained sound as Colin tightened his hand on hers so hard she felt a knuckle crack.

Oops, I just called this man "Sir" after sniffing him. I must have a death wish, she thought to herself.

But she ignored his tight hold, speaking to the man anyway.

"I'm so sorry for interrupting, but what scent are you wearing?" Olivia bit out through the pain in her hand, throwing Colin a filthy look.

The man grinned. "Kingsmen Premium Holy Grail," he answered, smiling broadly at her.

Vanessa leaned in, smelling him herself while Johnathan and Colin looked rather irritatingly at each other. She gasped, her hand covering her mouth as she locked eyes with Olivia's watering eyes

"Well," Olivia said, "I'm sorry to interrupt you, but we've been looking for that scent everywhere for years. Excuse me." She stepped back and pulling out her phone.

"No, that's cool. I get so many compliments when I wear it." He smiled good naturedly, rubbing his hands together. "So, my name is Elijah and I'm with a local band here. Charles called me about two hours ago when you sang your first song. I hope that's okay. I'm so glad I could catch you before you guys left... I almost killed myself to get here." The man huffed out a breath.

Olivia looked him over, noticing that he did look rather disheveled.

She turned back to her phone, typing something in. Curious, Colin looked over her shoulder seeing she was searching for the cologne in her search engine.

He frowned.

"I'm sorry, who's Charles?" Johnathan asked.

"Oh, I'm sorry. Charles is the DJ here, we're connected. My band performs all over the state and writes songs for some celebrities. We'd love it if you could come to our studio and test a song with us. My information is on the card and our social media is on there too if you want to check our work out before making a decision."

Vanessa looked rather stunned, staying silent. She hadn't been able to talk ever since they'd smelled the man.

"I'll be in touch to let you know what we decide," Johnathan said smoothly, reaching out and clasping his hand. "Thanks for coming out, man. We appreciate it."

Olivia cut her eyes at Vanessa at Johnathan's use of "we," but Vanessa seemed a bit overwhelmed, clinging to him.

Colin's eyebrows raised at how effortlessly Johnathan took over. Especially so soon after being caught up in his emotions.

"No problem, please seriously consider it Vanessa. We'd love to have you with us. You've got a gift." The man nodded at the rest of them before turning and heading to the DJ booth.

"Seriously? What is with you two?" Colin said, turning incredulous eyes to Olivia and Vanessa, who were now staring at each other again. A tear slipped down Vanessa's cheek.

"He smells just like Dad," Olivia said, turning her eyes to Colin. Whose eyes narrowed as he tilted his head. She turned back to Vanessa.

"Sis, that *has* to be a sign. You gotta call them. This is like dad's divine intervention or something!" she said, reaching forward and grasped Vanessa's arm. Vanessa looked shaken.

"Olivia, I can't take off and join a band. What about Allison?" she said tightly.

Olivia paled, shuffling on her feet as that box of hurt start to shake violently.

"We'll help, Vanessa. Let's just see what this is all about before we start turning down opportunities, yeah?" Johnathan said smoothly, putting his hand around Vanessa and taking the card from her, slipping it into his pocket.

They walked to the vehicle and got in.

"I'm hungry again." Vanessa suddenly said, making the car erupt in laughter.

They stopped at a local fast-food restaurant and ordered a ton of food, eating in it the car on the way back home. Olivia twisted in her seat and fed Colin bites of his burger and fries, as he wouldn't eat and drive. She thought it was a little neurotic how he drove and the rules he'd put on himself, but she figured a way around it.

Not mentioning it, but wanting to ask.

There was something he wasn't sharing, and it bothered her. It nagged at her that, despite the intimacy of the evening, she felt disconnected from him.

They returned to the house when Jonathan out pulled out a joint, making Olivia smile. He and Colin had a long conversation about it, which Olivia and Vanessa thought was cute, before deciding to partake.

They all got so trashed that Colin made Johnathan and Vanessa spend the night, showing them up to the spare bedrooms and letting them sort it out. Colin carried a giggling Olivia to bed and undressed her.

I'm so thankful she isn't the paranoid high type. Jesus that'd be awkward, he thought to himself, as he gently maneuvered her dress over her head, smiling at how her hair tumbled wildly around her. He pulled his shirt and shoes, leaving his pants on and pressed his lips to hers, silencing her giggling.

"You feel good, baby?" Colin whispered against her mouth as he laid himself on top of her.

He didn't want their first time to be drunk.

And not only was Olivia dunk, she was high, and her arm was still bothering her. He didn't feel like she could consent to any sexual act and didn't even feel right asking her to. He did have morals. They might be loose, but they were there.

Colin breathed deeply, loving the feel of her breasts squished against his chest.

"Yes." She giggled as he kissed and nibbled her neck. "Colin!" she squealed breathlessly, shaking him to get his attention.

"What, baby?" Colin groaned as he sucked the skin at her collarbone.

"*Vanessa's going to be famous,*" she cackled with glee as if it was the funniest thing in the world.

"You are adorable when you're inebriated," Colin chuckled, bringing his lips back to hers and kissing her-cutting off her laughter.

"Do you think they're screwing?" Olivia moaned into his mouth, the words coming out garbled.

"You can't hear them?" he said, pulling back and catching her eye as she panted for air. Her nipples pressed into his chest as she turned her head. Her eyes widened as her cheeks turned red.

There was muted screaming coming through the door of their bedroom. Her eyes flew to his as she put her fingers to her lips.

"Jesus Christ, what is he doing to her that makes her sound like *thaaaat?*"

Colin rested his head on her shoulder as he shook with silent laughter. Because knowing Johnathan's background, he could only imagine what was happening right now.

He probably had her strung from the ceiling fan or something crazy, he thought.

Paired with his celibacy since his wife died, he was actually feeling really sorry for Vanessa, to be honest.

Colin went quiet, thinking about what they could be doing to his bedroom. Eyes screwing shut, he threw himself down onto his back next to her, groaning.

"Man, my *bedrooom.* Fuck!" he lamented, placing his hands on his face and rubbing.

Olivia placed an arm across her chest and bit her lip. She'd come to find how much he loved his home, his assets, and didn't like a thing out of order. The fact they were probably indeed tearing up his room made her heart tug for him.

"Come on, it can't be that bad.. can it?" Olivia said, looking at him with a teasing look in her eye.

Getting up with a groan, he turned on their fireplace and disappeared into the closet.

"What are you *doing*?" she called out, pulling the sheets back and getting under the covers, snuggling down deep and sighing. He reappeared a second later in pajama pants, the sight of his hard muscles arousing her further. She licked her lips and purred at the sight of his tattoos.

Colin stopped in his tracks, his pajama pants tenting at the sound coming from her.

"*No*," he said roughly, standing still on the other side of the room. "You stay on that side of the bed, and I'm staying on the other side. I'm not fucking you tonight."

Wish I could, wish I could, wish I could, he chanted.

An offended look passed over her face. "*Colin!*" she whined, sitting up, her hair falling over her shoulders and breasts. "You mean to tell me my sister gets laid before I do? And I've known you longer!" she almost hissed at him, her green eyes flashing.

She recoiled as he rounded the bed and fisted his hand in her hair, tilting her head back to look at him.

"What did I *say*?" he growled down at her, his eyes narrowing at her wild ones. They stared each other down for a tense heartbeat.

Olivia felt her cheeks redden at the look on his face. "You said no. *Sir*," she said between tight lips.

His brow lowered. "That's right. You don't dictate *anything* right now. Stay on your side. You're in no state for what I have in mind for you." he said matter-of-factly before letting her go.

She moaned and threw herself back on the pillows before rolling over away from him.

Colin got in on his side of the bed and turned away from her as well, covering his head with the pillow to drown out the sounds of Vanessa's cries from down the hall.

Vanessa and Johnathan were both gone the next morning before they woke up and Olivia had to comfort Colin when he saw the state of the room they'd left. Olivia stood in the room with him, and her eyes roamed the snapped post of the four poster bed, the drywall was broken in pieces out of the wall behind the headboard, and the nightstand was fucked.

She rolled her lips, staying silent. Praying Vanessa was okay.

Giggling quietly, she put her hand in his and led him out the door where they went to his study to discuss the upcoming week. Olivia shared with Colin that she needed to do some research for a design she wanted to implement into a drawing she'd been working on. She would be driving to work in the morning with him, but then would have to leave right away to go to her destination.

Colin was half listening to her while he tapped on his tablet, scowling at something as he worked. Olivia let him be. He'd been working tirelessly on their latest project, and she knew he and Johnathan had several irons in the fire they were working on.

Exhausted, they fell into bed before having to wake up early for work the next day.

TWENTY-FIVE
I'm Not Evil

THE NEXT MORNING, OLIVIA parted ways with Colin without going up to his office and was gone for hours with no contact. Colin, trying not to panic, tried to call her several times with no luck.

Standing by the window with his brow lowered, he watched the street carefully as he called her phone again and again. "Fuck!" he cursed roughly shoving a hand through his hair and throwing his cell to his desk.

It was getting to be almost afternoon when he finally lost his mind having called Olivia's cell repeatedly and not getting an answer. She was supposed to be back at his office almost two hours ago, and never showed up.

God fucking damn it. Where is she? he thought.

He paced his office, breaking out into a cold sweat. Feeling his heart pound.

Okay, don't overreact. Maybe she got caught up designing. Maybe she doesn't have good phone reception.

He checked his phone for her location, seeing her a a little over an hour away, her location dot steadily moving. His eyebrow raised. "*What fucking cathedral is she at?*" he muttered to himself, trying to remember.

Eventually, her phone went dead after a few more hours, and Colin left so many voicemails that they filled up her mailbox. Rendering him unable to send out another one. He went downstairs repeatedly, asking the receptionists if there was any chance they'd seen her. They all responded no every time he asked.

Colin went back to his office, feeling insecure and worried for her, suspecting he'd done something wrong. He knew he'd been working overtime, but he tried to make it better by bringing her with him.

His anger mounted.

Did she run away? I thought we were doing so well.... Did I do something wrong? She wouldn't leave me without at least telling me, would she?

His receptionists' lack of concern burned him to his core, and he had to go through the day with a heavy lead feeling in his chest, weighing him down. As the hours passed, his breathing began to be affected. Uncomfortable, he had to massage his chest several times to help ease the god awful painful ache that had settled, making its home in the spot he knew his heart to be.

Colin was so pissed that he thought about firing his receptionists, but then quickly corrected himself. Because rationally that wasn't fair, and he wasn't thinking right, obviously.

Continuing to call her just in case she'd found a way to charge her phone, he cursed audibly at every automated "We're sorry, the person you are trying to reach has a mailbox that is full."

As he looked out the window at the sun going down, anger settled deep inside next to that heavy, uncomfortable feeling in his heart. Amplifying into a terrifying emotion that he hadn't felt in two decades.

Now truly panicking, Colin called Vanessa and Mary back for an update, and his anger burned brighter when they reported that neither of them had heard from Olivia. He refused to leave, staying at the office just in case she'd returned. As it became dark and there was still no sign of her, he broke down and called the police, officially thinking the worst.

Almost an hour later, he was outside the office in the dark giving the cop a report. His despair mounted when the cop told him that he couldn't file a missing person's report until Olivia had been missing for forty-eight hours.

Keeping his back purposefully to the cop's vehicle, Colin was trying desperately to ignore the police lights lighting up his office building, making his chest tight when he'd spotted Olivia walking up the long street towards them. Her long red hair whipping in the night breeze.

She was limping slowly in her green heels with her arms wrapped around herself, looking like she'd been crying. His heart stopped at the almost unbearable sensation of relief, and he fought hard to keep from falling to his knees at the sight of her, and for a moment, he wondered if he would be able to hold it together in front of the cop.

Colin ran to her, snatching her up to him, burying his face in her neck. Relief washed over him in waves making him feel slightly sick. Olivia let out a strangled sob and wrapped her arms hard around him, shaking.

"Oh fuck, you're so cold," he gritted against her ear, clutching her tight to him.

Olivia sagged against him, trembling.

"Where the hell have you been?!" Colin rasped, putting her down gently onto her feet, grabbing her face and kissing her roughly, visibly trembling.

Olivia started crying harder, trying to talk, but he couldn't hear her pass the blood rushing through his head. She was gripping his shirt desperately, making the material stretch uncomfortably across his chest. It was suddenly too much, the hours of worrying, the police lights giving him flashbacks, the cold sick feeling settling deep in his stomach.

He placed a hand on the side of her face as his eyes roamed, assessing her carefully, and mentally tamping down the rising anxiety and memories that were trying to break through his mind.

"*Amor*, are you ok? Did anything happen to you? *Are you hurt?*" he swallowed thickly past the terrified lump in his throat, feeling himself break out into a sweat at the thought of her being injured, assaulted, possibly violated.

Tears streaming down her face, Olivia shook her head no. Colin pulled her quickly over to the cops, his hand hard on hers, urging her tell them what happened so she didn't have to repeat herself again. He needed to get out of there, and quickly, before he had an anxiety attack.

He listened to the sharp cracking and scraping of her heels on the concrete as he pulled her up to the officer, the familiar noise momentarily calming him.

"Ma'am," the older police officer spoke kindly to her. "Can you tell me what happened? Mr. McDermont was worried about you. Are you well?"

The momentary calm dissipated as soon as she began speaking.

Colin felt nauseated as she started explaining herself. He clenched his fist hard, leaning into the uncomfortable feeling of his knuckles straining. He briefly thought about taking his friend Johnathan up on boxing with his psychiatrist friend Alexander.

He needed more than a boxing bag in his gym to get out his aggression.

"I got on the wrong *bus,*" Olivia said tearfully, gripping his forearm, her nails digging in painfully at the look on his face.

She knew she fucked up big time. So badly that she contemplated not even coming back as she was terrified of what her punishment was going to be, but then dismissed the thought quickly. Remembering their contract, and everything Colin had done to help support Vanessa and Allison and changed her mind.

She was stuck.

"I was trying to get to the other side of the city, a-and I mistook what bus I was on. It was my first time taking public transportation... they took me *two hours* out of the way. And when I got off at the stop, I realized I forgot my purse with my phone in it on the bus in my hurry to get off!" Her voice cracked with a sob, pressing her fists hard to her eyes, and that sudden need for pain was not lost on Colin.

He instinctively placed his hand on the back of her neck under her hair and squeezed down hard.

Grounding her.

"I had to hitchhike back and use their phone to call the transportation department to find the bus with my stuff. Luckily, they had it, and I convinced the lady who drove me around to bring me to get it. I was able to give her some cash for her troubles when I got my purse back." Ending her story, she hiccupped, trembling.

For her troubles. Colin mentally seethed, standing there with every emotion imaginable violating him, and that sentence was the one repeating in a torturing echo in his brain. Somehow, he was only able to process said sentence with irritation and anger.

He raised his head to the sky.

Peace. Just give me peace. I don't ask for much. I can't lose it, he thought, breathing deeply.

"*Baby,*" Olivia's fingernails dug deeper into his arm, and he tore his gaze from the sky, looking at her instead. Her term of endearment tugging at his heartstrings, and he reached forward to brush a tear from her cheek but he couldn't bank the fire that started inside of him. The one that told him he was done waiting.

"Please don't be mad at me," she whispered to Colin, her voice breaking. She brought up a hand to wipe her eyes. "It was an accident."

The police tipped his hat at them and walked away, thankfully turning off his lights before driving off. Colin let himself take a deep breath of relief, however that tight uncomfortable feeling in his chest wouldn't ease up.

Colin folded her in his arms, pressing his lips to her temple. *She didn't leave me. She's here. She came back. She came back...*

Conflicting emotions hit him at once; relief for her safety, anger that she was so remiss that she got on the wrong bus and carelessly leaving her belongings, upset that he almost lost control of his looming anxiety in front of her and the cop.

Desire to punish her for making him be on edge all day.

He pulled away warily, caressing her cheek and preferring not to say anything and led her firmly to his car, opening the passenger door and placing her inside. He leaned into her and kissed her softly, his tongue lashed out, searching deeper. He groaned when she parted her lips for him, and he shivered hard when her hands went to the back of his neck and clutched him to her desperately.

Their breaths sounded loudly between them, and his control almost snapped.

He wanted to crawl on top of her and mount her right there in the passenger seat. Frustrated, he pulled away reluctantly and buckled her in.

Colin rounded to the back of his vehicle and paused, gripping his hands into a hard fist, the tension in his body radiating through him and getting the best of him. He stood there for a long moment, at war with his body, and feeling so out of depth for the first time at almost thirty-nine years old.

Grimacing at the pain in his hand he shook it, walking the rest of the way to the driver's side with ease. Schooling his face into a picture of calm, knowing that he needed her to have him as she knew him, in control, with no room for weakness.

But she was turning into his weakness.

So what the fuck was he supposed to do with that?

On the way home in the dark he called Vanessa, Johnathan, and Mary, letting them know that Olivia was ok and just had a minor incident. He instructed Mary to go home, as she'd stayed behind at the house after her shift just in case Olivia showed up, or she was needed somehow. The woman was thoughtful.

But you do not need to be in the home for what's about to go down.

Johnathan probed him, "You ok bro?" his simple question making him unbelievably pissed off.

Colin bit the inside of his cheek in irritation because the fucker made sure he stayed in therapy every Monday; he didn't want other people probing his feelings and emotions.

He cursed, hanging up on him without answering the question, placing his hand on hers and thumbing the back of her delicate hand. His eyes flickered to hers, seeing her blue veins standing out in sharp relief. At her slight shiver, he turned her seat warmer on before replacing his hand back on hers.

He stayed silent for the majority of their drive. He wasn't positive he even had it in him to reassure her of anything, because how could he reassure her when he couldn't even convince himself he wasn't about to do what he knew he was about to?

"What are you thinking about?" he said gruffly, trying to see where her thoughts were. He didn't turn his head to meet her eyes when he felt her gaze on his profile.

"I... I don't want to be punished for an *accident*," she said to him softly.

His heart skipped a beat.

"I'm not going to punish you. I'm going to bury myself so deep inside you that it's going to *feel* like it, but tonight is not a punishment," he said quietly. Already imagining her scream the first time he thrust his cock inside of her.

Man, I hope it hurts, juuussst enough to calm me down, he thought, rubbing a hand across his jaw and breathing deeply.

His dick swelled against the fly of his zipper, twitching uncomfortably.

Olivia stayed silent.

"Where were you trying to go?" he asked, though, he already knew, he was merely attempting to keep the conversation going to help center his emotions.

His eyes scanned the road ahead as she turned to look at him again, her eyes wary.

"The famous Cathedral on the other side of the city. I was going to take pictures and practice measurements this week. I'm struggling on a specific design.... and I thought it would h-help...I tried to tell you last night on the plane but you were busy, so I just left you alone to work," she replied softly, bringing her hand up again to wipe an errant tear away and sniffing.

Colin squeezed her hand, knowing the small gesture was just that. Small.

He knew she knew that he was barely holding it in.

"Have you been taking your birth control pills every day?" he murmured in a low, level voice, placing an elbow on the driver's door, and stretching out his left leg, desperate to relax his body in any way possible.

He was bent to the breaking point.

Colin spent a precious few seconds breathing deeply, not wanting to scare this woman. In his mind's eye he replayed the red and blue sirens flickering across his office building.

A flashback quickly overtook his mind; sirens reflecting off broken glass littered across the black asphalt as he lay there struggling to breathe after the crash he'd caused when he was sixteen years old. Bodies being carted out in black bags, a child's arm flopping lifelessly as they put him into a bag of his own. His breath burned in his lungs as the memory came back viciously, unable to keep it at bay.

"Yes, every day. Why?" Olivia swallowed hard, feeling his hand stroking hers deceptively soft.

He glanced at her, giving her a wry look.

Turning her face from his sharply, she glanced ahead, her cheeks going pink as his words registered. "We're getting straight in the shower when we get home," he said absentmindedly. "Did you eat while you were out, Amor?"

She looked at him with wide eyes.

"Yes. I had a sandwich... The lady kindly got it for me while we were trying to locate my purse..." Olivia's eyes suddenly welled up as she gritted her teeth to stop a sob from escaping. She hated feeling so small and weak next to him.

"Stop it, please." The amount of effort it was taking to not unleash himself the way he wanted to surely should be worthy of some sort of medal. The noble peace prize maybe?

His own jaw clenched when he figured he could have hauled her back up to his office to fuck. They didn't even have to drive home. He warred inwardly with his sadistic tendencies, forcing himself to consider her feelings, instead of throwing her headfirst into what he knew was going to be an intense sexual relationship.

She doesn't deserve that, though, he thought. *She hasn't had a fuck since she was a teenager. She's sweet, she's special, she's different.*

His sadistic side was winning, however, the more he mused. *But she signed the contract. She knew good and well what she signed up for. You can do whatever you want to do to her. You don't even need a reason to hurt her.*

He shut the direction of his thoughts down quickly. Reminding himself to maintain control.

He wanted her to enjoy everything he did to her, even the pain, and the way he wanted to ruin her. Make her question her very identity when she looked at herself every morning in the mirror, knowing that wanting that was wishful thinking.

"When we get home I want you to go get the shower ready. I'm going to grab a piece of fruit before I come up. I haven't eaten today," he stated, causing her cheeks to go even more pink with shame. "Don't blush. It's not your fault. There's no fucking way I could have eaten, thinking something happened to you."

"That's all you're going to have?" she inquired quietly as she stared at him. "I can warm you up some leftovers for dinner."

Colin didn't reply; the sexual tension thick between them.

When they pulled up to the house, he parked the car in the garage, undoing his seatbelt, and stilled her from opening her car door with a hand tight on her wrist. Olivia's green eyes met his reluctantly.

"I'm going to fuck you all night Olivia. You're all I want. So, no. I don't need dinner," Colin said, his voice deep and husky.

Olivia's breath caught in her throat, excitement causing her pupils to blow wide. He let her hand go and grabbed her bag, following her into the house where he laid her bag on the countertop, and jerked his head in the direction of the home elevator. Not touching her or saying another word.

He'd bit into an apple as she walked slowly to the elevator, slipping inside, and disappearing to the top of the house. Walking into his office, he opened his drawer, taking an anxiety pill even though knowing it was going to prevent him from ejaculating for a long time. He sat there in the light of the lamp on his desk, breathing deeply and silently willing the memories to the back of his mind.

He didn't need this tonight.

Colin came into the bedroom and methodically running through his nighttime routine.

He put their phones on their chargers, turned the house alarm on, starting the fireplace and surround sound. Thinking he wanted to throw her off the usual vibe, he carefully picked a sultry, slow, carefully curated playlist of all men vocalists. A jaw ticked in his cheek while he worked, and his desire mounted high; he was so over being gentle with her.

By the time he'd finished, his cock was swollen painfully tight. Lowering his hand he cupped himself, squeezing hard around the thickness of his shaft.

Taking a deep breath, he stripped himself of his clothes before walking into the bathroom, joining her in the steamy, hot shower.

Olivia had her back to him and was currently rinsing her hair. The wet, dark mass tumbling down her back. She startled, looking over her shoulder when came up behind her, running his hands down her front, and pulling her to him as the first melody of the song started.

"Colin," she spoke hesitantly, tilting her head up to meet his eyes. "I *really* am so sorry I had you worried." She wrapped her arms around herself, her shoulders curled in as she began to cry silently.

Colin turned her to face him, leaning down to take her mouth harshly, placing them both under the spray. He traced her ribcage, firmly pressing his fingers in, feeling how tiny her waist was in the span of his broad hands.

He pulled back.

"Let's get something straight," he said, glaring into her eyes. "I wasn't *worried*," she flinched as he slapped the side of his hand into his palm, the noise echoing around the tile, "I was fucking *sick* thinking that something happened to you. And the only thing saving you from getting your ass completely ripped to shreds tonight is the fact that I'm ready to end this little waiting game between us, and I don't want to scare you. You haven't had a true lover before, that one time *romp* in high school doesn't count. I may be a sadist, but I'm *not* evil. Yes, I have an insatiable appetite, but I'd rather not throw you off a cliff headfirst. I said this to you in the very beginning." He paused, his eyes flickering between hers. "Do we understand each other?" he asked, seeing her eyes growing wider with each sentence.

TWENTY-SIX

Hurts Just Enough

OLIVIA NODDED AS SHE wiped a tear away with a trembling hand. Her crying ceased, being firmly replaced by a flame of desire. She tried to peek down at him curiously, but he stopped her with a finger under her chin, lifting her head back up preventing her from looking at him below his chest.

"*Say it,*" Colin growled harshly, his eyes hard on hers.

The water sluiced off his hair, running down his body in rivulets. The dark hair on his body under the spray enticed her to touch it. He was just so male. Viral. The age difference between them was suddenly glaring, and she licked her lips as she realized that made her even more lustful.

"I understand, sir." Her breath hitched excitedly.

"I'm going to fuck you pretty hard, Amor. Let me know if I start to bother your arm," Colin said, searching her eyes.

Olivia nodded again, her desire amping up to a deep, hot burn incinerating inside her belly, causing her muscles to tremble with anticipation. He took his finger away and stood back, letting her see him for the first time. When her eyes lowered, she went still as a statue, riveted. She swayed as she suddenly became lightheaded.

She was semi-aware that Colin was speaking to her, except she couldn't hear... couldn't process his words. He'd folded his arms, going silent as she blatantly ogled him, unable to do anything but stand there and blink. He could see so many thoughts race through her at once.

Olivia licked her bottom lip before biting it, mesmerized.

His dick was impressive column of flesh. Long, fleshy, and veiny. It hung low and heavy looking, weighted down by its girth. Her sex clenched painfully when a rather desperate whine escaped her throat, scaring her. She glanced up when he snapped a finger at her.

"See something you like, Olivia?" his voice echoed off the tile.

Swallowing hard, she nodded, feeling her ribs contract with each ragged breath she took.

"What was that?" Colin's eyes burned into hers.

She suddenly had a flashback of their first date, the way he sat back in his tailored clothes watching her so sexily over the rim of his liquor glass. His eyes had that same flash, and she became even more aroused; her nipples hardened even more, and she squeezed her legs together to try and ease the ache between them.

She was mentally kicking herself for being so innocent, the past few years being so distracted with killing herself with work, ignoring this magnetic man who'd been pursuing her for over a month while she denied him.

"Yes, sir," she said louder, holding her chin up to meet his hard stare with one of her own. "I don't think it's going to fit, *sir*." she whispered, sucking in a sharp breath of air at imagining him spreading her-

"Is that a challenge, *mama*?" Colin rumbled in his deep voice, his Latin flair thickening his voice. He closed the foot of distance between them.

Olivia shook her head and stepped back the tiniest amount, feeling her heart crawling into her throat at the look on his face. She'd started panting in earnest, her breathing being drowned out by the sudden blood rushing into her head.

"Because it's *going* to fit, Olivia. I wondered what thoughts were going through your innocent little head when I warned you that you were going to be screaming and clawing while you were beneath me." He tsked as he advanced closer, trapping her against the shower wall. "Poor baby, time's up."

Colin's chest met hers at the same time her's hit the shower wall. He planted his hands on the wall on either side of her head, leaning down into her space. Lowering his head, he got eye level with her, his chocolate eyes drilled into hers, the softness gone.

The way she was gasping, almost choking on her breath, made his desire wind tight. He smiled almost tenderly at her.

"I love that sound, baby. It's almost as good as what the real choking is going to sound like," Colin said.

The bass of the song reverberating loudly through the bathroom, and Olivia's knees shook as she tried to hold herself up under his intense stare. Without warning, he lowered his head and took a bite out of the juncture between her neck and shoulder, clamping down hard and shocking her. Olivia cried out as he spent a minute roughly sucking and pulling at her skin before slowly moving up her neck.

She made a pained noise and put her hands to her neck, trying to jerk away, instinctively trying to protect the spot she knew he wanted.

Colin moved quickly, startling her. He slid his hands in her hair and roughly snatching her head to the side before biting down slowly where he wanted and growling deep in his chest.

Olivia squealed, pushing against his chest futilely as Colin persisted, tightening his teeth even harder, and then harder. She jerked, then sagged, moaning long and slow, feeling her sex spasm as she orgasmed weakly.

Colin pulled away slightly to regard her panting and trembling body, helping to hold her up as her knees buckled. His eyes fell to the fresh mark on her neck, and he wet his lips as his blood rushed in his veins, and his chest expand with pleasure. He put his lips to her ear.

Olivia placed her hands to his chest, digging in her nails slightly.

"You like pain I've been noticing. Not many women can come just from having their neck bitten baby. God, I'm going to enjoy making you into my little slut. It's going to be my greatest accomplishment *ever*," Colin whispered in her ear, his hand tightening even more in her hair as he traced the shell of her ear with his tongue.

Olivia's hands went to his shoulders and dug in, her sharp nails making his erection jerk between them.

He bent and picked her up, forcing her to wrap her legs around his hips. He spun them around, slapping his hand against the shower control blindly and turning the water off. She caught a glimpse in the vanity mirror of him carrying her slight frame out of the bathroom and her mouth parted in shock at how erotic they looked. An image she'd never associated with herself before.

Colin carried her to her side of the bed, ripping the blankets down harshly, and laid her down onto her back.

He leaned down to suck the water beads off her breasts, enjoying the little moans of pleasure that erupted from her, and the feel of her fingers sinking into his hair. Pulling away, he turned, putting the digital clock that was on the nightstand on it's face, obscuring the time before casting her a dark look.

"You don't need to worry about time. Do you, baby?" he asked, cocking his head at her, wondering if she caught his hidden meaning.

Olivia's eyes widened as she blinked, slowly shaking her head no.

"Why?" he rasped. "I want to *hear* it."

"Be-because it's not my decision," she replied.

"Bingo. She's learning. None of it's your decision, even if I let you think it is."

He regarded her slowly before crawling up the bed and settling between her legs.

The sounds of the music beat sensually through the speakers as he roughly grabbed her in the bend of her knees, bending her legs back so far her knees were almost touching the mattress by her shoulders. Lowering his hand, he agitated her clit in the way he knew she loved. "God, your cunt is so juicy, baby," he whispered darkly, becoming more excited by the muted, wet sound of his fingers swirling in her flesh.

Olivia arched and moaned, her face pinching tight as Colin spent long minutes carrying her to the edge before flinging her off.

He reveled in her soft cry of orgasm, loving the flush that came over her face and chest as she was pleasured. She reached down and grabbed his hand to still his movements, rolling her hips deliciously for him.

"What's your safe word?" Colin asked, looking down at her flushed face.

Olivia sucked in a breath, making a cute whistling sound. "Bunny," she whispered.

"Say it again. Louder."

"*Bunny.*"

"Now promise me you're going to use it if you need it," he said harshly.

"*Col-sir.*" Olivia cried, rolling her hips.

"*Fucking say it,*" he said, a violent look in his eyes.

Her eyes widened, fighting to stay locked on his. "I promise to use my safe word if I need it, sir," she promised, swallowing hard.

Oh my fucking god, she keened inside her head, mentally crawling to her box that housed those deep feelings, and checked it. She frowned when she realized it was cracked.

Pausing, he lowered his head and bit the sensitive flesh of her inner thigh at the junction at her knee.

Distracted, she'd gasped at the little bite of pain, not realizing he'd lined himself up with the slit of her sex. He nibbled hard, causing her to cry out in shock before he suddenly slammed his hips forward on a guttural grunt, putting all of his weight into his lower back, splitting her apart.

His fingers tightened around her legs as he firmly sank into her before stopping halfway.

"Fucking God," he groaned, his skin immediately misting with sweat.

His breath froze in his lungs, feeling her warm, tight flesh contracting around him, strangling him.

Her mouth dropped open on a wail as she closed her eyes and dug into his forearms with her nails. He waited till she was done, before repeating the movement and pressing himself mercilessly the rest of the way in. Hitting the back of her pussy and then some, grinding deep.

Fresh, shocked screams ripped from her throat. Her nails drew blood this time as they sank into his forearms.

"NO! You're too big," Olivia screamed sharply, panicked.

Her body fell out of control, and she began heaving big panting breaths, crying out his name over and over. Her hands left his forearms and flew to his neck and shoulders, gripping tightly. He turned his head slightly to protect his face as she was attempting to grab at anything to ground herself.

Again, Colin waited till she came to her senses. It took a solid couple of minutes while he prayed for patience.

"Do you need to use your safe word?" he asked, thinking he wouldn't survive it if she did.

She shook her head no, her eyes meeting his. They were dark and wild staring up at him.

Her legs were trembling, and he flexed his fingers, firming up his hold on them, looking down between them and seeing the pink lips of her sex spread wide at his root. He tilted his head, feeling feral, fighting the desire to pound into her straight away.

"There's that sound I've been craving to hear. Your pussy is *divine*." His eyes flicked up, and he waited until her green eyes met his once more before pulling back, grunting as he drove forward on a harsh slap of flesh, jolting her up and down. He gave her a few relatively easy thrusts before speaking.

"When it's like this, and you become sore, crazy with need, out of your mind sensitive, and I still won't stop and give you mercy, I want you to remember that day you were in my office. The way you were signing every fucking thing over to me that was important to you. I *own* you. And right now, I want you to shut your fucking ass up and *take* it. Otherwise, I'll fuck you harder, Olivia. Don't test me," he growled deep in his chest, picking up the pace, spurred on by the sound of their slapping flesh echoing loudly in the room.

Olivia's face tightened with orgasm, and she threw her head back, flinching as he placed his hand over her mouth, muffling her screams.

"Enjoy it. That's the only one you're getting for a long time." He nipped her ear roughly, his hips churning through the hash clasp of her pussy.

Colin fucked her so hard they wound up on his side of the bed.

"Sir, oh my God! *Sir* please slow down." She buried her face into his forearm, just for him to pull her back by her hair.

"You need to come to terms with the fact you aren't in control, Olivia," Colin said, adjusting his knees and feeling his hips settle into a comfortable rhythm. "All you need to concentrate on is learning to take it."

His hands fisted into the mattress next to her, following her up as he repeatedly beat into her flesh, causing her to cry out for mercy. But he wouldn't give her any. He leaned down and licked the sweat off her collarbones, feeling like an animal as he dragged his tongue straight up her neck and settled his teeth on her jaw, stilling her from thrashing her head.

He continued for hours. Edging her. Bringing her to the brink and then back, not giving her the benefit of an orgasm he knew they both needed.

Torturing them both.

Sometime during the night, Colin moved them to the floor of the lounge so he could be closer to the drink's cabinet. He pressed his hips firmly into hers, her legs spread wide. Looking down between them he could see how engorged she was. He wrapped his hand around her throat to keep her still while he made them a drink one handed before hauling her up with a hand around her neck.

She sputtered around the liquid, moaning as it burned going down her throat.

"More," he said, his brow going low as she met his eyes tiredly. Olivia sipped, whimpering when he removed the cups from her lips and placed it to his.

Colin took a deep drink before putting the cup to the side and lowering himself over her once more.

He started off slow, giving her a brief reprieve from being so rough. He groaned as he felt her clench hard around him as the liquor settled into her system. He reveled in each smacking thrust, his pace becoming increasingly faster and more brutal as he began to work her up to what he selfishly prayed was a seriously painful orgasm.

He smacked and squeezed her breasts hard enough to leave red marks.

He lowered his lips to her nipple and took it between his teeth and sharply biting, ignoring her crying out. The floor had no give, and her hips beat hard off the wood as he pounded into her. Just like he'd described when he had her against her apartment door weeks ago.

Olivia tried to keep track of how long it'd been by the songs, but it'd been no use. Colin was an all-encompassing lover and a selfish one she'd found. There was no way to disassociate from him, as he'd notice immediately and shut it down, often becoming more vicious as he used every part of his body to dominate her.

Every muscle was straining to use her body the way he was. The muscles in his arms and chest stood out in sharp relief, betraying his stamina.

Olivia started begging for mercy, and he reprimanded her, giving her sharp slaps to her face, and then more to her breasts which were red and stinging. He sucked them till they hurt, then he used his teeth to make it worse. She burned everywhere; the sensations were as painful as they were pleasurable.

The heady mix of the dueling sensations making her crazy, and there was no relief in sight. She tried manipulating him by crying and was quickly told tears wouldn't help, so she cried for real, and then he started talking to her.

She mentally went inside herself to feel if that box of hurt was staying closed, pressing it deeper into the shadows.

Colin seemed to have this strange ability to tap into that subconscious part of her brain, driving his words straight in and rendering her senseless. The playlist switched and Colin slowed for the next song, removing his teeth from its grasp around her neck, circling his hips deep as he threaded his fingers through her hair and kept her head still so he could look into her eyes. Speaking to her in a sex-rough, deep voice.

"Should you have left without telling me where you were going?"

"No."

"Should you have even *thought* about taking public transportation with no experience?"

"N-No."

"Should you have been so remiss as to leave your purse by accident? Where the fuck was your head, Amor? You're lost, and then lose your belongings at the same time?"

"No, I didn't know." Olivia whimpered with tears in her eyes. "It won't happen again, *sir*."

"You're damn fucking right it won't. Why didn't you ask to take my car?"

"I didn't want to bother you," she whispered, closing her eyes to him and looking away.

That sentence took him back to the point where he ceased all movement and just stared down at her. Her eyes popped open and widened when she realized. There was a tense minute while he just stared at her, and her heart began to pound painfully at the emotion swirling in his eyes.

"I'm adding an extra eight months on our agreed time."

He started thrusting again, the feeling rougher after the slight break.

She looked up at him in shock through the insane mind numbing pleasure as the words processed.

"No wait, Colin! Please no! That's not fair!" her words came out incoherently, sobbing in earnest now.

"Yes. What you did to me today *wasn't fair. Now shut up."*

"But you're talking to me!"

"Oh, so we're back talking, now?"

Olivia squealed as he pulled her hair back and strained her throat so hard, she couldn't talk if she wanted to as she could barely pull in a full breath.

Surprisingly, the pain transformed into something special for her, and her body felt like she was engulfed in flames, same as if he'd poured gasoline and dropped a match on her, lighting her up. She jerked, suddenly orgasming so hard she almost knocked the drink cart over when her arm swung out for stability.

Colin wrapped his arms around her to keep her still as he worked over her relentlessly.

Olivia arched against him hard as he let go of her hair and she threw her head back on a high-pitched scream, feeling her body shatter to pieces. Her eyes squeezed shut as she gasped. Gulping breaths of air that felt like fire in her lungs. Unbeknownst to her she wet everything, squirting everywhere as she orgasmed.

"*Yeeesss,*" he growled, "*breathe* baby. God, you're so fucking gorgeous," he put a hand against her neck, stroking her throat firmly, slowing his pace. Removing his hand, he began slapping her on her arms, her breasts, her hips and thighs, her legs. Everywhere he could reach, scratching that itch he needed.

"Oh my fucking God, it *huuuurrrrtttsss,*" she screamed, trying to curl in on herself but he wouldn't let her, keeping her wide open, unable to close herself of from the sensations.

"It needs to, so you'll always remember. You're such a *good* fucking girl, taking my cock so well," he said to her, his eyes narrowed as her fists beat against him. They grappled with each other's arms briefly and she cried out incoherently, feeling like one delicious throb, still caught up in the wild grip of her orgasm.

"*I caaannnt! I can't take it,*" she cried, her head thrashing.

"You orgasm so strongly for me beautiful."

Pinning her wrists to the floor next to her head, he lowered his mouth to her nipple once more, his incessant sucking making the throbbing between her legs somehow more intense.

The floor was soaked with her juices, and he didn't care. Still giving her those punishing drives.

As the sharp edge of her orgasm faded, Olivia crawled inside her mind. Willing herself to relax and fall into this insane sexual trap that Colin was spinning her into, as if his dominant energy was a tangible web he was weaving. She whimpered at every hard suck of his lips around her nipple, and her legs went limp and she moaned weakly as her pussy spasmed uncontrollably, almost like she was in a constant state of orgasm.

Her feet bobbed in the air with every jolt of her body as he worked relentlessly to get his own. His mouth left her breast and then settled against her lips, sucking and biting at her lips and tongue greedily, groaning loudly and making her feel like the most desirable woman in the world.

A few minutes later he let himself find release within her body with one last harsh thrust. His thick cock spurted deep inside her, and she weakly stared up at his face, breathing harshly as he groaned a pained sound deep in his chest.

He was beautiful as he orgasmed, and seeing the harsh set to his face, she realized how much him fucking her like this cost him physically. She sighed as her body twitched with a weak orgasm again at the feel of his seed spilling hotly inside of her. He buried his head in her neck and they rested like that for a while, utterly spent.

They were both soaked in sweat. Shuddering against each other.

She ran her hands down his back as soothingly as she could. But her fingers were trembling.

After a few minutes, he carried her to the bed, still inside her.

"You did so good baby, I'm so proud of you." Colin took her mouth in a sensual kiss as he rubbed his hands down her body in long, soothing strokes, keeping his gaze on hers while she recovered.

Only when her heartbeat was back to normal, and he was sure she was relaxed, did he disengage himself and settle in the bed next to her with his hand curling possessively on her breast.

TWENTY-SEVEN
As You Are

THE NEXT MORNING, OLIVIA woke up to the smell of fresh crisp air. Her body tightened quickly, and she inhaled in shock. She struggled to make sense of the sensations as they all hit at once.

Closing her tired eyes and moaning, she turned to her side, feeling weighted down and boneless at the same time. She opened them quickly, hearing a sound next to her, seeing Colin regarding her over a cup of coffee. He took another deep swallow, groaning appreciatively before placing the cup on his nightstand and turning his eyes back to her.

"Good morning, beautiful." A slight smirk graced his face as her eyes met his, then flickering away immediately.

He looked refreshed; his brown eyes bright and not so tortured this morning. He sat with his back against the headboard, dressed in dark jeans, and a black t-shirt that showcased his muscles,. His hair adorably mussed. Content to sit in bed and enjoy a cup of coffee.

She narrowed her eyes enviously at him seeing he'd had a shower. She scrunched her nose.

"How long have you been up?" she accused, refusing to meet his gaze as she bristled. More importantly, how was he already up, showered, and dressed after pile driving into her all night. Having the nerve to look refreshed at that.

"Are you ever going to tell me good morning back? What is with you not greeting me?" Colin teased, trying to take some of the tension off her.

Olivia was obviously battling with herself at what happened last night, how thoroughly he fucked her all over the bedroom.

He made a mental note to go to the hardware store and buy something to lock their bedroom drinks cart down. He took another deep drink of his coffee, exhaling at the warmth. Feeling content in more ways than one. He jerked his head towards her nightstand.

Olivia looked over, seeing a bottle of water, her birth control, and some extra strength ibuprofen sitting next to a cup of coffee that was still steaming thanks to being placed on a coffee mug warmer. She glanced at him out of the side of her eye, feeling her face go hot as to why he'd suspect she'd need the ibuprofen.

"Thanks," she whispered, twisting, and popping the pills in her mouth with some perfectly creamed coffee.

Olivia winced as they went down, scratching uncomfortably against her sore throat. She pulled the covers off and went to get up, wincing again for a different reason. She'd looked down and her mouth fell open.

Bruises the size of fingertips dotted her once unblemished skin, blooming bright next to her creamy skin. A smattering of bruises along the top and sides of her knees, on the sides of her hips, a few shadows on her breasts. Her nipples were redder than normal.

She hissed as she pressed into the viscous bite mark on her neck, the skin deeply red and turning dark. Her eyes slowly turned to the full-length mirror across the room, and she saw him staring at her through it, his hooded eyes riveted to the sight of her body.

Olivia blushed furiously, making her way into the bathroom to get away from his assessing stare. Drawing up short, she melted whee she

saw a hot vanilla scented bubble bath drawn. Breathing in the heavy
humidity in the room, she stepped in, moaning in relief as the hot
water penetrated her sore muscles.

"Thank you," Olivia called out to Colin.

"You're welcome."

"God." she whimpered, running her wet hands up and down her
arms, soothing herself.

She soaked for a long time, appreciating that he let her have her
privacy. Feeling uncomfortable with his piercing gaze when she was
feeling so vulnerable.

She turned the jets on in the tub and attempted to mentally tally up
how much time she'd added to their agreement in just the month she'd
been with him. She grimaced, leaning her head back on the rest behind
her. Her eyes turned to the big picture window, seeing a beautiful fall
day through the glass pane, wondering how she managed to live so
long in that windowless basement apartment.

"A penny for your thoughts?" She heard Colin rumble in his deep
voice, having joined her in the bathroom.

He entered the room to put away some sort of spray cleaner under
the cabinet, collapsing the mop and storing that away too. He stood
up, leaning his hips in that increasingly familiar stance against vanity,
his arms and legs crossed as he studied her.

"Were you cleaning? Where's Beth?" Olivia asked, ignoring his
question.

She tightened her lips as he flashed that dazzlingly bright smile,
feeling this man was miles away from the beast that he'd unleashed on
her last night.

Colin rolled his sleeves down, smoothing out the crinkles, not responding right away. He cleared his throat, ended on a deep hum in
his chest, as if he was remembering something delightful. The words

he spoke to her last night echoed in her head, and she blushed deeply, grateful the water hid her shaking hands.

"The floor by the lounge needed to be cleaned, and I moved the drinks cart temporarily. Seems we made quite the mess. I don't want Beth to clean that sort of thing up as it's not exactly in her job description. I'll take care of that for us, usually," he replied simply, his eyes falling to her lips momentarily, a slight smirk on his face.

Olivia blushed in embarrassment, slipping her head under the water. She held her breath until her lungs burned before popping back to the surface, gasping for air. She looked over, blinking water out of her eyes, still seeing him there watching her.

A look passed over his face that he hid quickly. Gone so soon, she almost wondered if she imagined it.

"I was thinking how I managed to stay in a windowless place for so long. It was miserable. Like a prison. And I didn't even realize," she said softly, glancing at him through her lashes. Sighing, her eyes went once more to the big window next to them.

Colin pushed off the vanity and walked to her, squatting down and placing his hand on the side of her head. His eyes roamed her face greedily.

"I'm going to pick you out something to wear," he stated after a few seconds. "We're going on a field trip."

She nodded and then watched quietly as he stood back up and walked out of the bathroom, leaving her alone with her thoughts once more.

Activating the plug to the tub, Olivia awkwardly clambered out and wrapped a towel around her body, moving slowly. Her body's soreness mixing with the relaxation of the bath made her feel like she was moving underwater. Taking her time, she blow dried her hair.

Spraying it and putting it half up and half down, leaving wispy tendrils to frame her face.

Eyeing the dark bruises on her neck and collarbone from Colin's mouth, she contemplated how to cover it.

Dismissing it for a second, she applied a very light makeup to her face, preferring the look that brown mascara afforded her. She carefully gelled her eyebrows, giving her face a very vibrant and fresh look. Miles away from the way she felt from the neck down, and they'd only done missionary.

How was she going to feel when they got to some of the other stuff she'd read?

Wrapping the towel around her body, she ventured off into the bedroom, seeing he'd laid out a beautiful dark blue La Perla lingerie set. Along with a lengthy soft cashmere white turtleneck, and similar dark blue jeans to what he was wearing. Her's fit skintight and showcased her legs amazingly. The turtleneck hung slightly long, skimming her hips.

Pensively looking at herself in the mirror, she'd noticed in surprise that she took on the expensive aura that Colin often possessed, and decided she liked the feeling of the clothes transforming her.

She walked back into the bathroom and applied a very gentle nude pink gloss to her kiss swollen plump lips to finish the look off.

Grabbing her hot coffee, she took it downstairs along with a pair of stylish flats with red bottoms. She padded into the lounge, where Colin was busy flicking through the channels on the television.

Hearing her approach, he spoke over his shoulder, not looking at her. "There are cream cheese bagels with smoked salmon in the kitchen," he said, finding the news channel he wanted and concentrating for a second.

Leaving him to it, Olivia ventured onto the terrace and leaned against the iron railing, noticing that at some point a cover had been placed over the pool. She gazed over his yard again, observing the deep mow tracks in the lush grass and let herself admire the beautiful landscape. The colder weather was slowly turning the white strawberry hydrangeas a deep pink, giving the landscaping a beautiful depth of color against the white house.

Smiling, she pulled her phone out to text her sister, confirming their plans for Sunday.

A pang shot through her. She missed Allison so much.

Though they lived closer, she hadn't been able to do their usual pick up and go to daycare routine. Vanessa had found a better paying job closer to their new home. And under the pressure of Colin, had found a local mother's group who had children who were also dealing with kid medical issues, and had started to integrate play dates into Allison's routine.

Though she was so happy for them both, she missed their routine.

Pulling up her photo app, she picked a video of Allison playing, mesmerized by her beautiful hair. She'd restarted the video, watching it a couple times before she realized Colin had come up behind her silently, watching her. He placed a hand around her waist comfortingly, his fingers grasping slightly at her ribs and rubbing.

"You miss her," Colin acknowledged, not wanting to break her peaceful moment.

Olivia swallowed past the lump in her throat and turned to him with a small smile. "Where are we going?" she asked brightly, with feigned excitement, determined to give Colin his money's worth.

If she was going to sacrifice time with Allison, accept their lifestyle changing, and Colin was going to insist on this agreement and the investment he'd put into her, then she was damn sure going to make sure it was worth it to the best of her ability. He wouldn't want her puttering around his house miserably for the next four years.

Colin regarded her quietly. "I thought we'd go to the cathedral you were trying to see yesterday," he answered her, a slight apology in his eyes at how viciously he knew he'd taken her yesterday. His anger and terror had mixed into such a breathtaking inferno that he couldn't help sucking her into the fires with him. "I wanted to stop at a store and get you a professional camera, it'd be much better than your phone."

She went to open her mouth, but he just hushed her with a look.

"I won't put any extra time on. Think about it as an investment into your future business if that would make you feel better," he said, conceding slightly.

Olivia's mouth twitched. "Okay," she giggled, her earlier sadness easing as she bumped his shoulder with hers as she walked back into the house.

He let her take her Porsche this time, wanting to see how her arm fared while she drove. The look she had on her face as she slid behind the wheel for the first time seared into his brain. He groaned quietly to himself when he became rock hard as she stroked the wheel with both hands. Her slender fingers softly caressing the supple leather.

"*Wow*," she said almost to herself, a goofy smile plastered on her face as she glanced over at him, breathless with excitement.

Colin showed her how to open the garage doors and only had to reprimand her one time for hitting the gas too hard and almost backed into one of his expensive bikes. With his heart thudding anxiously in his chest, he instructed her to continue. Almost thankful for the distraction as it killed his erection but only temporary. However, it came back when she was crawling and laying all over the cathedral trying to get pictures of every inch of the venue.

Colin found she was quite chaotic and beautiful in her element.

He took her for a nice lunch afterwards at a Spanish restaurant. They ate their food, sharing a quiet laugh at a boisterous family of tourist that came in dressed inappropriately for the climate. They both watched in amusement as the tourists fought over the breadsticks, and members of the family teased two teenagers at another table who couldn't keep their lips away from each other.

Olivia caught Colin watching her, giving her a wink as he sipped from his glass of wine. She quickly snatched the bill that the server placed down before he could grab it. Sticking her tongue out at him, she hurriedly placed her card in the sleeve and gave it back to the server.

"Gotta be a little faster than that, *sir*," she said with glee, blowing him a kiss before finishing off her own wine.

Olivia's breath hitched as Colin got up quietly and rounded the table to her. He cleared his throat gently as he pulled out the seat next to her and slid in smoothly. He stretched out his arm and placed it alongside the back of her chair, scooting her closer to him with a smile. However, his eyes told a different story.

Her cheeks stained pink as he leaned into her ear, his deep voice rumbling, scratching across her nerve endings.

"You're going to get it for that, you know that, don't you?" he said softly, placing a kiss on the shell of her ear, his teeth scraped her earring, making a little clanking noise. Olivia's breath hitched as she felt her panties flood, his actions arousing her. He took his wallet out and thumbed out three-hundred-dollar bills, giving it to the waiter as he came back with the receipt for Olivia to sign.

"*Thank you*, sir," the waiter said as he stared at the cash in surprise.

"Don't mention it, man." Colin took the little black wallet from Olivia and grabbed the pen, scratching out the tip section and writing his name in the signature line.

Olivia blushed furiously, pouting.

"Let's go," he said, getting up and pulling out her chair, giving the tourists a little wave as they stared unashamedly at them.

It seems like they had put on quite the show of their own.

Colin wrapped his arm around her waist and walked her to the Porsche, holding the passenger door open for her, taking the time to adjust himself discreetly. They were quiet on the way home, both simmering in the sexual tension building between them.

TWENTY-EIGHT
Don't Give Up

"*SHRRRR*." OLIVIA'S EYES ROLLED into the back of her head as she arched hard.

Her moan crescendoed into a sharp scream as she felt Colin's teeth latch onto the sensitive flesh of her calf and bite down sharply as his hips slapped rhythmically against hers, her new Porsche rocking hard with their movements.

Whimpering and shuddering, her breath froze in her lungs as she bit her lip to stop another cry from escaping. They were back at the house, in the garage.

Letting go of her calf, Colin groaned and pressed his forehead into Olivia's, panting heavily.

"You going to be a brat again? Huh?"

"No!" she chocked out, tensing up.

He unwrapped his hand from the door where he'd gripped it, and wrapped his fingers around her throat, still thrusting and circling between her legs. He worked her hard, rubbing out every inch of come and pleasure.

Colin listened enraptured to her whimpers. Knowing her pussy was sore. Knowing he should have eaten her out instead of taking her like a damn animal in the back of her car because he couldn't even wait for them to get into the house. But fucking her tender pussy like this so soon after ravishing her the way he did was too much of a temptation to resist.

He'd rounded her car after Olivia parked carefully at home and snatched her up, throwing her into the backseat before ripping her shoes and jeans off. He crawled between her legs, shoving up her sweater and ripping her new lace bra in his haste to get to her naked skin. She'd hissed as he latched on tightly to her nipple and didn't let go the entire time he was beating into her flesh.

Her nipple and breasts now sported fresh teeth marks.

He'd been spurred on by the wet suctioning sounds of her pussy gripping him, and the slapping sounds of his hips meeting hers repeatedly, not able to be gentle. Even after last night.

Consumed by lust, he hooked one of her legs around the passenger seat and her other foot around the backseat headrest, and then yanked her hips down, making her spread impossibly wide for him. Ignoring her wild screaming that echoed throughout his garage as he fucked her harder than he did last night, taking full advantage of her splayed body. He pressed deep, circling and gyrating his hips.

Colin leaned down to her nipple once more, giving it a rather harsh nibble before tugging it away from her body and letting it pop out of his mouth. Refusing to finish, he met Olivia's eyes while he roughly licked the tip with long slow laps, waiting for them both to relax before he let them up. He fastened his jeans, grabbing her new camera bag and purse as she started pulling her clothes back on, cursing as he was still hard.

"Leave them off," Colin ordered, closing the door and giving her a hard look as they walked into the house.

He set the bags down before picking her up and depositing her on the island briefly, ripping off her sweater and bra, and pushing his jeans down below his hips. Picking her up with his arms under her legs, he reveled in her excited shout as he firmly jammed her back onto his cock. He gritted his teeth as he had to work hard to push through her swollen and abused muscles.

His own muscles bunched and contracted as his arms lifted and dropped her fluidly, roughly onto him.

"God, your cunt is so *sweet*, baby," Colin praised, gripping her hips as he stared into her face, drinking in her look of pure bliss.

Out of the corner of his eye, he saw Beth come around the corner to see what the noise was before her eyes widened, and she did a smooth pivot, quietly retreating quickly back the way she came. He made a mental note to give her a bonus on her next check.

He chuckled when Olivia suddenly jerked in his arms, trying to recoil away from him as he fucked her through the shock of what sounded to be a rather hard orgasm.

She was throbbing around him, and he became drunk with the feel of it. His body burned with the need to make up for the weeks of denying himself her body, unwilling to let go of the lush confines of this woman no that he had her.

He fucked her a while more there in the kitchen, holding himself back. Waiting until she'd succumb to another orgasm before walking them to the elevator. He whisked her upstairs and to their bedroom, where he spent most of the afternoon fucking her with his cock, his fingers, his mouth. She began to beg for him to cease, her face pink, her voice hoarse, and her hair sticking to her face.

Satisfied, he finally orgasmed himself before letting her up.

"You're not going to let an old man outlast you, are you?" Colin said to her teasingly as they lounged on the bed. He reached over, checking his phone to see that Mary had texted him that she had made dinner, and had left a bit early.

"*Whatever*. I guess it's true you've had years of practice. *Many*, in fact," Olivia replied, slithering off the bed slowly.

"Trust you're going to reap the benefits from all that practice." Colin chuckled as he watched her wobble her way to the closet, her hair wet and stringy in places against her head from him having fucked her yet again for a couple hours straight. "Mary's gone. Put a nightgown on so we can go downstairs and eat dinner," he called out after her, replacing his phone on the nightstand before getting up himself.

He padded to the bathroom on bare feet, feeling a slight burn in his abdomen and lower back, making another mental note to add more back exercises to his workout routine. He snagged a brush and took it to her in the closet, finding her pawing through the nightgowns.

"They're all mostly see through," Olivia muttered in a displeased tone.

She froze, wincing slightly as Colin began brushing out her hair softly, feeling the coolness of her sweat on the strands. She stood there jarred, her eyes suddenly pricked with hot unshed tears. Her shoulders hunched before she recoiled away from him.

"S-*Stop*, Colin. Stop it!" Olivia whispered, her heart constricting. She reached her hand back and grabbed the brush, surprising him as she whipped around suddenly with tears in her eyes. "Please don't do that." The tears slicked down her face as his clouded with concern.

"What's wrong, baby?" Colin asked, his brow furrowing in concern.

They stared at each other for a tense minute while she wrestled internally. She was torn, not sure how much of herself she wanted to reveal to him. The more she revealed, the more attached she was going to get, and she wanted to make it out of the agreement in one piece.

Closing her eyes briefly against the sudden sickening realization that she probably wasn't going to.

For the first time, she regretted signing the agreement.

This man was getting too close to her heart. Her breath hitched as another tear dripped down her face and she inwardly crawled inside her head, bowing her body over that box she kept so neatly tucked away. A pained whimper escaped her throat at her vulnerability. Her lips quivering as she stood there shifting her weight from foot to foot, wanting to flee.

"Hey, hey, hey! What's happened?" Colin whispered, placing his hand against the side of her face and wiping her tears away. She jerked back, slapping her hands across her face, roughly scrubbing the tears off. His own eyes narrowed at her harsh response. *"Olivia?"*

Closing herself off, she threw the hairbrush suddenly on the island and turned, ripping a sweater dress off a hanger and yanking it on, not bothering with putting a bra or underwear on.

"I need some air," she snapped.

"Can you please just tell me *what happened*?" he snapped back, running his hand through his hair. *"Olivia*? Please don't run," he pleaded, placing an arm on her chest of drawers.

She turned, her green eyes narrowing. He raised a haughty eyebrow at her as she walked the two feet to get into his face. His eyes turned stormy as he regarded her.

"I signed that agreement in exchange for a kinky sexual relationship with you... in exchange for *money*, because my niece and sister desperately needed it. Not to spill every damn emotion and secret I have. Leave me alone, I said *no*," she hissed at him.

Bending to grab a pair of sandals, she shoved her feet in them.

"I'm going on a walk in these fucking *ridiculous* sandals. Wasteful. You can adopt nine freaking children with how much money is in this room!" She nastily threw the words over her shoulder as she stomped out of the door.

"You don't have any underwear on!" Colin yelled, pissed at how she'd so easily closed herself off from him. Shutting him out.

He glanced at the brush, his eyes narrowing as he heard their bedroom door slam rather roughly. He cursed, going after her, wrenching the door open and seeing an empty hallway but she was already gone.

Walking to the spare bedroom, he looked out the window at the front drive, seeing her walking towards the long drive. She was curled in on herself, head bowed, hair whipping in the chilly wind. He closed his eyes, gripping the back of his neck hard, struggling as to what do to with this woman who seemed to be just as hurt and damaged as he was.

Thinking about her snapping at him in the closet, his eyes narrowed. Her mouth was nasty.

Apparently, she bit hard when she felt cornered.

Can I blame her for wanting to hold on to pain when I haven't let my own go? Talk about being a hypocrite, Colin chastised himself.

He walked quickly back to the closet, roughly pulled his clothes back on before going downstairs into his study, He grabbed his laptop and slid on his glasses., walking into the formal dining room that had the view of the drive. He placed it on the table and sat facing the window, groaning as he rubbed a rough hand down his face.

He was pissed that she'd walk out on him after he was worried about her for hours yesterday, but understanding that something triggered her, and he needed to allow her space.

Even if he didn't want to.

Forcing himself turn his attention to the upcoming holidays, he contacted a lighting company and scheduled work for Halloween, Thanksgiving, and Christmas.

He loved the holidays despite not having any family to celebrate with, and he found solace in decorating his home. He got a natural high off pulling up to his home and seeing everything that he'd accomplished with his life, knowing how hard he'd worked to redeem himself from the accident that changed his life when he was sixteen years old.

It wasn't always this way; it took years of therapy to settle him enough to be able to be normal.

He used to sit at home, numbing his pain until Johnathan found out and threatened to pull him from their business deal if he didn't enroll himself into a mental health program. He even had to sign a release of information so Johnathan could occasionally check in to make sure he was following through what he said he'd do.

Colin was proud of his growth, but suffered from occasional nightmares that were debilitating. He was diagnosed with PTSD from the accident that left a family of five dead, and him alive. His eyes flickered briefly from the screen to the window, seeing the sun almost finished setting.

His anger flared up, and he truly debated grabbing his bike and going out and looking for Olivia when he saw her petite form walking back up the long drive. The white sweater dress molded to her perfect legs as the wind whipped it against her body. He observed her movements carefully.

When Olivia got closer to the house, she looked up and saw Colin at the table, the glow of his laptop reflecting in the window.

Their eyes locked, and he could tell she'd been crying hard as her eyelashes were wet and her nose was red. His heart pulled, but still he made himself sit, needing her to come to him. Needing to feel that trust between them that only she could reveal. He wasn't going to make her, even though he was within his rights to do so technically if he wanted.

He wasn't going to push in that way.

If she'd allowed him to do what he wanted with her body, he could at least give her the safe space for her emotional autonomy.

After what felt like forever, Olivia resumed walking to the front door, opening it and closing it softly. Her lithe form appeared in the big frame of the dining room, just off the foyer. He took his glasses off with a deep breath, sliding the chair back to face her, and sank deeper into the seat, spreading his legs slightly, waiting.

Colin met her stare calmly, willing her silently to be the first one to speak.

Come on baby. Please. Give me an inch, something to work with, Colin thought, but he just sat there unmoving. Relaxed in the chair, the tip of his glasses in his mouth.

Her face pinched as she bit her lip, a sob breaking through, and she advanced the few feet to him, closing their distance. Olivia sank to her knees and placed her head on his thigh, sobbing. The scent of sex mixed with crisp fall air surrounded him, enveloping him in a comforting cloud.

Surprised and delighted at the submissive gesture initiated by her, Colin stayed quiet.

Instinctively knowing he didn't need to talk, just to let her cry.

He placed his warm hand on her head, her shiny red hair chilly from the air, and stroked her steadily. Lending her his strength as she let it out. Her arms went around his waist, and she snuggled into him even closer, her tears now wetting his shirt.

Still, he stroked her hair, waiting. Unwilling to push this woman, who had obviously been through so much that God only knew what hurt she'd hid away deep inside. A place he was determined to crawl his way in and share in with her. However, knowing if he exercised his control and force those secrets from her, she would never forgive him.

Emotionally, this would have to be on her terms.

He decided then and there to always be her emotional safe space.

Colin made a soft sound and his chest tightened painfully as he realized he loved this woman too soon. And that was the true reason he hadn't wanted to have sex with her right away.

He stiffened when his mom's words suddenly echoed in his brain. "A man always knows when it's love. It doesn't take long, mijo." she'd said when he asked her about love ater he'd had his first date. When he realized he wasn't normal sexually like the other boys.

Putting that memory away, he concentrated on the woman at his feet.

Olivia sniffled, looking up at him as raw pain etched her features, plain as day for him to read. "My mom," she whispered.

He put his glasses down to lean forward and press his lips to her forehead, breathing in her scent. "Yeah?" he said quietly. "Tell me about her."

"She was the last person to brush my hair. Mom did my hair every single morning and at night before bed. She used to put my hair up in pigtails and called me Pippy Long Stockings. Sh-she was so *proud* of my hair. Proud of *me*." Her voice cracked as her haunted eyes stared up at him, swimming in tears that seemed like would never end.

He cocked his head at her and nodded slightly, willing her to continue.

"After she died, I never let anyone else brush my hair again. I felt like that was the only thing tying me to her after her death." Olivia paused, taking a deep breath, shuddering at the force of the memories. "The night her and my dad were killed by a drunk driver was my homecoming dance for high school. She had done my hair in this elaborate style." A wince of pain flashed across her features as she bit her lip, going quiet for a second. "Mom and dad decided to go on a rare date when it happened... the accident."

Colin made a soft encouraging sound and placed his hand on her cheek, pressing gently, his eyes softening.

"And I kept my hair like that until their funeral. I know it was silly but... I wanted her to feel like *she'd* done my hair for such an important ceremony. I looked absolutely horrible, but it was the last gift I could ever give her," Olivia said, her head once more falling to his lap.

Her tears ceased.

"Come here, baby." He leaned forward, grasping her under her arms and pulling her up to him. Her legs curled under and she slumped against him as he held her tight, giving her space and warmth before he spoke.

"I know that was hard to share...I'm so thankful you trusted me enough to tell me. I apologize for triggering you; I never would have done it if I'd known. I hope you know that," he said deeply in his smooth voice, pleased when he felt her tiny nod under his chin.

"Thank you," she whispered.

He stayed there like that with her, stroking his hand down her back and side with one hand and holding her hand with his other.

She eventually stirred, tilting her head up to look at him, resting her head against his shoulder.

"I miss my mom too," Colin said softly, giving her a reassuring smile.

She blinked at him in surprise. "Yeah?" she whispered, her eyes flickering between his.

"Yes. Every day I think about her. Miss her. Wish I could hear her voice."

Colin placed his hand on Olivia's neck, his thumb caressing the vein there, just looking at her. Feeling his heart squeeze painfully.

Acknowledging that he had the feeling, he just didn't know if he was ready, despite years of therapy. He barely knew her, but she called to him that night he was out in the storm and ready to end it all over guilt. He'd caught a glimpse of her red hair in the window of the diner, drawing him to her like a candle.

A moth to a flame and Jesus, he scared of being burned.

"Are we okay, now?" he asked quietly, not breaking her eye contact. Olivia nodded slowly and he swallowed before pressing. "Would you like me to help you with brushing your hair?" His fingers still stroking slowly, but firmly. "You let me blow dry these gorgeous locks... that's a little trust between us starting right there, right?"

It wasn't lost on him that she'd let him touch her hair, blow dry it, and even pull it during sex. But the boundary was drawn firmly as to brushing and manipulating the strands. He'd wanted her to know that he'd recognized the difference, that he paid attention to things like that. That he cared about her to consider her in that way.

Colin knew from therapy that triggers really had no definite rhyme or reason, and he stored this away in his brain as he waited for her response. She held his stare. A heartbeat... ten heart beats... twenty...

"Yes," Olivia said softly. "I can try, but I won't promise anything."

He nodded his head, understanding immediately.

Olivia rose off his lap, clearly embarrassed at being vulnerable. He smiled gently up at her before standing up.

"Can I show you something?" she asked, back to being shy.

He nodded. "Anything you want."

He followed her upstairs and back into their closet, where she reached into the top drawer in her chest that housed her clothes, and pulled out a small bottle of cologne, and a handkerchief.

"This was daddies," she whispered, a sad look passing her face as she pressed the handkerchief to her nose and closed her eyes. "It used to smell like him before the scent finally faded. Vanessa and I searched everywhere for this cologne, and we could never find it. We gave up looking about three years ago, and the night that man came in the karaoke bar to proposition Vanessa was the first time we've smelt *him* since the scent on either of our handkerchiefs faded."

Her words dissipating, she handed him the piece of cloth.

Colin gripped it tightly as his eyes suddenly stung with tears.

He thought about his mother and how he would give up all of his wealth for the opportunity to smell her one more time. To have one more hug, share one more laugh, hear one more word from her lips. He held the cloth to his nose appreciatively, vowing to buy her a hundred cologne bottles so she'd never have to feel like he did.

The pain of grief was debilitating sometimes, and he didn't want her to suffer in this way.

"Your father had good taste," he said, smiling at her.

"Yeah, he sure did," Olivia smiled fondly.

She took the cloth back from him and carefully wrapped it around the cologne bottle and placed it gently amongst her belongings. Unbeknownst to her, inside the recesses of her mind, the lid on her box of hurts tumbled off.

"Let's eat dinner. How's your arm? Do you think you're up for playing a little game of pool later?" he asked, wanting to do something fun with her to break up the tension and put a smile on her face.

"I'm shit at pool," she giggled, turning and leading the way out of the closet.

He slapped her sharply on her ass. "I'll be the judge of that."

She was in face shit at playing pool and he teased her mercilessly about it, unashamedly.

Happiness tightened his chest as he beat her game after game, seeing her determination and her drive to not give up. The feeling caressed over his skin like a soothing balm and that night, they went to bed, limbs entwined as they talked intimately.

Not having sex, but sharing a different level of intimacy instead.

TWENTY-NINE
Can't Be Good At Everything

THE NEXT COUPLE OF weeks ran by quickly. Colin worked longer hours trying to prepare for the holidays, sometimes bringing Olivia along, and sometimes she stayed at home depending on her mood.

The lighting company Colin hired set up orange lights all over the exterior of the house. He'd paid to have huge blow-up pumpkins on the property, along with an elaborate pumpkin decoration at the front gate, fountain, and the front door. It cost, but he felt it was pretty.

He took her home late that night, wanting to surprise her with the decorations while it was getting dark.

He'd waited for Mary's text, informing him the decorators were done before he took her home. Not able to help himself, he recorded her reaction as they pulled up on the property.

She squealed with excitement, laughing hard at the monstrous blow up monsters and pumpkins. She'd launched herself at him in joy as they drove slowly up the drive. His eyes sparkled with amusement as he took her phone out as they got out of his SUV, stepping into his arms and sharing a slow sweet kiss with him.

They both laughed as they recording them kissing with all the decorations in the background of their video.

Colin picked Olivia up, setting her on the hood of his SUV kissing her soft, warm lips.

Feeling her curves pressed against his body, he almost said he loved her. Yet, he stopped himself, still probing this new feeling of his. The first time he knew that he truly felt it in his adulthood. He buried his face in her hair and inhaled her unique scent, trying to shut down these feelings that plagued him, scared him...

Made him feel alive.

***

A week and a half later, Vanessa, Allison, and Johnathan all came to the house to dress for Halloween. They planned to take Allison trick or treating in Colin's neighborhood and Johnathan was especially excited, wanting another chance to be around Vanessa. The poor man had caught some serious feelings for the curvy, fiery redhead.

Olivia caught him staring at Vanessa on multiple occasions, looking quite lovesick.

They were all currently crammed into the primary bathroom where Vanessa was helping with Johnathan's costume. He'd dressed up as the joker and required a lot of green makeup, causing Colin to threaten him with an additional renovation bill if the green shit didn't come out of his vanity.

He'd hit him across the shin with his expensive cane, causing Olivia to roll her eyes at Vanessa, mumbling "billionaire problems" causing the men to cast a narrow-eyed gaze at them instead of fighting each other.

Olivia donned as a woman's costume version of Chucky the killer doll, complete with the wild hair style that took a whole can of hair spray to accomplish. Vanessa dressed up as Anne of Green Gables with a straw hat and basket of books. Colin chose to step out as Robin hood, and he topped off the look with an expensive bow and arrow set.

He smiled when Olivia slowly raked her gaze down his form with a seductive look in her eyes. He knew he looked devilishly handsome, and her approval did much to stroke his ego.

Allison was dressed as Pippy Long Stockings, and Olivia was currently braiding her hair with a small smile on her face. Colin knew she was thinking of her mother at that moment, and in a quick motion that no one noticed, he snapped a picture of them together.

They took a golf cart instead of walking, mindful of Allison's illness, and the huge distances between properties.

A couple that lived on a property a few homes over wanted to take a picture of Johnathan and Olivia. Colin got a kick out of Johnathan raising Olivia over his head as she brandished her fake bloody knife in the air screaming with terror, afraid he was going to drop her.

After taking another snapshot of them all posing together as their respective characters two hours later, they made their way home.

They made out like a bandit with candy, tossing it all on the kitchen island and divvying up the proceeds. Colin disappeared to the patio to start the fireplace and heat lamps, and Vanessa disappeared to put Allison to bed.

Johnathan, Colin, and Olivia went upstairs to shower off their costume makeup and get changed into comfortable pajamas before reconvening on the patio. Each of them spreading out on the plush patio couches. Colin noticed that Johnathan and Vanessa were getting rather cozy, and she was leaning back on his shoulder, sharing the Hermes blanket from Colin's lounge.

Olivia leaned back against Colin as he stroked her damp hair. He wished she'd let him blow dry it before they went back downstairs, but she didn't want to keep them waiting. They made her in charge of picking a slasher movie, as she dressed like the most violent character to dress up as.

She reluctantly picked a scary one, not wanting to seem like a chicken. Colin noticed Vanessas' side eye and small smirk before she burrowed deeper into Johnathan and the blanket.

They both watched as Vanessa sighed contentedly, sipping from a glass of wine and taking a small bite of candy. Olivia checked the baby monitor she'd set up for Allison, making sure it was turned up before the movie started.

Johnathan silently motioned for Colin's attention, prompting him to check his phone.

> Hey bro, do you mind if I stay over and Vanessa and I use one of the spare bedrooms again? -J.Dawg.

Colin glanced up sharply.

> "Bro, I will fucking kill you if you damage my room again. The shit cost 9 grand to fix the damn room." -C. Kent.

Jonathan flipped him off secretly as he texted him back on his phone.

> Why are you acting like you don't like spending money, bro? Besides, I paid you back, didn't I?-J. Dawg

Colin rolled his eyes, jostling when Olivia's elbow dug into his ribs. He grunted softly, waiting for her to settle before he tapped out a response.

> Whatever man, can you just keep Vanessa quiet this time? You know what, just use the guest house please. And don't touch ANY of

my equipment. We will keep an eye on Ally tonight. -C. Kent.

Johnathan nodded his head.

Colin put the phone down as Olivia suddenly gasped and jumped so hard she almost tipped her drink on him. He'd caught her in surprise, glancing over at Vanessa, who was laughing her ass off at them. Her grey eyes sparkled in delight as Olivia suddenly started crying, making him look at her in alarm. He turned furious eyes on Vanessa.

"You're literally not going to sleep for the next three years," Vanessa gasped, gulping down her wine. "She's *terrified* of scary movies." She giggled, leaning back again against Johnathan with a self-satisfied smirk.

"Oh that's wonderful, because I wasn't expecting us to sleep much anyway," Colin said as he grinned down at Olivia. The comment broke through the fear momentarily and made her smile.

"And you can't send her to my house when you can't get her to sleep either." Vanessa shot over at him, grinning wickedly.

Such a lovely big sister, Colin thought, shaking his head at her.

Turns out, Vanessa hadn't been exaggerating.

Olivia was curled up into a ball on top of him by the end of the movie, her arms wrapped hard around his shoulders and her face was buried as deep as she could get in his neck, not able to get any closer. Colin didn't mind. He got to feel her boobs squished against him, content to lose sleep for that.

They finished the night watching a rom com show to calm Olivia down and get her mind off the movie. At the end, they' bid Vanessa and Johnathan goodnight, and snagged the baby monitor.

Colin waggled his eyebrows suggestively at Vanessa, causing her to blush and hurry into the house with Johnathan following closely behind.

Olivia and Colin brushed their teeth together before crawling in bed. He chucked with amusement when she'd moved all the way to his side. She ended up sleeping almost under him and making him balance on the edge of the mattress. Colin tamped down the slight irritation, kissing her before silently moving to her other side, settling in the middle of the bed.

He drifted off too, soon after he got comfortable. However, he woke up around four in the morning, restless, and noticed the bed was empty and the door was open.

Sitting up, he realized the bathroom was empty too. Pulling on his sweatpants, he'd padded down the hallway, seeing the bedroom Vanessa and Allison usually slept in with the door open. He walked in slowly, seeing Olivia curled around Allison, fast asleep. Her lips were pressed against her temple, her arm thrown across the little girl's body.

They were snuggled deep in the covers, the glow of the night light illuminating their red hair faintly.

Colin smiled and backed out gently, closing the door. Crawling back into bed, he turned up the baby monitor to full volume before falling back to sleep.

***

The next morning, Olivia and Colin were downstairs with Allison, making a full non-pork breakfast. A kids playlist was playing over the surround system when Vanessa came through the side door, Johnathan right behind her.

His brows raised, seeing the both of them looking a little worse for wear.

Colin was taking a sip of coffee in his usual stance against the counter, staring as they'd settled on the stools at the island.

"Good morning sunshines. Sleep well?" he said over the rim of his coffee cup, holding back a chuckle by clearing his throat.

Vanessa moved gingerly, biting her lip as she carefully settled against the seat. He laughed to himself silently and kept the coffee cup to his lips as he sipped. Truly terrified to lower it and embarrass the couple. He was hopeful he'd get a chance to really rib them one day soon without Allison present.

He noted Johnathan's stiff movements and lowered his brow.

"Yo', is my guesthouse okay? Anything broken?" Colin suddenly inquired, his eyebrow raising in concern for his possessions.

Olivia looked over at him, amused.

"Man, I'll just write you a check, alright? We don't need to always *talk* about it," Johnathan responded, accepting a cup of coffee from Colin wearily.

Jesus, Colin thought. *What'd they do to my shit?*

He turned his attention to Olivia, who was studiously making Allison's plate at the stove. Her shoulders were hunched, and she was making little breathy sounds trying not to laugh. He chewed the inside of his lip hard as she turned and hurriedly placed the plate on the counter in front of Allison, then swung back around to face the stove again.

A hilarious giggle escaped, and she slapped her hand over her mouth quickly. Her shoulders shuddered as she pulled down several more plates to sit next to the stove.

He couldn't help but to let out a little chuckle at her antics, which caused her to burst out laughing. She squatted down and pressed both hands against her mouth, trying to stem her sounds. Her face was bright red and tears were rolling down her face.

Colin held his coffee cup up to his mouth, and laughed properly now at the sight, causing her to give up and fall on her back, laughing hard. She grabbed her stomach and pulling her knees up to her chest, gasping for breath.

"What's wrong with Auntie Ollie, momma?" Allison asked, ripping her gaze from her tablet and rising on the stool to look at Olivia.

"She's a *biatch*," Vanessa breathed quietly; Allison was no longer paying any attention to her.

Colin let her exhaust herself before bending down to grasp her hand and help pull her up. "It's funny, isn't it?" he said, still chuckling.

Olivia nodded, unable to speak, swiping tears from her eyes. She took a deep breath and finished plating their food, ignoring Vanessa's embarrassed scowl.

"That's what you get for making fun of me last night," she whispered, sliding the plate to Vanessa and winking.

They ate breakfast together, discussing Thanksgiving plans. Vanessa suddenly looked at Colin in horror, and shook her head at him when Olivia happily announced that she was going to cook. He raised a questioning eyebrow at her, and she motioned his phone discreetly.

Seriously, what's with them and these phones? he mused, pulling up his text and seeing she sent the message as an S.O.S. Which he got a real kick out of. He took a bite of eggs as he read it.

> Colin do NOT let her cook. -Nessie.

Smiling slightly around his bite of food, he replied.

> Why not? It's just turkey, basically a roasted chicken. What could go wrong? -C

Please, please just listen to me. Cater something and store it in one of your refrigerator's downstairs. When she's not looking, I'll help you swap the whole meal out secretly. Just please listen to me. -Nessie

...come on, are you trying to get me killed? -C

No, it's *you* who's going to an early grave if you let this woman cook. Do not let her cook. Pay Mary a retainer or something for the holiday cooking. I'm so serious. Please don't do this to us. -Nessie

I gotta give her a chance if she's going to truly ever like me. -C

Like you? That ship sailed long ago, my friend. Cater. The. Fucking. Thanksgiving. Dinner. Bitch. -Nessie.

You need your mouth washed out with some soap, Ma'am. Is 'bitch' your favorite cuss word or something? I'll teach you how to curse in Spanish, it'll sound prettier. My God. -C

Colin put the phone down and shot her an incredulous look. Johnathan roared with laughter, having read the text exchange over Vanessa's shoulder. Colin's eyes narrowed slightly as he began to really pay attention to their interaction.

Olivia, who had been talking to Vanessa and Johnathan about a new recipe she wanted to try this year, was oblivious to the secret exchange.

Johnathan was nodding at her intently, his usual humorous self feigning ignorance. He politely asked Olivia questions about what she normally cooks for the holiday, because he needed everything to be 'halal,' of course. Vanessa chuckled under her breath and rolled her eyes, doing a better job at hiding her laughter than her sister had.

Then Olivia said something absolutely atrocious that made Colin frown and Johnathan's eyebrows raise on a slight head tilt, and he pulled up his text quickly again.

> Hell no, we aren't eating that. Send me the company you usually use. -C.

Vanessa broke out in peals of laughter. Stemming it quickly, she took a huge bite of food and glanced at him with humorously big eyes. He leaned forward and kissed Olivia on the side of her head, giving her ass a firm pat.

Can't be good at everything, he thought to himself, finishing his coffee.

THIRTY

Threats All Through

THE WEEKEND WENT BY in a blur, and Olivia spent a few days at the home while Colin worked from the office. She spent her free time swimming laps in the pool, trying to strengthen her arm more.

She didn't even complain when Colin added extra safety monitors, wanting to be able to check from his phone to make sure she didn't injure herself and drown while he was gone. She'd spent her days swimming laps, and then going upstairs and practicing making focaccia bread with Mary, finding solace in decorating the bread.

She surprised Colin one day when he'd come home from work with a gorgeous bread design, kissing him senseless when he came into the kitchen.

Colin felt at peace for once in his life and found himself relaxing more. Enjoying Olivia's company and the lack of anxiety that had been his ever-present companion since he was sixteen. He spoke with his therapist about how he felt settled, and went through his days feeling almost like a new person.

Day by day Olivia found her initial anxiety over their arrangement easing, but also finding that this new peace brought time to think. And when she had time for her thoughts, she ruminated on the past. About her parents, Vanessa and Allison's situation.

Giving up a grueling schedule for four years, she wasn't used to having so much free time.

Colin came home one time to her in the attic dusting. Another time to her having all his car doors open, and detailing each one. She'd begun to fall asleep on top of her architectural studies due to wearing herself out during the day. He wore her out further by making love to her most nights a week. Though she orgasmed, he'd got the niggling feeling that something was wrong.

He just couldn't put his finger on it.

One day, he came home, and Mary pulled him to the side in his study.

The older woman looked at him with raised eyebrows.

"Sir, she's cleaning *everything*. I've caught her cleaning multiple bedrooms and their bathrooms this week, and today she was polishing the leather seats in the *media room*. Yesterday she was scrubbing the grout in the mudroom with a toothbrush! I don't feel right accepting a paycheck if I'm not even able to do my job," Mary said softly, placing her hand on his arm. "Something is bothering her, *mijo*."

He leaned against his desk, regarding the house manager who'd been like a mom to him for the last ten years.

"*Mary*," Colin said affectionately, giving her a grin. "You know I'd pay you even if all you did was come sit in the house. Come on." He laughed before turning serious. "I'll talk to her."

"Mijo, you know I stay out of your business, but I've come to care very deeply for Olivia. I hope you aren't doing anything that... affects her. Colin. Women are sensitive creatures."

Colin smiled at her kindly.

"Thanks for the advice, Ma. I'll handle it. Don't worry, please. I'll talk to her."

"Okay, Mijo. I can't walk in on her cleaning anything else. I'll scream," she joked, giving him a wide smile and walking out of his study.

He followed shortly after, walking through the house until he found Olivia in the gym, walking on a stair master. He watched her briefly through the glass door before walking in.

"Hey beautiful. How long you been on that thing?" he asked conversationally.

He studied her, observing she was drenched in sweat.

She threw him a little smile before she huffed out a breath. "An hour, almost," she said with difficulty.

"Well, then that's more than enough. This is a stair master, not a treadmill," Colin rebuked her sternly, tamping down his rising irritation.

Olivia bit her lip as he leaned forward and punched the stop button, bringing the machine to a halt. She hopped off before bending into a deep stretch, stretching her quads and calves. He waited patiently until she was done.

"Olivia, what's going on with you?" he asked softly, turning to prop himself against a weight machine.

"What do you mean?" she asked, taking a towel and wiping her face and neck. Her breasts were heaving, the material of her tank top clinging to her curves indecently.

"I mean exactly what I said. What's going on with you? And I want an honest explanation as to why you've been breaking your body down doing unnecessary things. Like dusting the attic. That's not normal Olivia." He folded his arms.

Olivia snorted, turning to sit on one of the steps on the machine. "And neither is being a billionaire. Yet, here we stand." she said cheekily.

A muscle ticked in his jaw. She stared at him silently, challenging him.

"Kneel at my feet right now. I see you've forgotten your place," he said sternly, holding her gaze as she slowly get onto her knees.

"Sex between us is good, but something is off with us there, too. And I want an answer," he bit out.

Olivia's eyes widened. "Do I not please you?" she said, tilting her head to the side. She leaned back onto her heels, propping her elbows behind her and shoving her breasts out suggestively. His eyes stayed tight on hers, refusing to be manipulated. His hands went to his pants and unbuckled his belt before whipping it loose.

He rolled it up in his hands.

Her fingers clenched, barely but he noticed it.

"One more time."

Her eyes stayed on the belt in his hands. A look flashed across her face before it was gone as soon as it appeared.

"I miss being *tired*," Olivia sighed wistfully; her eyes flickering up to him as she sat up straight onto her knees and huffed. He narrowed his eyes. "It's the truth," she said softly.

"Maybe. But your truth is missing something though." He countered.

"What?" she said, scrunching up her nose.

"Trust. I can't give you what we need until I feel like you trust me."

There was a pregnant pause. "I will *never* tell you. That is something you can trust." She stared at him, unmoving.

They stared at each other for a few heartbeats of time, their battle of wills vicious. Averting her eyes on a scoff, she got up off her knees slowly, throwing down her towel before walking past him.

Irritated with her lack of response, he grabbed her arm roughly, leaning into her ear. She stiffened against him and made a warning noise in her throat. He tightened his fingers and growled back.

"Little girl, I could eat you up and spit you out for breakfast and keep going throughout my day like nothing happened. Do not mistake indulgence for weakness. I will take us there when I am ready. Not a minute before. *Do you understand me?*"

Olivia tensed, her eyes slowly meeting his. Her breathing came out low, and labored.

"I will not be manipulated; I will not be had. You need to learn to ask me for what you need. To trust me to give it to you." He put a finger to her temple. "If you don't figure this mental *shit* out soon, I will reach inside your brain my damn self and yank it out. That is a threat, Amor. Now, I'm going to give you one. More. Chance."

They stared at each other for several heartbeats, their breathing the only thing in the room.

She leaned forward an inch from his face.

"I'd like to see you try," she said, her eyes going hard as she met his stern stare with one of his own.

Colin dropped the belt, hearing it hit the gym floor. He moved lightning fast and grabbed her by the hair, snatching her to his front. Olivia's face winced with pain, and she closed her eyes briefly before opening them, the green in her eyes turning dark and stormy. He pushed her backwards, crowding her into the small two-person sauna he had in the corner of the gym. He ignored her pushing against him.

"*Colin, I don't want to be in here!*" she bit out angrily as he slammed the door behind them. The room steaming up quickly, he was glad, only bringing her in here because he knew she didn't like to be hot.

"You had better be glad we need this skin pretty for the gala in a few days because I truly want to fuck you up right now. What. Is. My. Name?" he growled down into her face, pressing her into the wall with a hand against her breastbone.

"Sir!" Olivia gasped, pushing against his chest.

Colin's mouth came down in a crushing blow onto hers and she retaliated, biting his lip hard enough to draw blood. He snarled, kissing her back just has hard. Their kiss was messy, their teeth clashed together as they both struggled to hurt the other. She moaned as he took her tongue between his teeth and bit painfully.

Colin stopped, feeling like a key slid into a lock. He pulled away, looking at her quizzically. She was panting, still struggling against his hold.

"Olivia," he said, his brows furrowed.

No way. We can't be this lucky, he thought.

"Olivia, look at me." She stopped struggling and met his eyes. "Baby are you a masochist?" he asked in a low tone, his jaw ticking.

Her nose scrunched. *"What?"* she said, seemingly offended.

"You heard me. Answer the question."

"No. No. I can't be. That doesn't make sense, because..." she cut herself off, her eyes widening.

Colin tilted his head. "Because why?"

She paused.

"Because it doesn't make sense," she said slowly, almost like a question.

"Honey, I don't think you want to work yourself to the bone to be *tired*, I think you like pain. I've been seeing the signs but not connecting the dots," he mused. "You get wet when I spank you, when I give you pain it turns you on. Everything you do is challenging me to hurt you, and when I don't, you get restless. I've been noticing, hell even *Mary* has been noticing something is off. Just now, the look in your eyes when you saw my belt, the way you're violently kissing me. You *like* it."

"No. I can't be like those people," she whispered, her eyes looking far away for a second.

He scrunched his brows in confusion. "What do you mean, like *what* people?"

"People who get off on pain, that's... not what nice people do. It's a *sickness.*" She swallowed, her eyes flickering back and forth between his.

"Baby, it's just a sexual *kink*. It doesn't mean because you're a masochist then you're a bad person," he said, his hand loosening in her hair. He caught the look of disappointment in her eyes before he tightened back up watching her nipples harden even more.

"But-"

"Why do you think this? What's the reason?" he asked softly, instinctively knowing something happened that colored her perception of her sexual identity.

She shook her head against his hold. "I can't tell you," she said angrily.

"Does it have to do with one of your side hustles?" he pressed.

"Bunny," she whispered.

Colin let go of her immediately.

They stared silently at each other.

"Whatever happened to make you feel this way, doesn't make it any less true. I can make you love it, Olivia. This side of yourself you don't want to see. I can give you what you need. I thought maybe you didn't trust me, but now I'm seeing its *you* that you don't trust. You need to trust yourself; you can lose yourself in me. I promise. I'll take care of you. We can be so amazing," he whispered.

Mi Amor, the word almost slipped out. He bit his tongue, watching her shake her head and quietly walk out the door.

He sat on the bench and put his head in his hands, wondering how he didn't catch it earlier. A sadist's best friend was a masochist, and the heavens just gave him one for free?

A masochist who didn't *know* she was a masochist.

"Fuck," he cursed, sighing.

THIRTY-ONE
You Must Have Me Confused

COLIN FELT LIKE SPENDING more money.

So, he spent time considering Olivia's nasty words to him weeks ago and had her call five orphanages and made her donate five hundred thousand dollars to each one. He was happy with this idea, because who could be mad when you're donating to help children's lives?

Surely not Olivia, he thought, pleased with himself.

Afterwards, he took her shopping again for their upcoming Thanksgiving charity gala, settling on a red, slinky number, loving the way it accented her body shape and fell across her breasts and hips.

The event was a few days before Thanksgiving, and she'd been waxed, primped, and exfoliated within an inch of her life, but she couldn't help not relaxing. Even when the manicurists told her to stop tensing her fingers during her manicure. She'd spent most of the day doing her own hair nervously, wondering if Colin would like it.

Colin had been working diligently for the last three weeks. A new country was in demand of his software and Johnathan's cars, and he was at the office late having meeting after meeting. Olivia began falling asleep before he'd even come home because she spent the day working herself to exhaustion anxiously. She'd begun going to Vanessa's house to spend time with her and Alison, not wanting her niece to feel like she was abandoning her.

Olivia knew something was majorly off with herself and didn't want to bother Colin with it, not after the conversation they'd had in the sauna. He was getting too close to her secret.

Smoothing down her red silk dress, she turned once more in the mirror, making sure it hung just right.

She slipped on a pair of nude high heel shoes before finding Colin in the bathroom where he had lined his beard and was busy buttoning up his white dress shirt.

His eyes met hers in the mirror as she appeared in the doorway and froze when he glanced down.

Olivia stepped into the bathroom looking like sex incarnate. The dress flowed over her curves like water, not leaving much to the imagination.

The dress was held up by tiny straps that looped over her shoulder and down the sides of her ribcage, holding up the dress low on her hips. A big bow graced her backside, just slightly above the seam of her ass. Her full breasts curved lusciously against the neckline that laid whisper soft against her cleavage. Her back was bare, her hair tumbling down in heavy waves down her right side.

Her eyes were heavily smoked out, accenting the bright green irises. She'd left her lips nude and for that, he was so thankful. He didn't relish the thought of cleaning lipstick off his dick later that night.

Colin grunted softly as he turned to stone in his pants.

Heart pounding uncomfortably in his chest, he stared at her as he began threading his tie, struggling to right his sudden rush of emotions.

Olivia cleared her throat gently before she raised an eyebrow at him. "Well, what do you think?" she said coyly, making another slow turn for him, clearly expecting him to say something. His eyes snapped to hers, and her cheeks warmed at the look in his eyes.

"I think I'm trying to invent new ways to fuck you. You in that red dress is going to be the death of me. I knew it when I picked it out." Colin confessed, his voice thick with desire. "Actually, I'm thinking about not even going."

He'd been gentle with her in the last couple of weeks since their talk in the sauna, as he wanted her to have time to get to know him before he really unleashed himself. He planned on taking advantage of their agreement soon, hoping that it would open her mind to her sexuality. The niggling thought in his head pierced hard, warning him that he required his pound of flesh, and soon.

Colin just didn't want to go about it in a way that would damage her psyche.

Despite the peace her presence bought him, it was costing him to hold himself back for her sake.

He tore his gaze away as he bent an arm to attach a cuff link, glancing back up again when her soft hands replaced his., attaching it and the next one before smoothing up his shirt to fix his tie. She gave it a cheeky tug.

"I'm so nervous." Her eyes flickered to his before lowering again to fuss with his shirt, smoothing down his collar unnecessarily and fiddling with a button.

He caught her hand tight in his before leaning down to place a kiss on her fingers.

"You're exquisite. There's nothing to be nervous about. I'll be right there with you the whole time. We'll go, eat expensive food, drink expensive wine, and then dance. I look forward to twirling you around in this dress on the dance floor."

And peeling it off later with my teeth, Colin thought.

Olivia pressed her lips together and nodded. She reached over and grabbed his beard moisturizer and took time to rub it into the hair on his jaw, taking a tiny comb to comb it in. her eyes were bright as he reached over and snagged something off the vanity.; a great big dirty emerald stone attached to an elegant chain.

She gasped, reaching out to caress it gently with a finger. "*Ohhhh Colin*. This is breathtaking." She turned when he instructed so he could place the emerald and fasten it around her neck.

He caught her eyes in their reflection in the mirror, pleased to see it highlighted her eyes perfectly. He smiled at her pink blush high in her cheeks. "Thank you so much," she said breathlessly, touching the emerald again, with a look of wonder on her face.

He bent, kissing her shoulder. "You're welcome. Let's go have some fun. The driver is here."

***

Colin escorted Olivia up the stairs carefully and into the grand building and checked her shawl and her clutch in.

Leading her into the great dining room, he paused for a minute to let her take it all in.

There were florals everywhere. At every table, on the big stage at the front of the room, dripping from the ceiling. And there were dozens of wait staff walking around with flutes of champagne and small glasses of whiskey.

He grabbed one of each, handing her the champagne.

"*Sir*," Olivia gasped, trying to keep her cool. "This is so beautiful. Thank you for bringing me." She smiled softly, pleased when he leaned forward and placed his lips to her temple.

They made their rounds and Olivia basked in how easily they worked a room together. Leaning into him while he introduced her to several people. Some she recognized from the media, and others she'd never heard of but knew were just as important. She was grateful to see that so far there was no one familiar in the throngs of people nestled all over the room.

She was on her second flute of champagne when Colin finally led them to their table, holding out her chair for her to take her seat.

"Thank you." she said, picking up her refreshing drink and sipping as she scanned the room again in a fit of nervousness.

A disconcerted feeling settled in her stomach as she saw a man towards the stage who looked a lot like her previous Saturday client.

She tensed, trying to remember if there was any time she didn't wear a mask with him. Shaking her head, she tried to convince herself the man was just a look alike. Their table filled up slowly, soon distracting her, and Colin wasted no time introducing her to the party there. She laughed, conversed, sipped her wine, and ate daintily as she was terrified to get food on her dress.

Before she knew it, they were three quarters of the way through dinner.

Colin leaned forward, his hand on her knee.

"Are you having a good time, beautiful?" he asked lowly, his mouth brushing her ear.

She blushed, looking at him and giving him a smile. "Yes, I'm having an incredible time. This feels like a fairy tale," She admitted.

Her initial terror of attending the event had dissipated, and she found she enjoyed conversing with the others at the table. She didn't feel awkward or out of place, and found she held her own easily. Not needing Colin as a buffer near as much as she feared she would.

The lights went low before the speaker came on stage and gave a long speech about the cause they were all there to support. Before ending, the speaker announced the last event of the evening would be a raffle, all the proceeds going to a charitable cause. She'd announced the winners quickly, Colin nor her winning anything, before opening the dance floor.

A few minutes later, Olivia was in the middle of a bite of a creamy éclair she'd when her worst nightmare came to life; she'd been busy laughing with Colin at something, when she'd suddenly a familiar voice rang out, "McDermont! Is that you, son?"

The hairs on the back of her neck stood up as Colin turned to address a man who'd just approached him.

Glancing up slowly, she paled, seeing Judge Carmichael standing there with a young Asian American woman. She swallowed hard and turned to the front, trying to find a way to escape. Feeling sick, she placed a hand to her breast, trying to stifle choking gasps. Her heart had crawled into her throat and was busy strangling her windpipe.

"Olivia," Colin called. "I'd like to introduce you to Judge Carmichael. He sits on the supreme court bench." He held out a hand to help her from her seat, and she stiffened as she faced the Judge head on, a small smile on her face.

Though she wrestled her face into one of calm, inside she was holding back hot, stinging tears. Her night effectively ruined.

The Judge's eyes widened slightly before narrowing as his brows furrowed in recognition.

There was an incredibly tense and awkward silence before he held his hand out for her to take. With effort, she froze her facial muscles into an impassive look.

Why, of all people, did it have to be him? she thought.

Her fingers trembled as she clasped them together tightly before unlocking her grip and reluctantly stepped forward, not wanting to appear impolite in front of Colin, and placed her hand lightly in the Judge's. Barely touching him.

Her teeth ground as he bent down to kiss the back of her hand, lingering. Olivia saw Colin give her a sharp look, noticing the noise.

Her relief dissipated, and she died a million deaths when Carmichael's eyes slid to Colin's briefly before leaning forward towards him.

"I didn't know you *dabbled*, McDermont? Kat's good isn't she?" Judge Carmichael whispered conspiratorially with no regard for the woman next to him.

Olivia made a low sound in her throat when Colin's hand suddenly tightened on hers painfully. Her heart let go of its grip on her windpipe, deciding to free fall into her stomach instead. She tensed as her mouth went dry.

"My name isn't Kat," she said weakly, but Colin spoke over her.

"I'm not sure I know what you mean, Carmichael," Colin said. Her hand started sweating, and she tried to extract it discreetly from Colin's once more. Desperate to turn around and grab her champagne. He didn't let her. "I don't dabble in anything. My tastes are well above board." Colin drawled smoothly in a deceptively calm voice in direct contrast to his grip around hers.

Sneaking a glance at him, she'd notice that his eyes went from cool to hard in a nanosecond. The edges crinkling, betraying his emotion.

The Judge tilted his head at Colin before cutting his eyes to Olivia's once more. She broke out in goosebumps as his gaze lingered longer than was necessary before his sharp eyes did a smooth perusal of her body, lingering on her breasts. Her chin quivered.

Olivia felt one of her knuckles crack and gasped in pain before covering it up with a small scoffing sound in her throat. She attempted to speak, clearing her throat of her nerves.

"I'm sorry?" she lightly laughed, uncomfortably, feigning her nonchalantness. "You must have me confused with someone else, I've been getting that a lot lately. My name is *Olivia*, not Kat," she smoothly lied, attempting to twist her hand out of Colin's grip before he accidentally snapped a bone.

He didn't let her go, so she switched tactics, rubbing her thumb along his fingers, trying to soothe him.

Judge Carmichael's eyes now blatantly roamed her hair and body greedily, lingering on her breasts longer than he'd previously had. She sucked her teeth as her hand suddenly went numb.

She felt her face go numb right after from the strain of keeping her expression neutral.

Keep it together, keep it together, keep it together, she chanted inside her head, mentally attempting to retreat inside her brain.

"I'm sorry, Judge Carmichael. You *must* be mistaken. Olivia is not from around here," Colin interjected once again, his smooth voice like silk against her ears.

He didn't appear to be outwardly affected by the judge.

Colin didn't seem to be intimidated by much at all, she suddenly realized. Olivia felt rather than saw the Judge's date eyeing her with spite.

"Oh please. I would recognize that hair and those *eyes* anywhere. There aren't many green-eyed redheads loitering around the area," he said, giving her a pointed look and nodding sharply to Colin before turning to Olivia and smiling.

Colin tilted his head slightly, his eyes flashing as he dismissed the Judge's words.

"Well, in any event. You have made me miss my dear friend *desperately.* She'd rather *rudely* and *abruptly* blown me off a few months ago. You're a kind reminder of what her presence still means to me. We had something quite special, *irreplaceable*, in fact." The man's teeth gleamed brightly in his face as he licked his lips. "Well, it's a

pleasure to make your acquaintance, *Olivia*. Have a good time. *Colin*."
Carmichael said dismissively, before turning on his heel and escorting
his plus one back to their table.

THIRTY-TWO

Make Me Forget Them

OLIVIA STOOD STILL FOR a second, feeling sick, her heart pounding in her throat before she gently sank back into the seat. She struggled to regain control of herself.

With her eyes watering, Olivia fought back desperate breaths, standing up from her seat immediately, and excusing herself before fleeing the table. Not giving Colin any reason to delay her.

She hadn't even looked at him while she sat down.

Rounding the corner, she hastily making her way into the restroom, and pushed into a stall. She gasped, bending over the toilet, and began dry heaving in panic. Her tears fell hotly down her cheeks and she pressed a trembling hand tight to her stomach, waiting a minute before standing up and grabbing tissue.

She dabbed at her eyes carefully before exiting the stall.

Olivia walked slowly to stand in front of the mirror, lamenting her lack of clutch that held her face powder.

She wet her fingers and carefully pressed them under her eyes, trying to hide the fact she'd been crying. Giving herself a once over in the mirror and a few minutes to breathe deeply, she waited to leave until she felt calm. Giving herself a firm head shake, she turned and walked out the door and straight into Judge Carmichael, who'd been standing rather close to the entrance of the ladies' restroom.

Olivia stumbled back a step, her eyes widening in shock.

Her back hit the door she'd just closed, making her feel trapped. Her blood pressure skyrocketed once more, and she felt goosebumps dot her flesh as her nausea came back.

"Excuse me, Judge Carmichael," she whispered, trying to step around him.

She gasped in fear as he quickly stepped in front of her, blocking her escape. She glanced around nervously, seeing no one in the little area with them. Her arm came up to wrap around her torso protectively, suddenly feeling very naked.

Strains of the music from the ballroom bleeding out into the surrounding area, highlighting her helplessness just mere feet away.

"So, that's where you disappeared to? I'd been calling Gypsy for weeks trying to get another appointment and she said you were gone. *Poof,* disappeared into thin air," Judge Carmichael said nastily, his lip curling as he regarded her from top to toe. "How much did it take? I guess the money you were getting from me wasn't enough, eh Kat?" he spit out angrily and took a step towards her.

She blanched, feeling the blood drain from her face seeing the evil look on his.

"Get *away* from me. I don't know what you're talking about and you're *scaring* me," she whispered, desperately hoping that she sounded as weak as she currently felt. Thinking it would throw him off.

During their sessions, she was always cool, confident, and in control.

She never showed weakness, never insinuated that she couldn't handle herself. Her mouth was her greatest asset in Esmerelda's Ring. It was how she was able to get by without using sex, unlike a lot of the other women who didn't have that luxury.

Carmichael took another step towards her, placing himself into her personal space. Desperate, she recoiled, her arm swinging out to slap him across the face.

His face cracked sharply to the side, her slap resounding loudly through the tiled area.

Giving him a filthy look, Olivia went to step around him, but he'd stepped even closer, leering at her in excitement as he caressed his jaw almost lovingly. Her eyes welled with tears and her breaths came in short.

Glancing around again, her heart sank as she still didn't see anyone. She'd made the wrong move.

Oh God, why would I do that? she thought. Her skin crawled as she swallowing bile, trying to inch to the side away from the door. Suddenly terrified he would push her through it and follow her inside. Though she was strong, she knew she wouldn't be strong enough to overpower him if he chose to violate her.

"I would've paid more, you know. If you'd just opened your cunt mouth and *asked*. The thing's I would've done to you." His voice dripped with disdain.

Her head tilted back and to the side as he pressed so close his breath brushed over her collarbone. She gaped at him in horror, pushing against his shoulders, trying to step back, but she was trapped flush against the door. Her heels clanked against the wood as she shuffled anew, trying to escape.

He grabbed her upper arms roughly, leaning in further.

"Get the fuck away from her," Olivia heard Colin's deep voice from behind the judge.

Her lip trembling, a shocked tear rolled down her cheek as she turned to face her lover.

"*Colin.*" she cried out, mortified to be found in this position, yet relieved. She rushed to his outstretched hand with a quiet sob, thankful that Carmichael hadn't had time to push her into the restroom.

"You'll be hearing from my people, Carmichael," Colin threatened, taking a single step in the older man's direction.

Carmichael's jaw ticked as they stared off for a long, drawn out moment that almost had Olivia dry heaving again. She placed a trembling hand to her stomach, wetting her lip and pressing harder into Colin.

Colin gave him a cold look over the bridge of his nose. Unwilling at the moment to break this man physically and risk himself going to jail and upsetting Olivia, he would just have him removed from his seat. Unbeknownst to her, he'd recorded their interaction, knowing something was horribly off when he was speaking with the Judge earlier, and her reaction to him.

He pulled her close, trying to comfort her while struggling himself, holding back from being violent with the judge.

Visibly seething with anger, he turned with a hand on her back and escorted her out of the exquisitely decorated room, away from the tables and dancing. The sounds of the band sounded loud in their ears as he rushed them through the room and out the side door.

He stopped abruptly in front of the coat check, jaw ticking as he handed the woman their ticket.

Colin's face was slightly dark, betraying his fury. "Are you okay? Does your hand hurt badly?" he asked gruffly, without looking at her.

Her own watered as she wanted him to acknowledge and verify what happened. Not knowing that he was already plotting releasing the video and killing the man mentally as he ruined his whole life's work and took everything from him.

"Yes," Olivia said, her own voice quavering, betraying her emotion.

Colin finally looked at her, swaying in her red dress, unsteady in her heels as she'd tried to pull it together.

He took her arm rather gently and caressed a soft hand down her hair before turning and taking her affects from the clerk. She followed him out silently as he flagged down their limo and made her slide in first. Gracefully getting in behind her and snatching up the vodka bottle to pour himself a finger of liquor in his glass.

His blood boiled, a breath away from losing it.

He tossed it back quickly, not even wincing. "Home, thank you. And raise the partition, please." He instructed the driver.

Olivia's eyes flickered everywhere nervously as the divider rose. Colin poured a double vodka before leaning forward and handing it to her. She looked at the glass skeptically, before taking it from him with a scrunched look on her face. She readjusted her dress and looked at the glass again, moving it to rest it to the side.

"Oh, you're *going* to want to drink that," Colin bit out, pouring another drink and tossing it back. Again not reacting at the harsh burn. Olivia flashed her green eyes at him, opening her mouth to speak, closing it quickly because she could not find the words.

He put the glass down, giving his leg and his hand a rough shake before placing his ankle on his knee.

Colin exhaled deeply, leaning his head against a fist with an elbow propped up on the window, watching her with his piercing stare. Not saying a word. Olivia's hand trembled badly as she tipped the vodka to her lips, swallowing it and wincing, not having a chaser.

"Drink it *all*," he ordered softly, referencing the glass still in her hand.

His finger was now tapping at his knee, as was the toe of his shoe, betraying his agitation.

Olivia licked her lips and sucked the whole thing down with a gasp, feeling the liquor go straight to her pussy. She felt it thudding harshly as it swelled with need, and she closed her legs to attempt to stem the uncomfortable feeling. She took a deep breath, feeling the fabric of her dress strain across her breasts.

"Colin-" she started, but he interrupted her.

"Has that son of a bitch ever fucked you?" he asked suddenly, holding her stare with his eyes.

Fury unlike she'd ever seen on him since she met him tainted his chocolate eyes. She shivered, suddenly afraid, but indignation and offense broke through the fear, stabilizing her.

Her lips parted in shock at his brazenly crass words. "You *are* aware that the man almost *assaulted* me tonight?" she hissed at Colin, her eyes flashing at him as she scooted forward in her seat.

His face settled into an impassive expression, and her heart began to beat wildly.

"I *said*, did that man fuck you, Olivia," he repeated, his voice lowering dangerously as he ignored her question in favor of her answering his first.

He stayed completely still in his seat, feeling his lungs burning with anger. Images of Carmichael's lips at her collarbone and his hands wrapping around her upper arm seared into his brain, making him feel murderous.

He got to smell her, touch her, damn near taste her.

"N-no. Colin I *told* you-"she said, pressing her hand against her chest. *"I told you about the only time I'd had sex."*

"He felt mighty comfortable getting in your space tonight," he barked, making her jump in his seat. Her eyes widened as her heart raced even faster, and a trickle of trepidation made it's way up her spine as she realized she'd never seen him angry. "Has he ever touched you, in *any* way?" he asked again, cocking his head. "I know you know him. *The gig is up, Olivia.*"

His intense stare was so uncomfortable she looked away to find a semblance of privacy.

It didn't matter though, the heat from his gaze continue to sear her across the limo.

She brought narrowed eyes back to his. "You and my sister are so fucking *stupid*. You don't listen to anything I say," she hissed, taking her glass and throwing it in his direction.

He didn't even flinch.

The glass hit close to his arm and bounced off the back of the seat, clanking dully against the leather before rolling off and bouncing on the floor.

Colin stared at her silently. His lack of reaction scared her.

Her eyes narrowed. "*No.* he's never..." she said simply, bending down to pick up the glass before placing it in a holder and rubbing her stinging stinging hang.

"Don't *fuck* with me. I won't be manipulated by you. You will finish *every* goddamn sentence I let you speak from here on out," Colin growled, leaning forward to hold her stare with his.

His chest was tight, his entire body was tense.

Olivia knew he was serious. She couldn't half ass with him, couldn't manipulate him, he wouldn't allow her to treat him like her former clients. He was not weak. She trembled under his stare, feeling as weak as she wanted to make him feel.

"Now, he's never *what*, Olivia? Finish the sentence and use your *words*," he shouted, making her cry out and jump back in her seat.

"He's never touched me, never f-f-fucked me," Olivia panted in her seat, her eyes were wide with shock, she pressed her back harder against the leather. "I promise, baby. I promise. I promise I'm not lying. I never let anyone touch me. I never let any of them see me naked. I swear, I swear it on Allison's *life,*" she cried out, pressing her fingers to her throat, a pained sob escaping her as she stared at him, trembling.

A pained expression crossed his face before he sat back and waited several minutes before saying. "I'm proud of you," he said softly. "It took everything in me to not rip his mother fucking face off."

Her eyes turned to his in renewed shock as he checked his watch. She glanced out the window, seeing they were almost home. His gaze stayed on hers, searing her with his intensity. She met his stare back silently.

Make me forget him, please. Make me forget I ever had to lose myself to those people, make me lose myself to you instead. Like you said, like you said I could, she pleaded with her eyes, but her mouth refused to follow her command to speak the words to him.

Her body burned with desire and warred with itself as she inwardly searched for that familiar box, making sure the lid was on tight. Finding a temporary comfort with the pain of the past taunting her.

Olivia breathed a sigh of relief when the limo slowed and came to a stop. But that relief was short-lived when he stepped out and held his hand out to help her out of the vehicle.

Olivia paused, unmoving, looking up at him and contemplated staying in the limousine, the look on his face terrifying her. She slapped his hand away, squealing when he reached in and yanked her out roughly by her arm before leading her to the front door and unlocking it. He grunted, shoving her through the door before closing it.

THIRTY-THREE
The Closet

OLIVIA STAGGERED ACROSS THE foyer table on her heels, pressing her free hand against her stomach, gasping and trying to still the trembling.

Colin moved, his hand gripping hers as he took her clutch and tossed it carelessly on the foyer table before backing her up against the glass double doors. He stared down into her face, breathing hard, and she knew his control was shattering.

Desperate whines escaped her throat through her ragged breathing.

"How many? How many men were there?" he whispered, his lips close to hers, forcing her to crane her head back to meet his angry gaze.

Olivia's heart beat unbearably loud in her ears. Her eyes flickered back and forth between his, and her lips trembled as she parted them to attempt to take a deep breath to calm herself. However, there seemed to be no air to suck in. All the oxygen was gone.

"Six," she bit out, feeling her heart crack, and closing her eyes against his. "Colin, I don't want you to know that part of m-me," she said thickly.

Not speaking, he bent slowly and grasped the hem of her dress in his hand, standing up and dragging it up her legs as he went. Overwhelmed, and grown tired of his intensity, she reached forward and pushed him away from her, crying out in surprise as his hand flew up and popped her in her mouth.

Her hand flew to her lips, feeling them quiver as she met his stare.

She inhaled on a gasp as she realized that the slight pop turned her on, but then was incredibly confused by the emotion. She opened her mouth and narrowed her eyes in anger. She stepped forward, her green eyes furious, her lithe arms reaching out for his face. "You *fucking* bast-"

Colin reached out and grabbed her face, squishing her lips together in his harsh grip.

She growled in her throat, fighting his advances. Her blows fell off his hard arms as he yanked her by her face to him. Glaring down at her harshly.

"*You're not allowed to speak, Amor,*" he gritted harshly, his eyes flashing, his jaw was tight. He crowded her hard against the door, subduing her easily as she struggled against him. "You may only speak when I ask you a question. You don't want me to know that part of you? You think it's too dirty? Too shameful?" his eyebrow arched as he looked down at her, his own face flushing.

Olivia mumbled against his lips, but he tightened his fingers even more.

"Too. Fucking. *Bad.*" Colin slightly banged her head against the glass with every word, his hand flexing against her mouth.

Olivia heard the dull thud of her head hitting the glass and whimpered as arousal began to bleed through her anger, the actions driving the words even deeper into her brain.

"I'm working my way in sweetheart, and you're going to let me."

He began to shrug out of his jacket, his hand still on her face, dropping it with a thud to the floor and yanking off his tie.

"I don't want you clean," he said, his voice rough with emotion. "But I'll spend the rest of forever cleaning you up if that's what is required. You think I'm fucking scared of you? Well think again. You and your little bullshit side hustle do *not* intimidate me," he snarled at her, his chocolate eyes melted slightly as he regarded her face.

Her blood sung with excitement at his words.

He dipped again, grasping her in the bend in her knees and raising her. Olivia placed her arms around his neck and leaned back away from him, refusing him out of a sudden bid for feminine propriety, recoiling from his harsh embrace. He shook her roughly, forcing her to look at him.

"Wrap your legs around me, Olivia. Do it the first time I tell you to, or I will drag you up the stairs by your hair. Do we understand each other?" he said threateningly.

Olivia whimpered as she flinched under his harsh administration. Gasping when she felt herself throbbing excitedly at the thought of his hands tugging at her hair. And in that moment his words about being turned on by pain came to the forefront of her mind.

She gasped.

He was fucking right. I'm a masochist, she thought, blinking slowly as the lock now turned for her.

Colin's fingers bit painfully into the back of her thighs as she willingly complied. He carried her up the stairs fluidly, her weight of no consequence to him. When he got to the top, he stopped. She glanced at him nervously, staring into his eyes, her own widening slightly at what she found there in his depths.

Anger. He was so angry.

She paled, biting at the unfamiliar expression on his face. Was he angry with *her?* Because she wouldn't tell him all of her secrets?

She struggled through short, panting breaths as he resumed walking them to the bedroom. She squirmed, expecting him to throw her on the bed, but he just veered left and into their closet, closing them into the small space.

She backed up hastily as he put her down, rounding the island. He turned and typed in a code into the keypad at the door, and she flinched at the snick of the lock as it slid into place.

He turned to face her, leaning his back against the door and crossing his arms. Olivia felt on fire with need the longer he maintained her gaze. and they stared at each other for a long, tense moment.

"Take the emerald off."

Trembling, she reached up to unclasp the heavy necklace, stepping forward quickly to drop it gently on the island. She kicked her heels off before backing up once more. Her eyes bored into him, waiting. Her brain raced with too many thoughts at once, mentally flicking through the agreement she'd signed in his office, trying to gauge how crazy it was about to get.

"Colin," she whispered. "You were right, the other day in the sauna. I didn't realize."

He inhaled sharply, his facial expression hardened until it looked like he was carved from stone.

His chest visibly expanded with pleasure at her words. He loved hearing he was correct about something, but nothing took the cake like his lover admitting her kink to him.

He nodded once.

Leaving Olivia with her inner turmoil, Colin turned his attention to his cuff links. Taking them off one by one and tossing them on the island along with his keys and his wallet. The careless tossing and the thudding of his personal effects on the marble top echoed loudly in her ears, pulling her back into the present moment.

He pulled out his phone and placed it down gently before sliding off his shirt and under shirt, revealing cords and slabs of hard muscle, tendons, tattoos, and veins to her gaze.

Olivia watched silently as he sat on a nearby bench to take off his shoes and dress socks, seemingly content to let her wait for him. Her blood rushed in her veins the more he revealed himself. Her body letting her know she needed to be satiated.

Colin was strong, muscular, and not the kind of muscle that one strives to get in the gym; he was built strong. It was evident in the thickness of his wrists and fingers, his chest and shoulder width. And he was about to unleash it all onto her.

Olivia's heart beat heavily, almost drowning out any other sound.

Her skin burned, her delicate flesh pebbled and sensitive, waiting for him to decide what to do with her. A hundred thoughts ran through her head however, she didn't need to wait long. He graced her with his gaze once more, his demeanor deceptively calm. She sparked when awareness hit her with the knowledge that she did know not to trust *this* Colin.

He was wicked with territories uncharted, and the thought oddly comforted her because she truly did love a challenge. Her eyes turned to his as he spoke, his buttery smooth voice filling the room.

"I'm going to fuck you hard, Olivia. Because I need it, and you need it too." His jaw ticked hard as he got closer, betraying his fading restraint. "I want to apologize in advance if the *way* I go about it makes you feel any kind of way. You're going to get some pain tonight," he said sternly, walking towards her.

She whimpered, her toes digging into the soft carpet of the closet as the sheer intimidating energy rolling off of him made her quickly lose her nerve. Her hands went behind her back and clasped tightly. Her eyes flickered from him to the door as she debated her chances of getting out of there without his permission.

Olivia's chin quivered as he continued speaking, his smooth voice caressing over her.

"What are you going to do to me, Colin? I'm scared," she whispered, feeling a lone tear trail down her cheek betraying her truthfulness. She wanted him to lose control, but she was terrified that he would burn her up with him.

"I'm going to break you in half, because I can't break that piece of shit in half, and you're my next option. This is what we agreed to, is it not? It's time to pay up, Amor." Olivia's eyes widened at the honest admission as he towered over her.

Her nostrils flared as she caught ahold of his flagrantly masculine scent, causing need hit hot in her belly as he got closer. Her back hit a wall and some clothes, and she watched warily as he reached into a drawer and pulled out a belt with lots of holes in it. Her breath froze in her lungs.

"No! Please don't h-hit me, I didn't d-do anything," she stuttered, but she could barely contain or hide her own excitement.

"I need to anchor you to something while I do this. I can't tie you down the way I would normally and risk re-injuring your arm," Colin said darkly, stepping forward.

Her heart pounded an excited tattoo at his words, even as she instinctively pressed herself harder against the wall as he reached forward.

The next few seconds went by so fast she barely had time to register anything past her shocked screaming. He'd looped the belt around her neck, fastened it, then hauled it up, forcing her to stand on the balls of her feet for air. She gaped at him, clawing at the belt, but her brain did not seem to understand what was happening.

She jerked hard, not able to move.

Olivia tilted her head slightly and saw that he had pressed the belt opening onto a small hook within the closet that was used for hanging hats. She swiveled her head to look at him as he picked up his phone and leaned against the island, crossing his ankles in a relaxed stance, and concentrating on his phone, ignoring her.

Something about seeing that familiar stance, his "I'm in control" power move that had been carefully ingrained into her for the past few weeks, made her feel safe. Lowering her heels to the floor experimentally, she gasped as her air was cut off, forcing her back up onto her toes again. Her calves were beginning to burn and ache. Especially after being in heels most of the night.

"Colin-" she bit out, struggling slightly.

The same odd warmth she'd felt when she laid her head in his lap, and he was stroking her back, suddenly washed over her. Mixing with the burn in her calves and feet, and it was quite overwhelming. Like in the way you have a revelation of discovery. The disconcerting feeling you have when you try to pick at and analyze if this is really you.

Sometimes, those initial revelations were raw to the touch.

"I didn't say you could speak," Colin said, still not looking at her as he tapped a few times at the screen.

A second later, strains of one of her favorite songs filled the small space, and he turned up the volume slightly. He looked up from his phone to watch her trace the belt around her neck with her slender fingers.

"Is it too tight?"

Colin stared at her, assessing her as her breathing quickly changed. Her skin warmed, turning dewy. He continued to lean patiently as he observed her.

She glanced back into his eyes, and he'd seen that hers turned cloudy.

Olivia debated, inwardly wrestling with herself. And figured if he had the balls to tie the belt around her neck, then she could have the balls to ask for what she needed. Even if she was embarrassed. She'd be damned if he was the only one getting something out of this tonight.

Now understanding that he wasn't angry at her, but angry at the Judge, and was jealous of the men that were attached to her past, and needed to take it out on her.

He was marking her.

Inwardly she retreated, taking the lid back off her box of hurts, and let him step in with her. Giving him a tiny bit more of her trust. Her heart squeezed uncomfortably.

"I need it tighter," she said simply, her eyes falling from his to glance at his bare feet.

Her heart beat pounding in her chest.

Colin straightened, and walked to her slowly. Gazing down at her with his hot stare for several long seconds before unlooping the belt from the closet hook.

She glanced away before his eyes incinerated her completely.

"One more loop only," he said, catching her eye and holding it as he tightened it minutely, before replacing it back on the hook. He'd watched her carefully as she'd slowly raised up on her toes to take away the slack that was there when she was on her heels, giving him that bit of power back that made him growl with need.

Olivia moaned as the sensation immediately overtook her, and she shuddered hard.

Tears fell from her eyes as it almost became unbearable.

Arousal slammed into her body, making her feel off kilter. She whined as she tried to cope. He leaned against her, placing his lips to her temple and lending her his strength once again as she clearly struggled with complex feelings. He briefly picked her slightly off the floor with a hand under her ass, giving her calves a temporary reprieve.

She hung limply. He spoke against her ear as he rocked her gently to the music, calming her.

"This playlist is for you, to give you comfort for however long I need to fuck you to get the thought of that man and you out of my head...a gift for you to rest your mind upon," he finished, pressing his lips to hers and licking into her mouth. Their lips smacked wetly together, causing shivers of pleasure to slide across her skin.

His thick arm underneath her ass felt so good as he cradled her. The sudden domination beating hard into her flesh and making her cry out, she clenched her thighs together as she felt more of her wetness squeeze out of her body. Her sex pulsed hard, feeling empty, before he set her back down onto her toes.

He walked over to grab a decanter of alcohol that he kept stocked in the closet, and placed the bottle on a shelf close to her head where his colognes were stored. He watched her with his dark gaze as he unscrewed the top and placed it off to the side. Her heart pounded, her vagina felt heavy and hot, stealing what breath she had in her lungs.

He poured a small amount into a glass before pressing it to her lips. She jerked her head away.

"*No.*" she bit out, clenching her teeth hard. He waited a few heartbeats as she came to the decision on her own, opening her mouth for him, gagging slightly and moaning as he poured some liquor in. She swallowed it, tears leaking down her face as he repeated the motion. She shot him a filthy stare.

"No chaser, huh? Didn't you tell me that ladies use chasers?" Olivia taunted him, just not able to help herself.

Her eyes flashing defiantly as he cocked an eyebrow at her as he set the bottle onto the shelf next to the top. A muscle twitching in his neck. She paled further as she realized he was settling them in the room and wasn't meaning to stop to leave for nothing.

"Well, I'm not going to *fuck* you like a lady. I thought you would have gotten that hint in the limo, when you didn't get a chaser then either. Keep up with me, baby," he taunted back. Mind games were what got him off more than anything. That's why his stare was so intense, as if he could see into the deepest recesses of your mind.

If you can manage to crawl under someone's skin, you can control them more than you ever could physically because the body could only take so much.

But the mind was a strong heady thing.

Olivia's breathing came harsher as the liquor settled. She groaned as the burn ignited hotter deep down in her belly, making her pant in earnest now. He reached into another spot within the cabinet and pulled out a tiny pair of scissors, snipping the straps on her gown. His fingertips brushed briefly against her skin, making goosebumps appear.

The silky gown caught on the tips of her nipples as it fell from her bosom. He'd stared at her again with a half-smile on his face.

"It pleases me greatly that you enjoy this," he said, reaching forward and pulling the dress the rest of the way down with his fingertip. He placed his arms above her on the frame, leaning in and ignoring her trembling from standing on her toes for so long. She gasped as she lowered, desperate for relief, choking on the belt once more, and again flew back up on her toes.

"Are you going to fuck me like a good boy now?" she hissed through the tightness around her neck. She giggled humorlessly, goading him.

Colin tilted his head at her, a wicked smile breaking out across his face.

She moaned as he put his nose to her throat and inhaled, unbothered by her dilemma and her words.

"Oh baby, I think you're sadly, *sadly* mistaken. I'm not the *good boy* hero in this story of ours. What book have you been reading? Whatever it is, it's the wrong edition. I'm the fucking *big bad wolf*, mama. And I eat little girls like you for a *snack*." He lowered his arms and, with a flick of his wrist, undid his pants and pulled his erection out.

The massive column drooping down slightly under its weight. Saliva filled her mouth instantly at the sight, and she attempted to swallow as she began to struggle anew. He caught her eye again as he reached above and grabbed a tie. He was determined to wait her out.

The beat of the music created a sensual atmosphere, the bass engulfing them both as he stepped into her and put the tie to her mouth. She jerked her head away, nervous.

"Colin, *please*," she tried again, her eyes now imploring as he held the green fabric up to her mouth.

"Open. You're done talking without permission," he ordered, a muscle clenching in his jaw.

She parted her lips on a defeated whimper, the fight gone from her body. Her legs shook hard, the feeling slipping from her toes. Her eyes flickered between his, her breath shooting out hot and fast from her nose as she panicked.

He leaned down to kiss her forehead before slipping the tie into her mouth and securing it at the back of her head.

A couple of tears slipped from her eyes as he stepped away, and she felt her ribs and belly contracting with every ragged inhale. She was terrified, and extremely turned on. So much so she could feel her wet panties rubbing uncomfortably between her legs. He slid them down and off her feet before straightening back up, holding them to his nose.

His eyes flashed at her as he inhaled her scent.

"Ah!" she yelped sharply as he slapped her breast hard enough to sting. Then repeated with her other breast.

The burn spread to join the heat of her arousal.

"Did he ever get a chance to smell you?" Colin whispered darkly, placing the little scrap of fabric against Olivia's nose. Her scent infiltrated the space between them, and she whimpered, shaking her head no. More tears leaked out, falling into the tie around her face. She relented, relaxing her calves to bring her heels to the floor, needing to relieve her straining muscles.

She held her breath, wiggling her toes and bending her calf back to stretch it, crying out again as he slapped her outter thigh, *hard*.

She struggled under his watchful gaze, enduring him slapping her randomly on her thighs, her ass, even her arms. And right before she went back on her toes to inhale, he snatched her up and roughly slammed her on his thick cock. Relentlessly pressing all the way in until he bottomed out inside of her and still pressed harder, grinding, getting it all in.

Colin dropped his head to her shoulder, giving her another little grind as he listened to her muffled screams of pleasured pain echo around the room, mixing with the music.

He inhaling sharply as her fingernails sunk into his shoulder blades. He paused for a second and rocked them deceptively gentle, to the music from side to side. Giving her just a slight second to recover, since he'd impaled her rather roughly before she even had a chance to suck in air after strangling herself on his belt.

Colin pulled back to catch her eye. She was panting and crying as her fingers continued to claw painfully into his shoulder blades. Her eyes wild and unfocused.

He smiled slightly. "Look at me," he demanded softly, his fingers tightening on her hips before he pulled out to the tip, waiting.

His body was absolutely burning to push back into the hot tight clasp of her body, but he held still, waiting for her. Lost in sensation, she refocused her green eyes and found him easily. Colin smiled briefly, seeing they were wide with fear and excitement. Nodding at what he'd found there within its depths, he purposefully gripped her even harder, wrenching a cry out of her throat before he rammed back in on an animalistic grunt.

He mercilessly pounded her up and down on his engorged dick, growling with every hard thrust.

Olivia's mind raced hearing the sharp slap of their bodies meeting and echoing around the room, mingling with their sex sounds and the music. Colin watched her creamy breasts slap against her ribcage, adding to the swirl of lust that congregated in his brain like the perfect storm to fuel his jealousy, anger, and lust.

He fucked her like that for several rotations of songs. Until her wild screams and moans lessened, sounding hoarser and more sparse until he noticed she'd lost her voice. She'd orgasmed several times, her cum dripping down and slickening them both.

He chuckled darkly as Olivia started mumbling through the tie around her mouth. Clearly deep in subspace.

He alternated the brutal strokes with getting down on his knees underneath her, wrapping her legs around his shoulders and sucking her off softly. Giving her a brief reprieve.

Colin serviced her body until his arms strained with exertion and sweat dripped down his back, making her nails feel like razors digging into his skin. His lungs burned, and his broad muscular chest was rock hard with tension. The cords and veins throughout his arms and torso visibly sticking out harshly against his skin.

A glance in the mirror showed him that the back of her thighs were bright red from the tight bruising grip he kept on her.

Colin put the discomfort of his body into the back of his mind, stopping briefly to take a drink of vodka, gasping at the burn, welcoming it. He placed his hand back under Olivia's hip and readjusted his grip slightly, looking down at her. He'd long since let her close her eyes, and she'd tilted her head back and was currently hanging there, her pretty mouth parted. Her hair swishing like a waterfall of fire behind her back.

He bent down and took a distended nipple between his teeth, now moving them side to side with the beat as he circled his hips deeply. Hearing her fresh cries as he pressed painfully all the way to the back of her pussy. She cried out weakly and orgasmed again, her muscles rippling and clutching tightly at the massive dick inside her.

He ended their slight break, resuming the brutal pace he'd had started with.

Outside in their bedroom past the locked closet door, muted sounds of flesh slapping, sobbing, his harsh redirection, reprimands, and the sultry beats seeped out into the room for the next two hours until he'd ejaculated inside her with an animalistic growl.

When the pain of fucking her so intensely blacked his mind out, and he no longer thought of the man who had the nerve to step into what was his earlier that night, he finally let himself find release.

Ungagging her, he cradled her limp body in one arm as he released her from the belt with the other, his hand quickly going to her neck to rub and massage the abraded skin there. He kissed her softly, sealing his mouth over the soft moans escaping her lips.

Colin carried her straight into the shower and quickly rinsed them both with her still in his arms. Not washing them up, but rinsing the night away.

Laying her carefully down on her side of the bed, he crawled in behind her. Firmly wrapping his body around her now silent one.

He pressed a kiss to her lips and breathed deeply, feeling the ache in his body already. He rubbed his hand down her back repeatedly. Murmuring to her what a good, brave girl she was.

Waiting patiently until her breathing deepened, and her chest rose and fell rhythmically in sleep, before he allowed himself to follow her into slumber.

***

Colin woke up a few hours later with a panicked groan, panting, feeling his heart racing.

His legs were tangled in the blankets, and he wrestled with them, trying to get free.

Colin yanked himself free of the bed, hitting the floor on one knee before he stumbled to the bathroom. He closed the door, crouching down on his haunches for a second, trying to regain his senses. He was struggling. His mind still gripped on the edges of his nightmare, and all he could hear was screaming, sirens, and glass crunching.

"*God*." he groaned, squeezing his eyes shut tight, mentally battling the past trying to come through into his present.

Standing up, he walked to the vanity and placed his hands palm down on the cold white marble of the sink and looked at himself in the mirror. A pulsing vein was sticking out in his neck. The lights of the bathroom threw his features in sharp relief as his chest heaved. Turning the faucet on cold, he splashed some water on his face and put his head down.

He took a second trying to count, attempting to breathe, anything to make the nightmare fade.

"Colin?" Olivia called out, her soft voice bleeding through the door. She tapped two times on the door quietly before cracking the door open slightly. "Can I help? Are you okay?"

She cautiously poked her head in, and he noticed she'd put a silky robe on. His head turned slightly as she shimmied her way through the crack in the door, her gaze meeting his hesitantly. Her face tight with concern.

"No, go back to sleep," he said hoarsely, turning back to his reflection in the mirror.

His shoulders were tight, and he was struggling to get it under control this time. Not like the other times when he could will himself to calm down. She ignored him, inching her way over, and put a hesitant hand out.

His haunted, empty eyes found hers in the mirror.

"If you touch me, I'm adding six months onto our agreed time," he bit out harshly, his body tensing up as Olivia got closer.

Tears pricked the back of his eyes as she inched closer to him despite his threat, her green eyes turning dark with worry. He groaned and closed his eyes at the first touch of her fingers on his shoulder. She leaned in and placed her lips on his skin next to her fingers as his body suddenly wracked with tears.

"Olivia," he said, his voice cracking as he reached out and snatched her to him desperately.

His arms banded around her almost painfully as he gripped her, his arms wrapped around her back and clutching at her ribcage. He buried his head in her neck and suddenly hauled her up on the vanity.

He got a welcome hint of the hard sex that they shared, still on her skin.

He placed her down harshly, the items there clattering as they fell to the side. She wrapped her arms and legs around him tightly, ignoring the burn in her thighs for being held open for hours. Olivia's fingers stroked his hair and the back of his neck. She ignored how hard he was squeezing her and shushed him gently. Rocking him, and also ignoring the twinge of pain at that simple movement.

She stared unseeing at the ceiling of the bathroom as her mind searched for a way to calm him.

"There once was a *fierce* and rather handsome gentleman named Richard Todd," she began softly. Sweeping her hand in broad strokes down his back, her other hand still cupping and squeezing the back of his neck. "Who broke away from his fellow noblemen and joined a band of merry foresters who were outlaws."

His shudders subsided, and his heart rate slowed, the fog finally lifting. Her body and her voice enveloped him into a soft, safe cocoon. She worked to open her robe to press her naked skin against his, wrapping her arms around him once more.

"He worked with the thieves to take the money back from the evil men who stole from the people in their land, and so they named him Robin Hood. The giver of thieves." She whispered, not remembering much of the story but trying so hard for this man.

Not even caring in that moment if he thought she was silly for ad libbing a children's story.

She continued with the tale. Making up an elaborate tale of sword fighting with sheriffs and close calls with bandits, her hands caressing him tirelessly the whole time. She used funny voices, and even mimicked animal sounds to surprise him and try to get him to laugh. Which he did once.

After a bit, he picked her up with her still wrapped around him, and carried her back to bed where she climbed on top of him and kissed him sweetly. Running her hands along his body and rocked him back to sleep.

His nightmare was firmly and decidedly dissipating.

THIRTY-FOUR

Need To Feel Normal

THE NEXT MORNING OLIVIA opened her eyes to her birth control, two ibuprofen, and a warmed cup of coffee. Colin was not in bed with her. Fighting rising disappointment, she looked over at his pillow and seen he'd written her a note. She picked it up slowly, pushing her hair behind her ear as she sat up.

Any thought she had about waking up with him after last night and discussing his nightmare dissipated in a flurry of disappointment. Was he even going to talk about it with her?

She read the note.

> Olivia,
> Take your medicine, take a bath, and relax. I'm in the down-stairs study handling a couple last-minute work-related things before break.
> Colin

Colin wrote the note hastily, knowing his words were true. But it was also the truth that Colin needed to call his doctor's office and get a slightly higher dose of his anxiety medicine. Knowing to get a handle on it so Olivia didn't have to worry about if he was losing his mind or not.

If he was in control or not.

Olivia whimpered as she swung her legs over the side of the bed. The heavy, hurt feeling settling deep into her bones and giving her that exhausted feeling she missed when she worked herself to death every month for Allison's medical expenses.

Olivia arched her head back, taking pleasure in the feeling and reveling in the soreness. She thought about her sudden epiphany last night, however; she was still unsure of her feelings around identifying as a masochist.

Doesn't that make me just like my clients? she wondered.

A fresh wave of confusion and insecurity broke over her consciousness. She just didn't feel like she related to the men that she beat. And because she wasn't disclosing that piece of information about her life to Colin, the one person that could probably help her, couldn't.

She bit her lip, sighing as she sank into a melancholy state.

Sinking into the bath, her hand flew up to her throat as she recounted the events from last night. She'd remembered how helpless she'd felt as she was strapped to the wall by her neck, and how freeing it felt that she'd been forced to give up control. She thought about all the other times she and Colin had been together. Not being able to help not to compare the ones where he'd taken her relatively regularly, versus when he'd stepped in with his dominate side.

She admitted to herself that the feeling she had after he was particularly vicious with her was definitely more satisfying. And she still couldn't force herself to pick. All were sides of Colin, and she cherished each one. Her brain easily turned that thought over and tucked it away somewhere remote where she'd stored all the things she didn't want to inspect too closely.

Taking the loofah, Olivia absentmindedly ran it up her arms.

Her eyes stared off into space as she thought about the rest of the agreement. How was she going to get out of this without a broken heart? He'd given her no real indication that he cared for her beyond a person he signed a contractual agreement with. For not the first time, she'd thought about the house she designed some years ago, asking herself if she'd known then what she knew now, would she have still designed it?

This thing between them was getting complicated, in more ways than one.

Her gaze narrowed, her thoughts now turning to once the agreement was over. He would be living in the house she designed, and where would she be?

Alone?

Biting her lip, she dismissed all thoughts, feeling herself getting upset. Once again shutting down her emotions in favor of putting on a front for this man who expected her to perform for him. Stepping carefully out of the bath, she blow dried her hair and secured the mass into a thick bun at the top of her head. She lightly did her makeup, smeared a light gloss on her lips, and dressed in all black today.

Like her mood.

Padding over to the bed, she grabbed her phone from the nightstand and opened her phone up to her text messages before finding Vanessa.

> Hey sis, are you free? -Ollie

She waited a second until she saw the three ellipses show up, indicating that Vanessa was responding. She walked to the lounge and sat down in a chair.

> Yes, what's up O? You ok? -Nessie

> Yes. -Ollie

She scrunched her eyebrows before typing back quickly.

> That's a lie. I'm not ok, I don't think. I'm con-
> fused. -Ollie

> Ok...what's up? What's bothering/confusing
> you? Is it Colin? -Nessie

> No..maybe. Sort of, but not really. Nessie, do
> you know what a masochist is? -Ollie

> Yes. Are you finally figuring out you are one?
> Lol. I've been waiting a long time for this
> conversaatttiiiooonnnnn! Did the man bring
> out your wild side finally? OMG bitch, puh-
> LEEASEE tell me the dick is good. That's all I
> want to hear!-Nessie

Vanessa sent about twenty demon emojis, five water squirt emojis, and a few eggplant emojis after the text.

Olivia's jaw hit the ground as she reread her sister's text exactly four times before she responded.

> I'm sorry, what do you mean you've been
> waiting years for this conversation? And I'm
> finally figuring it out? Like, you knew? -Ollie

Olivia waited forever for her to text back.

> Well, not explicitly, no. But come on, I'm
> your big sister. I've always noticed things.
> You would do weird shit like brush your hair
> too hard, hitting your head with every pass
> of the brush. Or you're always biting the shit
> out of your finger when you're stressed. You
> press your hands into your eyes hard when
> you're upset. You would dig your fingernails

into your skin. It's like anytime you needed relief from something, you would find a
way to hurt yourself. It was never like, serious enough for us to worry that you needed
to go to the doctor or anything but- even
grandpa Stephen mentioned some things a
few times and I then i knew I wasn't crazy for
thinking it. -Nessie

Olivia paused, rereading her message a couple of times. She waited, seeing the three dots indicating Vanessa was typing more.

Soooo can you answer my questions
please??? I'll tell you, Johnathan is just….
sigh like I would suck the fucking chrome
off his dick if he asked me to. The man is
beautiful. Fucking amazing. He is blowing
my MIND. He did this thing to my ass with his
tongue the other day that had me screaming for Jesus and you know I don't do that.
-Nessie

Olivia's mouth formed an 'oh' before she felt her face heat up. She pressed the back of a shaky hand to her mouth, trying to hold in a hilarious giggle.

Oh my GAWD Vanessa!-Ollie

I giveee…yes Colin is absolutely blowing my
mind too. Last night, he tied me to the closet
with one of his belts around my neck. Then
fucked me for three hours straight. It was
amazing. The best was when he made me
strangle myself before he picked me up.-O
llie

Vanessa sent about fifty shocked and then laughing emojis.

Oh my god. You are such a freak.-Nessie.

I really like him sis and it makes me scared. How am I going to get to the end of this in one piece? -Ollie

Well, does there have to be an end? Why can't this turn into something other than an agreement? Relationship > Agreement. Johnathan said the man is absolutely infatuated with you. -Nessie

Olivia put her phone down and looked up, thinking to herself. Contemplating her sister's words.

Yeah, well, if that's the case, why couldn't he wake up with me this morning and talk to me about his nightmare he had last night instead of running? The man wants to know my secrets but won't even tell me any of his, she thought, her sad feeling returning.

She looked at her phone again.

I don't know. I have to go Vanessa. Gotta run to the grocery store. Thanks for talking to me. Love ya. -Ollie

Grabbing her purse, she took the elevator downstairs, stretching her aching quads on the way down. The melancholy feeling magnified as she opened the elevator door, feeling Colin's presence somewhere in the house.

Walking with purpose, she'd rounded the bend and stepped into his office without knocking, finding him standing, leaning his hips against his desk, reading some papers. He had his reading glasses on, and the hair on his jaw looked slightly thicker, betraying his lack of grooming that morning.

His eyes met hers over the top of the papers, freezing on lips before flickering back to hers.

A tense moment passed between them before she swallowed, clutching her purse to her body tightly.

"I'm going to the grocery store to get the items we need for Thanksgiving. If you have anything special you need, please text me so I can get it on the way back in," she said hoarsely, her voice still scratchy from screaming for hours the night before.

Colin stayed silent as he penetrated her with his stare.

Her lips parted briefly as she figured out that's what it was. He was eye fucking her from head-to-toe with just his look. She blinked rapidly, looking away uncomfortably before turning awkwardly making her way out of the office. Not waiting for him to respond. Quickly making her way to the garage, she blinked back stinging tears, betraying rising emotions.

Upset because she was emotional, she'd gunned the gas a little too hard and flinched as she came just a hair away from annihilating his favorite bike. Why he kept it there so close to her car, she didn't know. Gritting her teeth hard, she correcting her car and pulling out smoothly, punching the button that let the garage door up.

Tears streamed down her face as she rounded the house and down the garage.

Her phone pinged. Vanessa.

Biting her lip angrily, she pushed the button to call her, knowing she was doing it because Colin wanted her to.

"Hey, babe. How's it going?" her sister chirped cheerfully over the phone.

She sucked in a deep breath, hating that she smelled fresh new leather instead of her car's old musky smell. She turned the heat off, preferring to feel the fridge air like she did when she was in her own car that provided her with no heat.

"Did Colin call you?" she asked, already knowing the answer.

"Yes, he's worried about you. Olivia, are you okay?" Vanessa prodded.

"I don't know. I don't know what I am anymore." She said, her voice thickening with tears.

"Well... you have to trust your heart." Vanessa's voice crooned over the phone.

"No offense, Vanessa. My fucking heart makes no difference. Never has, you know that," she said harshly, glancing in the rearview mirror she'd seen her nose and eyes were red. She drove down the streets slowly.

"That man loves you, sis. Why can't you just relax and let it happen?"

She wished it were comforting.

"*Because* every fucking good thing that happens to me gets taken away. You know that. I'm just so tired of being disappointed," she said with a strained voice, her breath hitching in her chest.

"Olivia, we can figure this out. There's still time. You're about to go back into school, the majority of our stress is over! You have options, we're in a better place than we were-"

"No. No! I'm not doing that, and I don't want to hear it. We've already talked about this, Vanessa. And you're wrong, time is the one thing I'm *solidly* running out of," she said harshly, thinking of all the time that's racked up the agreement between her and Colin, suddenly wishing she hadn't accepted the call.

In an extremely rare move, she hung up on her sister. Fighting the urge to throw her head back and close her eyes in agitation, she turned off the highway, merging onto another one a few exits down, heading to the diner, needed desperately to feel normal.

THIRTY-FIVE
Poison = Love Confessions

BELINDA WAS THERE WHEN she walked in. Olivia noted with some happiness that her old boss looked happy and refreshed, and the diner was spruced up rather nicely, with new paint, new floor, and new windows. The outside was updated as well, with fresh paint and some plants.

She bristled, knowing it was Colin's doing. Irritated that she couldn't seem to go anywhere without thinking of him, seeing him.

Olivia pushed the feelings aside and hugged the woman with a big smile. Laughing as Belinda leaned forward to smack a kiss onto her cheek affectionately, and motioned for her to sit down in a corner. The woman caught her up on all the going ons at the diner, and who was working there now and their gossip. They chatted over a nasty cup of coffee and a piece of pie. And she was once again reminded of Colin and the day he'd came into the diner and gave her his card for the first time.

Her phone pinged with a text from Colin, as if he'd felt her thinking about him.

> Where are you, are you ok baby? You ran out before we had a chance to really connect this morning. -C

> I'm fine. Just out, will be out for a while. -O

> Are the stores crazy? -C

Olivia debated her answer to that, realizing that she was at the diner and if he really wanted to timestamp locations, she was a sitting duck. So, she decided to answer simply, as she wasn't in the store. A lie by omission.

> No.-O

The three ellipses on his end appeared and disappeared several times before a simple text came through.

> *Let me know if you need anything. -C*

She'd tossed her phone on the table, annoyed.

Olivia finished her visit and said goodbye to Belinda, leaving the largest tip she'd ever left before heading back to her car and sliding in. Her car pinged as it connected to her phone, another reminder of Colin's presence in her life.

She turned off the highway, heading to her old neighborhood.

A bit later, she stood still in front of her old apartment door, seeing a yellow welcome mat indicating that another tenant had already moved in. Her eyes stung with tears as she stupidly put her hand on the door.

She bent forward and rested her forehead on her hand. Remembering tearing up the hundred-dollar bills that Colin gave her and how she tore it up and left it in front of the door for him to see. She cried genuine tears now, mourning her apartment and her old life. Knowing that somehow, someway, she'd needed to say goodbye to what she once was and find a way to move forward however that looked, with or without Colin.

Could they find a way forward together with so many secrets between them?

The future looked bleak to her despite the glitz, glamor, and ease of her current lifestyle. She'd been witnessing Vanessa becoming closer to Johnathan seemingly by the day, and she owed it to her to step back a little and let her explore what that was without her always inserting herself.

She quickly reminded herself that though she loved Allison more than anything, she had a mother who deserved to find her own slice of happiness.

Olivia wrapped her arms around her torso, her body lowering into a crouch as she pressed her wrists to her eyes hard. With some effort, she got it together, giving a lingering glance at her old door. She put her fingers to her lips, kissing them briefly before gently pressing them to the door.

Letting her old life go.

She turned to go back up the stairs and inhaled in surprise, her heart crawling into her throat when she saw Colin standing there at the top of the landing. He leaned against the brick wall, staring down at her with that penetrating gaze of his. Not speaking.

She shivered as he made his way down the steps, his big body quickly filling the small space. She tilted her head back slightly to look at him, his brown eyes stared warmly at her.

"How did you know I was here?" She swallowed thickly, fighting back a wave of tears.

The look on his face as he was fucking into her body the night before suddenly entered her mind and she blushed, looking down quickly. He placed his finger under her chin, raising her head back up.

"I'll always find you, Olivia," Colin said, his gentle eyes boring into hers. His hand wrapped around her waist, preventing her from stepping backwards away from him. "And I mean *always*." he warned, leaning further into her.

Her breasts rose and fell as she grappled with emotion.

He didn't close the distance, letting her make the decision but his eyes flickered between hers almost as if he was praying she'd lean into him.

"Touch me," Colin whispered, his lips a hairs breadth away from hers. His smell assaulted her senses, making her dizzy.

She let out a desperate gasp as she raised her hands slowly to his chest, feeling the hard muscles bunching underneath.

Giving in, she slowly raised her head, pressing her lips against his softly.

Olivia moaned, uninvited tears falling as he licked his tongue across her sensitive skin, searching. She pressed deeper into his body, parting her lips with a small sound and accepting him into her mouth, tilting her head back to give him further access to her. His hand came up to the side of her head, and he cupped her gently, letting her know that he could be both hard and soft. His other hand trailed down her arm and clasped her hand.

"We're going home," Colin said, brushing his thumb against her lips.

She nodded in agreement, following him up the stairs, and he followed her home. He pulled in next to her spot and led her to the hot tub, stripping them slowly. He grabbed his phone and put a song on repeat that expressed what he felt for her.

Olivia's heart thudded painfully as the singer began to sing in her haunting voice.

Colin placed her into the hot water and followed her down, covering her body gently with his. As he kissed away her tears, his heart broke in half at what he'd saw her go through standing in front of her old apartment. His chest ached as she wrapped her arms around his neck in a desperate hug.

He wasn't even sure she knew why she was clinging to him the way she was, there was so much unsaid between them.

I love her. I want to be her home, Colin thought to himself. But she wouldn't let him in.

He didn't have the key to her heart.

Tracing her curves with his hands, he pulled back and held her gaze as he took her leg and hooked it over his hip. The singer crooned as his heart thumped hard.

He groaned as he lowered her ever so slowly onto him, hearing her broken cries. He held her still against him, looking into her eyes. Images flashed of them in the diner, the night of the storm when they'd first met, the very first time he saw her red hair in the diner window while he was on his bike, and he pulled over just before he got ready to take a steep curve too fast in the storm.

He'd stopped to watch momentarily when she'd lifted her head and he saw a helpless, tortured expression in her eyes before she lowered her head into her hands again. Her hair reminding him of the family that he'd killed on that cold night, many years ago. A family of all redheads.

Would she be his redemption?

Colin shuddered, pressing his hand to the side of her face, staring deep into her eyes as she moaned, trying to close her eyes against his stare. His other hand went to her breastbone to feel her heart beating.

"Please look at me, baby, I need your eyes," Colin whispered, his skin pebbling as he pushed her wet hair behind her ear and caressed her lip with his thumb.

Admitting to himself that he loved this woman; it was going to be her or no one else. He knew she saw pain when she looked into his eyes. He sifted through more memories, placing his hands around her neck with his thumbs, stroking her throat.

Olivia in her apartment in her pretty green dress, her nervously rifling through her kitchen trying to hide just how destitute she'd become. The two of them standing side by side looking at her blueprints and drinking one-hundred-and-fifty-dollar wine out of fifty cent mugs. He and her at the Italian restaurant as he was translating the menu in English, and she'd still tried to order something cheap, thinking she wasn't worthy.

Colin moaned as she ground her hips against him, listening to her whimper. He fisted his hand in her hair as his heart went into overdrive, more memories flashing. The singer's voice was torturing them both.

He pressed his hips up into hers, grinding with her.

Them in the car when she'd set a grueling schedule designed to break her body and her spirit in the span of five minutes. Her, when she'd seen their agreement for the first time. The look on her face when she introduced Allison to him. The first time he entered her sweet body after he'd spent most of the day in a panic thinking he'd lost her. Her, the night before when she pulled him out of his fucked-up nightmare, thinking nothing could save him from his torment.

It was her.

It all came to the forefront of his mind as she sat perched on his lap, trusting him after he'd so viciously unleashed himself on her last night.

He moved gently, sitting back, and encouraging her to set the pace. Watching her swaying breasts as she gently rocked them to the beat of her heart. They were so entwined in that moment, neither of them orgasmed. Just wanting to be close. His hands held her tightly to him while he walked them out of the hot tub and back upstairs to their bedroom, where he'd held her for hours, giving her the care that he should have given her that morning. Not bothering to even figure out if she'd gotten her grocery order.

He'd already called the caterer, anyway.

***

A bit later, they ventured downstairs, where they settled into the lounge and ate cheap fried bologna sandwiches and chips and watched Hamilton. Colin got a kick out of watching her giggle at the king's song, not even minding when she rewound it several times. She sat on the floor between his legs and leaned her head back on his thigh. He stroked her hair contentedly, feeling rather raw and exposed after their lovemaking session in the hot tub.

"He *spits* when he sings! Haha! Look at him, Colin," she laughed, rewinding the scene again.

He chuckled with her, much preferring the joyful look on her face than the haunted, tortured one from earlier.

They fell asleep in the lounge, being woken up by Mary the next morning. Then, to Colin's delight and dismay, Olivia took him on the craziest grocery store shopping excursion he'd ever experienced in his whole life. He was so decidedly frightened by their fourth store run that he excused himself to the men's restroom to text Vanessa and Mary in secret. Unashamedly creating a group chat to ask them if this shit was normal.

Later that night, after they unloaded an insane number of groceries, Colin texted Mary again, to let her know that in case he didn't make it through the holiday that he loved her, and where the life insurance policy and living will was kept. He instructed her to bury his body, preferably alongside Olivia's, as she would be dead too, theoretically. She wrote back with a bunch of laughing emojis, telling him he got it bad.

He didn't need that reminder. He knew.

The evening before Thanksgiving, they all reconvened to hang out and be together. Johnathan's family lived across the world in the Middle East and didn't celebrate, and the two of them usually went on vacation to some obscure island and had general billionaire man fun.

But this year was different. Johnathan joked around with him, saying that he just wanted to see if Colin could do it-*be a normal family man.* And ironically, Olivia wanted to test a batch of pan of mac and cheese, just to see if she could do it.

They'd stood around the island, listening to Allison's show playing in the background. They all stared at each other crowded around the mac and cheese pan that Olivia worked so hard on. Attempted to wait each other out, the three of them holding a spoon and a small saucer plate. Each one waiting for the other to take the first plunge.

Colin looked at Olivia, who was smiling so proudly.

Vanessa was currently absolved, blinking back tears, Johnathan was sweating, having been filled in thoroughly by Vanessa, and then he in turned filled Colin in. Which made him so anxious earlier that day that he had to have a rare time out in the study to dissociate for a minute.

Olivia moved first, completely oblivious to the inner war that each person was fighting in their head over a relatively innocent looking pan of mac and cheese. It actually looked good, which made Colin felt a little better.

Colin grinned, before frowning.

He sobered quickly, knowing not to judge a book by its cover, scooping out a spoonful of mac and cheese onto each of their plates.

"Dig in!" Olivia sang happily as she beamed up at Colin. And he realized one of her rare joys was *also* the holidays. Catching Vanessa's eye he put a spoonful in his mouth, and then quickly corrected himself before he physically recoiled.

Oh. My. Mother fucking God, he thought, as every taste bud he didn't even know he had was activated at once.

He stoically stood there and chewed, his eyes watering. He groaned harshly on a swallow, hiding it with a moan that he'd hoped sounded like he'd enjoyed it. As he was currently struggling to clear his throat, fighting for his life, he noticed he wasn't the only one.

Johnathan's face turned a color he'd never seen before. Colin silently laughed to himself as he saw the big guy scootch his plate till it was completely against his body and hunkered down over it, hiding his face from all of them as he shoveled it down. Finishing on an incredibly alarming cough, he'd stood up quickly and grabbed a cup, filling it with water before sucking that down and then filling up and drinking another one.

He tossed Colin a single bottle of water before bringing one over to Vanessa. His color was almost back to normal.

"Well, what do you think?" Olivia asked breathlessly, tucking a thick lock of hair behind her ear and smiling.

"Oh my *gosh*, you did it this year, sis. You do it every year, in fact!" Vanessa quipped, saying a lot without actually saying anything at all. Colin noted that as a unique talent of hers.

Olivia beamed brighter.

"Yes Olivia, that was definitely mac and cheese! You do this *every year girl*? That's unbelievable," Johnathan answered quickly, following Vanessa's lead.

Olivia nodded proudly, completely oblivious.

"*And,*" Colin stated quickly, draping the foil over the pan and hurriedly putting it in the refrigerator. "Because you're so damn *smart,* you saved yourself time tomorrow from having to fix another one, so it'll be one less thing for you to have to do the day of. I knew I loved you for a reason," he let slip, the endearment coming out before he could even think.

Colin silently cursed to himself as he closed the refrigerator slowly. He paused, taking a deep breath before turning to face her. He stared at her as her face reddened, her eyes wide, the mac and cheese fiasco effectively forgotten.

"Aww, that's sweet." Johnathan chuckled, breaking the silence. Pulling Vanessa closer who suddenly stopped secretly trying to scrape her tongue on the side of her teeth, looking at Olivia with interest.

"You don't have to say anything," Colin whispered sheepishly. "I'm sorry, it just slipped out." He admitted, turning without looking at the others, grabbing their plates and taking them to the sink. Mentally slapping himself.

In the window's reflection he saw Vanessa turn and glance at Allison before slowly dragging her gaze back around, staring at Olivia with an expression in her eyes he couldn't place.

The interaction niggled at his brain, making him off center.

Olivia hugged him from behind, pressing her cheek to his back, not saying anything.

She rubbed her hands down his chest and stomach, stroking him unashamedly. Johnathan had thankfully changed the subject, boasting about how their vehicles and software had been picked up for distribution in Asia, and how some hot shot CEO there had wanted to buy the rights to the software if Colin was interested.

Johnathan knew Colin wasn't interested, but also knew that talking about work took his mind off things.

Colin listened quietly as he did the dishes by hand, not ready to turn around yet and face them.

Eventually the tension naturally dissipated, and they went back to normal. The doorbell rang, signaling the delivery of the Chinese food he'd ordered for their dinner tonight. They ate, putting Allison to bed before settling into the lounge with drinks, watching a movie. He'd noticed Olivia was drinking slightly more tonight, and when she tried to get her fourth drink, he'd slowly ran his hand down the length of her arm, quietly taking it from her and placing it firmly away where she couldn't get it.

Olivia got on top after they'd all gone to bed.

Colin drank up her breathless moans as she ground herself on him, falling forward and taking his mouth rather desperately as she worked over him to find her release. His hands were everywhere; in her hair, grabbing her breasts, her hips, helping her move.

Not having her on top often, he took time to appreciate how fluidly she moved. She didn't bother to jerk herself around on top of him like most women do when they're on top. She gyrated, really giving him a show, running her fingers through her hair, and down her body, caressing herself so he could see, making it so good for him.

And when he was ready for the curtain to close, he flipped her and gave her his best standing ovation, his lips devouring her cries as he circled nice and deep.

He went to sleep with that niggling feeling in his brain bothering him. He knew Vanessa knew something that was crucial, and those sly looks meant something. Instinct told him that maybe whatever she could tell him could unlock Olivia's heart.

Vanessa had the key.

THIRTY-SIX

Everybody But You

THE NEXT MORNING JOHNATHAN woke him up with a text. He'd slept in late, not able to fall asleep for a long time, his brain not letting it go.

> Bro is she freaking serious? Did Olivia tell you about this shit?-Big J-Dawg

> What are you talking about? I just woke up .-C. Kent

> APPARENTLY we can't eat until thanksgiving dinner, it's tradition. Oh and your girl is already cooking. It's 8! everything's going to be burnt by 5 And she's putting something in a pot that makes last night's mac and cheese look like a prime rib comparatively.- J.-Dawg

He tried to type as he got up to pull on his clothes, but Johnathan beat him to it.

> Get your fucking ass down here right now before I come up there and beat your goddamn ass through the floor and shove that nasty ass fucking mac and cheese down your throat and choke you with it. -J

Knowing he was serious, and slightly afraid of Johnathan's background as a torture specialist for the government, Colin's heart raced as he tripped down the stairs in his hurry. Recovering quickly, he rounded to the foyer to Johnathan trying to weasel pancakes out of Allison's plate, who was currently not in the mood to share.

Colin caught his eye as he turned the corner and saw Vanessa determinedly trying to work his espresso machine. His eyes widened, seeing Olivia placed the biggest turkey he'd ever seen in his life in his oven while she was speaking to Johnathan.

"You have really got to stop it with the *halal* shit. We *know*. We're not going to poison you; I bought beef to go into the greens, okay? Jesus." Olivia said breathlessly, closing the oven door and wiping her hands down the front of her apron.

Happy Thanksgiving balloons were blown up in the kitchen area nook, complete with taped on polaroid pictures of them all. It was cheap looking, but perfect. Colin rounded the island and greeted everyone, giving Allison a kiss on the top of her head. She was reluctantly holding out a sliver of pancake on a fork for Johnathan.

"Happy Thanksgiving baby," he whispered when he got to Olivia, who was furiously stirring something in a pot. She gave him a sweet kiss as he leaned over to peek in, his stomach turning.

"Happy Thanksgiving!"

Swallowing thickly, he turned and gratefully grabbed a pre-made mimosa.

He jerked his head at Johnathan, who was currently throwing daggers his way, absolutely seething.

"Hey, when Olivia's done getting the food together, we can go downstairs and swim while we watch the Macy's Thanksgiving Day parade on the television. I just had four big monitors mounted. We can put the game on, a Disney show, or both...whatever," he announced, letting the women know he and Johnathan were going to go the lower floor to get it ready.

They nodded, each distracted by their respective tasks.

He took the opportunity to sneak a couple cartons of leftover lo mien noodles from the fridge and exited the kitchen. They snuck to the lower-level full working kitchen where he'd had a couple extra refrigerators, a deep freezer, and a small dining room table.

"Dude, I've never in my life ate something like that before, how do you fuck mac and cheese up that bad?" Johnathan said, taking a seat and shoveling the cold noodles in mouth gratefully. Not even bothering to warm it up. "I mean, I actually got a migraine after we went to bed. Couldn't even touch Vanessa. I thought you were going to have to take me to the hospital."

"I have no clue. No one told you to eat a fucking whole plate. Vanessa and I didn't," he responded, checking his texts for the instructions that Vanessa had sent him about how to schedule the food warm-up process. So she knew how to start switching out different dishes.

> Is she going to notice the turkey is a slightly different size? -C

> No, I normally carve it, so we don't need to worry about that. Relax bro.-Nessie

"Well, excuse me for trying to impress the girl's sister," Johnathan said, rolling his eyes and going to the fridge to grab a bottle of water.

Colin looked on in amusement as his eyes widened in delight at all the catered Thanksgiving food he'd stashed there. Grabbing the bottle, Johnathan turned and looked at Colin up and down.

"And since where talking about screw ups, let's talk about that little slip up last night," Johnathan said lightly, landing his observant eyes on Colin's face.

Colin was busy trying to turn the oven on the correct temperature. Pointedly ignoring him. That niggling feeling came back full force at the mention of his "slip up."

"I mean, I've heard of women cooking so good that they evoke a love confession... but she managed to do that while she simultaneously poisoned us," Johnathan joked, trying to lighten the mood.

Colin continued to ignore him, stepping around him to grab the turkey from the refrigerator.

Johnathan moved closer, grasping his shoulder affectionately.

"Hey, do you really love her?" he probed, decidedly not letting him ignore his question.

Colin stopped in the process of putting the turkey on warm in the oven. He glanced up at his oldest, most trusted friend and nodded his head twice. Not quite able to say it again.

"Have you told her about the accident?" he pressed deeper, not letting up.

Colin gave him a deep, exasperated exhale. "No, *John*. I haven't. Her parents died by getting hit by a drunk driver. When she finds out about what I did, she won't understand. She'll hate me." Johnathan's eyes softened.

"But you weren't drunk, Colin."

Colin huffed a deep breath and turned to his friend swiftly. "It doesn't *matter*. Five people are dead because of me." His hard eyes met Johnathan's steadily, not backing down. "And no matter how much therapy I have, that won't bring them back."

His hands fisted slightly as he became anxious and agitated at the thought of Olivia leaving him if she found out. If he'd ever had the courage to tell her.

"I don't want to lose her," he said gruffly. "That's why I drew up that fucked up agreement."

Johnathan nodded. "You'd be surprised which demons dance very well together, Colin. You should give her a chance. She might surprise you. She's harboring secrets of her own."

Colin nodded. "Isn't it fucked up? We're living together and don't even know each other, really."

"But you know you love her, and love conquers all. Vanessa has alluded to the fact that she thinks that Olivia loves you, too."

"Yeah, but she hasn't *said* it," Colin shot back irritably.

"Give her time."

"Well, we've got plenty of time haven't we?" Colin said curtly.

Johnathan nodded, glancing at the various pans he'd put on low in the warmer, lost in thought for a moment. Colin could see the painful flicker that graced his face. His eyes softened towards his friend, his anxious mood receding slightly.

"Speaking of time, it's nice to see you moving on after... you know. I'm proud of you too," Colin said softly, referencing Johnathan's deceased wife Ezra who'd died of a freak heart attack eight years ago.

His dark eyes held Johnathan's, seeing his shoulders lower as he visibly relaxed.

"Thanks, man," Johnathan said hoarsely.

They threw away the empty Chinese cartoons in the hidden trash bin and went to the pool, setting up the hot tub.

Turns out, switching the food wasn't as hard as he'd expected. And he'd enjoyed laying his dining room table with the china he'd entrusted Mary to buy just for this occasion.

Olivia, in fact, didn't realize they switched everything and she ate with gusto, as did everyone else. Allison, who was not privy to their plans, ignorantly announced that this was the best Thanksgiving meal she'd ever cooked. And right then and there, Colin knew that he'd made the right choice spending an exorbitant amount of money commissioning a private Michelin starred chef to create this meal.

He shared a secret toast with Vanessa in his office as he snuck her in to congratulate her and show her Olivia's Christmas gift.

He'd bought an investment property nearby, and was going to have a prestigious architect company build another office, one he'd planned on gifting to Olivia so she could start her own firm when she was ready.

The Christmas gift wasn't necessarily the building itself, but he'd pulled some strings to get a meeting with the Architect's head CEO, Hendrix King. He'd shown him the blueprints and renderings of the house that Olivia had designed. He'd had those carefully copyrighted first, just in case.

Recognizing raw talent and potential, the CEO was so impressed that he'd offered a paid internship to Olivia when she was out of college. And then he'd turned around and asked to buy the blueprints to the house at a premium price of fifty million dollars so he could add it to their development plan, which he declined politely.

He'd wanted to be the only one in the world with Olivia's original design. So, he quietly funneled his own money into the property, choosing to invest in Olivia so there'd be no loss.

They agreed to a dinner right after Christmas. He accepted graciously.

Vanessa was stunned, trying to keep up with what he was explaining to her. Having no comprehension of business, but instinctively knew that what he was proposing was well outside of the agreed time frame for Colin's and Olivia's agreement. She'd told him so.

He dismissed her, not worrying about it. She gave him a slow look that he couldn't decipher before they left out of the office and rejoined the rest of them out in the lounge. That look ate at him.

It was the proverbial cherry on top of the cake.

And Colin decided he was over all the looks, and the secrets, growing tired of it.

His brain was straining all the time, trying to keep his sadistic tendencies at a minimum while he worked through whatever he was feeling for Olivia. He felt like he was being strangled, his heart swollen too big for his chest. His skin warmed.

Gritting his teeth watching Olivia playing on the floor with Allison, he suddenly snapped. The lack of sleep, the nightmares, and Olivia's rejection all accumulated in one fucked up tornado inside of him. He turned hard eyes onto Vanessa, who was sharing a smile with Johnathan who'd placed a hand on her tummy and was rubbing gentle circles under her shirt.

He walked to Vanessa and jerked his head back the way they'd just came.

Something in Colin's eyes made Johnathan jump up and follow them, slapping his hand against the elevator door that had started to close. Johnathan squeezed his broad body into the elevator with them, giving him a slow once over.

Colin couldn't stand it, feeling laid bare while everyone got to know everything.

The tension sharpened in the small space as his jaw ticked.

"What's going on?" Vanessa asked softly with wide eyes, confused at his sudden change of behavior after the pleasant conversation they had just had in Colin's study.

Her fear sharpened in the room, and she recoiled back into the corner of the elevator, her teeth biting her lip. He took a small step forward and narrowed his eyes as Johnathan suddenly stepped over, half covering Vanessa with his body.

"What's up, man?" Johnathan asked quietly.

But Colin heard the veiled threat under the question.

Colin struggled, his chest tightening further. "I need you to tell me what you know," Colin said softly to Vanessa.

"Colin, I don't know what she did, I promise! I swear it!" she whispered, her hand wrapping around Johnathan's arm, trembling. Clearly misunderstanding him.

"No. There's something else. I can't put my finger on it, but you know. Don't you? It's fucking big, and it's in the *way*," he said, the scent of her fear feeding that side of him that wanted to hurt whatever got in his way. "I need it *gone*, Vanessa. *Tell me!*"

Something flashed in his face that caused Johnathan to fully step in front of Vanessa, and press his back into her. Pressing her against the wall.

"*Mother fucker,* keep whatever you got going on with Olivia to yourself, and leave Vanessa out of it. She's not in that lifestyle," Johnathan spoke harshly, his eyes flashing at him.

Johnathan, who was not a sadist himself, had no problem going toe to toe with one.

Colin's eyes hardened further. "I won't be taken for a fool. She *knows,* Johnathan. Do you know?" He narrowed his eyes at his friend, stepping into his space. "You used to fuck with people for a living. Did you manage to get her to tell you and you're hiding it from me, too? Does everyone know but me?" he whispered harshly, seething.

Having the source of answers, the key to ending his torment right there in his face was visibly killing him.

"I said leave it *alone*. Allah himself won't save you if you fuck with me right now. She hasn't told me a goddamn thing. Now, get your motherfucking ass back!" Johnathan growled, stepping into Colin's face. His own brows lowered.

Colin looked sideways at Vanessa, who was trembling, holding her hand to her stomach.

His eyes narrowed as comprehension sank in. He glanced back at Johnathan, finally stepping to the other side of the elevator, crossing his arms in shock.

"Bro...what the fuck?" Colin cocked his head. "Where y'all going to say anything?"

"Yes. After the holidays. Ness, leave us alone for a bit, baby," Johnathan threw back over his shoulder, turning slightly to block Colin from her as she ran out of the elevator as fast as she could.

The door closed and Johnathan hit the floor to the basement. They stood off in the small space as it lowered slowly.

***

"*Olivia*!" Vanessa yelled, rounding the corner, and picking up Allison, putting her on the couch and turning on a cartoon.

"What is it, momma? Why are you screaming?" she asked, pulling at her stuffed animal.

"Nothing baby, mommy is going to go and talk to Aunt Olivia for a minute, okay? Stay right there and watch your show," Vanessa said, bending down to kiss her on the forehead.

She grabbed Olivia and pulled her to the foyer, turning and whispering furtively.

"Olivia, you need to tell him. It's getting too serious, and I don't like this -*this lying*," she begged, turning tear-filled eyes on Olivia's confused ones. Lamenting as Olivia once again shut her emotions off from her.

"No," Olivia whimpered, shaking her head. "No, Nessie. We agreed! You promised!"

"I'M PREGNANT!" Vanessa yelled, reaching forward and shaking her. Olivia's face flushed in shock at her sister's harshness. "And I'm done with secrets! I can finally have a life without secrets, Olivia. I refuse to go into a relationship without transparency. That man loves you; he *will* accept you; you need to stop being so fucking *stubborn!*"

There was a tense moment of silence where the two sisters just stared at each other.

"Congratulations. Allison's finally going to be a big sister!" Olivia said hollowly once she found her voice, ignoring her comments about Colin.

Blinking away tears and backing up, she blindly reached for the door handle of the front door, feeling her heart crawling through her chest.

"*No.* You're done fucking running from everyone!" Vanessa said, choking on her voice.

She lunged forward grabbing her hand hard and pulling her roughly towards the elevator. Olivia yanked against her hold as Vanessa tossed her in, using her heavier body weight to slightly overpower hers.

"Nessie, no!" Olivia shouted, lamenting to herself as Vanessa slapped the button and closed the elevator door. She felt her soul trying to leave her body as the elevator plunged downwards.

Olivia blanched, feeling like she was free-falling into hell.

"If you won't tell him, I will," Vanessa threatened softly, resolve settling on her faces as she turned to face the doors.

Olivia snapped, lunging for her Vanessa just as soon as the doors open.

They bounced violently off the wall before falling forward through the door frame. The women grappled, pulling each other's hair and screaming, rolling on the floor in a pile of screeching and cursing, flailing limbs and red hair.

The men rounded the corner in alarm, both covered in sweat from their own fight. They looked at each other before lunging into the fray. It took some time, but they were able to rip them apart. Struggling as they each had a fistful of each other's hair, and they had to manhandle them to get them to let go.

Colin pressed his fingers tightly into Olivia's wrist and he took his chance as her grip loosened on Vanessa's hair.

"Olivia, let go! She's pregnant, baby. You can't do this!" Colin yelled, struggling as she'd gotten another fistful of Vanessa's hair. Vanessa was currently gripping into Olivia's arm and yanking at her shirt. Johnathan put his hand around Vanessa's hair above Olivia's grip and yanked, pulling hard.

Colin hauled them apart, putting an arm hard across Olivia's chest, struggling to still her. Johnathan dragged Vanessa back, his hand banded around her chest and one arm around her hips, to not hurt the baby.

Vanessa screeched something inaudible in her high pitched voice, both women completely losing it as they attempted to scream over one another.

A weird beeping sounded in Colin's ears, and the back of his neck prickled.

Olivia broke through at his sudden distraction to grab Vanessa again, and it was clear she was trying to shut her up. He snatched her back with effort as the beeping kept overtaking his brain, touching the part of him that was affected by sirens. The place in his brain where his PTSD lived.

"Be quiet," he said, the women still struggling. Johnathan had resorted to picking up Vanessa, who was trying to claw and kick her way out of his arms.

"*I SAID BE QUIET!*" he roared so loud that everyone suddenly went silent.

Only the sounds of panting and that beeping remained. He gasped, his eyes going wild.

"Where's Allison? That's the alarm system. Where did you two leave her?" he spoke louder, releasing Olivia who had went still in his arms. She glanced at Vanessa before they all jumped into action, running to the elevator.

Olivia turned sharply and burst to the stairs, taking them two at a time. She tore around the corner into the living room, balking at seeing it empty.

The elevator opened, and she stopped them before they tried to get out. door

"Search the upstairs," Olivia ordered, closing the door, and sending them up.

Heart pounding, she ran through the main area of the house, yelling for Allison. She looked everywhere, seeing the study, powder room and the kitchen were empty. Olivia hurried back and checked the front door and saw it was locked. Pausing, her heart skipped a beat as realization shit her and she paled.

Turning slowly to face the terrace, she went to the door seeing the door cracked.

She walked out into the cold air, searching the grounds from above before her eyes landed on the pool.

Olivia felt her heart shatter, and opened her mouth in an ear-splitting scream, seeing Allison's small form sinking through the cover, being swallowed by the water.

Not struggling.

She burst into action and climbed over the railing, not even thinking about taking the stairs. She dropped herself onto the thick, cushioned couch below, knocking the wind out of her. Gasping desperately, she rolled, vaulting the furniture and tearing across the yard to the pool, screaming Allison's name.

Her bare feet beat hard on the grass before slapping onto the concrete by the pool.

She heard the back door crash open, glass splintering as a door broke and Colin emerged through, tearing off after her. Vanessa and Johnathan close behind, both of them yelling.

Olivia ignored them and dove headfirst into the icy pool, hitting the water and the pool cover hard, knocking the wind out of herself once again. Her lungs were burning from the cold frigid air and the icy pool. Heart racing, she struggled through the heavy tarp, attempting to find Allison with no luck. Trying to stem her panic, she emerged and took a deep breath and sunk under the tarp blindly.

The water was freezing.

Her lungs were burning for air as she reached her hands out frantically searching through the icy dark depths, refusing to give up.

Olivia maneuvered through the cold water blindly, ignoring her pain and pushing the tarp away and praying. She emerged again for another lungful of burning, icy air before lunging herself into the deep side. So far under the tarp now, she wasn't sure that even if she found Allison and got her to the surface, that either one of them would make it.

She shivered violently, knowing she was close to the entrance of the grotto, now far away from where she first entered the pool. It was pitch black and soundless as she searched blindly. But she wouldn't let herself lose hope. After several more bone-chilling seconds, her hand bumped into Allison's foot and she grasped it, pulling her to the surface where, thankfully, there was room to poke their head up for oxygen.

Olivia's lungs screamed for air as she emerged with Allison's limp body clutched tight to her.

Colin jumped in, leaving Johnathan and Vanessa to finish unlocking the ties to the cover and pull it out of the way, giving them space to not get tangled again. He grabbed Allison from her, putting her gently on the side of the pool before turning quickly to find Olivia, who was currently pulling herself out and at scrambling to Allison's side.

Putting her mouth. to hers, she performing CPR on Allison's unresponsive body.

Colin pulled himself out of the water, ignoring the freezing cold, and assessed Allison. Her pink tattered bunny was tucked into the pocket of her dress, the little destroyed ear sticking out and dragging on the ground.

She was blue.

Colin's heart shattered into a billion pieces. He put shaky hands to his hair and gasped, his chest feeling like it was caving in.

"Goddamnit it, *no*!" he whispered, his brain refusing to process what was happening. "No, no, no!"

He looked up sharply. Johnathan was on the phone with the police, instructing them on how to get to the house. Vanessa was currently on her hands and knees trying to crawl to them, crying awful gut wrenching sobs. Finally reaching them, she placed her shaking hands on Allison's head, stroking her wet, tangled hair out of her face.

Olivia's and Vanessa's breaths swirled in a white mist around them. But none escaped from Allison.

"No," Olivia's voice bit out. "No, Ally. You're not doing this to me. *Everyone* can fucking hurt me but *you,"* she said angrily as she bent down and blew breath into the girl's mouth.

Colin watched helplessly as he struggled with his own demons, dread filling him as he just realized he'd just caused the death of someone the love of his life cherished.

Another death because of him.

Olivia screamed incoherently as Johnathan tried to take over CPR, placing the phone on the ground on speaker as he tried to move Olivia out of the way,. She shoved him back away from her, refusing to stop. This went on for what felt like an eternity.

A tear slipped from his eye as he looked over blankly, hearing the sirens approaching in the distance. Feeling his brain shutting down to protect itself.

Johnathan tried again. Colin could tell Olivia was exhausted, but she wouldn't let anyone close.

"Get the fuck away! *Allison*!" she screamed, never ending those hard pushes into the little girl's chest. Water trickled steadily from Allison's blue mouth, yet still she didn't move, didn't attempt to gasp for air. She lay there, deathly still. Her hair a mass of red tangles around her face, her eyes refusing to open.

"Oh, God, *whyyyyyy*. My baby! Not my baby!" Vanessa cried.

Vanessa was currently curled up into a ball of grief, pressing her head against the side of Allison's, weeping silently.

Johnathan crouched over her, his hand on her hip. His own face wracked with grief. He reached over and placed his broad hand over Alison's eyes and forehead, lowering his head silently as he began to pray.

Olivia worked tirelessly over Allison's body as she screamed her name repeatedly.

Colin turned silently, walking to the gate and letting the emergency crew in. He watched them race past him, as if they moved in slow motion. He turned back, seeing them rip Olivia off Allison. She was screaming and crying, still on her knees, struggling to stand up as the crew worked over Allison.

They strapped her onto the stretcher as a crew member took over performing CPR on Allison's body as they hurried her away through the gate back the way they came. Johnathan cradled Vanessa's half limp body in his arms. She had passed out from shock. Olivia ran past him, following Allison's into the back of the ambulance.

Jonathan appeared next to him and got in his face, making him turn his eyes to his.

"Colin!" he snapped. "We gotta go to the hospital. I need you to snap out of it. *They need us,*" Johnathan said, his voice sounding hollow to his ears.

Nodding numbly, he'd jogged back into the house, grabbing his keys, a pair of shoes for Olivia, and his wallet and met Johnathan outside in his SUV. Sliding behind the wheel and pulling off behind the ambulance, seeing Olivia's red hair peek through the back of the ambulance window. His heart constricted painfully, and a choked sob wrenched from his throat.

He felt Johnathan's warm hand settle on his shoulder from behind. He'd crawled into the backseat with Vanessa, and she was slowly coming to herself, whispering "Oh my God," over and over.

Yeah, he thought sorrowfully. *Too bad he didn't seem to have invited himself to the party. Maybe Allison would have been saved. What God let a little girl die on Thanksgiving?*

Her time had been shorter than they all thought.

THIRTY-SEVEN

Also By

In You

Mounted (2026)

INTERCONNECTED WORLDS

The Romancing Me Series

Coming 2026

Alexander and Sarah's Love Story

The Billionaire's Assurance Series

The Pain We Nurture (Book 1)

The Pain We Allow (Book 2)

Unmasking Me Series:

Lola Unmasked part. 1

Lola Unmasked part. 2

Lola Unmasked part 3

<u>The King Dynasty Series:</u>

The Heir

The Spare

The Reign (2026)

<u>Christmas Novella</u>

Surrender at The Snowflake Inn

THIRTY-EIGHT
Acknowledgments

Where does a person even begin to start when there've been so many who have helped, encouraged, and just down right carried me through multiple areas of this project? I can try, but my words really won't do it justice.

To my parents, though you probably wont ever read this:

Dad, all those nights of you letting me read Poe, reading me my favorite books, the late nights running to the store at midnight to buy me my favorite book release. It wasn't ever about the books, it was about you. The time spent with you, the memories we made, the love we got to experience over a combined passion. Memories that will forever be cherished. I am so blessed to have a father like you.

Mama, the millions of times you asked me to spell a word for you (acting like you didn't know how), or asking me to explain a phrase to you. You were nurturing this passion and dream inside of me unwittingly. I could do none of this without either of you. I love you, and I hope you are proud of me. All those years you spent sacrificing and being an example of what could happen when you work hard haven't gone unnoticed or unappreciated. It's taught me my own drive, and now I get to see a dream actualized.

My bonus mommy, you are amazing, and I've been so incredibly blessed because you've been in my life. My sister, who pre-ordered with no questions asked. I love you forever.

To my family.

All the late nights, the take out dinners because I was writing instead of cooking. The times we've stood still in a grocery store so I could get a scene that popped into my head onto my notes in my phone. You all are my heart.

To Sara and Tina; the OG's. The ones who read this at its rawest and still made me feel like I could actually publish this. Sometimes it only takes one person to make a person's dream come true, and in my case, it was two. And started with you two. I love you. I adore you. I appreciate you.

To social media friends who have become so much more somewhere along the way. Des, Tia Fanning, Mari, Ashli, Jessica, K. M. Ryan, Janey, Haley, Cheryl, Red, Tris, Ericka, CC, Kaela, Jodi, Jen, McKenna, Kiwi, and others, I have never experienced such an outpouring of support, compassion as I have with you all. You are my sisterhood and you all motivate and drive me in ways that can't be expressed.

Brittany those pep talks kept me sane, and your unwavering positivity has upheld me many nights. Randi, and Gloria, you've made me laugh and have brought me joy. Doug, thank you for the help with the PR box Page III bookmarks, even if you did call me "nasty" for the pool table chapter in the sequel! Hahaha! I love to see you and Sara living out your own special love story, and it's so sweet to see.

To Dr. Patrick. Thank you for your help in manifesting the hell out of my dreams, as you live your own. It's been a pleasure to make your acquaintance. Thank you for the idea for the pavlovian pain response. It was a beautiful thing to add dimension to their relationship, and I hope when you read it, it makes you smile.

Last but not least. My book club girlies:

Gina, Blair, Erica, Dalia, Stephanie, and Jessica,

Those Friday nights we spent together laughing, joking about my imagination, sharing personal stories, encouraging each other, talking about nothing and everything, and discussing the what if's?

One of our 'what if's' happened. And it couldn't have happened without you.

Without all of you.

And Reader,

If you so happen to make it to the end of this. I hope you know that this obviously can't happen without you, either. Please continue to support and uplift other indie authors who are trying to get their stories out there. There are some amazing ones, and I hope that you give them a chance just like you gave me one.

Thank you for reading. And as always, stay safe.

Take care of yourself,

SKP